THE TEMPLE

NOVELS BY ARKADY LEOKUM

Send Me, Absolutely Free

The Temple

ARKADY LEOKUM

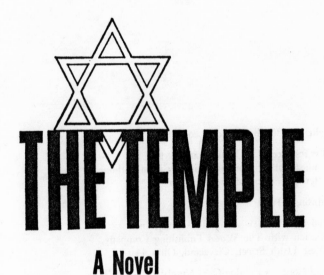

THE TEMPLE

A Novel

An NAL Book / The World Publishing Company
New York and Cleveland

Published by The New American Library, Inc.,
in association with The World Publishing Company,
2231 West 110th Street, Cleveland, Ohio 44102

Library of Congress Catalog Card Number: 75–93471
Printed in the United States of America

WORLD PUBLISHING
TIMES MIRROR

for Rose

F.A.F.A.S.D.

"The agreement entered into between a rabbi and his congregation is between a religious community and its chosen leader. It goes beyond the stipulation of a legal agreement; it also covers a spiritual relationship. A rabbi is not to be considered as an employee of the congregation. He is a consecrated servant of God called by the congregation to serve the religious, educational, spiritual and pastoral needs of the membership. His ministry shall not be limited to his congregational duties, but shall be left free to serve the larger community. The very nature of the congregation in Israel as a holy assembly and the lofty character of the rabbi's office dictate that the agreement between rabbi and congregation be preserved on the highest plane of mutual integrity, mutual respect and mutual devotion to the religious purpose for which the congregation exists."

—From the contract between a rabbi and a Reform congregation.

THE TEMPLE

Rabbi was missing.

Only one man in the room, as yet, gave this fact any special thought. For the others, no apprehension, no tension. They suspected nothing. Merely a general awareness that the meeting wasn't ready to begin, that Bob Barrett himself was still somewhere in another part of his house, and that when Rabbi finally did appear, late as usual, with a long, involved apology for his tardiness and with that intense eagerness of his, why, then another meeting of the Executive Committee of Temple Israel would proceed in its normal and discursive fashion.

True, Bob had phoned each of them at home this time to summon them, had spoken rather more solemnly than usual, had even designated it as a "special, emergency meeting," and had refused to discuss the purpose of it. But things were going well enough with the congregation and all its affairs even to imagine that a crisis was at hand.

So they stood about chatting amiably, laughing with indulgent exuberance at one another's jokes, and discussing the progress of the effort and drive that so preoccupied them all, the fund-raising drive for the building of the new Temple, the congregation's first, very own Temple in Greenlake.

Lou Mandel had put the architect's rendering of it on an easel for them to stare at, as he did at every meeting wherever it was held and for whatever purpose. As Chairman of the Building Committee, he tended at times to act as if this were his personal crusade and he did shove that drawing of the Temple into people's faces with missionary intensity and total unconcern for the appropriateness of the moment.

But everybody forgave Lou. Condemn fanaticism when it was for such a noble cause? Be irritated by absolute dedication to the building of a house of God? How could you not accept almost anything from such a man? They would look at his solemn, weary face, the lines in it carved deep by tragedy (his only son killed in an automobile accident just two years ago), and they would feel a sense of awe and respect for the miraculous spirit that had survived in him, the consecration of the man to this holy task. "Only he should relax a little sometimes and not have another heart attack! Without Lou heading the Building Committee, where would we be?"

And as a matter of fact, they did enjoy seeing that drawing of the temple, even for the hundredth time. Designed by Walter Wilcomb, the bearded, imp-like genius who was *the* Temple architect of our time, it had the kind of beauty and grace that offered a safe adventure in contemporary architecture. As the structural symbol of the Jewish community in Greenlake, they felt it was just right. Clean of line but not bare-looking, boldly modern yet properly restrained, and neither presumptuous nor self-effacing.

"I love it!" Jack Stern said, gazing at the drawing. "It's gorgeous! Look at those lines. And those curves on top!"

"Jack, you sound like you're talking about a woman." Dr. Greenwald poked his arm good-naturedly. "It's a holy Temple."

"So I'm in love with a holy Temple! God'll understand. The way I'm knocking myself out raising money, He better understand. Say, did I tell you about old man Jacobson?"

They all watched Jack with delight as he launched into one of his stories about an "extraction," Jack's word for obtaining a contribution from a reluctant member.

"I figure he's good for maybe thirty-five hundred tops, only it's going to be open-heart surgery all the way. So for a month I'm after him. He offers me two-fifty. I fall off the chair from laughing. Jacobson, you've got a sense of humor! A week later, five hundred. I slap him on the back. Jacobson, you could bring back vaudeville, you're so funny! Next week, he's up to a thousand, and it's like he's handing me a gallon of his own blood. So it suddenly hits me, his weak spot. I go right for the nerve. Jacobson, I say, not for yourself, and not even for us, the congregation. But just for the one, one person in the whole world —you should do it right! For your grandson! In three years that darling boy he's going to be Bar Mitzvah. You want to have that glorious event take place in a strange Temple that we share with another congregation? In another town, not even in Greenlake? Where your whole mishpocheh will look at that fine youngster and pity him? Or do you want that Bar Mitzvah in your own Temple, right here where you belong, where there's a place for you, where you'll look proudly on that boy and all your relatives and friends will say: now *this* is a Bar Mitzvah!"

"So he gave?"

"Five thousand smackers! Like I say, getting money is like extracting a tooth. You put the injection in the right place—it comes slipping out while they're smiling and still wondering what happened!"

No question about it, the congregation was lucky to have Jack Stern for Chairman of the Fund Raising Committee. How could you not like him? How could you not give and give and give when Jack came after you with that smile on his face, the lines all wrinkled up around his big nose. How could you refuse him when he gripped your arm so sincerely and stared at you with those big eyes under the bushy eyebrows, always with his jokes and his crazy stories, and underneath it all something you felt was honest and true—his love for the Temple. In the public relations business in New York, Jack Stern might be only a moderate success, working on the smaller accounts in the shop, but in Greenlake he was a hero. Of the $700,000 that was the goal of the Fund Drive, he had already raised $450,000, and there were still six months to go.

You could sense this appreciation among the other members of the Executive Committee as they stood there this evening, waiting for the meeting to begin. Even Dr. Greenwald had an indulgent smile for Jack's bantering. And from Dr. Greenwald that was something. For Emanuel Greenwald (the "Dr." was a Ph.D.) usually held himself slightly removed.

The second richest Jew in Greenlake (after Sam Beskov—but could you really count Beskov as a Jew?), white-haired Dr. Greenwald was a man people admired instinctively. Even his appearance was that of an elder statesman—an upright, adequately portly figure, a face at once intelligent yet benignly good-humored, he inspired confidence, if not awe, in all who met him. No wonder even the gentiles in Greenlake kept inviting him to attend this conference, join that committee. Had a Jew ever before been asked to give the Memorial

Day address in Greenlake? For that matter, had a Jew ever before given five thousand dollars to the YMCA drive in Greenlake?

Now, tonight, as they stood there in front of the drawing of the Temple that was to be built, they were subtly aware that one whole section was marked "The Greenwald Auditorium." Directly in back of the sanctuary, separated by sliding doors, capable of accommodating almost five hundred extra people ("What would we do without it on the High Holy Days?"), with a raised stage at the far end, a magnificent kitchen hidden away in the back, it would be a perfect place for meeting, conferences, performances, Bar Mitzvahs, weddings, a center for the social and cultural life of the Jewish community.

Technically, Dr. Greenwald was contributing only $200,000 toward the construction of the Auditorium. But everyone knew that this would be a very flexible figure. If the lighting system for the stage, or the refrigeration system for the kitchen, or the sound proofing, or the construction of the terrace outside the Auditorium should cost more than was anticipated, Dr. Greenwald would come through without a murmur. The Greenwald Auditorium was going to be built *right*.

In fact, Harry Brody was already working on Dr. Greenwald regarding the backstage facilities of the Auditorium. As President of the Men's Club, Harry had such beautiful dreams about using the Auditorium that it made his eyes pop when he talked about them. Dances with name bands. Father-and-son Sunday breakfasts where they'd break the world's record for bagel consumption. Lectures to a packed house by such personalities as Allie Sherman, one of the few Jewish coaches in pro football. Performances by the Theater Group of complete musical comedies with costumes and the works. All this would need space backstage, lighting equipment, storage closets, maybe even dressing rooms.

The chances were that Harry would get what he wanted. Maybe he wasn't the intellectual type, not even what you would call a well-educated Jew. But what he believed in was sound as a rock. And that was the simple, basic concept of "get 'em together." To Harry, the Temple represented "activity." A place where people would meet to enjoy each other's company. "What's better?" he used to say. "Is a Jew a better Jew when he sits home alone and reads the Talmud— or when he gets together with other Jews and they *do* something?

That way they get to know each other, appreciate each other. That's what Judaism is all about!"

Harry Brody was so dedicated to his concept of what was right and good for the Jews of Greenlake, he worked so hard at being President of the Men's Club, that the organization had tripled its membership in the last year alone.

All this was a matter of relative disinterest to the final member of the Executive Committee, Danny Cole, who stood next to Harry in front of the drawing and saw a totally different Temple there. Though he tried not to, he resented what it represented to the other members of the Executive Committee and probably to most of the congregation. For Danny, religion itself and Judaism in particular, was a great discovery he had made at the age of thirty. Rabbi had led him to the peak and pointed out this whole new world that lay below, waiting to be explored. And he had plunged into it with an eagerness that was incredibly rewarding to him. In the process, he had become more than a disciple of Rabbi, he had become his close friend.

Danny saw the Temple as an instrument in Rabbi's hands, the means to accomplish Rabbi's goal of bringing the Jews of Greenlake closer to the true essence of Judaism and thereby making their lives meaningful. Musical comedies in the Auditorium, catered weddings with live bands, even the use of the Temple for "cultural" affairs, were to him peripheral to its basic spiritual function.

Danny alone felt apprehension about this sudden emergency meeting of the Executive Committee. Bob Barrett, as President of the congregation, had the right of course to call a meeting for any purpose at his discretion. But Bob was the kind of man who took pride in operating Temple business smoothly and calmly, always conveying the impression that all problems were under perfect control in his administration. Words like "emergency" were psychologically unsound to Barrett. When he used them, it must be because he wanted to create a particular atmosphere. Yet here they all were, joking and chatting comfortably. It was, Danny felt, going to be an unusual meeting.

"Does anybody know," he finally asked, "what this emergency meeting is about?"

No one had an answer.

"And where," Danny persisted, "is Rabbi?"

"Where's Rabbi?" Jack Stern wrinkled up his big nose. "He's home writing Friday's sermon. What else?" It was said without malice, but touched on a point to which they were all sensitive.

"You mean he *writes* those things?" Brody held his cigar poised in the air.

"No, he makes them up as he goes along. Of course he writes them!"

"—and writes them—" Brody continued the cigar up and down like a deadly hammer, "—and writes them. That last one—I slept through it like a baby."

Greenwald didn't like the tone of all this. "Now gentlemen . . . *gentlemen.* Rabbi gives fine sermons. Excellent sermons. A little long perhaps . . . a bit involved intellectually at times . . . but full of meat."

"And I say," Brody insisted, "there's lean meat—and there's *fat* meat."

"And *I* say," Danny was becoming irritated, "some people can't appreciate the difference between a hamburger and a steak."

"And *I* say—" Brody was ready with a big one, but at that moment Bob Barrett walked in and the tension of the argument hung unresolved in the air. They all turned to him.

"Sorry I'm late," Bob said, not really apologizing. Everyone moved toward a place to sit and there was, quite suddenly, silence. They waited.

The Barrett living room was impressive not only because of its tasteful decoration, but unusual because of its size. There was a seating area in front of the huge fireplace, with two long couches facing each other, tables and lamps behind them, deep, comfortable armchairs nearby. Over near the floor-to-ceiling window looking out on the terrace was another couch, still more comfortable chairs, everywhere you looked an invitation to relax.

But as they all watched Bob arranging a chair for himself in exactly the position he wanted, a nervous impatience began to show. They glanced at each other. Dr. Greenwald cleared his throat, Lou Mandel leaned forward with hands clasped tightly on his knees. He had a way of looking utterly dejected, the lines of his face sagging woefully around his mouth whenever he was concerned.

Barrett at last was seated, with his legs crossed. He looked slowly around the group, only the habitual gesture of slicking his hair back betrayed his tension. Then unexpectedly he smiled.

"You won't believe this, but Elaine is out tonight, so I had to read a bed-time story to the kids. No story, no sleep. That's why I'm late. Sorry."

Lou couldn't help breaking in. "Bob, whatever this meeting is about, can we start with the Building Committee report first? We've run into some real trouble—"

"—and what Building Committee in the history of the Jews," Bob interrupted, "didn't have troubles? That's why putting up a Temple is in itself an act of dedication to God."

"I only thought, since Rabbi is late and while we're waiting for him—"

"We are *not* waiting for him." Bob said it calmly, but there was an awareness of the shock value in the way he paused.

Greenwald cleared his throat, a self-appointed delegate expressing their reaction. "This is an Executive Committee meeting?"

"That's right." Barrett remained impassive.

"And Rabbi—"

"—Rabbi was not invited." Barrett rose suddenly. "Since Rabbi won't be here, we'll start without him. I will offer the opening prayer."

No chance to express bewilderment as they all rose and lowered their heads. Bob looked upward, formulating it slowly.

"Bless us, O Lord, our God, as we meet here tonight. Guide us and inspire us to think with clarity of mind . . . to ponder with wisdom of heart . . . to act with honesty of purpose. Give us your blessing, O Lord, so that what we do here shall be truly representative of your will and reflective of the needs of your congregation. . . . Amen."

Slightly subdued amens from all as they sat down. Again they were waiting.

"I would like," Bob said, "to dispense with the reading of the minutes of the last meeting. Do I hear a motion to that effect?"

Greenwald, with an almost impatient gesture: "I so move."

"Second." Lou's hands were clasped tightly again.

"Any opposed?" Bob didn't wait. "Carried."

Well, here it was at last, and they leaned back to receive it as Bob rose and walked a few steps toward the center of the group. He was going to do it standing up. No question now, there really was something.

"Gentlemen, this may well be the most important meeting we've ever had. I ask you to bear with me and allow me to say what I have to say in my own way.

"I am not being deliberately indirect. I merely want us all to be completely aware of the background, the context so to speak, within which we must consider what I have to tell you.

"We are now a community of almost twenty-five hundred Jews in the town of Greenlake. That's only—what?—about ten per cent of the population. But we all know that *this* ten per cent is not an ordinary ten per cent. The way we live and act is watched very carefully by the rest of the town. We live, you might say, under a huge social microscope. We are observed like specimens.

"In effect, to the people of Greenlake, we represent the Jews. All Jews are being judged when we are judged. All Jews succeed or fail as good citizens, as human beings—in us.

"But we have another obligation too, and perhaps even a deeper one. And this is to ourselves. To our own sense of right and of decency, to the moral and spiritual values that are at the heart of our religion.

"And finally, we are now engaged in building a Temple here. A house of God, a symbol of our faith, a spiritual home for ourselves and our children.

"It is with great sadness that I must tell you that all three aspects of our existence here—the image of the Jew in this community—our devotion to the ethical standards of Judaism—and the building of the Temple itself—all are endangered! Gentlemen—" he gave them no pause, no opportunity for reflection, "—I have called this meeting for the purpose of taking action regarding the removal of our Rabbi from office."

Bob Barrett sat down. It was as if he wanted to allow the oncoming shock wave to pulsate back and forth and spend itself before he continued. Questions, indignation, horror, whatever that wave carried toward him, he would sit it out patiently. The reactions came.

"Tell us what it's all about, for God's sake!" Lou Mandel pleaded.

"*Why?*" demanded Danny Cole. "*Why* do you want to remove the Rabbi?"

"In the middle of the Fund Raising Drive? Oh my God! It better be a good reason, Bob!" Jack Stern was making it personal.

Dr. Emanuel Greenwald seemed more shaken than anyone had

ever seen him. "Such a statement . . . such words . . . they must not be spoken lightly. The removal of Rabbi from office, this is of momentous significance. I must tell you, Mr. Barrett [Greenwald's shift to another level], that what you have said not only demands an immediate explanation, it requires the fullest justification. For what you have uttered here has already become a fact in our lives. The President of the congregation, by merely presenting the Executive Committee with the *suggestion* that Rabbi should be removed from office, has created a situation that we—and the entire congregation—will from this moment have to live with and deal with. You have committed an act, Mr. Barrett, not merely made a suggestion."

"It is not," Barrett was the calm account executive with all the answers for the client, "intended to be a suggestion. It is a resolution I am presenting to the Executive Committee for you to vote on."

"Wait a minute!" Danny was bewildered by the direction the talk was taking. "Let's not get sidetracked by *what* it is! Let's get to *why*! Bob, will you tell us right now why you want Rabbi removed?"

"I don't like being badgered, Dan."

"Badgered? I'm just asking you—"

Greenwald raised his arm toward Dan with restraining authority. "Mr. Barrett, let us hear your reasons. Now."

Barrett sat quietly, his left hand covering his eyes and forehead. A slight shaking of the head showed the turmoil, reluctance, even sorrow.

"Gentlemen, this is the saddest thing I've ever had to say. Rabbi Gordon has shown himself to be unworthy of being our spiritual leader."

Danny simply could not accept it. "That means nothing! What kind of charge is that? How has he done that? How?"

Even Lou Mandel persisted. "Surely there's something more specific, Bob?"

Greenwald moved so that he stood directly in front of the President of the congregation. "Mr. Barrett, I insist on a complete explanatory statement, and I insist on it now."

It was the moment for Barrett to rise, to stare at them with the strength of his knowledge.

"Gentlemen . . . Rabbi Gordon has shown himself to be a man of . . . of immoral character."

Now it burst out of them—

"Rabbi Gordon?"

"Are you out of your mind?"

"I don't believe it!"

"Impossible!"

Greenwald was the one who spoke quietly. "By merely saying those words, Mr. Barrett, you have already created a terrible human tragedy. They will be linked with Rabbi's life to the end of his days. My mind is dazed at the thought . . . I can't accept it." He sat down slowly, everyone watching him, aware of his anguish.

Jack Stern leaned forward. "Can I have the floor? Just a minute, everybody. Before we go any further, I want to say something. We're at a very delicate point just now. We have to decide: Do we go on—wherever this takes us? Or do we stop? Now I don't mean we shut Bob up and say we don't want to hear what he has to tell us. But we might consider: Is this, is now the time to bring it all out? We're right in the middle of a fund-raising drive to build our Temple. Everyone realizes what that Temple means to us. And we're all smart enough to know that if something like this gets out—the Rabbi of immoral character—the whole damn thing may blow up in our faces. We've got too much at stake. All of us Jews in Greenlake have too much at stake. So I'm just saying, Bob—Rabbi's only human—if it's a little twisting of the truth—a broken promise or something—God knows—income tax—maybe he bets on horses? If it's—"

"Jack," Barrett was shaking his head, "It's far more serious."

Danny's incredulity was changing to anger. "What do you mean by immoral character?"

Barrett responded with his first intensity. "I mean *sexually* immoral!"

Something like a pain ran through all of them. A great regret. A sickening inside. And a silence.

"I am saying," Bob spoke slowly, as if stirring it about, the emotional mess in them, "I have evidence that Rabbi Gordon has become involved . . . with a woman who is not his wife."

Greenwald asked with reluctance: "You have *evidence?*"

"All that's needed."

Lou's voice was close to breaking. "You have . . . proof?"

"Proof! Proof! Of course I have proof! Am I the kind of man who would bring this up if I didn't have proof?"

Danny said flatly, "I don't believe it!"

"It's completely unimportant whether you believe it or not!" Greenwald spoke solemnly now. "What kind of proof, Mr. Barrett?"

"A person who swears she saw them together."

Danny was insistent, unable to give up. "Who is this person? I'd like to know that!"

"Why? What's the difference? Does it matter?"

"Goddam right it matters! Rabbi has enemies who—"

"Danny! Don't make me go into details. She saw them kissing! In each other's arms! Isn't that enough?"

"Who saw them? Why don't you tell us?"

"Because . . . it's my decision not to. Because there's no need to. We are concerned with the Rabbi—and that's all."

"And this . . . this other woman?" Greenwald reluctantly. "Will you tell us who—"

Now Barrett grew suddenly silent. As if his thoughts were far away, in a painful other world. Then almost in a whisper.

"No."

"Why not?" Danny was unable to stop.

"Because I choose not to."

Brody tried to make it easier. "You're protecting her, right?"

"If you want to call it that."

Danny on his feet. "This is unbelievable! A charge like that against Rabbi, and all we have to go by—"

"—is my word. That's right! My word. That I have the evidence! The facts!"

Greenwald was shaking his head sadly. Almost to himself. "Rabbi Gordon . . . whatever his faults as a rabbi . . . he's a good man . . . a sincere, decent man. . . ."

"But he is a man!" Barrett answered bitterly. "Rabbi is also a man, it seems!"

"Well, that's a surprise!" Brody smiled. "Who would have thought he had it in him? He's supposed to be so spiritual! So high and holy! So far above us. And we find out—he's only a man."

Lou Mandel sat clasping and unclasping his hands. "My God, if this gets out—what will happen to the Temple?"

"That—" Jack stood up again, "that's what I want to talk about. Before we get all panicky and do something we'll be sorry for . . . I want to ask a sort of tricky question. Now listen. Bob, aside from you, and this person, whoever she is, who saw them—does anyone else know?"

"No."

"All right. Nobody. This committee and nobody else. . . . Now please just let me sort of think out loud. . . . I'm in the public relations business, which is why, I suppose, you made me chairman of the fund raising drive. I know a little something about how people react. . . . Now. We're building a Temple. Raising money, getting support. . . . A year from now, with God's help, when the Temple is built—all this push to get everybody together will be finished. We'll be able to settle down like any other congregation, with its troubles, its little scandals, its problems. So—I'm just thinking out loud—so what would happen if we waited until then? What would be the great tragedy?"

Barrett clenched his fists. "What are you suggesting? That we keep a Rabbi who has done what he's done—as our spiritual leader?"

"I'm only saying we should consider everything involved."

"There's only one thing involved! We can't have such a man as our Rabbi!"

Greenwald, with authority, on his feet. "Bob, just a minute. Just a minute." (Back to "Bob," everybody noticed.) "Let's try, all of us, to be intelligent, responsible people. Let's see if we can't bring a little reason and judgment to this awful problem we must face. We're the Executive Committee and we have the responsibility of coming to a decision. It seems to me that we have to get two things straight. The first is, Bob—you are not going to tell us who the person is who saw them . . . or who that other woman is?"

"That's right."

"All right. This is something we must face. We're going to have to accept that condition—or say no to it.

"Now I come to the second thing. Who makes the accusation against Rabbi? The President of our congregation. The man who has led us for four years. A man we trust with all our hearts—as we trust him with the future of our Temple.

"So I address myself to you now—the Executive Committee—and I say we must make clear to him and to each other that we accept without question the truth of what he tells us. If not—we must say it now."

Nobody was quite prepared yet. Except Danny.

"I want to say something. Bob has talked about high standards and ethics. Where is our sense of ethics if we can condemn a man—*our Rabbi!*—without giving him a hearing? A chance to defend himself? Maybe completely deny this accusation? Is this a way to make a decision that can ruin a man's life?"

Greenwald, his face now expressing the wisdom and judgment expected of him, spoke with quiet authority. "Danny, you are right. In the abstract—you're perfectly right. We all believe in giving a man a chance to defend himself. . . . But this is not a court of law. We're not dealing with abstract principles. We are dealing with a situation that endangers the good name of all Jews in this community . . . the building of the Temple . . . the very future of our congregation. Our responsibility is to that—to protect that holy cause!"

"But if it's not true, what are we doing—"

Greenwald interrupted with his raised arm. "Danny, think. Just think. If Rabbi is faced with this charge publicly, and denies everything, and then Bob has to prove it publicly, how much more tragic that will be for everyone! And if Rabbi is faced with it publicly, and admits it—how much more shameful that will be!"

"You left out one thing! What if Rabbi denies it and Bob Barrett *can't* prove it? Then what?"

Barrett spoke quietly, with calm emphasis. "Let's get this straight once and for all. If Rabbi denies it, then I'll give you facts, names, places, anything you want."

"Well," Greenwald looked around at all of them, trying to evaluate reaction, "so this is where we are. A tragic moment in the history of our congregation . . . a heart-rending moment for each of us personally. . . ."

Bob felt the need to cut through this. "Having reached this point, I think we should move on to specific action, and quickly. Here's what I propose to do if the Executive Committee approves. I will approach Rabbi personally. Alone. I will confront him with the facts I have. I will tell him that the Executive Committee has taken a vote authorizing me to request his resignation. The reason for that resignation is never to be disclosed by us or by him. We will pay out the remainder of his contract. And we will expect him to leave this community as soon as he can."

"And what," Danny asked, "if Rabbi doesn't resign?"

Barrett's iciness penetrated to all of them. "I guarantee Rabbi will resign."

Silence. Apparently Greenwald felt the need for something more. "I think that, in view of the importance of this matter, each of us has the right, even the obligation, to express his thoughts before we take a vote. Let us reach a decision fully aware not only of what we are doing, but why. Do you object to that, Bob?"

"Of course not. We'll speak in turn around the room and we'll begin right now. Harry?"

Brody shook his head unwillingly, the cigar sliding from one corner of his mouth to the other. "You all know how I feel. I have nothing to say."

"You can't duck it like that!" Danny glared at him. "Let everyone speak!"

Barrett turned to Brody again. "Harry, whatever you think or feel, tell us now."

Brody leaned forward, irritated. "I'm not ducking anything! You want to have it? I'll be honest! As President of the Men's Club, I can tell you what our members feel about this Rabbi we got. You want the truth? They think he's no good! I'm not talking about how smart he is, or how much he knows. He's no good as a Rabbi. As a man who's supposed to lead us! A man you want to go to in trouble. A man you feel understands you, who's part of his people—the ordinary people—and shares their activities, their life. He's no good for this congregation!"

Danny raised his arms in disbelief. "What does that have to do with—"

Brody turned on him. "I'll tell you what it has to do with it! I say if we've now got a reason—if Rabbi has handed us a reason on a silver platter—for getting rid of him, we're lucky! Let's grab it and act!"

"And what about justice for this man? What about—"

"Danny!" Barrett motioning to him. "You'll have your turn. Sit down." Barrett looked at Mandel. "Lou?"

Great weariness in his face, Lou spoke in a heavy voice.

"Danny . . . I first want to say to you that I know how you feel. Justice? Who doesn't want justice? The life and future of a human being? Who doesn't feel sad? I've led a decent life. The best I could. I have tried to do what's right, always. Not to hurt anybody. Not to be insensitive to the suffering of others. . . . But for me, there is also something above all this. And that's why I have tried—and am still trying with all the strength I have left—to do something important for my fellow-Jew, for the future of this congregation.

"So for me, all other considerations—even what we call justice—must be secondary. For me, what matters most is the one thing that has taken up my life these last years—the building of the Temple. You all know that I had a heart attack four years ago. You all know the personal tragedy that struck my family two years ago. But you also know that it hasn't stopped me one bit! And I do it gladly. And I will continue to do it gladly. Because that Temple is going to be built, and no man—not even our Rabbi—is going to stop it. That Temple is going to be built because it is the greatest need we Jews have . . . and because it will fill our children's need . . . and their children's. I say whatever, whoever, stands in the way *must* be removed. We have no choice . . . we have no choice."

"Thank you, Lou." Barrett said it quietly, gratefully. He allowed enough time for the respect and admiration to be sufficiently felt. Then: "All right, Jack—"

In the center of the room, silently, hands in pockets, that big nose crinkled up in the expected smile, Jack stood pondering a moment, then ran a hand through his hair, rubbing the scalp as if in self-surprise.

"My friends, get ready for something funny. Here I am—Jack Stern —the fund raiser. With the wisecracks, with the jokes, with the slaps on the back, and the rah-rah speeches. But the funny thing is, what I want to say—it's serious. Because a very strange thing has happened. I've been going around talking to our people, trying to get 'em stirred up and excited. And you know what? These plain, ordinary people, they *are* excited! They *want* to give money. So help me, they want that Temple! They have the dream! The hope! You almost feel there's something holy when you talk to them. They want that Temple!

"My friends, Jack Stern isn't going to be the guy to let 'em down! And he's not going to let anybody else do it. . . . Me, I got about as much religion in all of me as the Rabbi has in his little finger. But right now—after what I heard tonight—I feel I'm a hundred times more religious than he is! At least I'm not doing anything that could destroy the faith and hope of our people. And I say a man who could do that . . . a Rabbi who could do that to his own people. . . ." He shook his head. "No, I say. No, my friends. No."

The appropriate wait, the others nodding to Jack in appreciation. The silence of agreement.

"Dr. Greenwald," Barrett turned toward him finally, "we are ready to hear from you now."

Greenwald spoke very slowly, his face gentle, almost soft.

"We don't have to compete with each other in expressing our dedication to the Temple and to our congregation. I want that Temple as much as any of you. Some people probably think even a little more—because it will have that Greenwald Auditorium. That 'monument' to me, as I've heard it described. Though actually . . ." he sighed, then raised his chin in pride and defiance, "actually it is a prayer on my part. Of thanks to the Lord who has blessed me.

"But even as we discuss the need to have that Temple built, we are asked to consider the tearing down of a human being. Our Rabbi.

"I have come fairly close to Rabbi Gordon at times. He seems to me to be a remarkable man. Hard to understand perhaps. Hard to know. But there is a basic decency coming from him that cannot be denied. A spiritual strength. A sincerity. And a commitment.

"I don't want to destroy that man. If—I say if—through some human failing or error, he has already destroyed himself, then that must be faced. If he is guilty of what Bob says, then he must suffer for it.

"But—he must admit that guilt . . . just as he must then forever live with it.

"I want this Committee to instruct Bob to go to Rabbi, confront him, and ask him to admit that guilt—if it exists. And only then, to request that he resign."

Greenwald looked around the room at all the faces, seeking their understanding and agreement. Jack and Lou nodded their heads, staring back silently. Brody looked down at the floor.

Barrett conveyed nothing of his reaction, as if merely conducting a casual exchange of views. "Danny, it's your turn."

Danny, trying to start the best way, pushing aside emotion, anger, bitterness, wanting to reach them and move them, spoke slowly in the lowest voice he could manage.

"We are all concerned with building the Temple. What is that Temple? It is the holy place where we come face to face with God. Where we take His teachings into our hearts, His laws, His commandments. To do right by our fellow man. To love mercy. To practice justice. This is why we build that Temple. To learn that again and again and again and to commit ourselves to it and to live by it!

"But if we build that Temple and destroy an innocent man to do it—what are we building? If we take our Rabbi—our teacher of God's ways—and destroy him to build a Temple—what are we building? Justice, truth, mercy, these are the foundation stones of our Temple. How can we deny them to our Rabbi?

"There is only one question that should be in our minds and hearts: how can we see to it that he doesn't suffer without cause? How can we save him from even one moment of pain—if he doesn't deserve it?

"An accusation has been made against Rabbi. That's all it is—an accusation. Our job is clear. How can we give Rabbi the most just, most merciful opportunity to cast away the shadow of this accusation? What can we do that is right for him? How can we practice justice— so that he may have it? That's the only thing that faces us. Nothing else!"

"My approach, I think—" Dr. Greenwald looked at Danny, "gives him that opportunity for justice."

"But Bob is *making* the accusation. He shouldn't be the one to act as judge—"

"Danny!" Bob interrupted. "We're not discussing that now."

"Why not? It's the heart of it! Is it right that you should be the one to go to Rabbi when you already think he's guilty? How do we know what will pass between—"

"Stop it!" Barrett was unable to control the outburst. "I resent that! How dare you imply—" Then he caught himself. Lowering his voice, he spoke calmly again. "I'm sorry. I understand how this upsets you. But don't you think we are all affected?" He came up to Danny, wearing an almost fatherly expression now.

"Danny, do you know why you're on this Committee? Because I

wanted you here. I said we need someone like you to represent the young spirit in our temple . . . the warmth, the idealism that you have to give. And we welcome it! But Danny, we also, we others, have something to contribute in this time of crisis. Our experience. Our judgment. And at a time like this, you have to be guided by that experience and that judgment."

"All I want," Danny was pleading now, "is justice for our Rabbi!"

"We all want it. But let me bring this down to reality. Let's stop talking ideals and abstract concepts and face the cold, brutal facts of life. Now listen to this. Listen! And then tell me if you have an answer. . . . If the Committee so decides, I will confront Rabbi. And when he admits his guilt, I will come back to this Committee and I will say: Rabbi has agreed to resign. *Rabbi has agreed to resign.* . . . What's the answer to that, Danny?"

Greenwald moved forward in his seat. "I think that everything that needs to be said has been said. Let us vote now. There is nothing more to be done."

Barrett turned away from Danny and walked back to his place. "We will now take a vote. Will all those in favor of what I have proposed, raise their hands?"

All the hands went up except one.

"Opposed?"

Danny thrust his hand up, the defiance in his eyes too.

"The decision is made."

Everyone was on his feet now, as if the momentum of what had happened was pushing them on. Danny walked quickly to the end of the room, to the doorway.

"The decision is made!" His voice was choked. "You say that as if it's the end! You really think it's going to end this way? A vote— and Rabbi is finished? Destroyed? This is only the beginning! This is only—"

He turned quickly and left the house.

Barrett spoke at once, as if wanting to cut off reaction, end it finally: "I will now offer the closing prayer. Gentlemen, please stand in your places in silence."

"O Lord, our God, we thank Thee for having guided us in this time of sorrow and crisis . . . for having given us the wisdom to act according to Thy laws and commands . . . for helping us to face with courage the terrible decision that was thrust upon us . . . and for blessing us with Thy strength to accept our responsibilities. Amen."

The others had never heard his voice so close to breaking.

RABBI 1

Sam Gordon came to the United States to succeed, and he failed. His brother, Nathan, already established with a dry goods store on 125th Street, provided the money that brought Sam and his wife, Ruth, from their home town in Poland to New York City. And Nathan offered to take him into the store, teach him the business, maybe even make him a partner eventually.

But Sam Gordon had a vision of success that was to be achieved by his own hands, his own initiative, and all he accepted was a loan from his brother so that he could open a little grocery store in the Bronx. After all, Ruth and he had operated a *kreml* in their home town and had made a living. Why not here? They would work as hard, be as clever at business, make as many friends, save as diligently, but here in America—God bless this wonderful country!—here in America the rewards would be a hundred times as great.

Another factor, not to be argued about, that prevented him from going into business with his brother, was that Sam was Orthodox and Nathan had become one of those modern Jews who observed nothing, practiced nothing, maybe even believed in nothing. Sam, on the other hand, had an involvement with ritual and observance that he could never conceive of abandoning. Sam wore a *yarmulke* at all times, even behind the counter of his store, said all the required prayers dutifully, went to *shul* on Saturday (the store remained closed, of course, until sunset), and lived the life of inner peace that such faith promised.

The store ("Sam's Grocery & Delicatessen") was actually a dark little hole on 169th Street near Third Avenue, and it always remained that. Instead of success, there was struggle. Sam opened at six-thirty in the morning to get the early business away from his competitors and charged a little less in order not to lose customers to the big markets. He gave credit to the poorer families who couldn't get it elsewhere (often losing these same families when their debts piled up and there was no longer any hope of paying), and stayed open an hour later than anyone else on the block. All of it Sam did with a mounting sense of helplessness and desperation, and then finally with acceptance and defeat.

When David was born (their first child, Sarah, was already three years old) there was a brief period of revived hope and concern with the future. Sam had once dreamed that having a son would provide that satisfying feeling of having someone to carry on, to turn things over to, of a destiny and way of life continuing on its good and rewarding path. But what was there to carry on? What in his own life could he possibly want his son to take over and continue?

No, Sam's purpose became instead to make sure that David would take his place in a totally different world. And since it couldn't be in business (he still thought of his dirty little grocery as "my business") then it would have to be in that other world which generation upon generation of Jewish boys had entered as the sacred alternative— the world of scholarship.

Thank God, David was a bright and studious boy—you could see that right from the beginning. Reading everything he could get his hands on when he was only eight years old so that he needed glasses by the time he was ten! In the Talmud Torah school, David was an outstanding student whom even the old Rabbis and scholars respected and took delight in. "He'll beat you in an argument," the Rabbi used to tell Sam, "and while he's doing it you look at those pink little cheeks and those shining eyes, and you're *kvelling*. When Dovidl does it, you feel good!"

On the block, David played a strange role in relation to the other kids. To begin with, he was frail, and wore glasses, and never got into fights. No matter what the controversy, no matter how natural it seemed to them all to line up and do battle and get it all settled with fists, David managed not to fight.

The other kids assumed a protective attitude toward him, as if there were an agreement among them to treat him with special consideration and concern. The fact that he was "smarter" than most of them made them regard him with the kind of respect young people bestow on heroes. When he supplied some information that no one else knew, or figured out an answer to what had puzzled them, there was a triumphant delight in their reaction. "I told you Dave would know what to do! He always knows!" David became a kind of arbiter of disputes, a final authority on obscure facts (from a baseball pitcher's record to the distance to the moon), and everybody's adopted wonder.

But there was another quality they sensed in him that was more important. This was an amazing, almost frightening intensity of spirit. In that thin little body of his there was a strange force generating a kind of passion, zeal, and involvement unlike anything they experienced themselves. When David became excited about something, and it might be only about settling an argument or choosing up sides for a stickball game, there came out of him such a fierceness of emotion, such overwhelming concern, that it would sweep them along and they would find themselves stirred up without quite knowing why.

This intensity, this total absorption that came pouring out of him and tore at people ruthlessly and tirelessly until they succumbed, became in time a serious problem to David.

By the age of sixteen, he was the undisputed, but resented, tyrant in his own home. No one dared oppose him on any matter. And while one might not expect much opposition from a girl like his sister Sarah, who was "too quiet" anyway and somehow gave an impression of gentle sadness, nor from his mother who felt incapable of making any kind of decision, it was shocking to see the way Sam yielded to him without a significant struggle.

"Is that what you want, David?" Sam would say. "You tellin' me it's *gotta* be that way?" They might be arguing about David's insistence that he have his own room, with everything in it arranged the way he wanted, and the family phonograph kept in that room.

"There can be no other way! It must! I know it has to be this way!"

"All right all right all right! Have it your way, David. You win."

And while David usually "won," not only at home, but in school, among friends, with whomever he became involved, he soon sensed that there was something he also lost in the process. This was a warmth in his relationships that he yearned for, an intimacy that he observed being shared by others, a closeness that other people had despite their arguments and fights. It was as if no one dared to be too near to him.

He felt their respect, even their admiration, but then a part of this would be a withdrawal too.

What disturbed him most, in addition to the loneliness, was that it seemed to be a rejection of the very essence of him. He was pouring out to them his deepest feelings, his ideas, reactions, whatever mattered, and this very act of communicating seemed to set up a barrier between him and others. Did it frighten them to see a human being so intimately revealed? Was it his passionate intensity that they couldn't tolerate? (Any kind of intensity, even a joyous one, becoming ultimately painful?) Or was it because he was so concerned with the very matters that upset their sense of security in everyday life, questioning their values and their purpose?

He convinced himself that they really didn't want to hear (were afraid of?) what he had to say. They didn't want the meaning of their existence examined and questioned. They didn't want to be constantly confronted with someone spouting a philosophy of life at them.

"What the hell do you want from me, David?" A friend with whom he had been talking about their future as adults exploded: "I'm not a saint! I'm going to get a good job, make money, enjoy life!"

"But then you're not even a human being."

"What am I?"

"An animal. You're going to exist only on the animal level. You're going to feed and care for your body. What are you going to do to feed your soul?"

Coming from a kid of sixteen, this kind of talk seemed not only ridiculous, but annoying, and the others frequently told him so. But for David, it only confirmed how important his "message" was, and how necessary that he bring it to them. In this way, and at quite an early age, he began to think of himself as a "man with a message" that set him apart. That he was an instrument for conveying this message to others was perfectly clear to him. It was as if he had no choice.

At the same time, he couldn't bear the idea that he might never be as close to others as he longed to be. He envied his friends who already had girls with whom they shared some kind of delicious intimacy. When he saw them merely holding hands, he had a need to turn away, it was too painful for him to watch. And he listened with anguish to their tales of ardent love-making, which were usually only fantasies, but presented as if the ecstatic truth. His friends relished torturing him in this way, describing their imaginary experiences in the crudest physical terms, the size and firmness of the breasts, the way the nipples felt, stiff and eager, the particular position she liked best. Listening to them, he felt torments of deprivation.

He wanted a girl with whom he would have everything—the sharing and exchange of each other's deepest thoughts and feelings, and also that whole physical explosion (as he pictured it) where his body would feel and feel and feel and touch and be touched and enter and be surrounded and embrace and hold and let everything flow in a great and passionate burst of one self into another.

He had sex fantasies as wild as anything his friends described to him, but they ended always in more longing and misery. Finally his frustration drove him into an experience that remained part of him, like the awareness of a sickness deep inside, for the rest of his life.

David met many girls in the normal way, through friends, at parties, dances. They were the daughters of neighbors, all of them nice, ordinary girls. But the romanticism in him, the image of the great wild relationship he was yearning for, made him treat them almost condescendingly. They sensed this and quickly turned from him.

But when Julia came along, it was a completely different matter. Julia was twenty-two, four years older than he, and worked as a secretary downtown. She was the most mature woman he had ever met. She had her own little apartment and was totally independent of her parents, living a life that suited her, indifferent to anyone's opinion of it. She was dark-haired, with an openly sensual face, soft, full lips, big, dark eyes, and she had a wonderfully frank, uninhibited manner about her. You always got it straight from Julia. No crap, no phoney evasiveness.

She was, according to reports, involved with a married man in her office and had hopes of breaking up that marriage in a reasonably short time. Meanwhile, she was more or less available, providing you could interest her. This wasn't easy. Most of the fellows were even a little frightened of her.

When David decided that all his dreams could be fulfilled in a relationship with Julia and began what was nothing less than a fanatical pursuit of her, she at first found it only amusing. She looked at this skinny youngster with the wavy, uncontrolled hair, who stared at her through his glasses with a ridiculous, intense passion, who tried so awkwardly to take her hand, hold her arm, touch her, be near her, and who seemed so desperate and terrified at the same time, and she laughed at the whole preposterous idea.

"You're a funny, crazy kid, David. Look at you! God, you tickle me!"

"I want you, Julia." He said it quietly, but with such feeling that she howled.

"*I want you, Julia,*" she mimicked him. "Listen to the little baby who wants a lollipop! *I want you.* So what do I care if you want me? I don't want you! Go away. Find a girl who'll play games with you."

"I want you."

Perhaps because he did amuse her, or maybe because she liked being the object of this adoration, she allowed David to see her often. He would arrive at her place sometimes very late at night, even after she had returned from her regular date, just to have the last few words of the evening with her and bring her a book.

She had a whole collection of David's book gifts on the table. Poetry (Donne, Keats, Shelley, Eliot), novels (Kafka, Joyce, Faulkner), and essays on art, philosophy, religion, from Bertrand Russell to Tillich. Julia never read any of it. Not a word.

Sometimes she would let him "lecture" her (as she called it) and then would listen with a quizzical or bewildered expression on her face as if trying to grasp what he was after.

"Just tell me one thing, you dopey kid. What do you want from me? What are you trying to do to me?"

"I am trying to reach the beauty that is in you, and have it emerge. I want you to touch and feel and know the wonder of life and make it part of you. There is a miraculous spirit in you that I want to reach . . . for your sake."

"You're driving me crazy, you know that? With that kind of crappy talk!"

"But I will reach you."

"Then what's all this about holding my hand and mushing around? Why're you trying to kiss me all the time?"

"Because I want you completely, all you are, in every way you exist."

"Like in bed?"

"My body wants your body, my mind wants your mind."

"You're a nut, that's what you are! An absolute nut! All that 'spirit' talk, and you're tryin' to lay me all the time. Well, forget it, sonny. I don't want to go to bed with you! I don't care for you that way, you understand what I mean? Uh uh! Nope. I just don't want it with you."

"If you let me make love to you, you'd change your mind."

She laughed and shook her head, blowing the cigarette smoke directly into his face. "No, baby. No!"

One evening, about a month after this conversation, David arrived with his little present of a book and sensed at once that she was in a strange mood. She moved about restlessly and responded sharply to everything he said.

"I brought you a wonderful book by Buber."

She snatched the book out of his hand without looking at it and flung it on the table.

"I don't want any more of your cockeyed books! I don't want any more of your crap altogether! It's driving me crazy!"

"You're upset about something. Let me talk to you."

"You upset me! You bother me! I can't stand your nuttiness anymore! It's getting me all mixed up. You tell me I'm this beautiful person inside—well, where is it? There's nothing inside! I can't even read those goofy books. Poetry, religion. What the hell do I care about that?"

"I want to make you care."

"But I don't! I can't stand you trying to change me all the time. Leave me alone!"

"I can't, Julia. I want you."

"There!" she whirled around, grasping at this. "I want you! I don't get it. All that stuff about my spirit and my soul—and always wanting to go to bed with me! What are you, for God's sake? Which one is you?"

She came up and stood in front of him challengingly.

"I'll show you what you are. You wanna see? I'll show you you're just like anybody else. Like any guy who wants to screw me. You're no different!"

She reached up and took his face in her hands, holding it, looking into his eyes, daring him.

"David, you want to go to bed with me? Now? Right now?"

He stared, unable to answer, afraid of some joke she was going to play on him.

"You've never been to bed with a woman, have you?" Now her arms twined around his shoulders, caressing, her body against his. "You want me to be the first? You want me to show you what it's like?"

He suddenly reached out for her arms, but she pulled them away, stepped back.

"You want to screw me, David?"

"Why do you say it that way?"

"Because that's what it is! For you—just like for anybody else!"

She walked over to the bed and pulled the cover back, down to the foot of the bed. "Okay?" she looked at him. "Okay? You want to do it?"

He watched her. He had to tighten his arm muscles to keep them from trembling.

"Well, what are you waiting for?" She had already stepped out of her dress and tossed it on a chair. "For God's sake take your clothes off. You're not going to screw with your clothes on?"

That word was a slap at him, a spitting at him. He felt her deliberately degrading him, making the moment dirty and ugly.

She was naked, her clothes in a pile on the chair. She moved to the table and lit another cigarette, her nakedness now something established between them, not to be given any thought. She was ready for the next step.

David stared at her, at the naked white body, and it was as if he didn't see it. Her breasts, which he had longed to touch, see, feel, were just two parts of the body attached to her chest. He looked at the mysterious black triangle he had envisioned a thousand times, and there was a hairy ugliness about it. Her behind curved more fully as she reached down for the cigarette, but it was like two lifeless layers of flesh.

"Well?" Now she was in front of him. "Do I have to undress you?" She had opened his tie and unbuttoned his shirt and pulled the ends of it out of his trousers. He moved his arms so the shirt came off, almost unaware he had done it. She lifted his hand and placed the palm on her breast. "Want to feel it?" She was watching his face, waiting for what she wanted to see there.

The flesh was cold to his hand, the bump of the nipple meaningless.

"Well, take your shoes off. You can do that!"

He stepped out of his shoes, using the toe of one against the heel of the other to extricate his feet.

"You want me to undress you, don't you? A lot of men like it. Gives 'em a thrill. All right."

She was unzipping his trousers. He stood with his arms hanging down at his sides, without even the strength to move them. She pushed his trousers down to the floor. He stepped out of the heap around his feet.

"More? Want me to do everything?"

She grabbed his shorts with both hands and pulled them down. They lay on the floor around his ankles, a white circle from which his naked body rose. She stepped back and started to laugh. He heard the laughter, saw the face laughing, the mouth open. He didn't have to look down, but he did. The cold, trembling feeling down there. The penis shrunken, withdrawn, as if trying to escape into his body.

"My God," she was still laughing, pointing at it now. "You can't even—"

The tears were running down his cheeks uncontrolled. His lips quivered as he stared at her, his face twisted with his pain.

She looked at him now, noticing, unbelieving. Was he crying? Was he standing there, this dumb kid, and crying? She turned away.

"For God's sake, stop it!"

He couldn't move, couldn't answer.

She walked about restlessly, confused, upset for the first time. She flopped down on the bed, on her back, and stared up at the ceiling, pulling on the cigarette. Finally she burst out with it.

"Will you go home! For God's sake, go home and leave me alone! Goodbye!"

He dressed without a word. When he was at the door, she sat up and called out to him.

"Hey!"

He looked at her, at her naked body outlined against the window. She turned away and fell back on the bed, unable to say it.

"Nothing. Goodbye. Go home, kid. Go!"

That night, in his bed, not really thinking of Julia or what had happened, not even of himself in relation to it, not feeling anger or pain, not doubting or questioning himself in any way, but feeling somehow that he was only accepting the inevitable, he decided to become a rabbi.

By the time Elaine Barrett returned from the movie in town (it was that French picture "for adults only" that everyone was talking about) the members of the Executive Committee were all gone. Bob had urged them to leave as quickly as possible, pledged them to secrecy ("No discussion of what's happened, even with your wives!"). He promised to report to them on his confrontation with Rabbi at the earliest possible moment.

Elaine didn't know they had been there. When a meeting was held at the house, she usually made a big pot of coffee and set out a plate of cookies or cake, then went off to spend the evening with a friend. Bob preferred it that way. Tonight, he had gently insisted she see this movie and she was pleased by his thoughtfulness.

Perhaps it was the picture, with its frank, close-up portrayal of physical love, perhaps it was Bob's gift to her of a free, enjoyable evening, or perhaps just the softness of the spring night and driving home in the open convertible, but she was conscious now of a delicious languor, of being so sensuously relaxed that she wanted to stretch right out on the bed and revel in the sensation.

At the same instant, as soon as her mind projected that image, there was the familiar tightening of anxiety, the awful sadness that came whenever she thought about going to bed with Bob. How would Bob react? Would there be the effort on his part, the struggle with which she was so familiar? All the outward signs and gestures, and at the same time the unconscious running away? The contrived busyness, the intent concentration on the work from the office, all aimed at avoiding the contact that he couldn't deal with?

Elaine knew that Bob considered her a strong, even a dominating woman. Occasional outbursts over trivial matters—"Stop telling me what to do! Don't try to run everything, Elaine!"—shocked her with their intensity and the revelation of emotions disturbingly close to the surface in him. But at the same time she felt that he must surely appreciate her understanding of him, her awareness of all the contradiction of drives and needs and anxieties that he now was.

At this point in her thinking she always went back to that caricature of a Jewish mother he had had. Fiercely protective, she guarded him so fanatically against what she considered a hostile gentile world that when he first went to school and saw *"goyishe"* children, he was frightened of them, convinced they would try to hurt him. His mother had made the whole outside world a place so dangerous, so threatening, that only the craftiest plotting and scheming could enable a Jew to survive.

His mother's perpetual struggles against her husband, Bob's giant of a father, were equally destructive for Bob. A tall, powerful, exuberantly dominating man, his father not only made the law that governed Bob's life, but enforced it with unyielding sternness. He made Bob feel that he could never compete with him, never learn to deal with such power, never overcome it and become a *someone* himself.

And the way his mother would slyly "get around" this man, with little lies and deceits, to get more money out of him, or make him spend the summer where she wanted to, or buy something for the house. All this Bob not only witnessed and knew about, but it disgusted him and made him feel ashamed for his mother.

And he had experienced, too, the inevitable reaction when his younger brother was born, the sudden loss of his mother's exclusive devotion, the actual physical withdrawal of her body, her encompassing arms, her breast against his face, and her substitution of this demanding stranger in his place. To make it worse, his mother had demanded of him when he was only two that he should now also play the role of protector to his little brother, help her provide love for the infant, be "big enough" to assume a role that to him was hateful. As if he had not been abandoned by his mother for this newcomer, the love he needed suddenly withdrawn from him.

All this Elaine knew, and in a sense used, in her understanding of Bob. It wasn't his fault that the struggles of his childhood had shaped him into a man who had a need to assert himself, to proclaim to the world his strength and virility. He had a need to do this in all his relationships, but perhaps especially with her. Had he picked *her*, she would ask herself, because she was in some way like his mother? A strong woman who could not be easily controlled. The mother-image he was determined finally to pay back and defeat?

Whatever the reasons, known to him or not, she was aware that he was involved in a kind of constant conflict with her. With almost desperate determination he tried to reach out to her, or respond to her own seeking of him, and at the same time he was somehow turning away, as if secretly accepting defeat in his effort.

It was remarkable, she felt, the way he never revealed any of this to the outside world. One reason was that there were so many positive and enjoyable things about him. A certain innate sweetness, at times an almost youthful charm, to which everyone responded. And he was considered a man of action, able to make and enforce vital decisions, functioning with strength and efficiency.

In fact, in the business world the word most often used to describe Bob was dynamic. . . . He was Executive V.P. of Evans & Hartsley, an advertising agency with 120 million dollars in billing, of which about 10 million was on the Lily Soap account, and Bob was supervisor of the account.

He ran it like a company commander who had a mission to lead his men to victory. Not ruthless, not unkind, but absolutely determined. He believed in thorough preparation, everybody knowing exactly what he would do and say at a meeting, and then sweeping the client back with facts, charts, statistics. He demanded of his people a presentation with every point covered, every question answered, every argument solidly supported.

Those who worked under him at the agency couldn't conceive of missing a deadline, even if it meant hours at night and weekends, and Bob would be right there with them, bouncing from office to office to check, approve, revise, or just provide the spurt of extra energy they needed. There would be a smile at the right moment, a joke to break the tension, encouraging praise precisely when it was needed. But the drive to get the job done right was relentless. And this "dynamism" of his brought results. When you worked with Bob Barrett you worked your balls off, but you knew the campaign would be sold, the marketing plan would be adopted, the budget would be approved.

In Greenlake, this image of him was sustained. How many **times** did other women say to her, with a suggestion of envy in their voices, "Elaine, you're lucky to have such a positive man for a husband." Or, coming closer to the area of their own frustration, "Bob is so intense— so with it—it must be great to have a guy who's so involved with you."

Involved? Elaine would smile wistfully. If only he were capable of the deep involvement she longed for, the complete sharing, giving and taking, the full, meaningful contact.

There was their custom of the half-hour cocktail, for example. When Bob came home and was washing up, she would bring out the tray, the shaker, the two chilled glasses, the olives, all prepared exactly as he wanted. Andy and Wendy were trained by now to respect this as the time when Dad and Mommy sat and talked together, and went off to watch television or do their homework. She and Bob would sit side by side on the couch near the fireplace, lean back luxuriously into the relaxing softness, sip their drinks, and talk about the day.

And Elaine, moved by this closeness, this relating to each other, might reach out for his hand and squeeze it. She would feel him squeezing back, the pressure of his fingers on her hand. There would even be a smile on his face that indicated his awareness of what she was expressing. Her heart would start to beat fast, but a cold shock would run through her as she realized he was only saying "I understand," and not expressing anything himself. Nothing was coming to her out of his own need, his own desire to reach out for her. It was all locked deep inside and covered over and protected by nerves that couldn't communicate, emotions that couldn't be stirred to life.

After dinner, when he reached for that fat, sleek briefcase of his and spread out all those papers and memos and letters on the desk, the evening's work, there was the implication from him that this was a burden, a responsibility he didn't really want. Yet it seemed to be a refuge too, a protective barrier between them that he hid behind, safe in his isolation, the distance between them justified, the shutting off of contact something he couldn't be blamed for.

She had come to know so well all these signs of his conflict. The way he would embrace her when they went into the living room in the evening, a quick, impulsive hug that said: I feel myself reaching out for you. And then he might stretch out on the couch "just to relax for a bit." It had been an exhausting day. "I'm drained. One crisis after another today." He would fall asleep lying on his back that way. Later she would see him on his side, facing into the couch, as if creeping into its depth for shelter, for refuge, for escape.

It might be one or two in the morning when, still lying awake in her bed, wondering, trying to argue against her loneliness and emptiness, she would hear him groping about as he undressed and got into his bed. If she stirred, he would mumble: "I guess I passed out. I'm sorry, dear."

Was he really asking her forgiveness? Or was he telling her again that it couldn't be helped. He didn't want the situation to be as it was any more than she did, but he didn't know how to change, how to "make it" with her.

He had used that phrase "make it with you," several times in bed. They would lie side by side, their bodies touching, their arms around each other, their lips a breath away, and they would both sense that instead of just lying there, they should be kissing, their mouths together, mingling and seeking. He would caress the back of her head gently, and sometimes run his hand softly down her back, along her spine, as if to soothe her, reassure her. And she would wait for the hand to wander elsewhere, a tightness of anticipation in her, a longing. But it moved only up and down her back, the palm gently caressing, stroking, slowly, almost absently.

She dared not take his mouth and kiss it, dared not draw him closer. That would be aggressive. That would be demanding. Forcing. She had to wait for him to summon whatever emotion, or freedom to show the emotion, that he needed. Her body would grow tense.

He would feel this in her at once and then stop even the caressing, as if she had spoken the words, the condemnation of him.

"What's the matter, Bob?"

"Nothing." He would sit up. "I think I want a cigarette. You?"

"No."

He would reach over to the end table and shake one out, light it, lie back on the pillow, the dragging on the cigarette like a punctuation to his thoughts.

"What's the matter, Bob?"

"You know."

"But there's really nothing the matter, darling. Not really. We have all the time in the world."

"What made you say that?"

"Because I know you need time and that it—"

"Why do I need time? Why should a man be this way with his own wife?"

"It doesn't matter. Everybody's different, and you—"

"I'll tell you what it is. I just can't make it with you. I feel . . . I don't know. . . ."

"Tell me."

"You want to know? I think it's a resentment. I feel the demanding by you."

"I'm not demanding anything."

"Not saying it—but feeling it. Waiting for me to perform. And I freeze up. Sometimes I just can't make it with you, Elaine."

It was not always this way, thank God. After a few drinks, or after a party, it seemed all right. Of course, he was somewhat uncontrolled then, not really himself, but at least the alcohol could bring out this urge. And sometimes, like a miracle, the sweetness that was in him, that was really always there, came out so fully, warmly, deliciously, that it was beautiful. But it wasn't easy. It had to be managed. But she was still willing to try.

This evening, easing the car into the garage, stepping out languidly, feeling warm and dreamy, she began to plan it carefully. The light was on in the den, which meant he was either working there or watching television. She would make some coffee and bring it to him and they would sit a while together and talk. She would tell him about the movie, amuse him, make him laugh. There would be no sense of pressure at all.

The instant she entered the den he looked up and asked: "How was the movie?" Almost as if he too had prepared himself.

"Wow!" she flopped into a chair. "What they didn't show about making love hasn't been thought of yet!"

He stretched his arms out over his head, yawning. "God, what time is it?"

No further questions about the movie, she noticed. "Eleven-thirty, dear. You must be tired."

"Tired? I'm dead! But I've got to finish this."

"Want some coffee? I'll make it."

"No!" The reply came a bit too emphatically.

She retreated. "All right. I know what you need." She came up behind him and started to massage his shoulders gently. He bent his head, allowing her to get at his neck, and then finally pushed back his shoulders and straightened up as a signal that he had had enough.

"Thanks for the rubdown. You better go to bed, Elaine. I've got to finish this."

"You've been at this all evening? That's four hours' work, Bob."

"Not all evening. I just started—" He caught himself and stopped. Now he stood up nervously. "Elaine, please go to bed."

Something uneasy in his manner suddenly seemed strange, something more than the ordinary tension.

"You haven't been working all evening?" It sounded more suspicious than she had intended. He was making meaningless movements behind the desk. "What *were* you doing?"

"Why do you keep asking?"

The words between them now had a different tone, there was a sense of sparring.

"It's simple. If you haven't been working, what were you doing?"

"Elaine, please don't cross-examine me. I was busy, whatever I had to do. Now—will you go to bed and let me finish?"

So? He was turning it off. And so obviously, so determinedly. Now she was certain there was something peculiar—an irritability, and a guardedness—about his manner tonight.

She went into the living room and sat back on the couch and lit a cigarette. When she turned to drop the match into the ash tray on the end table, she noticed it was full, not only with cigarette butts, but the ends of two cigars. She stood up and examined the other ash trays scattered about in this part of the room. All of them packed with cigarette butts. She knew Zelda had cleaned the room in late afternoon.

She walked straight into the den and sat down in the big leather chair facing the desk.

"There was a meeting here tonight, Bob. Why didn't you tell me?"

He hesitated, tapping the pencil against the desk, scrutinizing her for some kind of guidance.

"Well, so there was a meeting. You wanted to know what I did this evening—we had a meeting."

"Of the Executive Committee?"

"That's right."

"But no meeting was scheduled."

"So it was *un*scheduled."

"An emergency?"

"Elaine, don't pump me like that. There was a meeting. All right? Now let me finish my work, please."

"Something wrong about the Temple?"

"The Temple's going along fine. It's rolling along beautifully."

"Then what?"

He threw down his pencil. "Dammit, you're a persistent woman. If I wanted to tell you, isn't it obvious I would?"

"That is obvious. What intrigues me is why you don't want to tell me. Of course I realize now why you sent me off to the movies tonight. And if you felt you had to do that—I want to know why."

"Elaine, can't you let things alone? Just trust my judgment. I don't want to discuss it with you. There must be a reason, you can understand that. Now be sensible. Forget it, and just go to bed."

"All right," she moved towards the door, upset, feeling an undertone that frightened her. "I'll call Rabbi tomorrow and ask *him*."

They looked at each other, an indescribable understanding passing between them. Her mention of Rabbi, carried the hint of a threat. He reacted with the expected annoyance, even hostility.

"Elaine—" It was coming out now with reluctance and at the same time out of some need: "Rabbi wasn't at the meeting."

She was startled. "Of the Executive Committee?"

"That's right."

"He's not sick. I spoke to him this afternoon—was there some reason?"

"He wasn't invited."

Now she experienced a sense of danger, a strange fright. "Why, Bob?"

He managed to get back slowly to his chair, using the time to decide, to force himself to decide to do it. But he still couldn't.

"Elaine, I didn't—and I don't—want to discuss it. Don't force it."

"How can you go this far and not tell me?"

"I didn't want to go this far. You kept pushing and pushing. Now can't we let it go?"

"Why wasn't Rabbi invited, Bob?"

The curious need to reveal it all to her surged up in him. Despite the knowledge of what it would mean to them both, what it would place between them, he surrendered to an uncontrollable desire to get it out, have it over with, faced.

"The meeting was about asking Rabbi to resign his office."

"Oh my God!" Her hand to her mouth. A long, incredulous, agonized moment. "Oh my God—you've done it!"

"What?"

"You're going to get rid of him. Like you've always wanted to!"

She didn't understand. He kept thinking: she doesn't understand. She thinks it's because—

"All of you here!" She was continuing, putting it together her way. "This whole congregation has been after Rabbi. They don't appreciate him. They don't understand what he's trying to do for them!"

He couldn't resist it, the beginning of revealing it, the turning her in the right direction, the leading her to it with her own words.

"But *you* understand him?"

"Yes! Of course! I know what he wants to do here. For all of us."

"How is it that you know this so well, Elaine?" It had to be done, but there was a bitterness in it, a pain.

She was suddenly aware, her mind almost dizzy at the conclusion. "What does that mean, Bob?"

"There's no need to explain it. Is there?"

"What are you hinting at?"

"I'm not hinting, Elaine. I'm referring to it. How is it that *you* understand him so well? Better than anyone."

"Because I work with him!"

"That's what I mean."

She stared at Bob as if she needed to arrange his image in front of her, make him look normal, the head, the mouth, the eyes, the man talking to her.

"So I work with him. Will you in God's name tell me what's wrong with that?"

Bob was trapped now in all the ugliness of it, all that was to come and could no longer be avoided. "It's the *way* you've worked with him. Elaine, do I have to spell it out? The way the two of you are always together. Meetings all the time. Seeing each other all—"

"Bob!" She came right up to him. "What are you saying?"

"I'm saying, Elaine—and I didn't want this, remember that!"

"Say it!"

". . . That there's more between you and him than just work."

She stared at him, not knowing whether to turn and run or strike him or how to stop the tears or what to answer.

"What . . . do you think there is between us?"

"You tell me."

"Nothing!"

"That's your description of it?"

"Of what, for God's sake!"

"Of whatever it is. However far it's gone. Because it can't be just working together, Elaine. It can't be! All those meetings. Every day practically. Lunches. Seeing him late at night. And the two of you on the phone all the time. Are you telling me that's only work?"

She shook her head in utter disbelief, unable to accept the fact that he had actually spoken those words, actually said what had come out of his mouth.

"You must be crazy!"

"Yes. To have let it go on for so long."

"My God, stop it!"

"Crazy to have faith in you. To think you'd stop carrying on like a—"

She swung with all her strength and felt his face against her palm, the hot flesh of his cheek.

They stood in silence, not looking at each other. And suddenly they were like two beaten human beings, both battered, both hurt by the same blow. Her hand hung at her side, the palm glowing from the contact. Now the blow was his, part of him.

After a long time he stepped back. It was a struggle to open his mouth, create a voice out of his insides.

"Is that your answer?"

She was in the chair, sobbing, shaking her head, gasping for air. He continued talking, managing the words like great weights that he was putting down.

"We both know that such a reaction tells more about the truth than all your words do. . . . And it is not a denial."

"There's . . . nothing to deny. Nothing. Nothing."

"What's more . . ."—now he was going to push it all the way—"it would do no good to deny it. I have evidence."

She looked up. This was more than it was possible to believe. "Evidence of what?"

"Of your . . . let's call it involvement with each other."

She shook her head helplessly. "What evidence?"

"Zelda saw you kissing each other. Right here in this house. . . . Is that enough?"

"Zelda?"

"Your arms around each other. . . . You want more?"

"Oh my God!"

"That's not a denial either."

"My God, Bob! She told you that?"

"She swears it to be true."

"Zelda? She's . . . she's just getting back at me because I've been scolding her! I caught her drinking. I threatened to fire her. She's only—"

"She swears it! Now—now let's hear the denial."

"Oh my God!" Elaine covered her face, shaking her head, trying to make herself think, speak clearly. "She came in once, and. . . ."

"Yes?"

"Let me tell you! . . . there was a . . . a meeting scheduled here in the afternoon. Sisterhood. And . . . and it was called off . . . and Rabbi wasn't notified. Someone forgot. So . . . so he came expecting a meeting and . . . I gave him some coffee and we . . . we talked awhile. And . . . I was . . . I was very depressed that day. We'd had a quarrel the night before, you and I. It was when you went off into the kitchen after watching television all night, and you sat there and ate and wouldn't talk to me—"

"Come to bed with you. You can say it."

"You wouldn't come near me—just to be close. I needed you. I was unhappy. I wanted some comfort, some contact, warmth."

"So you turned to—"

"No! We were talking about something—just sitting there and talking, and he noticed how I looked, so he . . . he said: 'Is anything wrong? You look very unhappy.' And his saying that . . . I . . . I couldn't help myself. I started to cry. I cried and cried and couldn't stop. And finally . . . he wanted to leave, it was embarrassing for him . . . finally . . . we were standing there and he said: 'What can I do to help?' And I said: 'Nothing! Nothing! It's—my problem.

Nothing!' . . . And he . . . he put his arms on my shoulder and said: 'If I can help, please let me.' And he held my face for a moment, like a father, like a gentle, understanding father, and kissed me on the forehead. And I held on to him a moment because I was so sick inside, so desperate and miserable. And Zelda walked into the room and saw us. Saw that. She saw that. You understand? She saw Rabbi comforting me . . . trying to help me feel like a human being again. She saw that—and nothing else. Because there *was* nothing else! Then or ever or anytime, anywhere! *Nothing! Do you understand that?*"

"I understand one thing—that you turned to him then . . . and other times, God knows how often . . . in what way . . . for what reasons. You turned to him! To another man!"

"How am I supposed to feel about that? You tell me! How is a husband supposed to feel when his wife turns to another man to get—whatever it is—comfort? Understanding? Appreciation? Love? Am I supposed to accept that? What do you think it does to me? Or didn't you even care?"

Elaine sat in the chair, groping for some kind of clarity. What was he doing? What had he done? She was finally able to look up, her eyes swollen, her face a drained blank.

"What . . . happened at the meeting?"

"The Executive Committee has authorized me to ask Rabbi Gordon to resign."

"On . . ." it was hard for her even to continue asking, ". . . on what grounds?"

"On the grounds of immoral behavior."

"Oh God! Oh God, Bob! You told them?"

"I told them it was with a woman . . . who was not his wife. Don't worry. I had the decency to protect you."

"And they—believed you?"

"Oh . . . I'm supposed to get a confession from him or something. An admission. Then, I am authorized to ask him to resign."

"But what is he going to admit? There's nothing to admit!"

"Don't be childish. It's a matter of involvement! Of closeness with a woman who is not his wife. A certain kind of closeness no man has a right to have—least of all a Rabbi!"

"He did nothing immoral! That's not immoral behavior!"

"In a Rabbi—it is. In our supposed spiritual leader, establishing a special, private, close relationship with a woman not his wife—is totally immoral! Do you imagine he can still continue as a Rabbi here—with you and me here—after I confront him with that? If he has any integrity, he'll offer his resignation. I won't even have to ask for it!"

Now she began, consciously, deliberately, a desperate effort, using everything she could summon, all the determination left in her. She lit a cigarette, her hand shaking, unable to see the end of the cigarette, forgetting where the ash tray was.

"Bob—will you listen to me if I tell you something?"

"Isn't it useless, Elaine? If you want to stop me—don't you realize it's useless?"

"Listen! God, please listen. Listen with your mind, not your emotions. You know how . . . how we sometimes tried to discuss the problems we had. You and I. We didn't go deep enough perhaps, but as intelligent adults we did try. We talked. We tried to understand each other, understand what was at the bottom of it all. We tried to find out!"

"It didn't make it any better, did it?"

"But it can! Understanding what is happening, really getting at the truth of it, can help!"

"And you feel there is some kind of hidden truth here, don't you? As you always do. Something I'm not facing."

"Please, Bob—I'm not attacking you. I'm not pushing anything on you. Just trying to get at—"

"What?" He interrupted with irritated impatience. "You might as well say it!"

"Bob, you tell me now that I've hurt you. That my behavior—as it seems to you—was a rejection. A turning away from you to someone else."

"Not just someone!"

"All right, the Rabbi. And I can understand how that could hurt if it were true."

"If?"

"All right, even if you think it's true. Because I know that amounts to the same thing. But Bob—what you plan to do about it—how you plan to deal with it—is wrong!"

"Oh? I'm not observing some code or other? The 'injured party,' as they call it, has a formula to follow?"

"No! That's not it at all! If you could only put aside your hurt for a minute and try to understand what you are doing. You are going to confront Rabbi Gordon. Tell him what you feel—"

"What I know!"

"What you . . . know. Then you'll announce how he's to be punished for this. He's to be made to resign, be destroyed as a Rabbi. And Bob—now listen! Don't you know that it's not *him* you want to punish. It's me! Me!"

"Very clever. You're twisting it all so that—"

"I'm not twisting anything! Just asking you to face it. You want to get at me. Hurt me! Humiliate me! Punish me!"

"I don't have to punish you. Your own sense of guilt will do that."

"But you have to strike out at me. You have to do something to me. You need that!"

He stared down at his hands, opening and closing them as if there was a pulsation in them he couldn't control. Finally, in another kind of voice altogether, almost weary now, the weight of many sadnesses in it, he said slowly:

"What is this need?"

"Bob, we both know. Don't we? For whatever reasons, right or wrong—and there must be some right in it, I'll admit that—you have a need to tear me down. To show me that I'm not the strong, overpowering woman you imagine me to be. Or feel me to be. You need to show me your own strength, your ability to control your own destiny . . . and mine."

He turned away and sat down in the chair behind his desk, swinging in the chair so that it faced the window, away from her. She knew he wouldn't answer. She felt for him at that moment a strange sense of pity, of concern for his pain and his problem, of sympathy for his helplessness.

"Bob—all I ask is this: don't destroy another human being in doing this. Don't ruin a man's whole life—for this!"

He was looking down at his hands again. She stood there only a little while longer and then turned quickly and ran up to her room.

That night he didn't even come to the bedroom, and she hadn't expected him to.

RABBI 2

The problem was the five years it would take to complete the course in the Rabbinic school. The years from twenty-two to twenty-seven would be years of study and preparation, years during which he would need everything provided for him, every bite of food he ate, every pair of socks he wore.

Sam felt, in a resurgence of the traditional role of the father who had a scholar for a son, and a Rabbinical scholar at that, that the responsibility for solving the problem was his. Besides, he had come to accept the grocery store as the mark of his own failure in the world. All these desperate years of petty struggle, all the slavery of the body and of time in that dark, dirty hole of a place, had brought nothing but existence itself as a reward. Out of this dull gray existence he had wrenched no comforts, no security, no snug little accumulation in the bank to draw on for some critical need, no resources even to help his own son through these years of becoming a Rabbi.

It was a failure Sam could accept only with bitterness, but it was bitterness directed toward himself. And out of that bitterness he now drew the strength to act.

He went to his brother, Nathan, without humbleness or shame. For now there was a sense of duty involved, almost of sacredness in his purpose. The alienation that had developed between his brother and himself over the years didn't matter. So Nathan was successful. So he lived in a big apartment. So Nathan's son was already launched in the business and getting married soon. None of that mattered. The time had arrived again (as when he had helped him come to America) for Nathan to act as a brother, as a member of the family. A young boy needed help to become a Rabbi. That help would have to be given regardless of what had passed between the brothers over the years.

Sam approached it bluntly, as for a cause.

"Nat, I need your help. My David wants to become a Rabbi. For five years he's going to go to Rabbinic school. I don't have the money to support him for five years and pay all his expenses. God didn't let my own dream come true. I failed. I'm a poor man after all those years of slavery in the store. I want you to provide the money."

Nat put his cigar down. He studied his fingernails a moment.

"You want a loan? How much?"

"Not a loan."

"You want a loan from me, Sam?"

"I said *not* a loan! I'll never be able to pay it back, so what good is a loan?"

"Not a loan? So if a man is asked to give money—even to his own brother—maybe he's allowed a word to say? Whether it's a wise thing? The kind of sense it makes?"

"David is going to be a Rabbi! Can there be a question if this makes sense?"

"Ah!" Nat leaned back, his eyes up as if confirming it with the heavens. "The question is—does it make sense to become a Rabbi in America? In your old shtetl in Poland, that's altogether another matter. To be a Rabbi was to be a success."

"An honor!"

"I'm talking success, Sam. You heard this word before? In America it's the magic word. Success. People work, slave, for one thing only—success. If we send kids to school—it's for what? They should have success! You know what it means success?

"Money, it means."

"Not money in the bank only! Money on your back. Money on your dining table. Money in the way you talk, the way you smoke a cigar. A man who's a success, he has a nice home. He drives a good car. He wears fine clothes, his wife has a fur piece. He spends his vacations with other successes—Miami Beach in the winter, in the summer big hotels in the Catskills.

"Sam, don't you realize the wonderful thing about America is that we Jews—we can now do this too. Just like anybody else! God bless a country that opened our eyes for us, gave us something new to live for. We can forget the old world with its foolishness. That a boy should study and study—just to be a scholar. And that a great scholar, no matter how much Talmud he knows—*he* should get the highest respect. And that a Rabbi is *eppes* something special to look up to. That's gone, Sam. Finished! This is America."

Sam said it very quietly, but there was already a sense of hopelessness in his voice. "Nat, my David wants to be a Rabbi. That's all he wants to be!"

"So it's up to the father to show him his foolishness. That's why you're his father!"

"Nat, I need your help, not your philosophy."

"You need my money, Sam."

"David needs it."

"And because I'm his uncle, your brother, I can't let him do this, Sam. I'll give him the money just like that—I'll write a check in two minutes—if he'll go into a business. Even a profession let it be! A dentist, let's say, a lawyer. He could even be an engineer. But, Sam— a Rabbi? It's not right for him!"

"I'm going to ask the last time, Nat. You'll give the money?"

"Sam, it hurts me to see how little you learned in this country. How you still think and live like you're in the old world. For David's good I'm doing this, believe me, Sam. It hurts me—"

"It hurts you, Nat—but not enough."

The two brothers looked at each other with a sadness that neither could deny. Between them lay the knowledge that they were living in different worlds, that they could never again be to each other what brothers were supposed to be.

To Sam, it became another twisting of the rope of failure that bound him. Somehow, somehow he had to overcome this particular failure for his son's sake. This was the one thing he now had to do in his life, or it would all be nothing.

When he had made the arrangement, when it had all been discussed between himself and Al Margolies, he had to face telling David. But he wasn't really afraid. He was aware, with a combination of awe, bewilderment, and satisfaction, that there was something unusual about his son. The boy lived on another plane, in a world of strange attitudes and unexpected responses. He might not accept the arrangement, but he would understand. He would know deep inside why

Sam had done it. And it was important to Sam that David should understand.

"You really want, you decided and it's finished and definite, you really want to become a Rabbi?"

"There is nothing else I want."

"And no matter how, no matter what we have to do so you can go to the school, study—you'll do it?"

"There is nothing else I will do."

"So listen to me now. This is how it'll be. You know a Mr. Al Margolies?"

"The drug store on the corner?"

"He's been making good money. Good money. Two assistants, the lunch counter, everything."

"He's going to lend us the money?"

"Wait! Let me say how it'll be. No. Not loan us the money. Give it. All you'll need. For the whole five years . . . and it's not a loan. It's not a present. It's . . . David . . . it's what they call a dowry."

"A dowry?"

"David, listen to me. This is the way it'll be—if you want it. I can't force you. I don't even want to. You gotta want it yourself. But everything is arranged—if you only want it. Now listen. You know his daughter? Frieda? The girl Frieda?"

And so the dinner was set up for them all to get together, the two families, at Al Margolies' house. As it was done in the old country, David thought. A marriage arranged by the parents, the young people to meet when it was all done. Like the old days, Sam thought, when a sensible arrangement was worked out by the families and the children got together afterward.

Everything that one could possibly sit on in the Margolies living room was covered with thick, transparent plastic; still, one could see the beauty of the material underneath. The big couch in a flowered rose pattern, the two chairs in soft pink, the other little couch against the wall in delicate blue with huge woven roses arching across it. The money was evident everywhere.

All the Gordons came dressed in their best, Sam in the shirt with the cuffs, Ruth wearing the blue silk with the hand embroidery, Sarah in dignified black with the raised collar, and David in his blue suit, but somehow they still looked shabby in comparison to the Margolies.

It was the difference between taking out the best you owned from the closet and putting on something brand new and stylish.

Awkwardness was like a weight pressing down on the Gordons and they could only squirm under it. There was no escape. The Margolies were expansively at ease.

All except Frieda. She was a blonde girl of twenty-four (two years older than David) and there was a lack of grace about her. Her face had a kind of bigness to it, as if everything had been enlarged by a mechanical processer just one step too much. The heavy head of hair, the prominent nose with thick eyebrows curving down to it in two brown smudges, the large eyes that were more watery green than blue, the full mouth that formed a pout when relaxed—every feature— even her hands seemed too big for a girl and were constantly in her way. And yet one only had to look at her to realize that she was a timid and uncertain creature. One sensed her withdrawal almost physically. It was as if inside this overdeveloped framework there was a great empty hollow space and tucked away in a dark corner somewhere was the tiny, scared being that was Frieda.

David had seen her before, on the street and in her father's store, but now for the first time he actually looked at her and he felt a sense of pity and shame for her sake.

He wanted to take her hand and say: It's not your fault. Don't feel hurt. There's nothing wrong with you that a thing like this should have to be done to you. He wanted to show her that he understood, but he didn't know how.

They were placed side by side at the dinner table in the elegant dining room. She sat looking down at her plate most of the time, fingering the sterling silver teaspoon and turning it around and around nervously.

Mrs. Margolies, whose hair was swept up along the sides and monumentally arranged on top of her head, and whose voice seemed also to be lifted by the occasion, made it no easier for Frieda, though everyone realized her intentions were the best. She turned to David during the dinner.

"You like to eat? I mean you enjoy good food?"

David nodded.

"So you're lucky! My Frieda is a cook. I'm telling you! It could be fish, it could be meat. A *tsimmes* or chopped liver. She's got a touch! So what's your favorite, David?"

He tried his damnedest but just couldn't think of anything at the moment. Frieda tried to come to his rescue.

"Ma, don't embarrass me."

"It embarrasses you to be an outstanding cook? The way you make a *lokshen kugel*—that's an embarrassment?"

Sam squirmed in his seat a little. "David's a plain type eater. Whatever you serve, he eats."

Frieda and David exchanged glances. It was like the beginning of an understanding between them, for he sensed her relief at this and she knew he forgave her mother.

But Mrs. Margolies could not be stopped. "In a million years, David, you'd never guess what she wanted for a present on her birthday. Guess!"

David tried to think of something exotic. "A fiddle?"

Everyone laughed and there were a few moments of relief.

"Thank God not a fiddle!" Mrs. Margolies resumed relentlessly. "My Frieda's not for such foolishness. You know what? A sewing machine! That sensible girl, she wanted a sewing machine. Practical! To make her own clothes. To fix up a dress nice. Make drapes. Is that a sensible girl, I'm asking you?"

Now David felt the need to help Frieda out. "It saves money, that's for sure. Maybe she'll learn how to make a suit for me?"

Sam was glad David was taking it this way, good humoredly. Let Mrs. Margolies build up the girl, it was a mother's natural pride. And if it didn't bother David, that was a good sign.

"But it doesn't mean," Mrs. Margolies wasn't through yet, "my Frieda don't know how to enjoy. Like when there's a party, the boys know my Frieda's there, don't worry. The way she dances! Twenty-four dancing lessons, a regular course. She graduated one of the best in the class. You like to dance, David?"

"Rivkeh," Mr. Margolies finally interrupted, "he's going to be a *Rabbi*."

"And Rabbis are not allowed to dance? David—ha?"

"I think," now a certain embarrassment for him, "it depends on the dance."

"I understand—not some of these wild, crazy dances," Mrs. Margolies was really curious about this, "but nice social dancing I hope you and Frieda can enjoy together. A girl likes to dance."

"You know what?" Al Margolies said. "Why don't we let them get acquainted together alone? Let them go out, make a date. They'll find out about each other. They'll know what they can do, what they can't do." He turned to David. "So if you asked Frieda for a date, like to the movies or something, I got a suspicion she wouldn't object."

Everyone was staring at David. He looked at Frieda and saw her expectant eyes, waiting for him.

"Would you like to go to the movies tomorrow night?"

Frieda nodded quickly. Immediately there was a reaction of pleasure in the room, smiles, a flow of confidence and good feeling. It was going good! They pushed their chairs back and rose from the table. Al and Sam went off to a corner to congratulate each other and chat over the details. It was going to be a deal, no question about it.

The next night, David rang the bell downstairs and waited for her outside. When she appeared, he could see at once that she had dressed up for the occasion, as if they were going out formally instead of merely to a movie.

"You look very nice," he said. "You didn't make that dress yourself?"

"Oh no!" she laughed. "I wish I could."

They walked side by side down the street, still feeling like total strangers, afraid of each other's glances.

"You want to see that Cagney movie?"

"Sure."

"You like Cagney?"

"Yeah."

"Or there's that one with Charles Boyer. You want to see that?"

"Sure."

They walked on a while. "But which one? You have to tell me."

"Any one. I don't care."

"All right. Charles Boyer. It's—" he looked at her as he said it, "a lot more romantic."

He noted the quickest warm glance at him, even a little smile. And it didn't go away as they walked. Maybe she hadn't expected this. Maybe it was the beginning.

"Or better still—" he stopped, and she had to face him. She stood in front of him and for the first time since they had met they looked at each other as two individuals, her eyes openly taking in his face, his expression, and he aware of her as herself. "—Why don't we forget the movie altogether and sit somewhere and talk?"

She nodded her head. There was more than willingness, he thought —a kind of appreciation.

"Bickford's?"

"Sure."

"Do you mind Bickford's?"

"No."

"At least they let you sit and talk."

He brought the two cups of coffee to their table and sat down opposite her, so that she would have to look at him.

"Actually, I think Cagney is a better actor than Boyer. Don't you?"

She twisted up her eyes, thinking. "Maybe. But he's always the same."

"You mean a bang-bang tough guy?"

"Yeah."

"And isn't Boyer? I don't care what romantic part he's playing, it's that same damn Frenchman talking through his nose."

"Oh I like the way he talks."

"I know. Women do. You want another cup of coffee?"

"Uh-uh."

"Some dessert? Fruit salad?"

"Uh-uh," shaking her head. "I'm watching my weight."

"Fruit salad's not fattening. Besides, what's wrong with your weight?"

Her red face revealed the first real embarrassment, the secret shame. "I'm ... I'm ... well, I can't afford any extra weight."

"Nothing wrong with your weight."

"I'm watching it."

A long pause. The communication between two different worlds broken off for a while. They tried another code now, another language.

"You like to read?"

"Sure."

"Mysteries, I bet."

She smiled. "Well, I like them. But I read serious books too."

"Have you read Sartre?"

"Who?"

What he expected, what he knew, but determined to explore it. "Kafka?"

She was uncomfortable now. One more effort. "Tolstoy?"

"Oh!" Relief. "I started *War and Peace*, but gee, who could ever finish that? It goes on forever!"

So it was like this. As he had expected, had known. But she was also a little responsive. Not closed. Something to be awakened. Something to be nurtured. And so decent. So unpretentious. Honest, simple, gentle.

Finally, after they discussed the neighborhood (she hated it for its drabness, he loved it for its vitality), friends (she only had one real, good friend, he had many but not one real one), music (she liked jazz but knew about the classics, he liked the classics but knew about jazz), and parents (she respected her father's success, he respected his father's failure), they sat in silence a while, both knowing they now had to face it. And that it was up to him.

David pushed the coffee cup aside and leaned forward. "I think I'm going to make a speech," he said. "Not a sermon—a speech."

She smiled.

"About me, first—and then about you."

She waited.

"Frieda, it isn't just that I want to be a Rabbi. I must be one. I feel it as deeply as I'm able to feel anything. I want to reach people. Move them. Affect them. Help them. I need that . . . that involvement with people. And I think I have something to give them. Something good, and important. Something they should have that's missing in this world today. A concern with the *purpose* of life. A concern with its *meaning*. And the strength to make their lives richer that way. Through faith. That's what I want to do with my life. Do you understand?"

She hesitated. "I . . . I think so."

"Your father isn't religious?"

"No."

"You're not either?"

"I believe in God."

"I mean—you don't lead a life where religion is important."

"No."

"Would you . . . be able to?"

"I . . . I don't know."

"If I helped you? If I shared mine with you? Made you part of it?"

"I . . . think so."

"Would you try?"

She looked at him now, in need of her own answer. He reached out and placed his hand on hers. "Would you try . . . with me?"

Not the quick answer. She stared at his face, the intense eyes behind the glasses, the mouth open, waiting, the whole being of him surrounding her, pressing and seeking.

"I . . . could try."

"*Would* try?"

"I . . . would try."

He squeezed her hand a long moment, and then leaned forward again and she waited.

"Frieda, I want to say something that is very hard to say. I understand what you're going through. I feel it, and I feel for you. But let me say it, because . . . because unless I do, all of this means nothing and must never happen.

"Frieda, we don't know each other. We should. Two people who are . . . well, in the situation we are . . . should wait and get to know each other and be sure of a lot of things. One of them . . . maybe the only one . . . I mean with other people . . . would be to know that . . . that they love each other."

She was looking down and he felt her pain.

"But we can't say that. It would be untrue if we did. But . . . in a lifetime . . . when people are together for a lifetime . . . a thing develops and grows between them that can be good. It can be rich and good and have all the value to them both that anything else can bring.

"I want to promise you, Frieda, that I will try to make this happen. Nothing else will matter between us. How we met or why or anything. It won't matter! And I don't mean we'll forget it. You understand? It will be you and me. It won't matter! I promise you that."

He waited, but she could only look down, her big hands around the coffee cup, rubbing the edge, rubbing it, rubbing it.

He waited, unwilling to disturb the turmoil of fear and pride and uncertainty in her. He didn't even want to touch her. He waited, and looked at the bowed head, the hands rubbing the edge of the cup, comprehending the confusion whirling about inside her, the fear and shame and hope and doubt.

She looked up at him once, quickly, and then down again. And then suddenly, she reached her hand across the table.

He grasped it and held it tightly.

"Will you marry me, Frieda?"

She nodded her head. And he sat there as she cried, and he let her cry and he never took his hand away.

Danny Cole called his wife, Alice, from a phone booth in town to say he wouldn't be home for another hour or so, and then drove directly to the Rabbi.

It was eleven o'clock as he walked up the driveway and he suddenly realized he should have called Rabbi too, to say he was coming. But their relationship was close; Rabbi would understand. A tricyle blocked his way at the bottom of the three short steps at the front door, and he picked it up and put it aside.

Frieda opened the door, a dish towel in her hand. She stared at him apprehensively a moment as if she didn't recognize him. A few strands of hair had come down over the right side of her forehead, she was wearing an apron, and she had opened the door only wide enough to see who it was. Danny now felt like an intruder. He should have called first.

"Hello, Frieda."

"It's you, Danny. Come in."

"Is Rabbi . . . can I see him?"

"It's so late. Anything wrong?"

"It's important." He understood her apprehension, but didn't want to deal with it yet.

When he stepped into the living room he saw Rabbi in a robe, pajamas, and slippers, sitting at one end of the couch, reading. Frieda followed him in, still wiping her hands on the towel. Finally Rabbi Gordon looked up.

"Ah . . . it's you, Danny." Slowly withdrawing from the book, the long pull back into this other world. He placed the book aside. "Come in, come in!" Taking off his glasses, rubbing his eyes, he struggled to adjust. When you watched Rabbi do it, Danny thought, come back from a book, or from a deep tangle of thought, back into a room, to people, you sensed more than the reluctance. You knew how much was still away, left behind. "I was reading. Rosenzweig. The 'Essays on the Bible.' Translated by Buber. You know it?"

"David, it's eleven o'clock!" Frieda said. The relevance was clear to Danny, but Rabbi didn't even seem to hear her.

"You should read it someday. Wonderful! So come in, sit down. Frieda, maybe we can make some coffee for our friend?"

Danny and Frieda exchanged glances. "No, thanks. I don't want any."

"It's eleven o'clock, David." Frieda now stood in front of him, demanding a response, some awareness of the unusual circumstance.

"So? When my friend Danny visits me, the time doesn't matter. Besides, I want to talk to you, Danny. About Friday's sermon."

A dismissal of her, in effect. Instead, Frieda sat down on the edge of the chair, waiting.

"So come here and let me ask you something." Danny hesitated, but because Frieda was still there, expectant and apprehensive, he moved over to the couch and sat down. "I want your reaction. I think I have a really interesting point here."

Danny stared at him, controlling his sense of unreality. This was Rabbi. This was the uniqueness. The instant plunge into what concerned him, or whatever he was thinking of. A complete disregard or unawareness of the circumstances of the moment. If you awoke him at four in the morning to report some catastrophe and didn't start with your news, he would begin a discussion of whatever was on his mind before thinking to ask why you had called in the middle of the night. This was Rabbi. You had to accept it.

"I'm going to talk about expansion of the mind. That's right—drugs. What it is that people who take drugs—the kids, the grownups, whoever—what it is they really seek? And why—this is the important question—why they have a need for this experience. What vacuum in their life it fills. What satisfaction it provides. Because you see, the search for deeper experience, for deeper awareness of the self, is related in a very significant way to—"

"David!" Frieda interrupted. "Danny came here at eleven o'clock at night. Don't you want to know why?"

David smiled with slight guiltiness. He took his glasses off again and shook his head as he rubbed the edge of the robe over them.

"You know me, Danny. I'm sorry. I was so absorbed in—" he looked at him, "—so tell me. To what do we owe—" a meaningful glance at Frieda, "the honor of this visit at eleven o'clock at night?"

Danny clasped his hands together tightly and tried not to look at Frieda.

"There's something I'd like to talk to you about, Rabbi. . . . It's rather important."

"You mean alone?"

"Yes."

They both looked at Frieda. She folded the dish towel in her lap, neatly smoothing it out, her hand running over it and over it.

"I think I should stay," she said quietly.

"Frieda—!" Not a reprimand, a plea.

Still not looking up, her hand across the dish towel again and again. "I have an idea it's . . . some trouble." Then quickly to Danny. "Is it?"

Danny, surprised at her instinct, looked at David, who was smiling.

"Trouble, Danny? You never brought me trouble."

"Can't you see on his face?"

"Danny?" David was attentive now, for the first time.

Danny looked directly at him. He knew of no way to soften it. No way to evade it now. "Yes."

"I knew it!" Frieda was standing. "I knew it right away!"

"Frieda!" The Rabbi gestured gently, restraining her. "What . . . what kind of trouble, Danny?"

Danny looked down at his hands. In the delay, perhaps . . . perhaps. . . . But Frieda understood.

"He wants me not to be here when he tells you. But I'm going to stay."

"I'd rather you didn't, Frieda." Danny suddenly had the courage for this.

"And I feel I should stay."

This sparring, delay, challenging of each other, was now annoying to David.

"All right, stay Frieda! Stay! What can it be? Tell me, Danny."

The presence of Frieda made it impossible for Danny to speak. "I just can't. Rabbi—please allow me to speak to you alone."

"Frieda, please!" Rabbi had jumped to his feet, his arms outstretched like a sufferer, pleading.

She shook her head, smoothing the towel with her palm, across and across the damp, stained surface. "No. I'm your wife. If there's trouble, I want to know."

"I will assume the responsibility," Rabbi had come up to Danny, the tone not serious yet, the phrasing deliberately mock-legal, "of all the consequences of your saying whatever it is you have to say in the presence of my wife. All right? Now tell me, Danny. Please."

Wrong! Wrong! Wrong! But it had to be done now. "Rabbi, there was a meeting of the Executive Committee tonight at Barrett's house."

Frieda almost jumped. Rabbi stepped back.

"Tonight? Without me?" He turned slowly, heavily, all changed now, and walked back to his seat on the couch. He sat down like a man falling, the weight of it already on him, the significance. "I wasn't even notified."

"Deliberately." Danny watched him.

"And what . . ." David asked slowly, still taking it in, "what could they want to discuss so that they didn't want the Rabbi to be present?"

"You." Better this way, Danny thought, better to be blunt, get everything out.

"Me?" David spoke as if surprised. But the impact of Danny's news was evident; the fears already there in his voice and face.

Frieda had no ability for subtle prolongation. "They want to fire David, is that it, Danny?"

Always that instinct. That directness.

"What are you talking about, Frieda?" Rabbi waved her aside, and the idea and the fear with it. But it didn't work. "Danny?"

"Yes."

"Oh my God! I knew it!" Frieda bent over double, her head to her lap. "I knew it!"

"Danny?"

"Yes, Rabbi."

"They want to fire me?"

"Ask you to resign."

"It's Barrett," Frieda said to herself, to the hidden fear that had long been in her. "Barrett! I knew he'd do it someday. He was always your enemy, David. He hated you. I knew it!"

Rabbi only looked at Danny, the question in his eyes.

"Yes, Rabbi. Barrett."

"Because he doesn't understand what you're doing, David! He doesn't—"

"Frieda!" David said, standing. "Will you let Danny talk to me about this? Will you let him tell us?"

Frieda sat absolutely still. Only the hand moved over the towel, smoothing it.

"What happened at the meeting, Danny? Please tell me everything."

"Bob called an emergency meeting. He . . . he asked the Executive Committee to approve his coming to you and asking you to resign."

"And—?"

"It was approved."

"They're all no good!" Frieda was in tears. "They don't want a Rabbi! They want a messenger boy! You're too good for them, David! They don't understand—"

She was embracing him, clutching him, and David let her hold him and cry. He kissed her on the cheek; he held her chin a moment and looked at her, then quickly put his arms around her.

"Frieda, I know. I know what you're feeling. Now please, let's both sit down and hear the rest of what Danny has to tell us?"

She brushed the towel against her cheek and sat down. David moved slowly about the room, not pondering but absorbing, making Danny's words part of his reality.

"How," he turned to Danny finally, "did he express it? Inefficiency?"

"No."

"Did he cite a long list of failures? My inadequacy? My inability to function on the level required by this congregation?"

Danny was only aware of Frieda, the obstacle of her presence. But there was no turning back now.

"Rabbi . . . he made . . . an accusation against you."

"Of what?"

"Of . . . of immoral behavior."

The silence was like the breathlessness in the presence of a slimy monster that had slid into the room and lay there, alive in front of them, oozing filth.

Danny couldn't stand the anguish. "He accused you of immoral behavior with . . . with a woman who—wasn't your wife."

He stood up suddenly, the sight of the two of them more than he could bear. "I'm sorry! I'm so sorry, Rabbi, that I had to tell you this. Frieda—forgive me for saying it here like this, in front of you. I didn't want to. But I had to come here and let you know, Rabbi! I had to let you know!"

No one moved for a long time. Each was conscious of currents flowing through the room, toward each other, across and back, from one to the other two, from the two to one, across and back, the communication vibrating between them.

Frieda looked up. Her face was expressionless. The words came without passing through her face.

"David . . . I want you to know . . . I don't believe it."

David nodded. "Frieda, how could you believe it when—"

"I don't believe it!" She was standing. "You hear me?"

"I know, Frieda dear. How could—"

"*I don't believe it!*" To the sky, to the earth, to herself. She turned and ran out of the room, her hand over her eyes, wiping at the tears.

They listened to her run up the stairs, then heard the slamming of the door.

"Thank God," David finally said, "that she took it that way."

"Rabbi," Danny said, "let me tell you the rest of it now. He made this accusation, but wouldn't go beyond it. No names, no details, nothing. He refused. So that's all the Committee has. His accusation. His word."

David, standing up, began walking about in confusion, disbelief. "Of course, it's only a device. An excuse. Basically, they are dissatisfied with me. As their Rabbi. And this—this monstrous accusation—is only a means to—"

"No. Not entirely, Rabbi."

"Barrett *believes?*"

"I think he does."

"Immoral behavior with—"

"He must believe it or he wouldn't dare."

"But that's incredible! He's made up a horrible lie! It's a lie!"

"I know."

"Horrible, horrible! The thought of it! Such an accusation against me—"

"That's the point, Rabbi."

"That the accusation has been made?"

"Yes. For whatever reason—it has been made."

"And once made—"

"Yes."

"Of course! Of course! You're right. Once made. . . ." He was turning, walking, but with nowhere to go. "Then I have no choice, have I?"

"I don't see how."

"I must deny it. I must say and show it's a lie! Isn't that what I must do?"

"I was waiting to hear that, Rabbi. It's what I hoped you'd say."

"Of course! Can such a lie go unanswered? I have no choice! . . . But how? I don't know what to . . . Danny, what are they planning to do?"

"Barrett is going to come to see you. The way he put it—he's going to confront you with the accusation. And make you admit it. Then— after you do—the Executive Committee has voted him the right to . . . to ask you to resign."

"And if I deny it?"

"Barrett says . . . Rabbi, Barrett says you won't deny it."

"But if I do? If I say it's a lie! Which it is, God knows! Which it is!"

"Then . . . Barrett says he'll prove his accusation."

"Prove? How?"

"He says . . . with names, places, dates. All the evidence he has."

"This is a nightmare! What evidence? There's no evidence! There's nothing!"

"Rabbi, the horrible thing is that if you deny it—and Barrett is forced to try to prove it—it will be just as bad as if it were true. The accusation alone, if it comes out in the open, will destroy you as a Rabbi. And the Temple. That's what the others felt."

David sat down, all the weight of it in him, his head back, eyes closed, feeling all of it now.

"Do they . . . want so much . . . to get rid of me?"

"Some. I'm sorry, Rabbi. Some do."

"They're so dissatisfied with me? Have I failed so—"

"Only some, Rabbi."

"—that they would resort to this?" He spoke with his eyes closed, as if weary of it already, all the struggle. "Just imagine my position. If I resign, I admit to a false accusation. A horrible lie. If I deny it, I am still finished here as a Rabbi. What to do, Danny? What to do. . . ."

"Do what's right!"

"But what is right?"

"Expose the lie! Is there any question?"

"Expose it? Regardless of the consequences?"

"Of course!"

"Ah. . . ." The weighing, balancing. ". . . It isn't that easy, Danny. No. You see, it must be exposed only if that is the right thing to do. Not just for myself. For the congregation. For all the people here. To bring this out in the open—"

"Rabbi, there is right and there is wrong! A lie is wrong! My God, you're a Rabbi! You must do what is right!"

"And do you think a Rabbi has the ear of God and can ask Him what is right and wrong? I am a Rabbi, but like every man, I must find the truth myself."

"You know what's the truth here!"

"Yes. And suppose I were to fight for that truth? Who would gain by it?"

"Everyone gains by the truth!"

"Ah . . . not so. Alas, not so. Not every truth. Shall I fight for this truth—even though it will make the whole congregation suffer?"

"How?"

"When the Rabbi is smeared with dirt, all Jews become dirty. If this is brought out into the open, all members of the congregation will bear the shame. But if I resign . . . simply, quietly . . . no one will know."

"But you will know! You will be letting evil triumph!"

"Ah, how you put it. Evil triumph. Oh how young you are, Danny. Letting evil triumph, as you call it, is still intolerable to you. . . . But it is only an evil. One evil. Do you believe the world can exist without any evil? Even God has admitted he cannot eliminate all the evil from the world! . . . One must accept evil, Danny. Live with it. Understand what part it plays in the scheme of things. When this congregation is struggling so hard to make a place for itself here . . . to build a Temple for God—a Temple that must be built!—is this a time to be concerned with *one* evil? One man's right or wrong?"

"That Temple will be built on lies!"

"Does it matter? What house of God was ever put up with purity of spirit alone? What house of God doesn't have ambition, vanity, lust for power, even greed in its stones and foundations? But it doesn't matter! Because it still remains a house of God! Man's weakness doesn't make it less so. In that house of God there is at least a place where man can be lifted above himself!"

"Rabbi . . . I can't believe you're not going to fight this!"

"I'm saying I don't know, Danny. . . . I want time to think."

"Rabbi, I'm only your student. You've taught me many things, and I have tried to live by what I learned and what I believe. I'm going to do that now—live by what you taught me as my Rabbi. I'm going to fight this thing!"

"And I say—I must decide what will be done!"

"Rabbi, you can decide for yourself—but not for me."

"The fight would be for me!"

"No . . . Rabbi, not just for you. For me, too. So I can know I haven't betrayed everything I believe in. Everything you taught me!"

David reached out and Danny let him put his hands on his arms, hold the arms, and press them in against the body as if to hold in the flow, control it.

"Danny, you say you are my student. Then let me teach you something now. Listen to me. The greatest virtue of all is consideration of your fellow man. Not abstract principles of justice, but concern with the fate of your fellow man. . . . I say to you, Danny, as your Rabbi I say to you—this is what must be considered now. Only this! The congregation. Their good. Theirs—not mine!"

Danny pulled away from the hands holding him, from the pressure, the meaning. "Rabbi, are you afraid to fight it?"

"No! How can you—"

"Afraid for some reason you don't want to tell me?"

"*Danny!*"

"I'm sorry. . . . I'm sorry, Rabbi. . . . But I . . . I think you're afraid.

Oh, I understand! It would be painful. A terrible experience. Any man would be afraid . . . but . . . forgive me for this, Rabbi . . . it's the *man* who would be afraid. Not the Rabbi."

"I have told you, Danny, what I—as your Rabbi—"

"No! As a man!"

"*Rabbi* tells you!"

"No . . . No . . . I'm sorry. No!"

"Danny . . . listen to me."

"No!" He turned quickly toward the door. "My Rabbi fights for truth! For what's right! It's the man . . . the *man!*"

He opened the door and ran out.

The cloud of emotion still filled the room. Rabbi David Gordon put his hand to his forehead and stood there.

"The *man?*"

RABBI 3

What David had not realized, nor even been able to anticipate, was that the rabbinate was a profession. And the training for it included, naturally and inevitably, mechanical aspects, practical considerations, the learning of how to perform a job.

The study of Hebraic culture, tradition, history, was to him a joy, and each new subject a world to plunge into with the rapture of discovery. Midrash, Talmud, Mishnah, medieval philosophy, Maimonides, the *Halakha.* Even the reliving with ancient Jews the days of Roman, Moslem, Greek, and Babylonian times was an enrichment, the acquiring of new insight and identification.

But he had to accept along with this, the constant reminder that came with other courses that the rabbinate is a profession. And you had to train for it. A five-year course. During the first two years you're a candidate for the degree of Bachelor of Hebrew Letters. Then three years as a candidate for ordination. Finally you receive the *degree* of Rabbi. You become a member of the profession.

He would participate in these other courses without enthusiasm, almost without interest. Education, Human Relations, Speech, Homiletics—the art of the sermon. Preaching is, after all, one of the main functions of the Rabbi, so homiletics was important. You had to learn how to be effective in the pulpit.

The student sermons had to be delivered and then criticized by instructors and fellow students. As they sat there and listened they would take what they called the "pew posture," assuming the reactions of a congregation.

Perhaps a student Rabbi "telegraphed" his humor in the sermon by laughing before he told the stories. Perhaps another one read his sermons without looking up enough. This one constantly adjusted his glasses, that one kept his hands in his pockets. But the job had to be done right. It all had to be learned, practiced, performed.

Their role was defined for them explicitly. "The Rabbi of today is the teacher of the age-old teachings of Judaism and the spokesman for its ideas and ideals in the context of the world in which we live."

And during all the years of study and preparation, that world made itself felt. If not in the classroom, then in discussions, arguments with other students, in one's own consciousness of what was happening to people. Wars, demonstrations, strikes, movements, causes. One's own congregation would be a living organism, affected by all this, and the "ideas and ideals of Judaism" would have to be adapted to the atmosphere and spirit in which it existed.

"He must possess a passion for deep and continuous study, an ability to get along with people, and the desire to minister to their religious needs."

What were those needs? David had imagined that he knew, or hoped at least it was the Rabbi who would decide. But apparently it was the congregation that formulated those needs. A congregation in Los Angeles would have different needs than one in Brooklyn. It was the Rabbi's job to satisfy those needs.

What was startling to him was the discovery that it was the congregation that seemed to determine everything. When the committee approached the Rabbinical Placement Commission to obtain a Rabbi, they knew exactly what kind of man they wanted. There were categories, hiring practices. The congregation decided what areas were most important to it. Worship and Rituals, Religious School, Youth, Administration, Pastoral Activities, Temple Auxiliaries (Men's Club, Sisterhood, P.T.A.), Adult Education, Interfaith and Communal Activities.

And if a congregation felt that Temple Auxiliaries, Men's Club, and Sisterhood were what mattered most to them, that determined how one functioned as a Rabbi. The Rabbi met those needs.

Congregations differ. No two are alike, although there are patterns and trends, of course. The students had it all explained to them bluntly. Suburban congregations have a big business attitude—efficiency ratings, a computer approach to the hiring and firing of Rabbis. Every new congregation "murders" three Rabbis before they settle on one. There are statistics that prove this. One has to be prepared for it.

There are about 950 Reform Rabbis in the United States and about 700 Reform congregations in the United States and Canada. That's why certain procedures have been worked out. Newly ordained Rabbis and those with less than three years' rabbinic experience are eligible for recommendation to congregations numbering up to 125 members. After three years, the number stretches to 250 members; after five years, 600 members. And after ten years, one is deemed competent to minister to a congregation of more than 600 members. The profession is regulated.

Success in the rabbinate profession is equated with having a large congregation. Income can go to $25,000 or $30,000 a year. But a Rabbi starts at about $9,500, plus 10 per cent for pension.

When there is an opening in a congregation, the Commission never submits more than eight candidates. If one of the eight isn't chosen, the congregation has the right to ask for another panel of eight. And the congregation assumes the full expense of the interview, pays for the Rabbi's trip.

David went through all this indoctrination and training because he had to, because he realized that it was actually necessary, but he was impatient with it. He minimized it. All these practical considerations would work themselves out somehow. To him the important thing was his own enthusiasm, his eagerness to convey to a congregation what he felt and thought. He wanted to convey to others his concept of the significance of Judaism as a guide to life, the identification with it, even dependence on it. The restoration of the religious spirit and ethic to a meaningful role for today's Jews. The relevance of it even to today's nonbelievers, to the uninvolved, to the materialists, the rebels, the youth who saw no need for it, to the generation that had prospered without it. If he couldn't do this as a rabbi—then what else that he did would matter?

He went off in this spirit and with this ideal to his first congregation, a tiny one in Sioux Falls, South Dakota. And he quickly learned about a type of Jew he had never known. The ninety Jewish families who had founded the Reform temple had lost their Rabbi through death, and what they wanted was simply to carry on as before. Nothing disturbing, nothing radical.

They were a group of solid citizens in the community, storekeepers, small manufacturers, insurance men, lawyers, real estate brokers. They knew each other intimately (despite some social-economic stratification) because they were forced into continuous contact by the ghetto position of Jews in such towns.

Every Jew belonged to a synagogue or temple. Every Jewish businessman observed the holidays. Every Jewish family contributed to the fund drives. Every Jew functioned consciously and deliberately as a Jew. They had cohesion, unity, and involvement. And it was all on the simplest possible level.

They knew exactly what they wanted of him. He had merely to provide it according to their formula. Conduct the services. Deliver the sermons. Prepare the boys for Bar Mitzvah. Officiate at weddings and funerals. Keep the Temple running efficiently. The Temple was like a piece of religious machinery that had been set up in a corner of their lives, and while everyone wanted it to keep going, nobody wanted it to grow, become stronger, assert itself in any way within the structure of the total organism.

The single effort David made to break with their tightly satisfied, inbred concept of the Jews only led to a rebuke. The isolation of the Jewish community so disturbed him, gave him such a sense of unrelatedness to the world around them, that he suggested starting an interfaith program. Invite a minister, a priest, to come to Temple from time to time and preach a sermon. David, in turn, would appear at a church and by his words, even his mere presence there, help bring to the consciousness of these people the existence and significance of the Jewish community in their midst.

"Why must we live as if in exile here?" David asked. "Why must we be afraid to have them know what we are, what our faith is, what we represent in the history of man?"

A few of the younger members of the Board not only sympathized with his ideas, but became rather excited. They grasped at them as an answer to an indefinable restlessness in themselves, the urge to end the evasiveness of their presence as Jews in the community and speak out, asserting their identity with pride.

But the older, more solid members of the Board prevailed. The lawyer, the accountant, the shop owner only saw David's plan as a threat to the stability of a relationship precarious at best. Though the gentiles never expressed a negative reaction to the Jews in their midst, no action or word of hostility, one still felt this tension. There was an awareness in them of the Jewish presence that could erupt at any moment, inexplicably, negatively.

No, they said to Rabbi, we don't want your program. We don't need it. What can we gain by it? Why should we disturb things? Invite trouble? We are few, they are many. They don't need us to teach them anything. We need them to continue to exist here. Don't even bring it up with their people. Don't start anything. Do your job. You're our Rabbi. You've got your Temple. Stick to it.

David decided to serve out the three years that would be required for him to qualify for a larger congregation, and he endured them in a kind of agony of self-control. Nothing of himself, he felt, was involved. He was a functionary with the professional knowledge and training to fulfill certain routines. He didn't even feel close to them as Jews. They were Jews by necessity, by circumstance. For the first time he felt that Jews who lived as Jews only because that was the faith into which they were born were not true Jews. The outside world was the responsible factor, not their own spiritual awareness.

Frieda responded to this environment in a way that surprised him. After Joshua was born, she seemed to have found the true focus of her life and interest—taking care of the baby, keeping house, and having friends who did the same. The comfortable level of existence of the Jews in the community was to her taste. She felt at home with these people. She shared most of their attitudes, as well as the substance of their lives, which David used to describe as "the Jewish version of nothingness."

He tried to understand her response. After all, it wasn't easy to be a Rabbi's wife. And Frieda really didn't have her own involvement in religion to make it all seem worth while, the duties, the attendance at services, the meetings, the participation that was expected of her. She did all this with a kind of uncomplaining but unjoyous acceptance. But the house, the baby, the friendship of several women who had "adopted" her, this was something else. This was being a mother, this was being a woman, this was being herself, and all the hundreds of little satisfactions it provided were comforting.

When David told her that he was going to leave this congregation at the end of the three years, she was startled. It was only after a whole series of discussions with her, explaining his frustrations, his sense of uselessness, his rejection of the values and attitudes of the congregation, his need to lead his people to a richer development rather than just be the performer of ritual for them, that she realized he had a very special concept of his role as Rabbi, and that she would have to learn how to live with this.

When he went through the procedure of applying for another congregation, he specified that he wanted one that was more venturesome, less set and traditional in its ways, open to some leadership in meaningful areas on the part of their Rabbi.

The Pulpit Selection Committee of Temple B'nai Sholom in Atlanta was remarkably friendly and receptive. They smiled and joked and listened approvingly when he spoke of his concept of the role of the Rabbi. And they assured him they would support him and provide him with every opportunity to lead them along the path he chose.

The problem, David quickly learned after his installation as their Rabbi, was that while he had all the opportunity to lead, they had no intention of following. They had neither the desire nor the interest. The Temple, he felt, ranked as an influence in most of their lives considerably below the Chamber of Commerce, the country club, the bridge club, the riding and hunting society, the movies, TV, the Book-of-the-Month Club, and the Reader's Digest.

He had never suspected there was a *Jewish* Southern aristocracy, and now, as the stranger in their midst, he was constantly amazed by their ways and their values. No religious occasion, no holiday, ritual, celebration, even remotely approached in importance the social functions that dominated their lives. A party, a ball, a golf tournament at the club would arouse their excitement and absorb all their energy. Friday night services were a bore. Even High Holy Day observances were the fulfillment of an obligation.

David might have been able to accept a peripheral role for the Temple and for Judaism itself in the structure of their society (hoping in time to bring it closer and closer to them), but the plain fact was that it had absolutely no existence for them. Their relationship to the Temple was maintained out of some strange, subconscious sense of guilt perhaps, out of a remnant of historical and traditional memory. It was not religion, not faith, not even identification. It was a token payment to their forgotten past.

One Friday evening, eleven people showed up for services. David stared down at the six elderly faces (they came almost out of habit), at the two couples who were there because of the Yahrzeit commemoration (they owed this much to their mother's or father's memory), at the one member of the Board (it was a policy that one member be present at every service and David sometimes felt it was merely to keep an eye on him), and he saw that in truth, *no one* was there. No one had come to celebrate the arrival of the Sabbath, to renew the sense of faith, to acknowledge God's role in their lives, to experience the glow of religious involvement . . . or to listen to what he had to say to them. It was an empty Temple, with eleven bodies propped in their seats.

And he suddenly realized that the end had come for him. There was no meaning to his presence among these people. What he felt, as he stood there in the dead emptiness, was not disappointment or even rejection. He felt anger. He felt a great desire to strike out at all of these pseudo-Jews, and hit them with some weapon that would shock them, shake them.

He put aside the prepared text of his sermon, the fourteen carefully typed, painstakingly thought-out pages on "The Message of Job," and announced that he was going to preach on "The Negro and the Jew."

Not that the idea for it came to him suddenly. He had long felt the need to react to what prevailed among them, their indifference to this problem, their dissociation from the Negro, and even worse, their acceptance of the injustice and the misery that they witnessed every day of their lives. But it had been carefully marked out for him, by certain important members of the congregation, as a forbidden area. If we speak out, we're dead. We lose everything we've gained over the years. Our kids will pay for it in school, our neighbors will turn against us at home, our customers and clients will punish us in business.

For forty minutes, in the presence of the eleven restless, amazed, and frightened people staring up at him, he attacked the Jews' indifference to the fate of their black neighbors, their acceptance of injustice, their concern with their own welfare, their betrayal of their own ethics and values. And he threatened not only to preach on this subject again and again, but to participate in marches and demonstrations and to join Negro protest movements. He made them writhe in their seats, and his voice had never been so clear, his words so sure, his intensity so stinging.

The next day he faced the Board of Directors of Temple B'nai Sholom at the meeting that had been hastily called and was told that he was unwise, irresponsible, and unfit to continue as their Rabbi. He need not serve out the remaining six months of his contract. They would pay him the full amount and expect him to leave as soon as he had found another pulpit.

He told Frieda that he felt a great, beautiful sense of relief that this farce was over for him. And a kind of pride that he had finally struck at them in some way that reached a sensitive area, after all his failures to do so with appeals and exhortations about Judaism, God, tradition, the meaning and purpose of life. He had reached them at last.

But he had to face too the fact that in his five years as a Rabbi he had accomplished nothing. He had built nothing, created nothing, changed nothing. Pondering on this in hours of self-examination, searching for the explanation in himself, he came to realize that it was impossible for him to accept the blame. He was right. What he felt about his role as Rabbi was the only concept of it that had meaning. He couldn't alter that or give it up without destroying himself.

Then what was wrong? Judaism in America, he told himself, was wrong. The attitude of Jews toward their faith was wrong. Their relationship to the Temple was wrong. Their idea of the Rabbi's function was wrong.

And yet he knew that there were congregations where a true Jewish vitality existed, where an excitement prevailed because there was dedication and involvement. There were Temples where meaningful programs were being carried on—concern with the community, heightening of religious awareness, identification with Jewish tradition, study of Jewish thought, the creation of a Jewish cohesiveness.

And David determined not to accept another pulpit, no matter how long it would take, until he found one where such things would be possible, desired, cherished.

The Placement Commission sent him as one of the applicants for the Greenlake pulpit only because Rabbi Wolfson had developed a special interest in him. Rabbi Hiram Wolfson was a kind and gentle man with an active sense of curiosity. He had served fifteen years as

Rabbi in several communities, before coming to work in the New York offices of the Central Conference of American Rabbis as an official of the Placement Commission.

Efficient, well-organized, and practical, he was still open to the phenomenon of the unusual in man. And he responded to David's idealism with a secret delight. In their talks together (the congregation in Atlanta had written a rather violent denunciation of Rabbi Gordon, and Wolfson had called him in for a conference) a common sense of adventure developed. It was as if they both were plotting how to accomplish something desirable in the face of indifference and opposition. How to find a place for a Rabbi with zeal in a land of petrified pulpits. So Wolfson included David's name among the applicants whenever there seemed to be even a possibility that a congregation might be receptive to him. Greenlake was one of these.

The interview was conducted in the home of Robert Barrett, President of the Congregation. The atmosphere was responsive, warm, even eager. They were a relatively new congregation with no Temple of their own as yet, but their hopes and plans were exciting.

"We're going to be frank with you, Rabbi Gordon," Barrett said. "We're not sure of what we need. We're not in existence long enough to have a tradition, or a set of purposes, or perhaps even a well-defined approach to Judaism. But we do know what we *want*. And that is leadership. We want a Rabbi who has more enthusiasm than he knows what to do with. Who has more ideas than he can possibly ever execute. Who has more drive than any of us, or all of us put together. We want to be a dynamic congregation, and we want the Temple and the Rabbi to play an important, a critical role in our lives."

David listened to this, and a great deal more from Barrett and the others, with joy and almost disbelief. There was a certain slickness involved, and he was aware of it. They had about them the flavor of a group of men setting up a new concern that would be big and successful. But the openness of their approach, their receptivity, so excited David that he began to feel there was no question about it: they were right for him and he was right for them.

When he told them why he had been "fired" from his Atlanta pulpit, there was warm laughter in the room. It was as if they took enlightened delight in what he had done. When he asked if he could make a "little speech" about his concept of the Rabbi's role, they sat back and listened with nodding heads and agreeing smiles. And when he stood up at the end, and in the hushed room with all of them watching him intently, spoke of Judaism itself, its meaning and value and power, they listened to him as no other group of people ever had before.

"One thing more," he said, feeling them with him now, sensing their warmth toward him, "I am a passionate man. What I believe, I believe with all my heart and soul. What I do, I do with all my energy. If you offer me this pulpit, I tell you now: you will know I'm here! You and the whole congregation and the whole community. And no one will ever be uncertain about where I stand on any question. I'll be a pain in the neck to you sometimes, because when I start something—I won't let go. You might find yourself wishing I would, but I'll hang on and push and fight for what I believe in.

"If you don't want this kind of Rabbi, don't take me. If you want a Rabbi who's going to make a 'good impression,' who's going to represent you with a dignified façade, and who's going to lead you along a comfortable path, a man, in other words, who's never going to give you problems—then please, don't take me!"

Even though the Pulpit Committee was to meet on another day to go over all the applicants and make a decision, Robert Barrett stood up and said to David: "I know I speak for all of us here when I say to you, Rabbi Gordon, that we are deeply impressed. You have stirred and excited us, you have moved us. And you have made us realize, in a way most of us never did before, what a Rabbi can and should be."

At the meeting of the committee two nights later, it was evident that a few second thoughts had set in.

"I think he's right—we'd have problems with him."

"But the right kind of problems!"

"And he strikes me as maybe not yet altogether mature."

"What are you talking about? There's a genius touch about him, you know what I mean? That'll make up for it, don't worry."

"A leader I think he is—"

"—So he'll be attracting the young people to Temple. Get them involved, you know?"

"I liked that part he said about the community. We're not Jews in a vacuum. . . ."

And finally, Bob Barrett rose to sum it up in executive fashion, the arguments against, the questions, the doubts, and the points in favor, one, two, three, four, plus this, plus that, plus what was clear to everyone, and so, gentlemen, let us vote.

That week the Board of Directors accepted the recommendation of the Pulpit Selection Committee, and David Gordon was named Rabbi of Temple Israel of Greenlake.

IV

David sat down in the living room after Danny left and let his emotions sort themselves out.

Frieda was upstairs, probably asleep by now, and that was good. Her response, her faith in him, was the only comforting thing in the whole situation. She was a fine woman with the most decent instincts. Thank God their relationship had developed the solidity to withstand even such shocks. Perhaps she loved him in a way he could never love her in return, and depended on him more than he felt was healthy, but he knew their relationship provided a stability and security for a certain area of his life without which he would suffer.

Danny. He leaned forward, rubbing his hands together as he thought of the messiness involved. Danny's reaction didn't disturb him. He was young, inexperienced, and had a romantic idealism that was touching. Danny had only rejected him out of emotional immaturity. He would return to his side with even greater confidence. No, the problem about Danny was that he might do something rash. Take some step, try to organize some effort on his behalf that would be unwise and even harmful—to the congregation and to him. He would have to reach Danny as soon as possible and in the calm of a quiet discussion convince him to wait. Wait for *his* decision. So. That's what he would do about Danny.

Now. He leaned back against the couch, his eyes closed. Now to face the real significance of what had happened. To indulge himself in full awareness of it. The accusation, the charge, whatever they called it, that was only a trick. What mattered was that the Executive Committee wanted him to resign. There were one or two personal "enemies" on the Committee (Brody, for sure. Probably Barrett himself?) but the Committee surely felt that it was acting on behalf of the congregation. Not only in their interest, but fulfilling their desire. It was the congregation that didn't want him.

He had to face that. Was it true? Face it! . . . Yes. Probably true. Face it! It was true.

Because he had failed them? In their eyes, perhaps yes. Not perhaps. All right, not perhaps. But in God's eyes? Had ever a Rabbi in the whole history of—but wait. Are you saying you can see through God's eyes? Do you know what He wanted of you here? What He felt to be their need? But if not what I have given them—then what could He want of me?

David rubbed his forehead with his fingers, as if to press thoughts into place, arrange the confused ideas in his mind. Tired. He was very tired. To do this now. But you must. . . . All right, so you failed them. Are you—?

No! To doubt himself now would be to doubt everything. Judaism, its purpose, its value. Its need in the world today. That's what this was all about. He was only an instrument. A transmitter. He was passing on—not what he had created—but what five thousand years of wisdom and faith had shaped. What countless generations had died for. Had it all suddenly become worthless?

This was ridiculous. Sitting here and like a schoolboy going over his lessons. What was he questioning? Judaism itself?

He stood up, annoyed, angry. Enough! How to deal with the situation—yes, that required some thought. But to doubt himself, the rightness of all he believed in?

He decided to go to bed. Tomorrow he would figure out a course of action. Tomorrow would be time enough. Tomorrow!

He put out all the lights. The scene was over. Curtain. Thank God. Tomorrow.

Quietly he climbed the stairs to the bedroom. Frieda was probably asleep. No need to disturb her. Poor woman—how this all must have upset her.

Outside the door he heard her sobbing. He hesitated, faced now with the additional burden of consoling her, quieting her fears. He really didn't need that tonight. He was tired. Very, very tired.

"Frieda?"

No response.

"You're still awake?"

He walked over to her side of the bed and stood there a moment. She was stretched out on her stomach, her face almost under the pillow, lying there in her dress. She hadn't even got into bed.

He bent down and stroked her head gently.

She crept deeper into the pillow, twisting her head as if to deaden the pain. His touch, his fingers on her head, had set off a wave. She was sobbing again.

"You've been lying here all this time and crying?"

She turned to face him as if this were an accusation. "Is that wrong? The misery I feel? Don't you even understand?"

He bent over her and stroked her cheek, his hand on the wet cheek. "Of course I understand. Of course. How you must feel. It's a terrible thing."

He reached for some tissues in the box by the bed and gave them to her. She dried her eyes, wiped her cheek impatiently, as if her grief wasn't important now. For him to understand, that's what counted. What must happen now.

He looked at her, at the sadness in her face, at the way she was lying, curled up in the bed like a little child who had been hurt, and he leaned down and kissed her on the cheek.

"Thank you, my Frieda. Thank you for standing by me." It was hard for him to say it openly. "For not believing what . . . what they . . ."

"It's a lie! Don't you think I know that?"

"A horrible lie."

"But David—why do you think I'm crying? Why do you think it hurts so much?" She sat up and took his hands, looking into his face, his uncertain expression, confused now by what she was getting at. "Don't you understand?"

"That they wanted to do this? You're worried that—"

"No. Oh, I feel that too, but—David, it made me think of our relationship."

"Yes?" He was tense now, and bewildered.

"David, it made me realize that—even though I would never believe it about you—that it *was* possible. It could have happened, even though it didn't!"

"Why do you say that?" He stood up now, assailed by anxiety, confusion. What was she getting at?

"Sit down here, David." She moved on the bed to make room for him. "Next to me. Please?"

He sat a bit close to the edge and she slid over nearer to him.

"What I mean—I don't know how to put it—you would never do a thing like that because you're you. The kind of man you are. But David, that's not the same thing as . . . as you wouldn't do it because of how you feel about me."

"I love you, Frieda. You know that."

"What do I know? That you say it. That you show it. Yes. In every way a wife could ask . . . except one."

"What, Frieda? What are you saying?"

"David—" Afraid now of his reaction, of the difficulty he always had when this subject was touched on in any way, even subtly, gently hinted at. But she was determined now to be as explicit as she could, to bring it out and have him understand. "David—when was the last time?"

"What?"

"You know what I mean. When? Do you remember?"

He didn't know what to say. He remembered. He knew as well as she did. He felt a shame, a guilt, but not because of some deliberate act. It was like a secret defect in him that he didn't want to face.

"David—" she was holding his hands again, a way of forcing him to be there in every sense, "—it's two weeks."

"Frieda—" grasping quickly at anything, "I've been working hard. You know that. A million things on my mind."

"David, don't you realize what it makes me think? Two weeks, night after night, we lie in the same bed. We're normal, healthy people, and not once in all that time—"

He tried to pull his hands away, get up.

"David! Don't go. Don't run away."

"What do you expect me to do?"

"I hope . . ." she was caressing his hands, stroking them gently, looking at him, wanting to reach him, ". . . you'll make me feel that you do love me. That you feel something for me like I—"

She reached up to his face and kissed him, all her love for him in that kiss, in the caressing of her lips. He embraced her and she responded, coming closer, her body against his so that all the feeling in it could reach him.

They lay down side by side and she pressed against him, holding his face, wanting to kiss him with all the intensity of her being. He felt her mouth's wet openness, the tongue seeking. She took his hand and moved it down, opened his hand and pressed it down against her there, through the dress, alive.

He felt surrounded, enveloped, the openness of her like a deep warmth to enter, be embraced by, her love a taking from him and a shelter too, safe and right, all around him, holding him.

For him it suddenly became the most beautiful feeling of being needed and at the same time being protected that he had ever experienced. Of filling that need with all of himself, and of receiving the full outpouring of another's entire being.

Later, when they were falling asleep, lying close to each other, he thought: I love her and I am loved by her. That I should discover this tonight of all nights! But then, who can tell God how to perform His miracles?

RABBI 4

On the Saturday morning three weeks after Rabbi Gordon and his family had moved into the little house provided for them on Maple Lane in Greenlake, he found the dead rat in his mail box.

It was in a neat white box just a little larger than the rat itself, the sides sealed with brown paper tape, a typed address label on top, and it had been mailed from New York.

When David lifted the cover he saw a card in an envelope lying on tightly packed white tissue paper. He pulled out the card and read: DROP DEAD, JEW-BASTARD! Typed in capital letters, the comma after DEAD, the hyphen between JEW and BASTARD, the exclamation point. Very neatly done.

When he removed the tissue paper and saw the gray rat, curled comfortably in death, the long tail under its whitish stomach, a tiny sharp tooth showing in what was almost a peaceful smile, he dropped the box, and the rat bounced off the dining room table over which he had been standing. He had to brush the rat back into the box with the cover and he realized how large and heavy the loose, yielding, rolly body of the rat really was.

He covered the box and carried it to the little room off the garage where the furnace was and threw it in. He put the card into his pocket. Frieda was outside in the back with Josh, hanging some sheets and towels to dry in the sun.

David walked to his study, pushed in the button on the door lock, and sat down at his desk. He didn't remember Barrett's number, so he looked it up.

Barrett let him tell the entire story, then calmly informed him that he too had received a dead rat in the mail. The same message. The question was, Bob said, who else? And what had anyone done about it? He told David not to make any move, not to comment if asked to, not to discuss it on the phone if anyone called him. The Executive Committee would meet later and decide how to handle this.

In forty minutes Barrett called David. Six rats reported so far. Rabbi's, Barrett's, Dr. Greenwald's, Jack Stern's, one to a man called Philip Albrecht (a member of the congregation, but not especially prominent or active; probably a personal element involved there), and Sam Beskov's. That was it most likely, because the instinctive reaction seemed to be to communicate the news to someone at once, and there had been no more calls in the last ten minutes.

A problem had developed. Sam Beskov had called the Greenlake *Bulletin*, had gotten Leslie Fluter on the phone, and ranted furiously about this disgusting, disgraceful act of anti-Semitism. Fluter of course, was ready to make a big story of it.

"I know," David interrupted, "He called me for a statement. I told him I had received a rat too, but would make a statement later."

"Well," Barrett said, "Fluter called me and I suggested we have a meeting on how to handle this. He didn't want one. So I called First Selectman Stanford, who felt a meeting would be a good idea, and then got back to Fluter. So we're getting together in Fluter's office in an hour. I'm calling the rest of the Executive Committee. Meanwhile—no comment, no discussion. Right? We all want to be together on this."

"Bob—" Rabbi hesitated a moment before revealing it, "I want you to know that while I didn't issue a formal statement, I did give some kind of reaction to Fluter."

"What?"

"I . . . well, simply in human terms. I said I was shocked. In fact, horrified."

Barrett groaned. "Well, isn't that a statement? I thought we agreed—"

"Not a statement. A reaction."

"Rabbi, we have to deal with this exactly right! Fluter's going to use—"

"Bob, I have the right to say that when rats are mailed—"

"Never mind now! Rabbi, please, no more statements, reactions, *anything*."

David gripped the phone tightly.

"Rabbi?"

"I'll be there in an hour." And he hung up.

It was the first indication of differences between himself and Bob Barrett. And what was even more disturbing, a clear sign of Barrett's assumption that *he* was in charge of all matters concerning the congregation's position in the community. David prepared himself for an interesting meeting.

The fact was that if Sam Beskov hadn't called the *Bulletin*, the whole dead rat incident might have been handled in another way by the congregation's authorities. But Beskov was practically a renegade Jew. He always acted on his own, exactly as he pleased. Partly, this was because of his wealth and success. His syndicate owned three office skyscrapers in New York and was putting up a big condominium on the upper East Side. In Greenlake itself, on Main Street, Beskov had built the Cedarwood Shopping Center, whose ugliness was universally condemned and whose money-making capacity no one could dispute. If he was now disliked by most people in town, including Jews, it was because he was going ahead with plans for another shopping center on property he owned on the state highway at the southern edge of Greenlake, and had announced that this center would have a branch of Gimbel's department store with parking facilities for four hundred cars. He was currently fighting in court the town's efforts to re-zone the area to prevent him from going ahead.

Sam lived in the biggest mansion in Greenlake, on twelve acres overlooking the bay (from which he could see his sixty-foot yacht riding at anchor in his private harbor). He took obvious and uninhibited delight in his marriage to Gloria Gallant, who was his third wife and only twenty-nine years old (Sam was fifty-eight), and whom he had plucked out of the chorus line at the Sands in Las Vegas. In fact, he enjoyed everything he did with such gusto and such disdain for opinion, public or otherwise, that one might suspect he also took pleasure in setting up the shock waves that accompanied his actions. The Jews in Greenlake not only had nothing to do with him, but they cringed and suffered every time his name appeared in the papers—which was much too often. Leslie Fluter never missed a chance for a good Sam Beskov piece.

In this case of course, the rat that had been mailed to Sam was part of a larger effort affecting the entire Jewish community. Fluter would have to be made to see it that way.

The meeting was in Fluter's office in the *Bulletin* building, a small, red-brick structure opposite the Town Hall and half a block from the police station. The office was a corner one on the second floor, quite large and airy, and folding chairs had been placed around to accommodate a dozen or so people.

Leslie Fluter was thirty-six, quite handsome (some people even said elegant-looking), with smooth black hair, a comfortable, assured face, a confident manner, and he made no effort to conceal his ambition, determination, or whatever it was that motivated him in running the bi-weekly Greenlake *Bulletin* the way he did.

Basically of course, this meant providing a little something for everybody, as it must for all small-town papers that hope to survive. The *Bulletin*'s coverage ranged from gardening hints to detailed reports of church socials, not forgetting news for golfers, real estate deals, police court reports, and plenty of photos of prospective brides, college graduates, and the noble young men entering our armed services.

But in addition, Fluter had developed his own special formula, which he described as "the front page shock—the editorial page blast." According to the front page of the Greenlake *Bulletin*, not a week passed by in this little community without some startling occurrence that merited opening the readers' eyes wide enough to encompass a headline half-way across the page, and without the need to point out to these same readers, in a frank and fearless editorial, the implications of that occurrence.

How the *Bulletin* handled any event had become so important to its participants that the paper was now a considerable power in town, and Leslie Fluter, as the wielder of the power, a rather controversial figure. Which seemed to be what he wanted. Some people even said he had political ambitions, to which the only answer apparently was: why not?

Fluter now sat behind his paper-stacked desk in the corner of the office, in shirtsleeves, deliberately not rising as the people arrived for the meeting. He motioned them to chairs after a rather perfunctory greeting, setting a grim and unresponsive tone for reasons of his own.

Barrett had been able to reach only three members of the Executive Committee this Saturday morning, two of whom, Dr. Greenwald and

Jack Stern, had received rats in their mail. Harry Brody was at his carpet store in the midst of his Annual Clean-Out Sale and couldn't come.

Barrett waited downstairs in front of the building for Rabbi Gordon so that they could have a final brief discussion in private about unity of position and purpose. Rabbi listened to Bob's tense words in silence and managed to refrain from agreeing. There was no time for argument, however, so Barrett ended up with: "You're new in town, Rabbi. You don't know these people the way I do. So let me handle it." And they went upstairs, Rabbi Gordon still withdrawn and uncommitted.

The first shock was finding Reverend Robertson and Father Lemassey there. Sheldon Stanford, the First Selectman of Greenlake, had invited them.

"I felt," he explained to Barrett, "that their counsel and advice in this matter would be most helpful to all of us. When members of this community commit an act of hostility towards the Hebrew brethren in our midst, it is an act of religious vandalism, of defiance of the principles of religious tolerance as preached and practiced by our churches and their leaders. Therefore the guidance that Father Lemassey and Reverend Robertson can provide us in dealing with it will be invaluable."

Sheldon Stanford, even though it seemed difficult for him to use the word "Jews" in public and he always referred to them as "the Hebrew brethren," was apparently a sincerely liberal and even progressive individual. There was no question that he was sensitively aware of the "influx" of Jews into Greenlake (actually a growth from a dozen families to four hundred and fifty families in ten years), and that he was keeping a most watchful eye on the effects of this impact, but he never gave even the slightest hint of alarm or antagonism. His method was rather to "observe and control" the situation with a combination of dignified, subtle strategies. This included certain "understood" real estate restrictions, business arrangements, zoning regulations, club membership rules, property development policies, and whatever else worked in achieving the goal of keeping Greenlake the lovely place to live in that its "old settlers" intended it to be. His inviting Reverend Robertson and Father Lemassey to this meeting had been an act of statesmanship in his mind. A delicate situation, potentially dangerous, conceivably harmful to the good name of Greenlake. Their restraining influence would be helpful.

Bob Barrett, however, had to exercise considerable control not to show his irritation at their presence. To him this was "their" problem, the Jewish community's own private concern. Surely they had the right to decide what to do about it without dragging in the Congregational and Catholic churches and their ministers.

It was actually Reverend Robertson that he objected to most. Father Lemassey was easy to deal with. Young, good humored, very popular with his own church and many of the teen-agers in town as a "fun" kind of priest who played baseball and organized great Saturday night dances at St. Mark's Hall, he was a man you could reach and who, in many ways, reached out to the Jews in Greenlake with understanding and warmth.

But Reverend Robertson was a rather rigid kind of religious leader. He had a manner and approach that suggested the superiority of his vision and understanding of the world. He somehow made people feel that it was hopeless and rather foolish ever to argue with him. (He wrote a weekly column for the *Bulletin* called "Another View," and it was indiscreetly suggested by some around town that it should really be called "The View From Above".) Reverend Robertson obviously felt he was on very good terms with God.

The meeting was now ready to begin, but it developed that Dr. Greenwald had actually brought his rat with him. He stood up and extracted the white box from a paper bag he had kept under his chair.

"As a scientist," he said, smiling, as they all gathered around to look at it on Fluter's desk, "I must say this is a rather ordinary species of the common city rat and has no special interest whatsoever. But as a Jew to whom this creature was sent as a symbol of hatred, I find it remarkable. Gentlemen, shall I leave it here to have before us as evidence of what we are dealing with?"

Fluter picked up the box. "I'm going to have it photographed."

Barrett stopped him at the door. "Les, just a minute. Why do you want to do that?"

"Because a picture of this in the *Bulletin* would be enlightening."

"Just a minute." Barrett still discreetly blocked his way. "Can we talk about this? In fact, isn't that why we're having this meeting?"

"Why?"

The undercurrent of hostility was evident. Still Barrett persisted. "To discuss what to do—and what not to do. To agree on the best course of action."

"Best for whom?"

Barrett licked his lips and the smile was an executive-to-client smile that concealed everything. "Shall we say for everyone concerned? Including the *Bulletin* and its readers?"

Fluter looked at him with a confident, unyielding stare.

"I'm going to have it photographed." He walked back to his desk and pressed a buzzer. "What I do with the photograph may, or may not, be decided at this meeting. But I want it." A fat little gray-haired man opened the door and stood there. "Joe," Fluter said, "have this photographed. Including the card inside. Thanks." He handed him the box.

Sheldon Stanford broke the tension. "In my experience, every meeting is a better meeting for having a chairman. And since being chairman at meetings seems to be one of my chief occupations in this town, I hereby volunteer to function as such."

"Hear! Hear!" Father Lemassey, smiling, meaning that as approval.

"No objection being audibly voiced" (Stanford's grin, his good humor overcame the pomposity, and through it all a firmness and leadership were asserted, obviously one of the reasons he was so successful in local politics), "I will now act as chairman and ask if anyone wishes to speak."

"It's a simple matter—" Fluter didn't ask, he spoke, "—a news story has broken and certain people are objecting to the way the *Bulletin*'s going to handle this story."

"Perhaps—" Dr. Greenwald's heavy voice was heard louder among the murmurings, "—perhaps it is not your right to handle this in any way you wish that is being, shall we say considered, but rather the desirability of the effect it might have on certain members of our community."

"May I—" Barrett impatiently, "please just—"

"I believe," Fluter tensely, "that the remark was addressed to *me*."

"The chairman," Stanford very sensitive now to what was developing, "recognizes Mr. Barrett." Characteristic of him, Bob thought. Always with Stanford one had the impression of fairness, understanding.

"Thank you." Bob leaned forward in his chair, resisting the urge to stand and deliver a speech. "Gentlemen, I would like to present our position. And by 'our,' I mean of course of the Jewish members here. A certain individual—perhaps more than one, we don't know—has mailed dead rats to six Jews in this town. With the rat, a card. Rather nastily worded. Now there's no question that this is an act of anti-Semitism. It's offensive, it's deplorable, it's shocking. But then, every act of anti-Semitism—and I'm sure all of us here agree on that—is offensive, and deplorable, and shocking. And unfortunately, such acts do occur in Greenlake from time to time. In some cases, it's only a gesture, an expression perhaps. Or a nasty word, a remark. Or an attitude, a position taken. It happens . . . it happens. . . . Now, this has happened. It falls into a certain context, it's part of a certain hostility felt by some people in Greenlake towards Jews. The question is: should we react to this expression of hostility in a special way? Make a special, big thing out of it? Exaggerate its importance? And what will we gain by it? Will that do more harm than good? We—and again I say, speaking for the Jewish members here, and as representatives of the Jewish community—we believe it will do harm."

"I am unable to understand—" Reverend Robertson half closed his eyes as he tilted his head back, "how a condemnation of religious intolerance—which I am sure Mr. Fluter intends to express in his newspaper—can possibly be considered harmful."

"I'll explain." Barrett was on his feet. "The people in this town who—"

"Now wait a minute!" Fluter was standing too. "Sheldon, let me say this!" Stanford nodded. "We seem to be discussing the possible harmful effects of what I'm going to print in the *Bulletin*. But does anybody know what I intend to print? Well then, let me inform you. Contrary to what some of you may have expected, there was going to be no news story. Nothing on page one, or anywhere. Only an editorial. I would now like to read that editorial. If I have the chairman's permission?"

Stanford nodded, as if oblivious of the sarcastic tone. Fluter sat down, found the typewritten sheets inside the desk drawer, leaned back and started to read.

"DROP DEAD, JEW-BASTARD!"

The above typed message, on a card that was enclosed with a dead rat, was this week mailed to a certain number of Jewish residents of Greenlake. That it was the work of a sick mind is obvious. That it is to be condemned as an act of violent anti-Semitism goes without saying. And that the decent people of Greenlake, and the community as a whole, are horrified that it could happen here, is certain. But the *Bulletin* believes there is something all of us can learn from this incident. And we had better learn it now.

Change is the essence of life. Nothing can stand still and survive, and that includes towns and communities. Greenlake is changing and will continue to change, in many significant ways. One of these, inevitably, is the arrival of new residents. Among them there will be Jews, as there will be Protestants, Catholics, and even atheists. That is the American pattern of growth and development.

If there are people in Greenlake who resent or object to any one particular group among the newer arrivals, they are not only expressing prejudice and intolerance, but they are standing in the way of progress.

Every group makes its own distinctive contribution to the life and future of a community. Jewish residents of Greenlake will make theirs. It will be a valuable and desirable contribution, because the Jew has much to contribute to the fabric of any modern civilization. The Jewish tradition, Jewish culture, and Jewish spiritual heritage are rich strands to be woven into that fabric.

To oppose it is a form of reactionary, self-defeating folly. To express that opposition by means such as this individual, or individuals, have taken is ethically wrong and morally sick.

The *Bulletin* condemns this on both grounds with all its conviction, and urges the whole community of Greenlake to do the same.

Reverend Robertson applauded. His hands clapped in the silence. "Mr. Fluter," he said, "I regard that as a magnificent statement, and I intend to read it at my services tomorrow."

Fluter flung the sheets down on the desk. "Now," he said, staring at Barrett, "are you telling me not to print that?"

"I am not," Barrett said, clasping his hands, back in his chair again, being very careful and controlled, "telling you anything. You know that, Les. I wouldn't dare and I wouldn't want to. But . . . I am hoping—and suggesting—that you not print it."

"Why?"

"Do you want me to go through that editorial and explain why?"

"How else can your objection make sense?" The tight tone, the look almost of disdain, Barrett accepted calmly. Rabbi Gordon shifted in his chair. "Oh yes," Fluter picked it up instantly, "I think we should hear from the Rabbi too, Rabbi—Gordon—is it?"

"Rabbi Gordon," David nodded.

"Your new Rabbi, I understand. I'd like to have *his* reaction."

"Of course." Barrett clasped and unclasped his hands, the smile on his face a supreme effort. He turned to Stanford: "May I now, briefly, tell you why that editorial is objectionable to us?"

"I'm sure we'd all like to hear it," Stanford waved his cigar.

"To start with a small point, that heading on the editorial—DROP DEAD, JEW-BASTARD!—while it quotes what was on the cards, is not something that we think should be repeated in print and given this prominence. It is an offensive thought, a painfully offensive thought and expression, and you can understand why we would rather not have it repeated.

"But to get to the main point. There are actually two. Mind you, Les, this is not intended to be a criticism of you, or of anyone who holds the same viewpoint as you do. It is a disagreement with that viewpoint.

"All right. Now you relate this incident to the arrival of more Jewish families in Greenlake. You make a point of it. You say—"

"The statistics," Stanford interrupted gently, almost kindly, "do indicate that this is taking place."

"What I'm saying," Barrett persisting, "is that Leslie's editorial makes a point of it."

"It is," Stanford still so smoothly, "a fact of common knowledge, is it not? And therefore Leslie's reference to it can hardly be considered provocative?"

"What I'm trying to say," Barrett holding on, "is that Les implies that the fact that more Jewish families have moved into Greenlake has produced a negative and hostile reaction."

Reverend Robertson said in a gentle tone, "Are you assuming it has not?"

"I know it has—in some cases. But the editorial makes it seem inevitable. It makes an issue out of that fact—when it needn't be."

"But it *is* an issue." The Reverend spoke with a suggestion of annoyance. "As I can testify, unfortunately, from conversations I have had even with my parishioners. And an issue to be dealt with."

"But by bringing it up in the newspaper—"

"I think," Father Lemassey spoke up for the first time, "that we are now either all on the head of a pin—or at a point of disagreement that won't be resolved here and now. I would like to hear Mr. Barrett's second objection."

"Bob—" Stanford motioned with an expansive gesture.

"The second point," Barrett closed his eyes a moment, pondering it, "is a more subtle one. It is really, when you think of it, something that we, as Jews, may feel and that we normally don't bring up publicly. It's concerned with an area of some sensitivity for us. And that is that we feel—about ourselves—that though we are Jews, though we do have our tradition and culture—we are as American as anyone in this country, and live as Americans, act as Americans, feel as American as anyone else around us."

"You are saying," Reverend Robertson had appointed himself as the summer-upper, "that you are *American* Jews."

"No. I am saying that we are Americans who are Jews, just as you are an American who is a member of the Congregational Church. And Leslie's editorial implies that we are a people apart—different and apart—from the rest of the community."

"The editorial—"

"Just a minute, Les. May I finish? The editorial brings up and stresses a separateness, a difference, that *we* find doesn't exist. And so we resent it, and that's why this editorial is something we'd rather not have appear."

"We seem to have wandered quite a bit from the basic issue involved here," Robertson observed pedantically. "An act of anti-Semitism, religious intolerance, has been perpetrated. It must be dealt with."

"But it was committed against us," Barrett turned to him, "and we are suggesting that you let us deal with it."

"Anti-Semitism, Mr. Barrett, may be your problem in terms of its effects on your people. But it is also our problem in terms of the ethical behavior and moral principles of our people. Surely you concede the right of religious leaders like Father Lemassey and myself to deal with this problem among our members."

"I would say though," Lemassey interjected with his understanding smile, "that we must do so in a way that respects the wishes of the very people we want to protect and help—the Jewish community."

"Thank you, Father Lemassey." Barrett glanced at him.

"You are assuming," Fluter said almost angrily, "that Mr. Barrett is speaking for the entire Jewish community. It so happens he is not. I received a phone call from a rather prominent and important Jewish resident of Greenlake—Mr. Beskov—who also received one of those rats in the mail—and he demanded that I expose and condemn the whole incident in the strongest possible way."

"Sam Beskov," Barrett answered as gently as he was able, "speaks only for Sam Beskov."

"It seems to me," Fluter was grinning, "that when he does speak, people listen."

"Some people listen." Barrett stared right at him.

"I feel," Stanford injecting himself almost physically with that cigar of his, "that a discussion of Mr. Sam Beskov is somewhat irrelevant at this moment."

"I'm only trying to suggest, Sheldon," Fluter still felt his advantage, "that Bob Barrett's views may not be representative of the entire Jewish community. As a matter of fact," this last was said as if it had come to him as an inspiration, "I would like to hear what Rabbi Gordon has to say."

"I'm sure he agrees—"

"I want to hear what he has to say!" Fluter's determination was strong in his voice.

Stanford detected something now too, "I think we all would like to hear from Rabbi Gordon. Rabbi?"

Barrett leaned back, his anger only partially controlled. David hesitated a few moments, then stood up, but as if realizing he shouldn't have done so, moved around his chair and held on to the back of it.

"As you probably know, I am very new here. I have been in Greenlake only a matter of weeks, so I can't pretend to know what's going on in this community. Attitudes, tensions, conflicts, I can't really speak about them. But I believe I can express myself about two things: one is what we have been calling 'the incident'—the mailing of the dead rats. And the other is the editorial Mr. Fluter has written.

"In my personal opinion—and I stress that—this particular act of anti-Semitism should receive the widest publicity possible. We all know that anti-Semitism manifests itself in many forms. Discrimination, various restrictions, and so on, and some of them will be overcome in time, and some perhaps not. But what has taken place now, this incident, is quite another thing. It is as terrible, in its way, as an act of physical violence. It is an attack, an assault, as brutal and inhuman as the fall of a Nazi whip on the back of a Jew. It is more than shameful, more than disgusting; it is a dangerous precedent. And as such, it must be condemned. Openly, unequivocally, forcefully. It must be pushed into the consciousness and awareness of the entire community so that Greenlake grasps the horror of it, so that it understands the evil of it, so that it determines never to allow it—or anything like it—to happen again!"

He gripped the back of the chair and looked down, reorganizing himself. A different tone, a different manner were needed now. He went on to a far more delicate subject.

"About your editorial, Mr. Fluter, I have this to say. And again I stress, this is my personal conviction. I happen to feel, and feel very deeply and proudly, that the Jew has something unique to contribute to society. Distinctive, individual, and very special. This is certainly not the time or place to expound on what that is. But for me—it exists in him, it expresses itself in his way of life, in his values, in his spirit, if you will. And it is the sum total of this, which I choose to call the essence of Judaism, that *does* make him different. Not, obviously, in the way he dresses, talks, looks. But in the overall human unit that he is, the amalgam, the totality. And that totality, as Mr. Fluter says in his editorial, is a priceless contribution he can make to the fabric of civilization. . . . That is how I feel."

Barrett knew it would be a mistake for him to say anything now. Everyone was silent. Father Lemassey stood up.

"I don't know how we're going to decide this, but I do know what I would recommend."

"I take it," Stanford stood up, and so did everybody now, "that you would vote in favor of printing the editorial?"

"I don't think a vote is necessary." Reverend Robertson was buttoning his coat. "The consensus is clear."

"One thing more," Fluter said. "In view of Rabbi Gordon's remarks, I'm going to do a news story on it too. A helluva news story."

"With a photograph, I assume?" Stanford was smiling, as if at the vision of the dead rat picture on page one of the *Bulletin*.

"With the photograph!"

When David walked out of that meeting and down the stairs, and as they all separated to go to their cars, he realized that neither Barrett nor Dr. Greenwald nor Jack Stern had spoken to him.

V

There were all kinds of special provisions and arrangements in the Mandel home made by each of them for the other's benefit. All activities, practically all of life, was organized around a response to the two overwhelming tragedies that had occurred: Lou's heart attack of four years ago, the death of their son, Mark, two years ago.

People said that Fay Mandel took it "beautifully." By this they meant that the essential Fay they knew and liked somehow survived. She managed to smile gently when the conversation turned to light things, she was still sensitively aware of people and their comfort when they visited her and would get up to refill a drink when it got low in the glass. She kept her neat, if conservative, manner of dressing, her hairdo, her make-up; even her fingernail polish (as some women noted) was the same color as before.

But it was in her eyes and in her voice that one instantly detected the difference. There was a remoteness in the way she sometimes sat and stared straight ahead, and one didn't have to ask why or what she was thinking of. She spoke so slowly now, heavily, almost wearily, the effort of it like the pushing aside of a great weight each time. Her face was drawn, the cheekbones out like a declaration of anguish, and sometimes one could see a little trembling of the lower lip when she was trying just to talk normally of ordinary things.

The loss of Mark so soon after Lou's attack, and with the concern for Lou's condition now an ever-present part of her life, had produced another kind of change in her. This was a form of detachment. Everything in life that people were involved with, all the things that excited them, didn't seem to touch her anymore. The dances and benefits, the Sunday School, the Sisterhood activities in which she had been a leader, were now pushed back in perspective. She came to the meetings and chatted a bit and listened and then got up and went home. One had the feeling she had not really been present at all. The women understood and sympathized, and glanced at her with little sad shakings of the head. Poor Fay. What she's been through, poor woman.

Even more, and understandable too, though not so easily acceptable, was the way she sometimes expressed herself about people and events. There was such great tolerance in her now that she seemed able to forgive everyone for everything, as if she understood the secret sorrows that prompted others to behave as they did, or sensed an agony in them that they couldn't express. "It's like her heart goes out to everybody," her friends began to say of her. "She knows suffering. She knows people are suffering all the time."

The visible, daily pattern of her own life didn't change much, and at least Lou could feel content about this. "Everything's just like before," he used to tell himself, "and that's the way it should be." But he knew this wasn't true. All he had to do to realize how their life had changed was to think of Mark's room.

Mark had been one of the happiest, "well-adjusted" boys in town. With his smiling round face, his sense of humor, and his playfulness, he had been popular with girls and seemed to have hundreds of friends. He was a pretty good tennis player, a member of the high school's baseball and basketball teams, a reader of serious books, an admirer of classical music, a son who always willingly helped around the house. He had been a source of pure joy and pride to Fay and Lou.

When he had gone off to college, his room had naturally been kept intact, exactly as he left it. This was to provide him with a sense of still "belonging" when he came home on holidays and vacations; it was a good way to give him a feeling of security. Then, when he got married, they converted it into a guest room, took out Mark's books, the desk from the corner with the world globe and the sports trophies on it, put up more feminine curtains, changed the bed cover, and hung a few pictures that Mark wouldn't have allowed when it was still his room.

A month after the accident, Fay changed it all back again. She herself got Mark's familiar things down from the attic and restored them to their old place. The desk looked as if he might come back to work there at any minute. Even the tennis racquet in its plastic cover stood in the corner where it had always been. And though Lou had never been upstairs since the heart attack, he found out that Fay sometimes spent hours at a time just sitting there, doing absolutely nothing, just sitting on Mark's bed and staring at the room, or sitting at Mark's desk and crying.

He didn't have the heart to criticize her for this. He couldn't even discuss it with her. It was as if he didn't know about it. This was Fay's world, her private ordeal. After all, she was—to use her word—"functioning." She was shopping, preparing dinner, going to meetings, living in the normal pattern in all those areas of life. How could he take away from her this painful fulfillment of whatever need it was, this indulgence in her sorrow? It made him uncomfortable, it "bothered" him to know she had re-created Mark's world in that room upstairs and still lived in that vanished world, but he felt he had to accept it.

He had to accept it just as he knew she accepted the strange and difficult world his own illness had forced on them both. The constant medication he had to take, which she made virtually her responsibility. The glance at her watch during a TV show or while visiting or in the middle of whatever they were doing: "Lou, it's time for your pill." The food she prepared that she believed was "good for him." She would move a chair before he could even attempt to do it, or go down determinedly to the basement to get the clothes out of the dryer and carry them up herself in the big basket. She drove the car now whenever they went anywhere together, hovered near the bathroom when he was inside taking a shower, shooed visitors home at an early hour. And always she did it so naturally, so simply, that he never felt there was a sense of sacrifice on her part, or that it was a burden, and most wonderful of all, she never made him feel that he, Lou, wasn't exactly the man he had always been, with the strength and authority and command of the situation that she respected in him.

There had developed between them a special sensitivity to each other's emotional state, an awareness of a mood, or even of a quick reaction to a remark, or sight, or association. It was as if each knew what the other was feeling.

They never quarreled now. They disagreed often, they even contradicted and corrected each other, but it was with a softness of manner, a gentleness that had become part of their relationship. It was just something understood by both. Nothing in this world anymore was worth a quarrel between them. Nothing could justify hurting each other now.

So when Lou came home after the Executive Committee meeting about the Rabbi, it was perfectly clear in his mind what procedure he would follow. Not a word to Fay. Let the matter develop whichever way it would, and when it was over, acknowledge his part in it. But under no circumstances upset her now.

She was asleep on the couch in the living room, stretched out with a small cushion under her head, the newspaper across her chest, some pages on the floor, the music from the hi-fi playing softly, the unobtrusive background music of her favorite FM station that she listened to all day because it "soothed" her.

She heard him of course and sat up almost painfully, her back struggling to straighten up. He hung up the light topcoat he always wore now, even in warm weather, put it away with his hat in the hall closet. He walked into the living room slowly, up to his big chair near the fireplace, the one that slid back like a lounge with a footrest, and sighed himself into it. There was a silence as Fay leaned her head back against the couch, her eyes half-open. They were both so weary. It was so hard just to be awake and alive in this world.

"So—?" Fay said finally.

"So—a meeting." He was going to reveal as little as possible.

"I'll get the hot chocolate."

"Never mind tonight."

"I'll get it. It'll just take a minute."

She pushed herself up and went into the kitchen. The pre-bedtime ritual. A mug of hot chocolate. It seemed to help him sleep. Still, he really would have preferred to skip it tonight, get into bed, turn off the lights, end the day and the thoughts of the day, close the flow of emotions in him.

"About what?" She was setting the mug, the two cookies, the paper napkin, all on the little round tray, down on the end table near the chair.

"What about what?"

"The meeting."

"What's the difference?" A wave of the hand. A big gulp of chocolate. He had no skill at parrying, no subtlety at disguise.

She stared at him, a faint, almost bitter smile just at the corners of her lips. Lou, Lou. Such a simple man. So honest, he could never hide anything.

"You might as well tell me."

That's Fay for you. Half asleep when you come home, knocked out, barely able to stand up, and suddenly the questions. And a stubbornness with it all.

"Tomorrow. It's late. I don't want to go into it now."

Oh the familiar feel of it, the pattern, like a physical thing in your hand that you could sense vibrating. You could even measure the vibrations, the intensity of them. How well they both knew it now, that there was no deception between them any more, that the little gestures, efforts, were only for a few moments or so, a kind of pretense at it, because the other already knew that there was more underneath, that the truth was soon to come out.

"Tell me, Lou." He knew she had seen the signs in his face, in his manner, heard it in his voice. "Tonight. Now."

"Well—." How do you formulate such a thing? How do you state the conclusion without conveying all the horror and agony that led to it? "We're asking Rabbi to resign." He tried to raise the chocolate to his lips for self-protection, but her expression made it impossible. She stared at him with such pain in her face, her mouth open, her face twisted, questioning, her eyes looking at him in disbelief.

"Why?"

"Why? Why? Fay, a lot of reasons. You know why. The whole business. Everything. The Committee feels he's not good for us. For the Congregation."

"Just like that?"

"No." There was really no use. She would get to it. "Not just like that. Bob had a specific reason. Fay—" he sat up straight, looked down at his hands, clasped them together. "Fay, Bob told us of something. Awful, awful. He said he had evidence that . . . that Rabbi had . . . was doing immoral things. Something to do with a woman."

Fay didn't move for such a long time that he finally looked at her. She was just staring at him with an expression of disbelief, puzzlement, pain.

"Fay, I don't want to discuss it, Fay. It's done, it's done!"

"Rabbi?"

"Rabbi! Rabbi!"

"Immoral? That man?"

"That man! Now stop it. It's over. It's done. The Committee voted —it's done."

"And you?"

"What about me?"

"You—also voted?"

He stood up, walked away. But there was nowhere to go. "What do you want, Fay? I'm not responsible for what Rabbi did. He's responsible. Bob said he had evidence, all the facts, everything. He said Rabbi would have to admit it."

"You believe this, Lou? Just tell me that."

"I think it's possible." He turned away. "I don't know! Am I God? How do I know?"

"Then how could you vote to—"

"It is possible, Fay! What are you—a child? Men do things. It's happened before. Men do things!"

"Not that man."

"That man!"

"You voted to—"

"I voted for the Temple! You understand? To save the Temple! Not against Rabbi—but so that we can build the Temple!" He came up to her. "Do I have to tell you what that Temple means to me?"

"And what has Rabbi—"

"Everything! If we keep him on after what Bob told us, if it got out—and it would, because such things always get out—it could destroy everything! Split the Congregation. Drive people away. Ruin everything. All the work I've done, all these years!"

"Why do I hear this word 'I'? 'I'?"

"Because that Temple is me! What else is my life now?"

"Me! Me! How can you talk only of yourself?"

"Fay—" he sat down near her. He took her hands. "Fay—don't do this. For my sake, please. It was a horrible agony for all of us. Everyone on the Committee. Nobody wanted to do the wrong thing. We just wanted what was best for the whole Congregation. And we had to decide. We had to!"

"You just told me why you decided. For your Temple!"

"Our Temple!"

"For your work! For yourself!"

"So it's for myself! I couldn't help it!"

"Couldn't you?" Fay moved away, covering her face for a moment. She turned to look at him. "I know you, Lou. Like I know myself. This isn't you. This is a desperate, selfish man talking. Not Lou. Not you!"

"Fay, it had to be done. The others voted too. Not just me."

"Don't tell me about others!"

"They all believed what Bob said!"

Now she stood in front of him so that he could see her eyes, feel them. "Do *you* believe Rabbi is an immoral man? Answer me that!"

"I . . . I don't know."

"*Lou!*" Her fists clenched, her arms raised. It was a cry into his face. "You do know!"

She turned and started to run. He caught her arm. "Where you going?"

She started to sob, and he held her, his arms around her. His heart was beating fast. That heart. That damned heart. He was holding her, clinging to her too. They were both so miserable. There was pain in this for both of them.

She pulled away finally, to the couch, and sat, her head down, crying. He looked at her helplessly. Despite everything, the sorrow, the anger, another thought was pounding in him now. His heart. His heart.

He walked slowly, carefully to a chair and let himself down.

"Lou," she stared at him across the room, "don't you know what Rabbi has done for me? Don't you remember?"

He nodded his head.

"After Mark—don't you remember? He was here with me every day. For whole days he sat with me, giving me the only thing I could hold on to. An understanding. A faith. An *acceptance*. I couldn't accept it, Lou. Mark's death hadn't happened. I couldn't accept it. Only Rabbi made me do it. Only Rabbi gave me the strength to live with it."

He nodded his head. Don't argue. No excitement. It's not good for you. Let her talk.

"Lou, if not for Rabbi—God knows what! You understand? That man was with me for days. He let me cry, yell, scream. And then when I was all empty, when I couldn't stand the emptiness inside, he filled it with understanding. Lou, I couldn't accept Mark's death, and he helped me do it!"

They looked at each other. "Fay, don't tell me that." He couldn't stop himself. "You don't accept."

"In my way, Lou—"

"In what way? You put all the things back in Mark's room!"

"For his memory! To be able to live with his memory!"

"No!" Now he stood up. "It's not accepting when you act as if he's still alive. When you sit there and cry with all Mark's things around you—as if he's still alive!"

"That's part of it. I have to go through that."

"It's crazy! It's sick!"

"It's what I need! Rabbi said I should do it if—"

"I don't care what he said! It's wrong! Sick!"

"I have to do it, Lou. Rabbi said I—"

"Well, to hell with Rabbi then! For what's he's done to you. Made you like a lunatic. Sitting there like a crazy woman!"

"Lou! It's to help me."

"Sick! Sick! I wish you'd never listened to him! I wish he'd never come here!"

She looked up, staring at him. The long silence of understanding.

"Oh my God! Lou—is that why?" She turned away, started to run upstairs.

"Don't go, Fay!"

"Stay away from me!"

"Don't go!"

Quickly up the stairs. He followed, running. Forgetting his heart as he tried to catch her.

She entered Mark's room and slammed the door. Locked it. He stood outside, panting, his heart beating against his chest like a frightened creature trying to get out.

"Fay!" He could hear her sobbing. "Open the door!" With his open hand against the door, beating at it. "Open the door!" It was then he felt the pain. The dreaded pain, the unbearable sharpness of the fearful pain.

Dizzy. Weak. Unable to stand. Hold on. Breathe. He slipped to the floor, his head sliding against the door downward to the floor.

Fay heard. The scraping, the sound of the body. She opened the door, looked at him on the floor, gasping, trying to breathe. She ran to the other room. The pill. The glass of water. She would force it into him, make him swallow it.

"Swallow it!" Patting his cheek. Forcing his mouth open. "Swallow it!"

He opened his eyes. A little nod. Yes. Yes. All right. He made an effort to open his mouth. She was on the floor, holding up his head. Swallow! Swallow! Lou—you must!

Down. Now let him lie. She ran to the phone. The special number. Dr. Kramer.

Finally. The voice. "Doctor Kramer? Fay. Lou's had an attack. Come right away."

She went back to where he lay. His eyes were open. She gripped his hand. It was cold. She kissed it, held it. Cold, cold. His face began to sweat, the lips blue. Now she was caressing him, wiping the sweat away, holding him.

"I—"

"Don't talk, Lou!"

"I . . . I'm sorry. What I said."

"Don't talk. Rest. The doctor's coming."

"If—"

"Please!"

"If . . . Fay. . . ." He tried to shake his head. "I did wrong. I did . . . wrong . . . wrong. . . ."

RABBI **5**

Rabbi Gordon's first Bar Mitzvah in Greenlake had been Richard Brody. He wished with all his heart it were somebody else.

The problem was not the boy, who was a quiet type, not so much subdued as overwhelmed. It was the father, Harry Brody, who practiced overwhelming people as if it were a mission in life. Harry was short, round-faced, almost totally bald except for a smudge of black hair across the back of his skull that sat there like a natural *yarmulke*. He wore round, silver-framed glasses that added to the impression of his aggressiveness, even though you couldn't explain how. He waved his arms all the time. Just listening, he waved his arms, the elbows fluttering out to the sides and back. And when he talked, there was a regular flapdoodle of arm-waving going on. People teased him, saying that if he only knew music he would be a great conductor. He also grabbed lapels, tugged at shoulders, poked ribs, and slapped backs. Harry made contact.

It was one of the reasons, perhaps, why Brody's Carpet Store on the Highway was so successful. It was a low building with an enormous glass front so that you could see right into the whole store and observe the great selection of carpets and rugs that were displayed like huge strokes of color from every wall and surface and stacked up in opulent thick piles like massive layer cakes.

Harry had two salesmen who knew the merchandise and talked persuasively and tried hard, but almost every big sale was clinched by Harry himself. At just the right moment he would move in and overwhelm. If the customer wanted to see a particular style or color, Harry would eagerly, happily pull a heavy sample of carpet from the midst of a pile and offer it up with the pride of a man presenting his virgin daughter in marriage. He would then bring the customer into such close contact with it, make him feel it, rub his hand over it, stand on it, scuff it, caress it, sometimes even lie on it, that by the time he was finished the helpless prospect felt it would be a betrayal not to buy the carpet with which he had established such intimacy. Then Harry would go to work on the woman from a completely different angle. Nothing technical. Just the glorious wonder of this magnificent color, the beauty of the pattern, the richness it would bestow upon the home, the envy it would create in visitors' hearts.

Harry Brody was making a lot of money in that carpet store, and he enjoyed everything that the money brought to him. The Brody house was in a two-acre zoned area of Greenlake. Their swimming pool wasn't the regular rectangular kind, it was the more extravagant kidney shape, and along the far end there were even three cabanas where guests could change. There were built-in speakers near the pool so one could listen to hi-fi music while sipping cocktails between swims. The Brody car was an air-conditioned white Lincoln; the second car (always parked in front of the store) was a red Thunderbird.

Neither Harry nor his wife, Gert, experienced any sense of guilt whatsoever in the enjoyment of their possessions and way of life. Not only did he work hard for it and therefore deserve it, but he considered himself a dedicated man. He was President of the Men's Club of Temple Israel.

Some people imagined this served chiefly as an additional outlet for his enormous energy. Others felt that perhaps he was using the office and the contacts it provided to help his business. It happened that both assumptions were partially true. To Harry himself, however, the Men's Club and his devotion to it were an obligation he had assumed in a good cause. And that cause was simply to bring together the community of Jewish men in Greenlake in every kind of social activity. "If you don't get 'em together, how're they going to feel anything for each other? And if Jews don't feel anything for each other, where are they? Sunk!" Then came a concept he felt had great profundity: "The Jew is linked to his fellow Jews voluntarily. No laws, no regulations, nothing forces them to join together. What I'm doing is making that voluntary link stronger!"

Harry had been one of the first of the important members of the congregation to call on Rabbi after his appointment. He came to

Rabbi's home ("More personal this way") and sat down in the living room and opened up.

"Rabbi, you don't know me and I don't know you, so let's get acquainted. Because I got a feeling we're going to work together real close, you and me. You're going to help me and I'll knock myself out to help you, and we could have a partnership here to give the Jewish folk in this town a lift like they never had."

Rabbi of course had heard of Harry Brody, seen him here and there, met him briefly, and in a sense been "warned" about him. His head sideways, he now squinted at the man in amused bewilderment. So this was Brody at work. The push, the drive, the enthusiasm. Well, he was nothing to be frightened of if you knew how to handle him. The idea was to put all this to good use.

"I'll be glad to help you in any way I can," he said.

"Good! Glad to hear that!" Brody actually reached out his hand to shake Rabbi's. He grasped it and squeezed hard. "If we understand each other from the start—we'll get along. Right?" Harry now rose and flapped his way back and forth in front of Rabbi, thinking aloud, talking, planning, organizing.

"What I want to do is make a marriage. Let me explain, Rabbi. I want a marriage between the social activities, the getting together for fun, play, talk, whatever—and a certain religious feeling. So it's not just *anybody* doin' this—it's *Jews* doin' it and it's got a religious quality too."

Rabbi still smiled, though he was completely confused. "I'm afraid I don't understand. Exactly how do you—"

"Simple! I want you there at every kind of social function I can get you to. Your presence, the Rabbi himself being there, participating, it already gives it a different touch, y'know? A meaning."

"Which functions? I still don't—"

"Which not? Rabbi, you got an idea what I got going here? With these men? You name it! The bowling group, that's every Wednesday. The golf, tennis, and swimming groups, that's the year round, believe it or not. If we can't play, we can talk about it! The theater group— that's I'm real proud of. We're going to put on shows I swear you'll think it's professional. We got a lot of talent here! Then there's the dances, the parties, the picnics, the lectures, discussions. Rabbi—what can I say? I got 'em hopping! There's not an activity we haven't got a group for it."

"What part are you suggesting I—"

"Participate! That's the key word. Be with it. I want you at the discussions and I want you at the dances. The bridge championship and the barbecue. We have a golf tournament going. So you swing a club too. We're doing a theater sketch? You'll suddenly discover you're an actor! The men need that, y'know what I mean? To see the Rabbi involved, participating. It makes it *Jewish* somehow. And you know what? You'll end up having a helluva time!"

Rabbi smiled at the thought. Golf, bridge, acting, dancing. How little this man knew him. But then he couldn't be blamed for that. In the suburbs a Rabbi is expected to be a suburbanite. If he didn't enjoy all the created activities and all the natural opportunities that suburban life provided, why had he chosen to be a Rabbi there?

He had been warned about this and it was his first confrontation with what he knew would be a problem for him. He decided to deal with it openly.

"Mr. Brody, perhaps you—"

"Harry!"

"All right. Harry, you might as well face something about your new Rabbi. He's just plain no good at that sort of thing. Bridge? The other players would want to strangle me in ten minutes. Golf? You're looking at a freak—a man who's never even been on a golf course. What else? Oh, acting, the theater group. The way I act I could make King Lear come across like a comedy. I'm a lousy dancer, I—"

"Wait! Rabbi, wait a minute! Who said you have to be an expert in anything? What I want, what would make all my members feel good is just you being there. Sharing it with them. They want to see they got a Rabbi who can come down from the mountain—you know what I mean?—and mingle with the people."

Brody was waving his arms with the enthusiasm of his image. Now he leaned closer, a look of almost conspiratorial slyness on his face.

"Let me tell you something else, Rabbi. You're new here, right? Everybody's wondering about you—what kind of man is this Rabbi? You want to establish yourself with the folks, right? Make them feel you're a regular fellow. A *mentsh*. So they'll feel closer to you, right?"

Rabbi shook his head, still smiling at Brody's inability to grasp his situation. "But Harry, the way I want them to feel close to me is as their Rabbi, not as their playmate. I'm their spiritual leader, not their cheerleader. I want to reach them on—well, a more meaningful level."

What made Harry Brody the man he was, now came out. He didn't argue, he didn't disagree, and he didn't give up.

"So okay—that's fine. You're the rabbi, you know your business. . . . Now. Will you make—let's say a gesture? Will you give it one try, just to see what happens? Who knows? You might be surprised! So will you come next Wednesday to the bowling tournament? This one time, just to see?" He was holding out his hand. "Do it for me? As a favor? One time? Yes?"

Rabbi looked at him and it struck him that the man was absolutely sincere. Totally involved in his own way. Unquestioning in his dedication. He held out his hand and Harry shook it warmly.

"Wonderful! Agreed! It's a deal! Hey, you know what I'll do? I'll get out an announcement right away to the members. Rabbi Gordon to join us in the bowling tournament. You want to bet there'll be a turnout like we never had? Oh, you're doing a *mitzvah*, Rabbi! I swear —a *mitzvah!*"

Tuesday night, Rabbi sat in the living room with Frieda after dinner and announced quite simply:

"I'm scared. I feel like tomorrow night in that bowling alley, they're going to see me naked."

"David, anybody can bowl. It's just throwing a ball. Nothing!"

"It's not just a ball—a *bowling* ball. I never even held one in my hand."

"So they'll show you how."

"I'll never hit a single stick."

"Pin."

"Pin?"

"They call them pins."

"See!" He rubbed his forehead nervously. "I don't even know what they call anything. Frieda, tell me honestly. Do you think a Rabbi can serve his congregation by making a fool of himself? Just tell me that!"

Frieda put her arms around him and couldn't help smiling. "Maybe it's good for them to see a Rabbi is human."

"I'll accept human. But I don't want to come out *sub*human."

"David, I've got an idea. They have bowling on TV. You can see champions there. Let's watch it—and you'll learn."

They turned on the bowling program at ten o'clock, and Rabbi sat there trying to learn—like a student in a classroom. Watching how they held the ball, how they moved, how they swung their arms. He became agonizingly bored in five minutes. The tense, confidential whispering of the announcer didn't help. He just couldn't bear to watch one man after another throw a ball down the alley, knock over the pins, see the next one throw the ball, knock over the pins, then the next one, and each with such a serious look, such concentration, all performing the same absurd act in the same way with the same results.

He turned off the television, laughing at himself, at the ridiculousness of it all, but in despair. "Frieda, if I have to learn to do that to get close to my congregation, I'd better find another profession."

She laughed. "The Lord did make men a little lower than the angels. If this is what they need from you—then this is what they need."

Wednesday evening, Rabbi figured out exactly what he would do. Show up, greet the men, perhaps make a joke or two ("I'm glad to see you fellows throwing the ball instead of the bull"), stand around for fifteen minutes or so, and then leave. After all, it was only intended to be a gesture. He dressed in the usual way, the white shirt, conservative tie, dark suit, black felt hat, and drove over to the Sunrise Bowling Lanes a half hour later than he was expected.

The twenty-five or thirty men had been urged by Brody to control their impatience for a few minutes, but they finally started without Rabbi. Brody kept an eye on the entrance and when Rabbi appeared he made a dash to greet him.

"They started already, Rabbi. I hope you don't mind?"

Rabbi shrugged, adjusted his glasses, and looked at the gleaming expanse of polished wood, the large black spheres moving like planets in strange orbits back and forth, a universe of weird click-clack sounds and stooping men. For a moment he felt completely lost.

"Over there," Harry pointed. "We're all down at that end."

As he walked with Rabbi toward the far end, he glanced at his suit. "You're not exactly dressed for bowling, Rabbi, I'll say that."

"For watching?"

"Oh come on, Rabbi. You'll throw a few balls, huh?"

"No, thank you."

"Oh you will! Come on—"

Rabbi shook his head. Harry clapped his hands to make them all stop. "Fellows, look who we got with us! Rabbi Gordon! The Men's Club is proud and happy to have you here with us, Rabbi. It's an honor, I mean that. But I want to tell you right now—you're getting no special favors when it comes to bowling, right?" A slap on the back that almost knocked Rabbi's glasses off. "We play to win, right fellows? So Rabbi—off with that jacket, roll up your sleeves, and let's see how good you are!"

Rabbi stared at Brody in such obvious agony that several of the men turned away in embarrassment. But Harry couldn't be stopped. He grabbed Rabbi's coat and started to pull it off his shoulders.

"Mr. Brody!" The struggle was lost, the coat was off, and now Harry was pushing him toward the line of balls.

"Just grab one, Rabbi—and let 'er go! Come on everybody—" the men had all stopped now to watch this, "let's give Rabbi Gordon a big hand!" He started the applause and some of the men joined in, the awkwardness of the situation inescapable.

Brody reached down and held up a ball to him. Rabbi looked at the three holes in the ball and in his misery they became three hateful eyes. Three sockets, mocking. Brody thrust the ball at him. The men watched in silence, shifting about painfully. Brody's glasses glinted up into Rabbi's face. "Gotta show 'em, Rabbi. That you're with 'em!"

Rabbi reached out finally and took the ball in his left arm, startled by the weight of it. He cradled it, heavy against his body, like a weapon that had been thrust into him. Then he inserted three fingers of his right hand into the ball and when he tried to hold it they slid out and the ball crashed to the floor and rolled off to a side. The sound was like a cannon shot.

Some of the men laughed, others turned away, not knowing what to do. The crack of the ball on the floor, the pain in one of his fingers, the laughter, Brody's grinning face still pushing at him, the perspiration on his forehead, everything now exploded at once and Rabbi stepped back, shaking his head. He turned in panic and walked to get his coat.

Brody pursued him. "Rabbi, don't go!"

"I'm making a fool of myself. This is ridiculous."

"It isn't! You're here. You're trying. That's what counts. We're seeing our Rabbi bowling with us. You're like one of the boys!"

Rabbi walked back slowly and the men stopped again, turning to watch him uneasily. Brody picked up the ball, showed Rabbi how to grip it. It seemed so incredibly heavy, so awkward there at the end of his hand, he felt he would never be able to swing his arm.

"And now, fellows!" Brody again, thrusting his exuberance at them, "Here goes Rabbi again! He may not be a champ—but he's a sport!"

Rabbi swung back his arm painfully, pulled it forward, and released the ball. It rolled down the side of the alley and hit two pins. The applause was that of sympathy.

"You did it!" Brody was exultant. "What did I tell you? All you need is practice, Rabbi!"

He threw three more times, taking his turn, and the most pins he hit were five. "I think I'll sit down and rest," he said, and Brody, triumphant in having brought this much about, smiled and nodded and agreed.

Rabbi watched the men, the intensity of their concentration, their total involvement, the almost violent giving of the self, and tried to understand it. He actually began to feel after a while that there could be a joy and reward for them in doing this well, in throwing the ball so precisely, in controlling the body so effectively. They were happy doing this, there was no question about it.

But why was *he* there? What difference did it really make to them? Would his presence, his "participation," lead them to a closer relationship with him? Would they accept him more, follow him more willingly, become more involved with Judaism?

He couldn't believe it. And he sat there like an alien in their midst, and felt a kind of self-pity. The Rabbi has to come to a bowling alley to reach his people. The Rabbi has to throw a ball to win their respect. The Rabbi has to act on this level to achieve some communication. He felt a shame at his presence there, a betrayal of his own identity.

When he stood up to leave after a few minutes, the men stopped again as if in observance of some formality towards the Rabbi. He stepped forward, and they were all turned toward him now. He wanted to say the right thing, not suggest the alienation he felt but convey his understanding of them.

"I came here just to be a few minutes with you, and I want to thank you for putting up with me. I read somewhere that bowling—some form of throwing a ball at an object—goes back so far in history that it was done even before the time of Moses. So there must be something to it. And the way you fellows do it, I can see it's not only a pleasure—it's an art! It so happens, bowling isn't exactly one of my outstanding accomplishments. Or did you notice that already? Anyway—enjoy yourselves, have fun! And—please don't judge your Rabbi by his performance here. Come to the Temple—that's *my* alley! Good night!" He waved his arm to them.

The men applauded, and a few of them smiled. Then they turned back quickly to their game. Enough time wasted.

Brody walked Rabbi to the door and Rabbi turned to him unhappily.

"So you see, Harry, it didn't work."

"Well—" Harry shrugged his shoulders, not denying it, "I appreciate your trying, Rabbi."

"The point is, Harry, I really have to do it my way."

"What?"

"Reach these people. Even the members of your Men's Club. Reach them with what I have to offer."

They looked at each other a moment, and Brody knew now the kind of man he would have to deal with. A Rabbi who, even when he tried, couldn't relate in many areas, a Rabbi who would essentially be a stranger to many, many aspects of the life of the congregation.

Rabbi, driving home, refused to feel a sense of defeat. This was not what he had to give them, no matter how much they felt they needed it. He was their spiritual leader, their teacher. He would come close to them in his way . . . and it was a way that had meaning.

There was no feeling of anger between Brody and Rabbi because of this incident, but it set the stage for the conflict that emerged later about Richard Brody's Bar Mitzvah.

The two of them, Rabbi and Harry, had to consult on the plans and preparations. Since this was to be Rabbi's first Bar Mitzvah service for the congregation, he felt it important to set the proper precedent, to indicate the manner in which such affairs would be conducted by him, and to make the congregation aware of his attitude toward this occasion. At their first meeting about it, he stated his viewpoint to Harry as strongly as he could.

"Harry, as far as I'm concerned, the Bar Mitzvah serves a strictly religious purpose. True, it started as a custom, and is not prescribed in the Bible, but its significance is simple: a young man—your son—has taken his first important step toward assuming his place as an adult Jew, a member of the community."

Brody was equally determined and decided the best course was not to yield anything. "I'm no scholar or anything like that, Rabbi, but it seems to me you left something out. This much I know—it's a *celebration* too. It's always been and always will be. The family, the friends, they always celebrated the Bar Mitzvah in a social way. Right?"

"I'm not implying there should be no celebration."

"Good! Then let's make it simple, Rabbi. You run the religious part and I'll take care of the social end."

"I'm concerned with the effect on the boy. On your son. What he gets out of his Bar Mitzvah—"

"Look," Brody stood up, his arms in the air. "You don't think my Richie's going to have his Bar Mitzvah and me and my family and all my friends aren't going to make a big thing out of it? What I want to do for my boy—that is one hundred per cent my business. And let me tell you something, Rabbi, I think you just don't understand how people feel about this. In fact, you want to know something? You're missing an important thing. This is one of the times we Jews feel good about being Jews. We feel proud we got a boy who's becoming a Jewish man. We're celebrating in a big way. What? Not some athletic accomplishment. Not something to do with business or social life. No—it's a religious, a Jewish religious event in the kid's life and we're celebrating that! And it's a good thing, a damn good thing we Jews still want to do it and feel excited about it! You should appreciate that as a Rabbi, not knock it. You ought to be happy as a Rabbi that Jews have this excuse to rejoice about their Jewishness!"

"Harry, I just say this: If the celebration overwhelms the religious aspect, the meaning of the occasion is distorted. Its value is destroyed."

"So all the Jews in the world are wrong? All the Bar Mitzvah parties for hundreds of years—"

"In all those hundreds of years, whenever the celebration became an ostentatious display, it was wrong! Did you know, Harry, that the Jewish community of Cracow, Poland—almost four hundred years ago, mind you!—imposed a tax on Bar Mitzvahs to discourage extravagant celebrations? It was wrong then, it's wrong now. As your Rabbi, I don't believe in having excessive—"

Brody waved his hand in front of Rabbi's face to stop him. "My son Richard is going to have the kind of celebration I want to give him! That's the way it's going to be!"

Brody walked out without another word and the two men didn't meet again until the Friday before the Bar Mitzvah Sabbath, when Rabbi instructed him in the procedure that would be followed.

During the preparation for this event, Rabbi made an effort to reach the boy, Richard, get him to respond to the religious significance of the occasion. He spent hours with him giving him instruction in history, Bible, prayer, Jewish belief and theology, Jewish practices, comparative religion. He tried to cram into the boy such a great awareness of spiritual values and tradition that he might himself reject the emphasis on the festival aspect of his Bar Mitzvah. But Richard Brody knew, from his father, of Rabbi's attitude and resented it. He sat there as Rabbi spoke and read and taught, and let very little of it touch him.

One slight victory Rabbi did achieve, and that was in the speech Richard was to make. Customarily the Bar Mitzvah speech is an expression of thanks to the parents for the care and love they have bestowed, and a statement that indicates the boy's awareness of the new responsibilities he will have. The boy usually writes it himself with the help of his instructor. Rabbi suggested another subject, and guided Richard so much in the writing of it that it was practically Rabbi's statement. And what he wrote was a brief dissertation against materialistic concern, against the success criteria of our society, and of the need for Jews to rise above them and search for deeper meanings in life. Harry Brody read it, understood, and said nothing about it. He let Rabbi win that small battle.

Because the congregation didn't have its own Temple, the Bar Mitzvah was divided into two parts. First came the religious ceremony in the Temple they were sharing with the neighboring Jewish community, and later the celebration at the Sprucewood Country Club. The club had the kitchen facilities, the dance floor, the parking space, and it was considered a beautiful "setting" for such an occasion.

Rabbi had made a decision, after much weighing of the situation, not to attend the celebration. His presence there, he felt, would be an endorsement of that kind of indulgence, a tacit approval of the Bar Mitzvah excesses that had made this occasion a source of ridicule of Jews. As their new Rabbi he wanted the congregation to know where he stood on this matter. Brody had tried to persuade him to come, and Rabbi's refusal had created a tension between them that was evident during the services.

They stood together in front of the Ark at the end of the services, ready to return the Torah scroll to its sacred place. Helping to replace the Torah in the Ark was an honor bestowed upon Brody as the father of the Bar Mitzvah boy. Rabbi recited the two verses of the Psalm:

"The law of the Lord is perfect, restoring the soul; the testimony of the Lord is sure, making wise the simple. The precepts of the Lord are right, rejoicing the heart; the judgments of the Lord are true; they are righteous altogether." Then the little prayer of praise for the word of God. "Behold, a good doctrine has been given unto you; forsake it not."

Brody, on one side of the Ark, his son on the other, pulled the draperies that closed off the Torah scrolls from sight. Rabbi turned to Richard and shook his hand. Then he turned to Brody and Harry gripped his hand tightly.

"Rabbi, I want you to come to the celebration."

"I can't do that, Harry."

The two men stood alone, talking. Everyone kept away, respectfully, assuming Rabbi was conveying his good wishes.

"It's part of the Bar Mitzvah, Rabbi!"

"I don't approve of it, Harry. I can't!"

No one heard. No one knew what was going on in front of the Ark.

"Rabbi, it will be a disgrace for my family and friends. An insult to us."

"I can't help it. I'm sorry."

They were whispering tensely to each other, bitterness, tightness in their voices.

Brody looked at him now with all his being. "Rabbi—please. I ask you—please. As my Rabbi, for my son's sake if not for mine, I *beg* you, Rabbi. Please come."

Rabbi stared at Brody, at the eyes behind the round glasses, at the suddenly humble face, at the anguish of the man. He felt now a pity for him, a kind of understanding and forgiveness.

"I will come."

The number of invitations the Brody's had sent out came to three hundred and twelve. There were old friends who drove from New York, relatives who flew in from St. Louis and Chicago, and of course all the people in Greenlake whom they couldn't possibly leave out.

The Sprucewood Country Club had been hired for the entire afternoon. A bar was set up in a small room off the main dining room, and there were three bartenders. In the space behind them and in the anteroom next to it, were stacked up cases of Scotch, bourbon, gin, vodka, rye, as well as Pepsi-Cola, Seven-Up, soda, and ginger ale. On every table in the dining room stood a flower arrangement, at every setting a souvenir card and gift (a handsome, imitation-leather address book and pencil), and in front of each plate a champagne glass.

Five uniformed waitresses circulated with trays of hors d'oeuvres, of which there were ten different kinds. The most popular were the shrimps to be dipped in a spicy sauce, and the tiny hot rolls of frankfurters wrapped in bacon. Twenty-five pounds of chopped chicken liver were available as a spread.

The dance band started playing as soon as the first guest arrived. Consisting of six men, it had been brought up from New York and cost Harry four hundred and fifty dollars, not including the tip he would give each man.

A statistically minded participant, after his third drink of Old Grand-Dad, one hundred proof, was heard discussing the affair with one of the other guests, who was a stockbroker. The statistically minded one estimated that there were one hundred seventy-five mink stoles, and twenty-five mink jackets, and probably one hundred pounds of solid gold and three hundred carats of diamonds on display in the rooms of the club at one time.

The stockbroker, a man in his late fifties, didn't like the imputation.

"There's nothing wrong with people dressing up for a Bar Mitzvah with the best they got."

"It just looks so damn vulgar. Everybody showing off."

"So? And when the Italians have a wedding—they don't show off? Or the Irish? And you never heard how the goyim wear a million dollars worth of jewels at one of *their* parties? Let me tell you something, most of these people here knew hard times too. Way back. So now let them enjoy!"

And basically, everyone seemed to be enjoying. It was as if they recognized that the Bar Mitzvah was in one sense an excuse, an opportunity to get together and indulge oneself in fine display, good food, and liquor, and yet the nature of the occasion wasn't totally lost on them. The Brodys had a Bar Mitzvah boy. The Brodys had worked hard and made it and had a lot to celebrate. Good for them! Mazeltov!

Among the guests were a number of weak tired little gray ladies who sat in the comfortable chairs and nodded approvingly to one another. There were men in small circles talking business, women going back and forth to the dressing rooms to touch up their make-up and comb hair back into place, and young people circulating about with obvious intentions and fairly good success. Harry Brody was having his hand shaken and his back slapped without a moment's respite, and Richard was having little envelopes thrust upon him wherever he turned, which he pocketed with accomplished swiftness, responding with "Gee, thanks!" in every case. It was all part of it.

Rabbi stood quietly in a corner and regarded the scene like a man in a strange country observing a local tribal ritual. Frieda had put on a nice dress, not quite formal, and she stood beside him sharing in the greetings directed toward them from time to time. Both of them seemed so out of it, so set apart, that people now and then felt an obligation to stroll over and say a few words just to be "nice to the Rabbi."

At one-thirty, the luncheon was served, and people sought out their tables and place cards and sat down to eat a meal of grapefruit or fruit cocktail, cold vichysoisse or chicken noodle soup, roast beef or broiled chicken with asparagus or string beans, baked potato with sour cream and chives or butter, mixed green salad with French or Roquefort dressing, coffee or tea with cookies (eight different kinds) or seven-layer chocolate cake, and cognac or a liqueur served at one's place, plus chocolate-covered mints on a plate in the center of the table. Cigars for the men were offered by the waiters directly from the boxes, and everyone noted they were Royal Coronas.

Then the band returned to its stand, people pushed back their chairs, and the sound of the *hora* was heard. A circle formed immediately in the center of the floor, getting larger and larger, people everywhere clapping their hands to the exultant rhythm.

Harry Brody came up to Rabbi's table and reached out for Frieda's hand. *"Rebbitsin,"* he said smiling, "come dance!"

Frieda didn't even have a chance to glance at Rabbi. Brody had pulled her out to the dance floor. Then Gert Brody came up to Rabbi, her pink gown aglitter, her eyes shining, her hand outstretched.

"Rabbi—it would be an honor for us to have you dance."

Rabbi stood up awkwardly, aware of people staring at him. He hesitated just long enough to feel his hand pulled forward by Gert, and then he was on the dance floor. Room was made for them in the circle, hands clasped and raised.

He didn't know what was happening, but he was suddenly part of the joyous movement, the twisting, stamping, surging. The free, vital, proud swinging of the body, the eyes laughing, the hands tightly clasping. People watching him, smiling, thanking, wanting him, his presence, his being with them. Embracing him with their eyes. Laughing with joy at his being there. Accepting, holding him. He couldn't resist, then he didn't try to; he let go. A wave of joy ran through him and out of him. The smiles, the hands, the eyes, the bodies swaying and exulting, the music faster, faster, the warmth, the spirit, the exuberance, the love, the closeness, excitement, happiness, triumph. The being with his people . . . being one of them at last. . . .

Everyone was saying they had never seen Rabbi with such a happy look on his face.

VI

Suddenly it was hard to think of a place to meet him just to talk. Elaine considered asking Rabbi to come to the house as the most open gesture of all, the clearest indication that there was really nothing wrong between them. But she imagined Bob's reaction when he would learn of it and decided it wasn't worth the anguish. Going to Rabbi's house would be difficult because of Frieda's presence. And of course meeting in a coffee shop or restaurant wouldn't allow them the opportunity to talk freely. Everything had been so innocent and easy before, and now there were problems and anxiety no matter what she did. She hated the situation. She ended up by calling Rabbi and saying she had to meet him at his office, that it was important, and that it had to be done that day.

Rabbi Gordon's office was a little room in the basement of Temple Beth El in Silvertown. It had been set aside for him by the Temple as part of the temporary sharing arrangement, and it was a depressing place. Almost no furniture, a desk, two chairs, an improvised bookcase. The basement was above ground level and the room looked out on the street, so the Venetian blinds on the narrow window were always kept drawn.

Rabbi used the office only when he had a need to be alone, and always in the half hour or so before services when the isolation and quiet helped him prepare himself for the "confrontation with God" that was to follow. Sitting there now in the cold drabness of the room, waiting for Elaine, he decided to use the time in a meaningful way. He was busy making notes on a new project when she knocked on the door and came in, and he had to tell her at once what he was working on.

Elaine was no longer surprised by this. Rabbi was Rabbi. When he became involved in something, he had to be pulled out of it to reality, to the present. He had to be made aware that you, too, had something to communicate. But first would come the flow of his own concern.

"Ah, Elaine, it's you. Sit down, sit down. Elaine—I want your reaction to this. Something very important. I have been thinking—"

He stood up now and walked about, his thoughts like electrical impulses that made him turn, stop, walk, and through it all forgetting that she had called him with a sense of urgency in her voice, that she had requested this meeting because she had something important to discuss.

"—I have been thinking of doing something as simple, as basic, as bringing Judaism into the ordinary life of the congregation. I mean into their existence and not just into their thoughts. It must be something they experience and not just something they believe in. And that cannot be done in the Temple alone. I feel that they go home after services and it's as if they had a small injection of the religious spirit. And like all injections, it wears off. So I want something that starts with them. Something they do themselves, in their homes, with their families. An act of devotion that they perform, and not one that is conducted for them. Elaine—my idea is to make the Sabbath meaningful again! Do you understand?"

Elaine was staring at him, at the excitement in his face, the joy in this concept. She couldn't stop him now. She would have to let him finish. This was Rabbi.

"I want to start a drive—" he didn't wait for her response, "a campaign—whatever it is—to make our congregation respect, observe the Sabbath! Cherish it as a special and holy day set apart. A day of awareness of God. It is the feast of creation, as Rosenzweig called it. God created heaven and earth in six days, and on the seventh day He rested. That's why it is the day of rest. We celebrate His work of creation. And even more, oh, so much more!"

He walked quickly to the bookcase, found the book, turned the pages.

"Listen to this. He's talking about the Sabbath. 'For what is redemption if not the concord between revelation and creation? And what is the first ineluctable premise for such concord, save man's rest after he has done the work of this earth! Six days he has worked and attended to all his affairs; now, on the seventh, he rests. Six days he has uttered the many useful and useless things the work day demanded of him, but on the seventh he obeys the command of the prophet: he lets his tongue rest from the talk of everyday, and learns to be silent, to listen. And the sanctifying of the day of rest by listening to God's voice in silence must be shared by all members of his house.' I want them to listen, Elaine! And that means creating the atmosphere to listen, setting the stage for it, preparing themselves for it. I want them, on the Sabbath, to dress differently. To act differently. To have a special meal. To have the family together. To know and feel that it is a day when they will come closer to God. I want the Sabbath to have meaning for them again! You understand? And this I will do by—"

He suddenly stopped and looked at her. Her hand was over her face, the fingers pressing against the temples as if to shut off the jumping nerves. It suddenly occurred to him that perhaps she hadn't been listening at all.

"Elaine? Do you think—? Is there a chance for this?" He stopped again and came over.

"I'm sorry, Rabbi." She looked up. His face was like a young boy's, still glowing with the excitement of creation, the sweet enthusiasm. "I'm sorry. I think it's a good idea—but my mind was on something else."

"Of course! Of course! I completely forgot! You called me to talk about something. I'm sorry. The idea of the Sabbath—"

"I understand."

"—carried me away." He smiled. "My fault. I'm sorry." He walked back to his chair behind the desk and sat down. "Please. Now tell me what it is."

Please now tell me what it is. Just like that! Jump from all that Sabbath talk to this. And sitting there behind his desk like a nice, friendly Rabbi willing to hear your little problem. And the fantastic idiocy of it all, the unbelievable twist of life was that it was all about him. All concerned with *his* life and future. And yet one had to think it out carefully, plan, organize, how to tell him. It was even hard to get his attention, to make him just listen! She smiled bitterly and he noticed it.

"Elaine, is something wrong?"

She moved her chair closer to the desk to be able to reach the ash tray on the corner, and rubbed her cigarette in it as if this act were an answer, side to side the burning end of the cigarette against the glass, saying yes yes yes. Was he with her now? Finally here from that other world of his?

"Rabbi, I don't know how to do this. Straight, blunt, frank—or gently and gradually."

"Straight. Whatever it is, Elaine. Whatever your problem, you know me well enough to trust—"

"Rabbi!" She cut him off. "It is your problem I want to talk about."

"Mine?" Sudden remoteness, concern.

"And I guess mine too."

"I don't understand." Now confusion, and a quickening of tension.

"Rabbi, let me just ask you this. Do you know about a meeting of the Executive Committee that was held yesterday?"

He hesitated. "How did you find out? Of course—Bob."

"Yes. Bob. So you know. . . . Do you know of the decision that was made?" She looked at him, the tightness in his face, the fingers to the lips as if to control a quivering. "I'm sorry, Rabbi. Of course you know. . . . Have you . . . decided what to do about it?"

Rabbi stood up, walking slowly back and forth behind the desk, his fingers through his hair as if to press out the thought, the response. Everyone was pushing him to do something about it. Danny. Frieda. Now Elaine. They had all the answers because obviously, on their level, the answers were easy. How could they understand that a Rabbi can never think of himself alone? He is the trustee of the congregation's welfare, the leader who must always consider their good before his own. Had she come to urge him to take action? He needed time, time to think and weigh everything.

"Elaine, I don't know yet. I must be sure that what I do is best for the congregation."

"Rabbi," he was the kind of man you had to guide toward facing certain truths, you had to press them on him, "do you know what they are accusing you of? What . . . Bob is accusing you of?"

"Oh . . ." Now he thought he understood. His good, devoted friend Elaine was naturally shocked at the mere concept of it, and had come to convey her disgust to him, her sense of repulsion at such an idea. That was understandable, and typical of her sensitivity and concern. "You mean—the ridiculous charge that . . . that I . . . something immoral? With a woman?" He took her arms and smiled gratefully at her. "Don't be upset. It's such an obvious lie it isn't worth thinking about. What's behind it, of course—that's disturbing. Using this to . . . well, to try to get rid of me, that's what is shocking."

Elaine stared at him and wondered how she could do it, how she could let him know. He was an amazing man, so concerned with all the important aspects of life, and so oblivious to certain truths about them. It was as if he knew that humans were capable of evil, but didn't know what their evil acts were. Elaine was tempted not to go farther, not bring it out in the open between them, but she was afraid it might later emerge somehow, through something Bob might do. It was better to face it now. Better to let Rabbi know it now.

"Rabbi, that . . . that woman is supposed to be—"

"What woman?" He waved his hand. "There's no one! It's a complete lie!"

"Rabbi—" It had to be done. "That woman is supposed to be . . . me."

He looked at her as if he hadn't heard her, as if the words had not been said. He turned and moved away toward the desk and then made himself lean back against the wall, needing this motion, this time to prepare himself. He folded his arms across his chest, cocked his head sideways with a look of apparent amusement, and said:

"Now, would you say again what you just told me?" As if he didn't really expect her to.

"Rabbi—it's supposed to be me. According to Bob—and of course I'm as stunned, as horrified as you are—there's some kind of . . . involvement he calls it . . . between you and me. I had to tell you! I didn't want you to find out in some awful way. I wanted you to know what he's up to."

Rabbi didn't know what he felt, what he was experiencing. More than confusion and bewilderment. A kind of anger that it had been possible for Barrett to characterize and judge his relationship with Elaine, to put a stinking, dirty label on it, and to use it against him. That this should be a weapon in Barrett's fight against him, this was upsetting him now as much as the lie of it, the deliberate distortion. And at the same time, standing there with Elaine, he could not think only of his own problem, his own despair. He was aware of what she must be feeling at this moment and of the need for him to say, do something, that would help her. But he simply didn't know how.

Elaine could sense the turmoil in him now, the clash of different anxieties. She wanted to make it easier for him. "What I want to say, Rabbi, what I want you to know is that you are in no way responsible for this. In no way! You have nothing to do with it. It's . . . it's Bob's problem."

Rabbi really didn't want to hear it. What difference did it make whose problem it was? The point was that it had been said. The concept now existed. It was like a living thing with a life of its own. It was there, between him and Elaine, between him and the whole world.

"Elaine. . . ." Suddenly it was so hard for him to talk to her. He sighed and started again. "Elaine, you don't have to explain it to me. Surely you and I don't need to explain away what we know doesn't exist. Bob's . . . problem . . . that's for you and him to deal with."

She came to him and there was a kind of pleading in her now, a desire for him to understand her need to go through it all. Now it was for her sake she had to do it.

"Rabbi, please let me say it. I want to, because otherwise you and I will never again be able to face each other with complete freedom. I must tell you why Bob . . . why he can do such a thing. Please, please let me!"

He sat down, not wanting to look at her, unable to face this emotional bursting in her. She moved about, talking to herself in some sense, summoning up the memories for her own examination as well as his.

"Bob and I . . . it seems like such a good marriage. People always feel we're such a good match for each other. And in many ways it is. Bob is a successful man. Everyone knows that. In business. President of the congregation. A leader. He has so much to be proud of. So much to feel good about in himself.

"But . . . in some way . . . for some reason . . . he feels threatened by me. Isn't that strange? I've tried so hard to be his support, his understanding, accepting wife . . . and it seems to come out as a threat. From a dominating woman who's trying to control him, manage him.

"I just don't know how to deal with this, Rabbi. God knows I've tried. Anticipating his wishes, being sensitive to his moods, making him feel secure and loved and appreciated.

"It just hasn't worked, Rabbi. He resents me. Maybe even—somewhere inside—hates me for the way I seem to make him feel. What can I do? I have needs too. I need contact and warmth and love and acceptance too! I need a sharing, a deep, rich life. I'm dead without it. What else is there, if you don't have that?"

She stopped a moment and brushed her cheek. Rabbi glanced at her. He didn't want this, but he knew he had to let her finish. It was part of his being a Rabbi. "Elaine, I understand. I'm sorry it's been this way for you."

"So—" she raised her head, determined to get it all out now, "—so I had to find something. To hold my life together. To give me some kind of sense of belonging. And I . . . well, there was the Temple and everything that came with it. I plunged into it. Into all the work. I began to feel good about myself. I was helping, and it was welcome. I was doing, and it was accepted. I was wanted, needed. I was part of something where I could give myself without holding back. And I . . . and I also turned to you."

He moved his hands in the air as if brushing that aside.

"No, Rabbi. I must say it. I turned to you! Don't you see—that's where the misunderstanding came. That's why Bob felt he could attack me. He couldn't believe it was only because you gave me the chance to be alive. That I did all the work for that. Volunteered to help you in everything. Typed for you and made notes for you and organized meetings. Came to your house, to wherever you needed me, whenever you needed me. I was needed—you gave me that. And more. So much more! Your warmth, your intelligence, your interest. Your sense of excitement. I loved that! I responded to your concern over what mattered, your intensity. You shared it with me. I waited for every meeting with you to feel that contact and warmth."

Rabbi was uneasy now, understanding what was happening. He tried to bring it down. "Every human being needs contact, Elaine. It's normal, natural. Nothing more."

"But I was so grateful for that, Rabbi! So grateful!"

Rabbi tried to smile, minimizing it. "It's a Rabbi's function. To help where there is a need."

"It was more, Rabbi! It was because you understood me. That's what was so wonderful. You gave me the chance to express, to share what mattered to me. To have it welcomed and understood. Rabbi— I was myself with you. Completely myself. And I could be, and you wanted me to be."

Now Rabbi stood up. He had to stop her. "Elaine, there's no need to go through all this. You've had this problem, and in some way I helped you. That's all."

"But I must tell you! I have to say what it's meant to me. Don't you see? You must know what you have meant—"

"Elaine!" He turned to her. "No more. Please, no more."

"Why? Let me say it, Rabbi. I need to—so much. To say it!"

"Elaine, this isn't necessary. We both understand."

"I have to say it! I don't care! What you have meant to me. I have to—"

She stopped suddenly. They were looking at each other with complete awareness now. It was all said between them, in the silence, in the staring at each other. Elaine felt frightened suddenly. She couldn't breathe. She tried to talk and the words came, but from some distant stranger and she was hearing them far away.

"What you . . . have meant to me. . . ."

Staring at each other in silence, unable to turn away, the communication was complete. Elaine stepped back, frightened. She tried to think, make herself think. What? Oh God! The hands over her face, uncontrollable sobbing. Oh God!

He waited, knowing, understanding it, feeling all she was groping for. He wanted to hold her arms, help her, give her the strength not to face it but to run from it. She had to run from it and didn't know how.

"Elaine, there is nothing for you to regret, to suffer for. Nothing. You must believe that."

"Oh my God!" She couldn't look at him, her hands still over her face, shaking her head.

He took her arms tightly, straightening her up. His hand went to her chin, tilting the face up, letting the tears flow straight down her cheeks now, the eyes half-closed with hopelessness.

"Elaine, I am your Rabbi!"

She looked into his eyes, his face, into herself. "Is that . . . all?"

"All!" He let her go. "I am your Rabbi . . . and that is all I have been to you."

She rose in silence, trembling. He stood with his back to her. She walked slowly, groping, toward her purse. The handkerchief, the tear stains wiped away, the purse snapped shut. His back still to her.

"What have I done, David?"

He couldn't answer. He couldn't, in the confusion of his own emotions, in the opening of parts of him he had never explored, in the presence of her nakedness before him, deal with this anymore. They were two human beings groping for a truth they didn't want to reach. He had to end it, but he had to give her something she could grasp, something she could live with.

"What have I done to you, David?"

He turned to her with all his strength, his arms raised without knowing it.

"You have done nothing! Believe that. Nothing. You have no guilt. *No guilt!*"

She kept shaking her head. "Will you . . . forgive me?"

He could only look at her. The misery in her was not to be reached now. Nothing could soothe it away for her now.

She turned suddenly and went to the door. One single moment at the open door, one turning to him with all her being.

"Forgive me!"

In the silence, he stood clenching his fists, crushing something tighter and tighter, squeezing it to nothingness.

But it remained inside him, and was alive.

When David came to Greenlake, Olga Sperovsky was the head of the Adult Education Committee of the congregation and she was a "live one" as her friends put it. At the Ferris Elementary School where she taught fourth grade, her classroom was a showcase. The walls were covered with drawings made by students, charts and cut-outs and collages about nature, astronomy, geology, trips they had made and activities they had pursued. Displays everywhere of objects they had collected, plus a cage with two white mice, an aquarium with eight goldfish and a sea horse. And a diorama of the town of Greenlake that had been a class project.

When Miss Sperovsky's pupils performed in the auditorium, it was a spectacle that delighted the whole school. The last play she had put on, for example, was about Mexico, and the costumes (made by eagerly co-operative parents) were colorful and enchanting, the sets were exuberant, the music was authentic, and the lyrics were original and charming and were written by Miss Sperovsky herself.

Olga was a tightly compressed bit of a woman, with straight gray hair that hung down in old-fashioned neglect, a pathetic unfemininity to her face, an old-maidish sweetness about her that should not have mainfested itself until years later. She lived with her sister (a widow) and the two of them led quiet lives of devotion to each other, to duties, and to family.

Olga's selection as head of the Adult Education Committee had seemed a natural and happy choice. She would give the position the same spirit and imagination she had brought to her classes in school. She would keep things humming. She organized theater parties to see Broadway plays that had anything to do with a Jewish theme or background. She brought together an exhibit of Israeli jewelry and handicrafts that everyone said was absolutely beautiful. She had a well-known actor who did semi-Yiddish monologues come up to Greenlake to offer an evening's entertainment. She had a local designer talk about "The New Look—From Furniture to Fabrics," with exhibits and actual models. She was a regular little live wire, and the members loved her.

At the first meeting of the Adult Education Committee that Rabbi attended, he felt himself surrounded by a warmth of spirit and a relaxed, almost jovial atmosphere. Miss Sperovsky made an amusing little speech welcoming him to the meeting, and beyond that, to the congregation and to their lives and hearts. The other four members of the Committee (three women and one man, Stanley Jacobs, who had a kind of scholarly look about him and was on the Committee because everyone felt he knew a lot about Judaism) all greeted Rabbi with smiles, handshakes, kind words, and the obvious assumption that he was there just to look in on things. Part of Rabbi's procedure of getting acquainted.

He wanted to see how they approached adult education, get a sense of what they were after. But also, he hoped to convey to them some of his own ideas. Adult education as part of the Temple's activities could be anything you wanted it to be. And he wanted it to be significant, a way of involving the members in Judaism itself. God knows, it was badly needed. So many Jews didn't even know what it should mean to be a Jew.

He sat back and listened to Olga outline the program for the next six months.

"What I have in mind is that it should be exciting, enjoyable, attract as many members as we can pack in, and at the same time give them something about being Jews that'll make them proud! And I think we've got it."

She was so excited, sparkling with her own enthusiasm, that the others smiled in anticipation.

"So here it is. We're going to call the whole program 'The Jew in the Arts.' And we're going to cover everything—music, theater, literature, painting, sculpture, and even entertainment! Because that's an art too. We're going to show them how the Jew is making a contribution to all the arts, all over the world. And in some cases—let's take novels for instance—we've got the best writers of them all!

"But wait. How are we going to do it? Not just with exhibits—we'll have that too, don't worry. Books, posters, samples of paintings and sculpture. Oh, we'll have exhibits! But more than that—we'll have the people themselves. Right here in person. The writers and the musicians and the painters. They'll come to talk to us. Explain what they're doing. Answer questions. It'll be a program for which we're going to have standing room only, believe me! Now—" she paused, and the sense of triumph was in her voice, "do I hear any questions?"

Rabbi had heard it all with a kind of remoteness. He wasn't surprised. This was the type of program Temples all over the country were carrying on and feeling quite happy about. It was so familiar to him, the content of it, the attitude toward it, he heard it as if listening to an oft-repeated story. The problem was how to deal with it, and with them.

But the first response to Olga's remarks came from the excited members.

"Olga—this is positively terrific! The best yet! The only thing I want to know—" the woman smiled in anticipation of her joke, "is, do we members get front row seats? I don't want to miss a single one!"

They laughed happily at the prospect she had raised.

"So who—" another woman asked, "are some of the people who'll come? You got any lined up yet?"

"Oh—" Olga had apparently been waiting for this, "I happen to have a partial list with me. Mind you, this is only a partial list." She held up the paper and read from it like someone bestowing riches on her listeners.

"For the 'Jew In Literature' session, we've got Herman Netrose. Only three best sellers, that's all! You all know the latest one—'It's Fun to Be Jewish.' And what a speaker! I understand he leaves them weak from laughing."

They chuckled their approval.

"For 'The Jew in Painting'—I've got not one, but two artists! Jay Garmish and Allan Allitone. They'll bring their paintings with them and have a kind of open discussion, the two of them, in front of us.

"Some of the other names—this is only so far, the list isn't complete yet—Lou Duborski, the producer of 'Happy Holiday'—and you know what a hit that is! . . . and, hold on to your hats—I think we can actually get Shelley Berman!"

Applause and cries of delight. Leave it to Olga—she was a regular impresario! The meeting was now becoming a mixture of conversation, jokes, congratulations, and a feeling of success and good humor enveloped them all.

Rabbi was watching them with a trace of apprehension. How would he be able to stem this flow, turn it aside, make them approach the whole subject from another viewpoint? He was rubbing his chin thoughtfully when Olga turned to him, exuberant with her success, and said:

"So, Rabbi, that's our program. I'm sure you can see how excited we are about it."

He nodded. "That I can see."

She looked at him just a bit tensely. "And you're not?"

"Well—" he stood up and then realized at once he shouldn't have done it. It was as if he was going to make a speech. He moved behind his chair and leaned on the back of it to look more casual. "Would you mind if I asked a few questions?"

"A privilege to hear them!" Olga still wasn't sure what to anticipate.

"Like a basic question such as—do you people feel this is adult *education?*"

"Ah!" Olga thought she sensed his direction. "I know what you mean. Formal education, it's not. But if education is learning, then it is! Because our members will learn about the arts, and they'll learn what Jews are accomplishing there. . . . Isn't that worth while?" Her question to him already had a note of challenge in it.

"Learning anything is worth while," Rabbi wanted to be very careful in the way he did this. "But I think we'll all agree that it's more important to learn some things than others. More—rewarding, shall I say? More meaningful."

Olga now looked directly at him and it was an obvious confrontation between them. "For example, Rabbi?"

"For example? Well—let me say this first. What the Jew is doing in the arts, we can find out about in many ways. From the newspapers and magazines. By going to museums and the theater. From reading the books they write. But there are things Jews need to learn that can't be obtained that way. So—for example—I believe the members of our congregation need to know more about basic Judaism. They should know—and most of them don't—about Jewish thinkers and philosophers and leaders who have shaped our religion. They should know how we arrived at our faith, what its essence is, and how to make it part of their lives."

By now there was a disturbed silence in the room, a sense of anxiety. Why was he introducing this now and upsetting everything?

"To me, as your Rabbi," he had decided to push this all the way, "that's the kind of program adult education should be involved with."

No one knew what to say for a while. Then Stanley Jacobs spoke up warily.

"You got like . . . something in mind, Rabbi?"

"Yes I have. . . ." He bent down to his briefcase. "As they say, I happen to have brought my music with me."

The smiles had an uneasiness about them. So, Rabbi had prepared for this. It was not going to be just a few comments from him, but a whole new program maybe. They shifted about nervously. Olga sat with her hands clasped tightly in her lap, restraining herself so far. Now this was something she hadn't expected. Well!

Rabbi took out two books and held on to them as he faced them again. "Maybe what you're going to hear is only a *Rabbi's* idea of adult education. At least, this Rabbi's. Your new Rabbi. And I'm not so new to this congregation that I haven't learned quite a bit about them. I feel—let me put it this way—I know that a great deal is missing here. Religion we have, but faith is missing. Activities are here, but involvement is missing. Jewishness is here, but Judaism is missing. I am going to try to supply what is missing. It is at the heart of all I want to do here.

"And I want to use adult education as part of that. So—I would like to start with a basic course. A series of weekly seminars or discussions built around these two books." He held them up. "One is called 'Great Jewish Thinkers' and the other is 'Contemporary Jewish Thought' and is a reader based on the works of those thinkers.

"Perhaps some of you have heard about these men. Ahad Ha-Am . . . Aaron David Gordon . . . Abraham Isaac Kuk . . . Hermann Cohen . . . Leo Baeck . . . Franz Rosenzweig . . . Martin Buber, and others."

For most of those present, he might just as well have been reading a list of ancient Chinese scholars. He was aware of this and it only confirmed his determination.

"They are the people who have dealt with the basic issues of

Judaism in our time. They have influenced our lives and their work is part of our history and belief and practice today."

He looked at them, at the withdrawn expressions, the tightened features, the skepticism.

"*This* is a program of adult education that I believe our members need and would benefit from. I would like you to consider it."

He sat down, so as not to force a response at once, to give them time to absorb it. No one said anything for a long while, perhaps expecting Olga to speak up for them. She finally managed it, and it was obvious she was disturbed and unhappy.

"Rabbi—do you really believe you'll get any kind of attendance for that program? It sounds very deep to me. Who would come?"

"Miss Sperovsky, if one man comes, just one, and gets closer to Judaism, it will serve God's purpose."

"But all these philosophers—or whatever they are—people aren't interested in them! They're interested in what's happening now!"

"And Miss Sperovsky, do you believe that what's happening now to the Jews is only their writing books, or painting pictures, or producing plays? Don't you realize they are also facing a crisis? Of their identity? Of their acceptance and understanding and involvement with Judaism?"

Olga swallowed and looked down. Stanley Jacobs broke the silence in his characteristically gentle, conciliatory manner.

"I think there's another question here we got to deal with. Rabbi Gordon is new to us. He came here to do what he thinks is right for this congregation. And it seems to me we should give him a chance at least." He looked around for agreement, and a few nodded their heads reluctantly.

"Thank you, Mr. Jacobs." Rabbi turned to Olga. "Miss Sperovsky, will you give me that chance?"

She tried to answer, but could only manage after a while to nod her head. The meeting broke up quietly, everyone subdued by this unexpected development, feeling uncertain and somehow disappointed.

A two-page mimeographed letter signed by Rabbi was sent to every family of the congregation announcing the new adult education program, explaining its purpose and scope, and inviting all to attend the first session which was to be on a Thursday evening at 8:30 P.M. in the auditorium of the Women's Club in Greenlake.

At 8:20 that evening, Rabbi mounted the platform and sat down at the table. There were eighteen people in the auditorium. Stanley Jacobs was the only one from the Committee. Among the others were Elaine Barrett, wife of the President of the congregation, and Danny Cole and his wife, Alice. Danny came up to Rabbi and said: "I want to thank you for giving this course. I feel like a lost Jew who is being shown the way. I feel I will know where I am going. Thank you!" And Rabbi looked into the intense, responsive face and said to himself: here is the one man. I am justified.

What Rabbi wanted this course to do was to raise in the minds of the congregation what he considered the basic problems of Judaism in America. What makes a Jew a Jew today? Does he play a unique role in society, or is he to be indistinguishable from the community? What part of his life, his patterns, his values, is affected by his Judaism? And so he selected from each of the Jewish thinkers they were studying the relative statements, the provocative thoughts that would stir up this kind of questioning and reaction.

From Ahad Ha-Am: "What, then, are those Jews to do who have nothing left but this theoretical religion, which is itself losing its hold on them? Are they to give up Judaism altogether, and become completely assimilated to their surroundings? A few of them have done this: but why should they not all adopt the same course? Why do most of them feel they cannot? Where is the chain to which they can point as that which holds them fast to Judaism, and does not allow them to be free?"

Search in your hearts, Rabbi exhorted them. What is that thing in you, in your own individual case, that keeps you bound to Judaism? Do you know what it is? And he made them contemplate themselves and discuss it and argue about it.

To him, this was reaching for the essence, this was the adult education that Jews needed today. But by the third session of the course, his class had diminished to eleven students. They no longer used the auditorium of the Women's Club, they met at Rabbi's home. They were a little circle, now bound together like a group of explorers on a private search for the unknown, intimately stimulating each other toward what they hoped would be the truth.

When they got to Hermann Cohen, they were already more or less in agreement. "Our survival depends on the spiritual, intellectual and moral power of our stock. But all of these have root in our religion. An even though modern culture must fructify our spiritual-intellectual nature, yet our ethical power is primarily rooted in our religious folkways and education."

Now they were all giving examples to prove it. Now the drive had become to enlarge on it, deepen the significance of Judaism in their lives by understanding it better. Rabbi felt a triumphant glow as they talked together, probed, and sought for answers. This was what it meant to be a Rabbi, to teach, guide, inspire!

By the sixth session there were five students left. They gathered with Rabbi on Thursday nights, like members of some isolated sect. What they discussed was like a secret dedication of the self, unknown to the world "outside."

Leo Baeck: "The religion of mere activity without devotion—this religion which becomes an ethic of the surface, or no more than the custom of the day—is not Judaism. The world of Judaism is to be found only where faith has its commandments, and the commandments its faith."

"You see," Rabbi said, "there must be a *why* we do good, and that why comes from God and His love for man. We follow God when we are concerned with our fellow man."

Rosenzweig said it for them: "It is something inside the individual that makes him a Jew, something infinitesimally small yet immeasurably large, his most impenetrable secret; yet evident in every gesture and every word—especially in the most spontaneous of them. The Jewishness I mean is no 'literature.' It can be grasped through neither the writing nor reading of books . . . It is only lived—and perhaps not even that. One *is* it."

Danny, eagerly probing, exclaimed: "He's right! One *is* it! One *is* a Jew. It's in every part of me. What I do, think, feel. It's the biggest, greatest thing in me, and yet I can't put my finger on it!"

Elaine said: "One just knows. It is a kind of inner knowledge and strength."

And Rabbi said: "But one still needs God. This is the final point. Buber writes: 'This is the ultimate purpose: to let God in. But we can let Him in only where we really stand, where we live, where we live a true life.' "

When they finished the course, the last session over, the last discussion, the last sharing of warmth and response and search, they remained a while in silence.

"Rabbi," Danny said, gripping his hand, "this is a beginning for me. I feel I have entered a new world—myself, and all that has made me what I am."

Elaine said only: "You have bestowed a blessing on us, Rabbi. There is no way to thank you." The three others looked at Rabbi with gratitude and shook his hand.

Next evening, Bob Barrett dropped in for a chat. He was as tactful as it was in his power to be. "So your adult education course finally finished up yesterday."

"The last session."

"Elaine tells me it was quite wonderful. She got so much out of it, she says, that she feels like a reborn Jew."

"I'm glad it meant so much to her."

"Rabbi, I know how you feel about the fact that there were only five people following this course for the last month or so. And I don't question the validity of such a viewpoint. . . . But we must do something for our other members too. They also have needs that we can help meet, and by so doing bring them closer to us. We must think of them too."

"They could have come."

"But didn't. I'm sorry, Rabbi, they just didn't. So we're going to give them something to which they will come. What they're interested in. We're going to go ahead with Olga Sperovsky's 'The Jew in the Arts.' It's all lined up, all arranged. It starts next month, and its success is assured."

He paused and looked at the troubled face of Rabbi, the remote, rejecting face, and knew of course that he was hurt.

"It is no reproach to you, Rabbi. It's dealing with a fact of life. The other side of the Jewish coin."

"The empty side."

"We can't all be spiritual explorers."

"We can try."

Barrett stood up. "I hope you'll understand, Rabbi. That's all I ask of you."

Rabbi understood. He had taken over the adult education program and it had been a failure. Now they would put on a successful program. One need not attack a Rabbi to destroy him. It can be done by ignoring him.

The news of Lou Mandel's second heart attack was known to everybody of course, and there was speculation about what had brought it on. Overwork, just knocking himself out as Chairman of the Building Committee, was considered by most to be responsible. "You know Lou. He holds nothing back. Day and night he worries about the building of the Temple."

Danny Cole, however, felt there might be more to it, and he decided to investigate that suspicion as part of his fight to save Rabbi. He called Dr. Greenwald and asked if he could come over for a talk.

Dr. Emanuel Greenwald and his wife Rebecca had never had any children, which was considered a shame by everyone who knew them. What a father he would have made! How much he could have done for a son or daughter. With his money, a Greenwald child would have been secure and comfortable for life. With his enlightened attitude toward life, he would have been able to guide his children toward a meaningful, useful existence.

But in seeking other outlets for his energy and devotion, Dr. Greenwald had done well. Greenland Chemicals Incorporated, which he had founded and built up over the years, was one of the most respected operations of its kind in the East. Originally it had been a manufacturing concern, producing basic chemicals for other companies, and then later turning out a few finished products of its own which Dr. Greenwald had created. There was a detergent spray for glass, a hand-cleaning compound, and a liquid that removed spots from rugs and upholstery. They were marketed successfully, and eventually sold to larger corporations in the field, which distributed them nationally. Greenwald made so much money on these sales that he decided to indulge himself in the kind of activity that excited him most—the creation of new products, the solving of problems. Greenland Chemicals became primarily a research organization to which other companies turned for help and ideas. And now one could stop Dr. Greenwald any time and ask: "What are you working on, Doctor?" and he'd wink his eye and smile and say something like: "I can't tell you the details—but don't be surprised if you'll soon be flavoring meat in a whole new way!" Or using a new kind of liquid to keep your hair down, or polishing your shoes with a cloth that will act like magic. He had a brain, that Dr. Greenwald!

His position in the community, as a sort of elder statesman without portfolio, was another outlet that took the place of concern with children and family. He tended, even in his manner, to be fatherly toward the enterprises with which he became involved. A five thousand dollar check to the YMCA drive was bestowed as if he were patting all the boys in town on the head. Helping the New Music Society promote a series of local concerts was like enabling young people to indulge themselves in a little worthwhile fun. When he was the honored guest speaker at an affair, he would stand before his indulgent audience and offer them sound and constructive advice out of the wisdom of his experience. And in the appropriate tones.

The greatest lesson in life, he would say, staring at them solemnly, is that what you do for others enriches you. Be prepared for disappointments in life, but never be disappointed in yourself. You are only one person, but what you do can become part of the lives of hundreds of people. This is a responsibility from which there is no escape. If you ever face a choice between trying something that is good, but might not succeed, and not trying it at all, make the attempt. The chance is worth it, and the reward is yours even if you fail.

These expressions of wisdom were all delivered with great seriousness and sincerity. Some people said (not meaning it unkindly) that Dr. Greenwald was a preacher by instinct, and that he could give benevolent advice even if he were only discussing the weather. "He is an intuitive man of God," Barrett once said of him.

Actually, this religious coloring to his outlook was a recent touch. A fiercely, aggressively independent young man, Emanuel Greenwald had broken away from his father's house and way of life and beliefs as soon as he went off to college, and he never returned. He once told

Bob Barrett, after they had elected him to the Executive Committee, that he had not been in a temple or synagogue even a single time since the age of fifteen. There had simply been no need for God, for religion, for any specific religion, for any aspect of any religion, in Greenwald's life during all these years, and it had never occurred to him to pretend.

He now felt otherwise. Pretense, acting as-if, was quite an important part of religion. He had learned, through his own experience, what was an astonishing truth about the development of religion: ritual preceded faith. And a certain prominent Rabbi with whom he had discussed this dilemma of belonging without believing, had told him quite frankly: go through the motions of prayer; the reasons for it will come to you later.

So there he was, honored member of the congregation, on the Executive Committee and Board of Directors, respected "Jewish citizen" of the community of Greenlake, and finding that all this participation in religious activities provided more satisfaction, and a different kind of satisfaction, than he had ever received before. What it did so effectively was to put everything into perspective. His company, his ideas, his inventions, his triumphs and success could be seen against the scale of man's needs and problems and tragedy, against the struggle of mankind to find purpose and meaning, against life and death itself, against the possibility that something existed that was so basic and true that man had to call it God.

The Greenwald Auditorium became, on this scale, the most meaningful gesture of his life. It was a statement to himself that he had reached out beyond the ephemeral accomplishments of a lifetime. It was a statement to others that he was searching for answers. It was a prayer to whatever there was to pray to, that he be considered other than he was, that the unforgivable be forgiven.

To a certain extent, his wife, Rebecca, had helped bring all this about. She was an attractive, graceful, intelligent woman of sixty. White-haired like her husband, neat, modestly dressed (the pearls around the throat, the diamonds in the rings, the gold bracelet, all in the best of taste), and she had a certain persuasiveness about her that was surprising when you considered that Dr. Greenwald was so articulate. She could make a point, defend it, stick to it, and yet never seem obstinate. And it was remarkable how often you discovered that she had indeed defended her point so well that you were won over. Rebecca had no individual ambition or even goal. She was Mrs. Emanuel Greenwald, and a happy woman.

Danny Cole had never visited the Greenwald home on Maple Hill Road, and he was somewhat overwhelmed by it. More than three hundred feet of high green hedge along the road, a beautiful metal archway at the entrance, the long curving driveway to the front of the house, the series of white columns at the top of the steps, all contributed to the spaciousness and serenity of the setting. A maid in black uniform opened the door. In the marble-tiled foyer that was practically the size of his own entire house, he glimpsed, through huge doors, the terrace and the acres of land beyond it. In the library where Dr. Greenwald was waiting for him, bookcases covered one wall to the ceiling, the rug was so deep his feet seemed to sink with every step, chairs sat like monuments to comfort, as did the elegant sofa, a magnificent table in front of it bearing a huge vase of flowers. Yet the room was uncrowded looking, quiet, with the sense of order, the atmosphere of control and power accepted as natural.

"Danny!" Not just a handshake, but both hands on his. "So good to see you. Will you have a drink?"

"No, thanks."

"Well, sit down, my friend. Sit down and welcome."

Rebecca walked in. Neat dark suit, a gentle quality, a smile.

"Rebecca, this is Danny Cole. You've met."

After the greetings, the idle words, hesitant chatter, finally they sat down.

"By the way, you don't mind Rebecca being here? I told her you were coming and she was interested. She likes to get in on everything."

"Of course not."

"Well, Danny?" Dr. Greenwald leaned back calmly, waiting, but attentive, interested.

He decided to do it bluntly, as if the atmosphere itself needed cutting through.

"Dr. Greenwald, you know about Lou Mandel."

"Of course. How terrible! He's in the hospital, I heard."

"Another heart attack. . . . Dr. Greenwald, I want to ask you this question: what do you think caused it?"

"The heart attack?" Greenwald shrugged his shoulders. "I'm not a medical doctor. Who knows?"

"But what do you think brought it on?"

"What are you getting at, Danny?"

"I don't think it was overwork, as most people are saying. I think it was something different."

"Yes?"

"Dr. Greenwald—it happened about two hours after our meeting. The Executive Committee meeting. Do you remember he made a statement—as we all did—and how upset he was?"

"We all were, Danny."

"Yes, but Lou's statement was a struggle for him to make. It was full of soul-searching. He was trying to justify what he was going to do."

"So? I don't understand what—?"

"Dr. Greenwald, I don't think he made it. I don't think he ended up feeling that it *was* justified. I think he's a man of such decency, and I guess really such honesty with himself, that he realized he had acted wrongly. I think it finally came to him that he was acting to destroy a man's life unjustly. And he couldn't take it—because that's the kind of man Lou is. It upset him so much that . . . well, that the emotion produced the attack."

Dr. Greenwald stared at Danny as if trying to penetrate into what was going on.

Rebecca stirred in her chair. "You're suggesting a sense of guilt did it?"

"Yes, Mrs. Greenwald. An overwhelming sense of guilt." He turned to Greenwald. "And we all know how much the building of the Temple means to him. It's practically his whole life. I think he wants that Temple more than anyone in the whole congregation. But I also think he had the decency—even the greatness of character—to push that aside and say to himself: I cannot destroy a man's life to do it. . . . I believe that, Dr. Greenwald."

"It's an interesting speculation, Danny. What is your point in discussing it with me?"

"For one thing, I believe that if he were asked now to act on the Rabbi as we were asked then, he would vote differently. I think he would even fight that decision."

Greenwald stood up as if to extract himself from the situation quickly. He walked over to the window and stared out, standing silently, his hands clasped behind his back. He didn't turn when he spoke.

"Danny, I think I would like you to go."

Rebecca sensed what was going on between the two of them and went over to him. "Let us hear him out, Manny. There's no harm in that."

"I don't want to engage in this discussion!"

Rebecca touched his arm. "Manny, I think you should hear him out."

"Why?" He turned finally. "Why?"

"Because—" she was all gentleness and firmness, "he is telling us something we ought to know."

"It doesn't matter to me what Lou Mandel thinks or feels!"

"Of course not, darling." She was just touching his hand. "But he's not really talking about Lou Mandel."

Greenwald glanced at her and she squeezed his hand. She gently led him back to his chair and he sat down heavily with a sigh, a reluctance, and a kind of despair on his face.

"What do you want, Danny? It's all decided. Finished."

"Nothing has been done. Bob Barrett hasn't even spoken to Rabbi yet. Nothing has been started that can't be stopped."

"Danny, Danny," he rubbed his forehead. He couldn't control his restlessness. "Danny, leave this thing alone! Can't you?"

"No. I can't, and I won't."

Rebecca turned to him, speaking gently, as if merely curious. "What do you want him to do, Danny?"

"I'm not sure, Mrs. Greenwald. Let's just consider this: if Lou Mandel has changed his mind, if he would talk and vote differently now, that would make a big difference to that Committee. And if Dr. Greenwald would do it too—what a difference that would make. We could ask for another meeting of the Committee right away, reconsider the decision, vote again, change everything!"

"Danny, Danny—" Greenwald's voice was heavy, weary of it, "you're being childish. Bob won't allow another meeting. Lou wouldn't be able to come anyway. Bob's determined to get rid of Rabbi, don't you realize that?"

"Why?"

"Why? For all the reasons he has in his head. Who can count them?"

"And this accusation—"

"—an excuse! Provided by Rabbi himself. Foolishly provided by Rabbi himself."

"Dr. Greenwald—" Danny faced him, wanting to hold his shoulders, wanting to focus into his eyes, "do you believe the accusation against Rabbi?"

Greenwald struggled for an answer, but then only turned away.

Rebecca came over. "You know that you questioned it when you talked to me."

"I said it didn't seem possible. But anything is possible!"

"Then let me tell you, Dr. Greenwald," Danny stood in front of him, "I know it is not true. Because I spoke to Rabbi. And he said it was a lie! A complete, horrible lie!"

"You—spoke with him?"

"Right after the meeting. I went there and told him the whole story."

"He denies it?"

"Everything. It *is* a lie!"

"Barrett wouldn't dare. Didn't he say if Rabbi denies it—he has proof?"

"Now! Now we're getting to it, Dr. Greenwald. Here's the point: he's counting on Rabbi to do nothing. To put up no fight, nothing public, no action, nothing. And he is right! His instinct is right!"

"What do you mean?"

"Rabbi—because he's that kind of a man—doesn't want to hurt the congregation, doesn't want to create a scandal, cause a split. Do you know what he said to me? This is not a time to be concerned with one man's right or wrong. Only the good of the congregation, only the building of the Temple must be considered now. That is Rabbi. And Barrett knows it. Rabbi won't fight for his life, for justice. Don't you see?"

Greenwald clasped his hands, his eyes down. "Rabbi . . . said that?"

They were all silent a while. Rebecca turned to Greenwald. "If there were a fight to save Rabbi, to clear him—would it endanger the building of the Temple? Are you sure of that?"

"It would split the congregation, Rebecca. And the scandal of it could destroy any chance of the Temple being built. I'm sure of it."

Danny, back in his chair now, leaned forward. "Which would mean —I might as well say it, Dr. Greenwald—that the Auditorium wouldn't be built. And I might as well say everything, now that we've come to it—I am asking you to take that chance. Because now you must know that Rabbi is innocent. Now you know a man's life is being ruined unjustly."

"Why do you come to me, Danny?"

"For two reasons. One is because you're the most important member of our congregation, the most respected. Because what you say and do counts more than what anyone else does."

"And the other reason?"

"Because, Dr. Greenwald, I believe in your integrity. I know the kind of man you are."

"I don't want to hear that!" Greenwald was on his feet again. He moved away. "I'm a man like anyone else. I reject that . . . that *image!* I don't want the burden of that great, noble integrity!"

"It is not a burden, Manny." Rebecca's voice was quiet, but she never took her eyes from his face.

"Isn't it? Always the great, noble, virtuous citizen. Upholder of justice. Dr. Greenwald—the living saint. I'm tired of that role! I don't want it! Do you know what I want? *I want that Auditorium built!* More than anything I have ever wanted. And that is the truth. I can be—I am!—just as weak, just as human, just as selfish as anybody. I've earned that right too! I'm tired of fighting for causes. I have my own needs. I'm entitled to them. I want that Auditorium!"

He sat down, his fingers at his temples, pressing the nerves, the emotions, the confusion, the shame. Danny looked at him and then, hesitantly, was about to speak, but Rebecca motioned with her arm. No one said anything for a long time. Greenwald wanted no more. Too much emotion, confusion. No more. No more!

Danny knew he had lost. He had come with only a little hope. Somehow, he had thought, something could be accomplished. It had seemed possible. But Greenwald was, after all, like everyone else. That's the world. Everyone is like everyone else. He started to rise. Rebecca motioned again. He leaned back, waited. What? She was watching Greenwald, her eyes on the face, seeking.

As if he sensed it, Greenwald finally looked up. They stared at each other.

"Rebecca—*don't!*"

She said nothing. He stood up angrily. "I say don't! You know what I am, if anybody does. Manny Greenwald. Nothing else! Slob! A selfish, no-good slob!"

"You've said—" Rebecca's voice was so gentle, "so many times that Rabbi was quite a man. Are you less than he?"

"Yes!" The bitter laugh. "Oh, how much less! But that is what I am!"

"Then—for him."

"What?" He turned.

"For him—you must do it."

"For him?"

"Yes. If you can't fight to save such a man, what can you fight for?"

"For—him?"

"For one of the rare human beings on earth, which you believe him to be! What can be more important than to save such a man? What in your whole life will ever have mattered more?"

She rose and went over to him. She reached out for his hand and held it. He tried to move away, but she held it. They were silent a long time. Then he looked at her, and gently, softly he embraced her. She looked at Danny.

"Go now, Danny. Dr. Greenwald will be in touch with you."

Danny walked out. His heart was pounding. There were tears in his eyes and he didn't know it.

Rabbi had been surprised at the resistence to his "Inter-Preach" idea, proposed about a year after he had come to Greenlake.

"The Jew is a mystery to them. They don't know us, they don't understand us." Rabbi was addressing the Board of Directors and the meeting was becoming more tense.

"And what do you expect to do, Rabbi—explain us to them?"

"At least acquaint them with us on a new level."

"Why? For what purpose?"

"So that our relationships in this community will be better."

"Inter-Preach" was to be a series of guest sermons by him in some of the churches in Greenlake, and return visits by some priests and ministers. It was his first innovation after six months in office, and this meeting of the Board of Directors was to decide whether to approve the plan.

"Why should we explain ourselves to them, Rabbi?" a member was asking. "They don't feel the need to explain themselves to us."

"Because it is they who have misconceptions about us. And because we have something to gain if they understand us better."

"Rabbi," Barrett stood up, "I think we're wandering all over the lot. Let me try to sum up the issue, the question. You have proposed this 'Inter-Preach,' as you call it, and the members of the Board have expressed some doubts as to the wisdom of it. Those doubts have to do with: one, will such a proposal be welcomed or resented by the other religious groups? Two, is the timing of it right, since you are new here and we, as a Jewish congregation, are hardly established here. And three, what would we gain by it? Would you please comment on those points and then maybe we can move toward a decision."

Rabbi felt a little heartsick at the whole business. He had proposed

"Inter-Preach" and had expected everyone to respond enthusiastically. He didn't even imagine the matter would have to be cleared with the Board of Directors. But the reactions had helped him understand new subtleties in the attitudes of Jews in the suburbs. The defiance in moving into communities where they were hardly welcome, and then living there with a deference to the sensitivities of the very people who didn't want them. A closeness and unity that made most of them aware of and responsive to each other, yet an insistence on individuality, a rejection of the concept that they were a "unit" in any sense. They retained an involvement with Judaism and religious observance, but also showed a determination to limit that to certain areas and occasions, so that their Jewishness would be recognized as an incidental factor. They took intense pride in their tradition and uniqueness, yet dreaded being considered "different" or apart. They exhibited an almost heroic attitude toward the survival of the Jew, so that they seemed ready to fight and die for that cause, yet displayed a fear of offending or stirring things up if they were asked to challenge mistaken concepts and counteract ignorant hostility toward Jews. In short, Rabbi concluded, the Jew in the suburbs, perhaps in the cities, perhaps in the world today, is not only split into organizational, doctrinal, theological, and cultural fragments, he is in spiritual and emotional conflict within himself. The Jew has lost his way, but pretends that his goal has changed.

Rabbi stood looking at the members of the Board of Directors, all earnest men, all so vitally concerned with the rightness and wrongness of the plan he had suggested, and he realized that the simple truth was that they just didn't know what to do. If he was to be their Rabbi in the sense that he thought he had to be, if he was to help them in terms of where he thought they needed help, he had to demand they follow him. Trust him. Depend on him. Allow him to do what he felt had to be done.

"Bob," he said, "I'm not going to answer your points one by one. I'm not going to try to win an argument with this Board of Directors. In fact, I'm not going to try to convince anyone here that I am right. This is not arrogance on my part. This is because, as your Rabbi, it is my job to do for this congregation what needs to be done. And as your Rabbi, I intend to function in no other way.

"I am going to have an Inter-Preach program to accomplish certain things. I want to establish an awareness in this community that a group of Jewish people are now part of it, and they are part of it on the same level of respect, recognition, and importance as any other religious group. My preaching sermons in their churches is going to be done on the basis of: the Jews are here among you. Here is what they have to contribute. I am not going to 'explain' us to them as freaks or outsiders, but I am going to make it clear to them who and what we are, and why. And if they've had other ideas about us, they were wrong and they might as well know it.

"And I will want them to come and speak to us so that we will learn whatever they want us to know about them. It's as simple as that. Plus one more vital thing: I want the spirit between us, the nature of our relationship, to be one where we communicate with each other openly and frankly. We must take that step. The Jew has nothing to hide from the world, but sometimes he acts as if he does. The Jew should have nothing to fear from the world, but he acts as if it's normal to be afraid. The Jew has something to give to the world—but he acts as if the world will not accept it. That is what I want to change. Here, in this town, with these people, and with our congregation."

The Board of Directors voted to approve the Inter-Preach program. Not so much because they fully agreed with Rabbi's reasoning and goals, but because most of them didn't want to create a situation of open conflict with their new Rabbi. "Besides," as one of them put it, "if it gets out that we turned down a program of getting together with the other religious groups in town, where would that leave us?"

Rabbi decided to start the program on a small scale, one sermon by him in a Catholic church and a Congregationalist church, a sermon in the Temple by each of their representatives.

Father Lemassey loved the idea. Rabbi approached him first because the attitude of the Church toward such attempts was frequently negative. But Lemassey was an individualist and he had a grand fighting spirit. He took on every issue, every situation, as a battle that he was going to win, and he engaged in these battles with all his strength. It was a personal triumph for Lemassey that his church took over St. Mark's Hall near the railroad station after it had been abandoned for years and turned it into a meeting place and the Saturday night spot to be at for young people in town. It was Father Lemassey who was the first religious leader in town to deliver a sermon on civil rights and who organized an educational aid program for the neighboring industrial community of Lanebrook, where there was a Negro ghetto section. Lemassey was the kind of man who could drink a quart of beer with you and belch in your face as he discussed *Finnegans Wake,* existentialism, or the Green Bay Packers.

Once he and Rabbi agreed to go ahead with the program, they sat down to discuss the details and Father Lemassey came up with a surprise. Rabbi, in his own energetic manner, announced what his service was going to be about.

"I think, Father, that I will call it: 'The Ethical Basis of Judaism.' I believe that's one of the most fascinating and unusual aspects of our religion, and the one that perhaps has the most significance for us. It should be very enlightening for your congregation."

"Ah, Rabbi—" Lemassey held his fingertips together, smiling gently, "—I don't think so. Or rather let me say, I can think of subjects more enlightening for my members."

"Yes?"

Lemassey never stopped smiling. The kind, sparkling eyes, the friendliness, the firmness and determination all in one, remained unchanged. "You see, you are flattering the intelligence of my people in assuming they want to understand such profound concepts as the ethical basis of Judaism. May I tell you, Rabbi, what is the real situation? They know absolutely nothing about the ordinary religious practices of Judaism! Oh, they have a few quaint notions about some things. A vague idea, perhaps, of what 'kosher' means. But no more. And they are so curious about such things. And so uninformed."

"You want me to explain *kosher* to them?"

"But why not? It is a part of Judaism they are aware of—and confused by. And there is so much more—your fasting on Yom Kippur, your circumcision rites, your—that thing on the door—?"

"The *mezuzah.*"

"Yes! The blowing of the ram's horn, what the Torah is, your holidays, all the things that Jews do and practice and believe in that they've seen and heard about and wondered at. What an opportunity to enlighten them! I only suggest this, of course, Rabbi. It is only a suggestion." But he continued to smile and looked at Rabbi expectantly.

Rabbi stared at him and finally shook his head. "Do you know that

I've been thinking of giving such a course to my own congregation? They understand so little of the background of their own religion."

"Ah—then how much greater is the need to give it to mine!"

"I'll tell you what, Father Lemassey. I'll speak on that, explain as much as I can in one sermon, if you agree to do the same for us."

"Ah, wonderful!"

"The mass, the trinity, the praying to saints, the veneration of Mary, the position of the Pope—all the things about Catholicism that mystify us."

"And sometimes us! But agreed, agreed. A wonderful idea!"

And to the surprise and rather satisfying pleasure of most members of both congregations, the Inter-Preach between Rabbi and Father Lemassey was an informative and harmonious success. During the discussion and question period, it was obvious that both audiences tried to be as tactful as possible, and just as obvious that they wanted to get at matters that disturbed them.

"Could you please explain, Rabbi, the concept of the Chosen People?"

Naturally that bothers you. How odd of God to choose the Jews and all of that kind of thing. "Well," Rabbi smiled, "don't forget it was the Hebrews who also chose God. Israel was willing to be chosen —that is, be the vehicle of His revelation—but in doing so it willingly chose to fulfill God's will, regardless of the difficulties, the agonies that might descend on them. There were no privileges that came with being chosen—only obligations. The Covenant with God that the Hebrews accepted was a willingness to face all the peril of defending justice and mercy and of battling against evil." He looked at them and smiled again. "And believe me, it hasn't been fun!"

Rabbi's own congregation was curious about the structure of Catholicism, as well as the tenets of the faith. What was the role of the orders, such as the Jesuits? What were the requirements for becoming a saint? Could the Pope ever make a mistake?

It was an interesting exchange between the two congregations, and Rabbi felt it had stimulated a deeper kind of interest and even a kind of acceptance of each other.

When Rabbi approached Reverend Robertson, there was apparently the same degree of interest, the same agreeable response.

"I am pleased, Rabbi Gordon, that you recognize the need for such communication and exchange. As you may know, I have always urged confrontation, a frank dialogue. It helps clear the air. I'm glad you see it that way too."

Tact, Rabbi kept telling himself, show tact with this man. He has a certain reputation for stiffness and self-satisfaction. He has to be handled. So he sat listening and smiled and nodded in agreement, and made no effort to suggest anything provocative. For Robertson was absolutely clear about how the program was to be conducted. When Rabbi began to outline the sermon he had in mind for the Congregational Church, Robertson cut him off with a wave of the hand.

"Oh, no. I don't want to know, Rabbi Gordon. That is entirely up to you. If you so choose, you may preach about the Ten Commandments. That will be your prerogative. Just as the subject of my sermon will be entirely my decision. Don't you agree this is the way it should be?"

Thinking about it, influenced probably by Robertson's attitude, and in anticipation of the kind of sermon he would give, Rabbi decided not to speak about rites and rituals and reverted back to his original concept of explaining the ethical basis of Judaism.

It was not very successful. In the restrained, almost cold atmosphere of the simple white church, talking to the politely still, remote audience, Rabbi felt the need to reach for greater emphasis, stronger argument, more dramatic presentation, and the sermon emerged as a comparative study and had overtones of making Judaism seem a superior religion because of its underlying ethical foundation. It may have increased an understanding of Judaism among a few of the listeners, but it also produced an unconscious resentment among many. In his nervousness and anxiety, Rabbi had overdone it, been too aggressive, and probably had left an image of the self-satisfied Jew.

As if to overcome this, Rabbi made every possible effort to fill the Temple for Reverend Robertson's appearance. He wanted the representative of the Congregational Church to realize that the Jews in Greenlake were eager to hear *his* views, and were receptive to whatever he had to say.

It was when Robertson rose finally and stood at the pulpit, that he announced the subject of his sermon: "The Problem of Anti-Semitism."

There was a glancing around, a tensing, a quick wave of surprise, and then a dreaded anticipation, a heaviness. Why this? Why such a subject?

Reverend Robertson sensed the quick defensive reaction. In his mind it was precisely for this reason that he wanted to speak to them on this subject. The Jew tightens up, bristles, the moment a gentile brings up anti-Semitism. How then can the Jews ever be made to understand the gentile view of this? They must listen with open minds and hearts to facts, opinions, even prejudices so that they can know the nature of this affliction that tortures them so. It will help them deal with it, or if necessary, live with it. Reverend Robertson had the feeling of being on a merciful mission to these people, and was prepared for their reluctance to submit to it.

"My friends," he was attempting a benevolent smile, "in speaking to you of anti-Semitism, I'm sure I need not stress that there is nothing whatsoever that can possibly justify it. So let's get that straight, shall we? Anti-Semitism is to be condemned outright and in all its manifestations. It is an unpardonable act of religious and human intolerance. My church is dedicated to eradicating it wherever it may exist.

"But my friends, our wishes won't accomplish that. Not even—I am afraid—our prayers. What then can we do about the horrible fact of its existence? The resentment of Jews that is found on every level of our society? The criticism that is expressed, sometimes privately, sometimes subtly, and sometimes in the practice of daily life? The antagonism toward the Jew that is found even among intelligent and well-meaning people all over the world?"

They listened to him and the anxiety in them wound tighter and tighter. He was speaking with such good intentions—why did it have such a false and frightening sound to them? Why did it make them so uncomfortable to hear it? A Jew doesn't have to be told that anti-Semitism is evil. He lives with that awareness all his life. Reverend Robertson was cutting the artery of their existence to show them what was in their blood. As if the taste of it had not been in their mouths for generations and generations.

"I believe," Reverend Robertson continued, "that it is important to examine what produces this reaction we all condemn. What it is that creates this attitude towards the Jewish people. And I mean that it is important for *you* to know and examine it."

The silence lay like a nausea in them all. Now the bitterness showed in their faces. The anxiety summoned from five thousand years away was in their hearts. Thank you, but who needs it? Thank you, but you don't have to remind us. Thank you, but get your hands out of our wound. Thank you, but stop it.

Reverend Robertson felt it all, and to him it was as if they had risen and run out of the room, run away from truth—when the truth could only help them.

"There is no question, my friends, that both in a historical and social sense, it is certain patterns of behavior among the Jewish people that have provoked the hostility towards them. Mind you, the Jews couldn't always prevent such behavior among themselves, they were often not in control of the situation and so could exercise no choice. But we must face the fact that the patterns do appear again and again, and it is these I want to discuss with you today so that we can better understand the phenomenon of anti-Semitism."

This was sick! To come to a Temple to tell Jews how they had been behaving wrongly. Rabbi and Barrett exchanged glances on the platform. People were looking at each other in anger and disbelief. What to do? Wasn't there some way to stop him?

Then, from Robertson, came the most incredible statement of all. The listing and elaboration of what to his listeners was every accusation, condemnation, charge, and libel that had ever been made against the Jews.

So few Jewish farmers. Why? So many in business and finance. Naturally it is noticed. Naturally it is resented . . . for competitive reasons perhaps, but the fact of their dominance in this field is undeniable. The choice of professions. Doctors. Lawyers. The statistics prove it. The question this provokes, understandable.

"Not the reaction, I repeat. To make this a reason for anti-Semitism is wrong. But it makes people ask themselves questions about Jews."

He went on now to Jewish involvement with radical causes. (Thank God he didn't mention Karl Marx! Too much of a cliché, even for him.) Jews supported extremist movements, helped organizations trying to produce changes in our society.

"For you see, people must then ask: if the Jews want so much to be a part of our society, our way of life, why do they work so hard

to change it? You see the contradiction this presents? I am only pointing out to you the effect of certain patterns."

He was speaking the basic truth as he knew and felt it, sensing only
his own purpose: to make these people understand what they must
cope with. Not wanting to hurt them any more than he wanted to
hurt his own congregation when he pointed out their weaknesses and
failures.

"And if we turn to personal factors, to those encounters between
individuals that provoke anti-Semitic reactions, of course they can
be explained. Jealousy, insecurity, the fear that rivalry produces in
weaker people. All explainable. And all, I repeat, to be condemned.
But human beings cannot avoid noticing differences among themselves. And so when they see the aggressiveness of certain Jews, the
desire to dominate in certain areas, those fears are heightened."

Jews tended toward an ostentatious display of wealth. They were
reluctant to join the armed forces. They involved themselves with the
foreign nation of Israel. My God, where did he get the list? All here.
Everything! The whole familiar rejection of the world summed up in
one speech. How he must have prepared for this!

His listeners were squirming, shifting, looking at each other, shaking heads. With the bitterness now there was anger. Why? Why?
What did he want them to feel? Guilty? And then finally, came the
basic accusation. The most ancient one of all. Separatism. ". . . for I
the Lord am holy, and have set you apart from the peoples, that ye
should be Mine."

"We are a nation of many peoples and races. That is the glory of
our country. That we have built one nation out of many different
origins and beliefs. One union. And to live within this union is more
than a privilege. It imposes an obligation. To join it wholly and in
full spirit. To be part of it in a true sense, without qualifications,
conditions, or the witholding of the self. An obligation to surrender,
for the sake of that greater unity, the particular and separate alle-
giances and differences. This sacred obligation rests upon the Jewish
people too. If they are to be part of this nation of ours, then they
must be part of it completely. Hold nothing back, retain no special
areas of vital differences they hold more sacred. There can be no islands
of separatism in our midst. There can be no uniqueness in a nation
of equals. And at this time in history, at this point, here and now, the

Jew does have a choice. He is not only free to choose to be one like all others among us, but he has an obligation to do so. I respectfully urge, I sincerely pray, that he will make that choice."

Rabbi shook his head. Separatism, the oldest charge against the Jews. The desire to deny them their identity. And as he listened, he looked at Barrett and thought: this is your position. Robertson is voicing your ideas. Let us Jews blend, mix, join our surrounding life and culture and reveal no separateness, no uniqueness.

But Barrett heard it only as a misconception by Robertson. Didn't he know that Jews had already made that choice? Look at how they lived in Greenlake. Like all other people, feeling, doing, acting, behaving like everyone else. How could he still throw this at them now? That was over, ancient history!

The Reverend wanted to sum up now, and he paused. In the moments of silence as he looked down at them, he saw the grim faces, the hurt in the eyes, the anger. And he felt pity for them, the way one feels for a child who has been scolded and who doesn't grasp the nature of his wrongdoing. Yes, they were like children. The Jews were the bad little children in the Universal Playground, always making it so hard for themselves to join in the innocent games and fun.

If he could only have reached them and made them understand it was for their good. To help them. And to them it was as if he were saying: you see why you're hated? Despised, reviled, spat upon? Persecuted, massacred? See how you have deserved it? He was being the classic friend of the Jew. The helper who never helps without hurting. Maybe because in him is all the suppressed desire to hurt?

"My friends," he leaned forward to be closer to them, "the truth about ourself is never pleasant ot hear. To see ourself with the eyes of others can be painful. I know that. But it is this way that we learn. That we come to understand ourselves—and this is even more important—to understand others and why they act as they do.

"Look into your hearts, my friends. If there is anger there now for what I have said—then you have closed the door to the truth and the knowledge that can help you. I know that I have spoken out of a love of justice and the brotherhood of man. Thank you."

Silence. Not even a stirring could be heard now. They watched him as he walked back to his chair on the platform. The calm, untroubled, satisfied look on his face. This was a man of God? Who had done this to them?

Bob Barrett rose quickly and came forward. Everyone waited.

"Reverend Robertson has delivered a sermon to us." He spoke slowly, the control tight, the face composed. But the voice was calm. "And I want to point out to our members that this is our Sabbath observance. This is a religious service. What we have heard is a sermon. Not a speech. It is for that reason that we will not have discussion or comment. Or answer. I believe—" he looked at them, his eyes over the whole auditorium slowly, "everyone here understands what I am saying."

It was enough. Release. Thank God! Good for Bob Barrett. Good for you, Bob! Good!

Rabbi finished the services with a prayer and a benediction.

Inter-Preach was dead.

VIII

The Executive Committee meeting had been on Wednesday, but it wasn't until Saturday morning that Barrett called Rabbi and indicated he wanted to talk with him. They agreed that Barrett was to come to Rabbi's home. They would be alone since Frieda had taken the children to visit her parents in New York for the day.

The delay until Saturday was deliberate on Barrett's part. He knew that somehow—almost certainly through Danny Cole—the news and substance of the meeting would reach Rabbi. And he wanted it to be absorbed thoroughly, to be examined and pondered, to become in a sense an accepted fact before he confronted Rabbi personally. The man, to him, was a curious combination of the impulsive and the thoughtful. Capable of instant and rather extreme reaction when provoked, yet by training, or because of his sense of dedication, he was equally capable of standing back to contemplate the wisdom of a particular move, able to force himself to be dispassionate. And what Barrett wanted and felt to be absolutely necessary was a dispassionate meeting and talk. Otherwise it could lead anywhere. So he waited until Saturday morning and then simply asked on the phone: "Rabbi, may I have a talk with you?" It didn't surprise him that Rabbi didn't ask what about. Of course he knew. And he sounded calm. It might, it just might, go off rather well.

Rabbi, for a while, had imagined that Barrett was putting off the confrontation for exactly these reasons. But he dismissed the idea. No, what Barrett was doing was preparing himself. Summoning courage. He must be figuring out how he could manage the ordeal of throwing a false accusation at him. Wondering how he could face the indignation of a man reacting to an obvious lie. The fact that Barrett had needed this time, Rabbi was sure, indicated how guilty he must feel.

And so he determined not to allow Barrett to escape the penalty for his malicious act. He wasn't going to make it easier for a man who could be so viciously immoral. But he would do it cleverly, let Barrett expose himself first. After that, he would give him his full response.

The duel began at once. Since the very first words would set the tone, Barrett decided to pitch it on a gentlemanly level.

"Thank you, Rabbi, for allowing me to break in on your Sabbath."

Rabbi lit his pipe slowly, blew out a few heavy, pungent puffs. "Since Frieda's away," he shrugged, "why not?" He walked over to the couch. "Sit down, Bob."

Barrett, on the edge of a chair, lit a cigarette. The silence was like a weapon they were both using against each other.

Rabbi broke it deliberately, and in a particular way. He focused on the meaningless. "She's gone off to see her mother. Isn't it amazing— how complex is the relationship a woman has with her mother? Do you know I believe a daughter can hate her mother in a way a son never can. And yet—she can also have an intimacy, a sharing, that to a son—"

"Rabbi." Barrett stood up.

"Of course. We can discuss women and their mothers another time." He puffed on the pipe. So Barrett was tense. Good. That would make it harder for him. "Oh—please sit down, Bob." The broad gesture. It is I who am trying to put him at ease. Good!

Barrett was in the chair again, jabbing his cigarette into the ash tray. Damn Rabbi's smugness! Acting as if he doesn't know!

"By the way, Bob, did you ever think of smoking a pipe? It's satisfying in quite a different way than a cigarette." The conversation was deliberately meaningless. Maybe to provoke him. "You see, a pipe actually provides a kind of physical support. You grasp it, you hold on to it, you almost lean on it. And at times—"

"Rabbi!" This time, something came through in the tone. Too much, but he couldn't keep it out. "I would really prefer not to discuss pipes and cigarettes."

"Of course. Sorry. I was merely trying to put you at ease."

"I'm quite at ease, thank you." Damn that streak in him, that way of trying to make you feel he was acting only for your benefit.

"Well . . . there was a note of urgency in your voice on the telephone."

"This is urgent. But I'm quite at ease, thank you."

The tension between them had begun to come out now. Neither of them was very good at controlling it. Let it all come out then.

"Yes." Rabbi's head to a side, the suggestion of a bitter smile. "I have long admired the ease with which you are able to handle urgent matters. Or even—unpleasant ones."

"Rabbi, unfortunately I am not able to return the compliment."

Well! This was going to be total. No pretense. Fine!

"Ah well, I am only a Rabbi. That's why we have Presidents of congregations. A division of labor, so to speak. The Rabbi deals with the non-urgent matters—such as God, faith, the meaning of life— while the President—"

"—Rabbi! Can we stop this please?"

"Of course." He puffed on the pipe again. "As they say in your sphere of activity—the meeting is yours."

Rabbi felt, in the mere presence of this man Barrett, a force that was alien to him. The tense aggressiveness, the controlled hostility, the total orientation toward another universe of involvement—and yet this was the man who was trying to change his whole life.

Why did it have to be? Why couldn't he have been an ordinary, decent, good-hearted man to deal with? Given the natural difficulties and conflicts, given all the problems and unanswered questions—a man to whom you could turn with openness and frankness and try to reach some kind of understanding or mutual tolerance. No, it was the Barrett species he had to deal with. The taut emotion, the intensity, the blindness of total self-confidence, the lack of sensitivity toward someone like himself. All right then, if this was the nature of the antagonist, he would use the appropriate weapons. He would be just as harsh and unyielding.

And Barrett, looking at Rabbi puffing defiantly on his pipe, felt an irritation that ran through his entire being. The very look of the man affronted him. That more than soulful expression, transcending ordinary life in its spiritual superiority. That crudely assembled face, the mouth petulantly thick, the eyes big and liquid behind the glasses, the nose like a finger pointing down to press a point. Was this the man he had helped choose as their Rabbi? How could he have been so deceived as to believe he was right for this congregation? It must have been the committee's inexperience and the effect of hearing him spout about his dedication.

Now, as Barrett looked at the Rabbi he had chosen, he saw not only the weakness in him, the lacks, the inability to function in whole areas that mattered to the congregation, but he saw also a man capable of strange behavior, of actions that were crude and deplorable. A man who could disregard the sacred role of a Rabbi to form attachments and associations that were shameful. No question existed in his mind now, this man was capable of it!

So there was no reason to be merciful with him, no reason to overlook anything he had done, deliberately or unintentionally. Now here he was, puffing on that goddam pipe, making nasty little jokes.

"Rabbi, has anyone ever pointed out to you that it's unbecoming for a Rabbi to be sarcastic?"

Rabbi answered with a wave of the pipe, an amused raising of the eyebrows. "Sarcastic? Really? And I had flattered myself that I was using wit."

"Whatever it is—it shouldn't be coming from a Rabbi."

Well! Now we're on standards of behavior for Rabbis. Getting closer.

"Apparently your image of a Rabbi is quite different from mine."

"Not just my image!"

"Oh?"

They were looking at each other, all the pretense gone now. Barrett turned away, jabbed the second cigarette into the glass of the ash tray, and rubbed hard, the burning end like an extension of himself, rubbing in, rubbing in.

"Rabbi, we seem to have come to the point sooner than I thought we would. So I'll go on—"

"As I said, your meeting."

He crossed his legs and stared at Barrett. There was, despite all the apparent amusement in his face and calmness in his manner, an anticipation of conflict that was creating as much fear in him as it was anger. How would Barrett bring it up? What would he throw at him, attack him with? What was at the heart of this man's willingness to force this all into the open? Desperation, hurt? A sense of humiliation? Personal animosity? It was as if he could feel himself about to be struck by Barrett, almost physically attacked, and didn't know with what it would be done, or how.

Barrett was the captive of his occupational training. In the business world you handled a crisis carefully. You organized your arguments. Prepared your position. It was practically impossible for Barrett not to conduct the present confrontation as a meeting, make a presentation.

"Rabbi, I haven't made a study of all the kinds of congregations we have in this country. And their differences and their problems. But I'm sure we'll agree there are differences. And each congregation has different problems."

"Agreed." He really had this all planned, didn't he?

"Now I do know the problems this congregation faces. In fact, we don't really exist as a unified congregation yet. We've been sharing a Temple. We don't have a sense of truly working together. We have no deep unity of spirit or purpose."

"Agreed." But only so far. "I think all that is coming along nicely. It's growing."

"And I know it isn't!" Oh no, Mr. Rabbi. Not so clever! "The truth is that our chief problem is precisely to build that spirit. Create that unity. To inspire a devotion and dedication among our members." Barrett stared at him. "Now, I'm going to be blunt with you, Rabbi—"

"Thanks for the warning."

And sarcasm won't save you either. "None of us here—not the President, the committees, the organizations—nobody can provide what this congregation needs except the Rabbi. It must come from him!"

Good of you to say that. So at last you realize it! "I had hoped you would say it is coming from him."

"No!" Then this is it. Now. "No, Rabbi. And that's why I'm here. The truth is that regardless of all your other qualifications, this is what you cannot give us! . . . I must ask you to face that, Rabbi."

He stood up, the pipe put aside. At least it was out in the open now. "But I don't feel that it is the truth."

"The whole congregation feels it!"

Dirty! Blaming them. "Do they?" He turned away. The whole thing seemed sick. Oh he was sick of it all. Everything. "Do they? Then

how is it that we are building a Temple? That we are growing? That
we are becoming stronger and more concerned?"

"You know how?" Barrett was almost shouting. "Despite you!
Despite you, Rabbi!"

He looked at this man who was pushing his failure into his face
and decided not to hate him. He would deal with him, but not hate
him. "If that is so . . . then let it be despite me."

"No! The congregation knows what it's missing! Everybody feels it!"

Suddenly there was a need in him to say it too. To say the stinking
truth! "And do they know what's missing in them?"

"That doesn't matter!"

"Oh doesn't it? As a Rabbi, I say it is all that matters! Because
what's missing in this congregation is the most important thing of all
—the spirit of God. True faith. The understanding and love of its
own religion!"

"Rabbi, these people have joined the congregation to get something,
and they're not getting it! You've got to face that!"

And what must *they* face? "They joined for only one reason—to
belong! Because it's the proper thing in this kind of society, in this kind
of town, in this idiotic creation called a suburb. . . . And what else?
Yes, something very important. To give their children some identification with Judaism that they themselves cannot provide at home. They
know that. Their guilt makes them do that. . . . But as for themselves?
They're a congregation of cynics and unbelievers."

Barrett turned away. He must do everything to control himself. "I
don't want to hear that from a Rabbi."

"But I am your Rabbi—and I will tell you! This congregation has
no interest in Judaism, no concern with God. Religion in their lives?
They just can't be bothered!"

"They are good Jews, Rabbi, and that's what counts."

"Are they? Are they good Jews when there are more men in the
bowling alley from the Men's Club than at services on Friday night?
When there are more women at the cooking lesson sponsored by
Sisterhood than came to all the Bible classes this year? You talk about
the chief problem this congregation faces. You know what it is? It's
the emptiness of their souls. The deadness of their spirit. No faith.
No understanding of Judaism. No love of God! This is what they
need to have brought to them!"

"That will come in time."

"From where? From the golf course? From the bazaars, the picnics, the dances? From the Bar Mitzvas with bands and catered food to impress richly dressed relatives—for boys who never even see the true observance of their Jewish faith in their own homes?"

No use! No use! Barrett wanted to stop, but there was no stopping now. "Don't blame all that's wrong with religion today on this congregation. We're no different from a thousand others!"

"Then I will make you different!"

"They won't follow you!"

Rabbi looked at him. How fully everything came out once the door was opened, the decision made. No holding back. No consideration of the pain. He was strangely calm now. "But as their Rabbi . . . I must try."

Barrett had grown calm now too. It was cold, dry business now, the facts of it.

"Rabbi, come down to earth and face the truth. We're not concerned with what you must do. We're concerned with what we need. And that means the kind of Rabbi we need."

"Mr. Barrett—who is the judge of that? You? Your committees? Your cynics and promoters? . . . I am the judge of the kind of Rabbi you need! You understand? I—your Rabbi!"

Barrett gave no answer. There was no more to say. Neither of them wanted to continue this. All had been said now. Barrett, standing near the window, was trying to organize the next step. Rabbi watched him, sensing it. Anticipate him. Bring it out. Why prolong it now?

"Bob—why are we pretending, you and I? Why are we engaged in this little fencing match? Is this what you really came to tell me?" Barrett stared at him. There was a bitter knowing in Rabbi's face now. "Did you really hope to get me to resign—without having to reveal yourself?"

"What are you talking about?"

He was pressing it, like something in the hand against the other's body. Pressing it in. "You came here to ask me to resign . . . but not for the reasons you've given me."

"Those reasons are enough!"

"Then here is your answer. Not to me! I reject them!"

Barrett looked into that face. How he detested the superior look of supposed spirituality, the armor of religion. The shield of dedication and Jewish virtue.

"Rabbi . . . are you determined to make this an occasion of shame and humiliation?"

"For me?"

"For both of us!"

"There is no shame and humiliation here—except what you bring with you!"

Barrett's fists clenched, the jaw gripping the words, the emotions. "Rabbi, what you are doing is wrong! I've given you a chance to do it cleanly, decently!"

"Thank you for your kindness. But, for God's sake—say what you have to say!"

Barrett still could not. "Rabbi, this is not *my* choice. Remember that!"

"So be it. My choice!"

"Rabbi, for the last time, think of what you're doing!"

God! Rabbi found himself shouting: "Say what you have to say!"

Barrett stared. The block! He turned away. "Strange. It's so strange. I . . . my upbringing . . . my sense of . . . I don't know . . . respect for the position of a Rabbi . . ."

"Say it to me as a man then!"

Barrett gave a bitter smile now, a smile conveying open hatred. "As a man? You know what I would say to you as a man?"

"Say it!"

"As a man . . . I say to you . . . *you are guilty toward my wife!* Do you hear that?"

Rabbi was utterly still. Not even his eyes moved from Barrett's face. Finally, his voice hoarse, the tension discoloring it. "Well . . . So you've said it."

Barrett gripped Rabbi's arm. "Is that your answer?"

Rabbi stepped back, the arm pulled away. "What answer do you want? You fool!"

Barrett followed, almost leaping. "Admit it, God damn you!"

There was sadness in it now as Rabbi, sighing, shook his head. "How terrible it must be for you—that you should come to this. That you should not only think it—but say it."

Barrett spat the words out into his face again. "Don't give me that! Pious talk, crap!"

All right. Then what, Barrett? "What is it you want, Bob?"

"I want to hear you deny it! Can you deny it?"

"Deny—what?"

"What was going on between you two! Together all the time. Everywhere. Private meetings. Lunches. You were seen by people!"

"Of course we were seen. There was nothing to hide."

Barrett was like a hunter, his prey twisting, concealing. "Did you meet with my wife in your office—privately—again and again— privately!—because there was nothing to hide?"

Incredible! Like a madman after him. "We met to discuss congregation business. Why do you think we met?"

Quick! "At night? Night after night?"

"Whenever there was time."

"Oh . . . oh, there was time! There was time for everything!"

No! Barrett had said too much now, had gone too far. "For what, in God's name? Do you know what you're saying?" Rabbi now reached for him. "Bob, how can you even think this? How can you believe it *possible* about Elaine and me?"

"How?" Pious crap-artist! "Because you were seen! Is that enough? You were seen—in my own home—with your arms around my wife! Kissing her!"

No. Stop. It must be stopped. There must be a way to stop it. "Bob —this is—my God! I can't believe what I'm hearing!"

"Then deny it!" Barrett shouted. "Deny it!"

Rabbi turned away. Where to turn?

"Deny you were kissing her!"

He looked at Barrett, at the face red with anger. Was there any use? "I . . . in the way you think of it . . . I deny it."

"What does that mean? Nothing!"

"Oh God, Bob! That I should have to explain—"

"To me, you do!"

"Explain?" He moved about, searching for a tone, a voice, a way of conveying the innocence and tragedy. "There was some kind of mixup about a meeting . . . and I showed up after it was cancelled or something. Elaine offered me a cup of coffee . . . I sat there and . . . and I noticed something was wrong. She was . . . almost in tears. I . . . I asked if I could help in some way. She said . . . she said it was about some problem . . . she couldn't talk. She started to cry . . . so I comforted her. . . ."

"By *kissing* her?"

Oh, pity for this man! Pity! "No, Bob. No. By holding a poor soul who was distraught with her misery. And comforting her. To give her hope. To give her strength to continue. I said: trust in God. He will care for you. And I . . . I kissed her on the forehead in a gesture of . . . of . . . of compassion for her suffering."

"You had your arms around her!"

Rabbi turned now on Barrett in anger and despair. "Stop it! Stop it! No—we will not continue this. Enough! No—I am your Rabbi and I say *enough!*"

He would end it now. "Mr. Barrett, there is no sense in continuing this. I won't do it."

"Well then, Mr. Gordon—just answer me this. Never mind what happened or didn't happen. Or why or why not. Just tell me this: are you in love with Elaine?"

"What?"

"A very simple question. Are you in love with her? You can answer that!"

Rabbi was looking at him, at the face probing into him, at the man reaching into his insides to grasp—what? An emotion? A thought, a sensation, a movement along some nerve that had passed through him somewhere, sometime? Was it there? Was it there?

"Are you asking if I felt anything for her?"

"*Love?*"

"Love?" My God, what is the answer to that? "I felt . . . I feel . . . an affection for her. Is that wrong?"

"Affection!" The cynical bitterness in his voice.

"Yes." And suddenly he knew it all and wanted to say it. Not more than it was, but all that it had been. The richness, the beauty, the good in it—so good that he had never known before that it could be like this with anyone. The realization at times, in her presence, or glowing from it afterward, that it could have been with her, with Elaine, with a woman like this. And that it would never be. That what he had—whatever else he had with Frieda—this would never exist for them. This complete sharing and joy, this understanding,

this joining of the selves in planning and working, this closeness. That
had to be said somehow. He needed to say it.

But how to utter the words? How to make them bear the essence
of what it really was, and not the misunderstanding that they would
bring? He bit his lip and tried to start and couldn't. Then finally,
quietly, almost with a gentleness, he said:

"I have a very deep affection for her. For her kindness, her eagerness to help, her involvement."

"That's a good word! Involvement! That's what you had with her—
an involvement. And she is my wife and you are a Rabbi! Now you
tell me if that isn't wrong! Immoral! For any man—but for a Rabbi—!"

It couldn't be done, Rabbi realized. It had to be played out on this
level.

"Not immoral, Bob. Not immoral. Warm and human and normal—
and nothing I am ashamed of or feel guilty about."

"Your sense of guilt doesn't matter!"

"It is all that matters, Bob. Because there is no guilt in this for
either of us, Elaine or me. And so there is nothing wrong. Can you
understand that?"

What Barrett felt now was strangely enough not anger, nor hatred
for this man. But a jealousy that was like a gnawing pain inside.
Jealousy that this man had reached Elaine and she him. That there
had been contact and response and a flow between them that had
such meaning for both. That it had been achieved where he had
failed. He had not found out how, but this man had. On whatever
level, however deep, it had been reached by this man with his wife.

He could only feel his own defeat, his own failure. This was the
tragedy for him. Not Elaine's unfaithfulness but the mere turning to
this man, not Rabbi's response to her but her reaching toward him.
And his own inability to make it happen for himself.

The only thing he could do now was to eliminate this evidence of
his own failure, destroy it, wipe out the image from his life so he
wouldn't have to face it in humiliation and shame, in every experience
of the conflict and agony with Elaine.

"Rabbi," he sat down, reaching out now for his weapons, his
strength, "I have given you a chance to resign in a way that would be
respectful and dignified and cause no problems. You have rejected
that way, so there is no other choice. The Executive Committee has

empowered me to request your resignation as Rabbi of this congregation."

"On what grounds?"

"On the grounds of conduct unbecoming to a rabbi."

"Specifically—?"

"You're a fool! You don't have any sense! Why do you do this?"

"Because we are in different worlds, Mr. Barrett. And I must know what that world of yours is that can do such a thing. I am entitled to know it to the fullest."

"All right then. They are asking you to resign on the grounds of immoral behavior with a woman who is not your wife."

Quickly, surprisingly calm, even with a sense of superiority in his voice, Rabbi said: "The request is acknowledged."

"Your answer! I want your answer!"

Still calm, the coldness in his voice the reflection of his separating himself from this, putting it all far away from him, he gave his answer: "I have received the request and I will consider it."

"What is there to consider?"

"For me, Mr. Barrett, there is a great deal. The good of this congregation."

"Don't give me that. That's why the request is made—for the good of the congregation!"

Rabbi looked into Barrett now, through all the swirling surface signs and motions and expressions, into the cold center of him, and said it very quietly: "Is it, Mr. Barrett?"

Then he walked to the door and held it open.

"I want you to leave now."

Barrett stopped at the door, looking down as he spoke the words: "May God be with you as you decide."

And then he was out and the door closed. Rabbi stood there unable to move, shaking his head, hands over his eyes, shaking his head. Is that what he had said? May God be with you?

God be with me? All right, all right. God—be with me! For it is all being done in Your name and will be done as with Your blessing. The lie spoken. The act committed. The evil deed accomplished. All in Your name!

Then help me, God! Let me also say: In God's name this is what I must do. Help me to know, so that I may truly do it in Your name!

RABBI 8

It had been a curious thing to Rabbi that when his mother died he could feel no more than he did. He actually made an effort to touch his own emotions, to reach them and stir them into awareness and response. He wanted to be able to cry, and couldn't. He wanted to feel a sense of personal loss, some anguish deep inside. There was none. He even went through the process of imaginatively projecting himself back in time to when he was a little boy, to when he would run to her in tears for the warmth and embrace of her arms, the shelter of her body, the acceptance and love.

Now she was dead. Mama is dead. Mom. Mommy. My Mommy is dead! He saw it only as if it were happening to a little boy on the screen in a movie. A visualization, not an experience. He couldn't feel like that little boy again. He really couldn't feel anything for her except pity.

What an empty, miserable life she had had. Everything revolving around the store, the business. Taking all her energy, almost all her emotion. In the shabby home, the moments of release and joy came so rarely, erupting suddenly when there was a holiday, Pesach, Purim, a relative visiting, a good week in the store, and the happy feeling in her was always so brief, over, back to all the problems and burdens she had to cope with.

She was a good mother who knew what had to be done. There should be enough food, healthy things to eat, fresh oranges, fish, meat. There was always enough. The children had to have nice clothes. They should be clean, neat. She washed and ironed them dutifully and with a certain amount of love and pride. The kids had the right to enjoy a movie every week, and she handed them the money herself, from her own purse, and sent them off with two extra cents each for candy.

But in a strange way he had never felt that she related to him, understood him, had been close in the ways he needed her. He recognized, thinking about it now, that the reason for it probably lay in him. The unusual way he had developed, even as a child. The reading, the involvement with ideas, the self-confidence of spirit, the search for purpose in life and for faith to live by. It had made him independent of his mother when he was still a boy. He had never really turned to her for anything that mattered. He had grown up not needing a mother as much as a teacher. And now that she was dead, he felt no loss. Only the sadness of death for her sake. Only for her loss.

It was a shock to discover how this death affected his father. The image he had of their life hadn't prepared him for it. His father had sold the store five years before, and the two of them had lived in their dark little apartment in the Bronx like creatures that had crept into a hole, the shelter of the winter of their life. They had never gone anywhere, even to a movie. They never visited anyone. They seemed to exist by making the least possible amount of effort, even the least possible motion. Into the kitchen, into the living room, into the bedroom, into bed. The lights out everywhere except the room they were in, so as to save money. They ate so frugally, sometimes a hard-boiled egg and sliced tomato for lunch, a piece of fish and bread for dinner, hot Postum to warm their bones. A television set (a gift from Sarah) their contact with, and perhaps vision of, the world outside. Shuffling about in slippers and robes. Hardly talking to each other. Hardly living.

This was the way their life had seemed to him. Yet now, with his Ruthie gone, Sam was a lost and bewildered human being. He had depended completely on Ruth for his existence and for all functioning. She had done it all, making the bed, cleaning the house, cooking the food and bringing it to the kitchen table where they ate, shopping for whatever was needed, seeing to it that he wore a sweater when it was cold, that the windows were open when it was warm, that they sat down in front of the television set at night, that they played a game or two of gin rummy after lunch, that he took his afternoon nap, that there was powder to keep his false teeth in place, that he had clean socks every now and then, that he got a haircut when it was time, cut his fingernails when they became too black, had a clean handkerchief to wipe his nose, that there was a *challa* Friday night and the candles and enough wine for the blessing, that a day had a beginning and that it had an end, and that in the emptiness and loneliness of life there was another soul nearby so that the sadness would not be too great.

What Rabbi didn't know was that in all this, there was so much more. That in the isolation of their lives there had developed an awareness of each other that was more than concern with physical needs. That there was the desire to be with each other everywhere, always, a clinging that had beauty to it. That each knew the other so intimately, so fully, there was a joy in the recognition.

They anticipated each other's reactions, whims, little quirks, even remarks, even expressions. She knew what he would say when she put an extra half-piece of gefilte fish on his plate on Friday night, how he would glance at her and smile: *"Eppes* a holiday tonight?" He knew how she would purse her lips when he turned on the television show she didn't especially like but consented to watch with him. "You wanna watch that, ha Sam?" "Would I turn it on otherwise?" "Every Thursday night? We can't miss it even once?" He would look at her, his hands behind his back, smiling, letting her go through the little routine. "So all right, one more time we'll watch it." And of course they never missed it a single Thurday night, and he wouldn't even mind her pretense to be sewing while she sat there. He knew she was looking at it sideways, not missing a thing.

They had dozens of such little games between them, played out with understanding and tolerance, allowing each other to act out the role. He would start out without gloves on a cold day. "Sam—no gloves? You want to have frozen hands?" "They say cold hands a warm heart, no?" "Your warm heart I'm not worried about. Put on the gloves and *shveig!"* It was as if he wanted her to notice, to care, to want to protect him in this little way. And she knew he relished this concern.

On Monday, the shopping day for the week, he gave her the twenty dollars, counting out the bills. Nine, ten, fifteen, twenty. "Sam, you made a mistake. You gave me twenty-two." He raised his eyebrows in mock surprise. "I did? So what can I do? Too late. Might as well keep it." And of course she knew he had planned it all along, and he knew that she knew, and that was the little warm joy of it for them both.

They would get into bed at night, the long day over at last, the weariness of just standing, sitting, moving about finished with. Now the nice feeling of the bed under them, supporting, warm, no demands, just lying there and letting the body and the mind feel at peace.

"So Ruth—you wanna say good night?"

"What should I say? Good morning?"

"So I'll give you a kiss now and you go to sleep."

"You too."

"You should sleep well."

"You too, Sam."

Who would have believed they still held on to this last kiss at night? At their age? It was just a kind of habit now—only it was also the final acknowledgment of their being with each other and for each other, and it expressed a quiet happiness for them both.

Mama. Mama. Mama. Always there. Always with you. Always knowing what to do for you. Always thinking of you. Always accepting you and understanding you. Always being part of your life.

Gone. All suddenly gone. And Sam had an emptiness inside of him he didn't know what to do with. For two weeks after sitting *shiva* was finished, he continued to sit in the dark emptiness of the living room, his hands quietly clasped in his lap, his head down, staring at nothing, sometimes dozing off, sometimes rousing himself to go into the kitchen to get a bite to eat but not eating, not hungry, not able to do anything.

Sarah had to go back to California finally, and he was left totally alone. Rabbi realized it was not a question of what his father would do now, but of what to do with him. The tragedy of the old. They no longer make the choice, it must be done for them.

Rabbi and Frieda had a long talk and decided Sam would come to live with them. In a strange way, Rabbi had been reluctant to approach her about this. It was only partly the guilt every husband or wife feels in imposing a parent on the other. It was, for him, also an enlargement, a deepening of the sense of failure that sometimes hung over their life. She had to cope with his problems with the congregation, his remoteness from her and even from the children, his noninvolvement with all the burdens of managing the house, all the domestic chores. And now to ask her to accept his father into the midst of this.

It was therefore a joyous thing to him to see how Frieda responded. Not reluctantly or even hesitantly, but with warmth and understanding.

"He's your father, David. He has a place here."

"It will mean problems. He'll be in the way. He'll—"

"—Whatever. It's your *father*, David! He'll have a home here."

He embraced her gratefully, and as they held each other close there was a sudden surge of affection, a realization of mutual need that had not been expressed often before. They were a unit. What affected one, affected the other.

"You're a very good human being, Frieda." He looked at the distraught face, now close beside him, feeling with him. "You're a good woman. Thank you."

"I love you, David." The simple statement, so simply uttered, that for her explained everything.

Frieda "fixed up" Rabbi's study into a bedroom. There was no other room in the house to spare, and it also meant Sam wouldn't have to climb any stairs. They bought a studio couch and a dresser, cleaned out a closet so he could hang his things, put a comfortable armchair in the room so he could have a place to sit when he wanted to be alone (or when visitors came and he was expected not to be in the way).

Sam moved in, and the strongest expression of his feelings about it all was: "Very nice. Very nice." Everything about the arrangements they had made was "very nice." No more. No great words of gratitude. No profound thanks. It was as if he expected all this, perhaps even felt it was due him. A father comes to his son when the time arrives to make it necessary. This was as it should be.

And now Frieda took the place of Ruth. She didn't enter as intimately into the personal, physical aspects of his life, the functioning and care of his body, the clothes, underwear, baths, haircuts, teeth. What she set out to do was to make him feel wanted and "taken care of." The soft-boiled egg or hot oatmeal for breakfast, the Postum, the whole wheat toast he liked, the soups, the boiled chicken, the heavy blanket on his bed and the electric heater nearby when he needed it, the constant questioning: "Are you all right, *Zayde?* Can I get you anything?"

Rabbi watched her at this continuous task of devotion and concern, and felt a delight in her for it. Perhaps it did provide another purpose in her life, a sense of sacrifice which is so satisfying to some women. Perhaps she was expressing to David a gratitude that was too painful to express in the ordinary way. But the gentleness and thoughtfulness that was emerging now added a new richness to their own relationship, and Rabbi found himself somehow touching her more, a hand on her shoulder, a caress of the arm when she stood in the kitchen preparing something special for his father, an embrace in the evening when he saw how tired she was.

And a remarkable, unexpected, and almost difficult to accept result of all this was the way he now wanted to make love to her. She would lie beside him at night, stretched out on her back in sheer exhaustion, just glad to be resting at last, and he would want to show her that he was aware of how she felt.

"Tired?"

"Uh-huh."

"Want me to rub your back?"

She looked at him, the eyes warmly responding. "Would you do it for me?"

"Of course."

"To make me feel good?"

"—and because I want to."

She would turn on her stomach and he would start by leaning on his elbow and reaching over to move his hand up and down her spine, the hand flat against the skin, rubbing gently, warmly, to soothe and ease the tired body. And she would begin to respond and move softly with pleasure and moan and shift her body about on her stomach so he could reach her shoulders, her neck, down the length of the spine, to the bottom of it, that tense triangle where the hand was so soothing, the mere touching so relaxing. He would finally move so he was directly over her, squatting over her back, both hands against the tight shoulders, rubbing away the weariness, expressing his gratitude, his awareness of her sacrifice, saying thank you, thank you, for my father, thank you for what you are doing for me, and kneeling over her, the body beginning to quicken beneath him, he would feel the surge of response and desire, the wanting of the body that was saying I want you to him.

So strange! He felt he shouldn't question it, but he did. His need to analyze everything. Was he feeling all this for her because of gratitude only? So strange that his father's presence in the house, her devotion to him, was bringing this out, bringing them closer, making his body express the emotion, the response. It didn't matter. For whatever reason, it was good.

And Frieda felt a new kind of importance in David's life. Taking care of the house and his own needs was an expected and common-place act. Caring for Joshua and the baby was only a normal and natural thing for a mother. But to provide her husband's father with a home, to make him feel welcome and cared for, that was another level altogether, and it made David regard her almost with awe. It overwhelmed him. It brought out a warmth and a love that she yearned for and was willing to do anything to receive.

The only problem was Sam himself. Not his personal habits, which they could put up with. The sloppiness of his dress, so that they had to remind him to comb his hair, to zip up his pants, to pick up his clothes from the floor, to use a napkin when he ate, to flush the toilet when he went. It wasn't even his assumption that he was now so totally a part of this home that he belonged anywhere and everywhere just as any of them did, in the kitchen whenever it suited him, in the living room as a natural place to sit and relax, with their friends and their company whenever there were visitors, talking, participating, being where everyone was. For how could one say to him: go to your room. Stay away from us this evening. Be alone in the little world we have set apart for you. He simply had no concept of such tactfulness or sensitivity, and they realized it and accepted it.

The problem that arose was that he had an altogether different approach to Judaism. It began with his shock at discovering that Frieda didn't keep a kosher house. She didn't have separate dishes for dairy and meat, which he not only considered sinful, but a scandal in a Rabbi's home. Frieda suggested to Rabbi that it would be no trouble at all to set up separate dishes and that she was willing to do it to please his father, and it was done. When Sam saw bacon in the refrigerator, he picked up the package and threw it into the garbage pail.

"Not in this house, David! Pork! You can't have it in this house!"

Again, Frieda willingly submitted to a "cleansing" of all the food that was in the kitchen and the freezer in the garage, and bought only kosher products from then on. They discovered that, after all, it really made only a slight difference in their lives.

But these were, in a sense, negative things and easily corrected to suit him. It was the positive things that Sam began to demand that created the difficult and painful problems. He insisted that morning prayers be said, that the proper blessing be uttered before every meal, that Rabbi and Joshua wear *yarmulkes* in the house, that all the observance of Orthodox Judaism be followed in every detail.

And he began to work on Joshua, who was now seven, to instill in him what he considered to be the attitudes and behavior expected of a Jew. He started to teach him the prayers in Hebrew, and Joshua, who was a bright little boy, responded to it as if it were a game and began to show off his new knowledge to his parents and want all the prayers in the home to be read from Grandpa's book. He talked to him constantly about what "a good Jew" does and believes, so that the boy began to question his father and demand explanations about how he could be a Rabbi and not act as a good Jew. He gave Joshua a prayer shawl and the boy wanted to know why his father didn't wear one. In time, because he spent so many hours with him, and because Joshua was attracted by the ritual, the display, the performance of so many prescribed observances, it was clear that he had won him over and that it was going to create difficulties in the family.

Rabbi decided it had to be stopped. "I want you to leave the boy alone," he explained one evening. "He is a member of this family, and we are Reform Jews. That's what he must accept."

"I'm helping to make him a good Jew, that's all."

"Dad, my idea of a good Jew is different from yours."

"Different it is—but better? I'm giving him a *Jewish* feeling. What you and all these Reform people got, that's not even Judaism. To me it's fifty-fifty Christian already."

"But not to me. And he's my son."

"And my grandson!"

"I want you to leave him alone! You've gone so far with him he doesn't even have respect for what I do now. And I am not only his father, I am a Rabbi."

"I don't blame him, David. Respect for what? For Jewishness that has nothing in it? No prayers when they should be said? No following God's word all day long? No doing what every Jew *has* to do? For thousands of years it's been the way. And I'm helping that boy to be a Jew for the rest of his life—in everything—not just a Jewish name. Not just on the outside!"

Rabbi might have managed in some way to accept this, even though he knew that Sam was really attacking him at the same time that he was working on Joshua. It created an awkwardness at home, it presented a constant split in the family, but he felt that as Joshua matured he would have no problem in winning him over again, in influencing him and enlightening him.

But the conflict reached an intolerable level in a completely different area. Sam refused to go to the services that Rabbi was conducting. To begin with, they were held on Friday night in the neighboring town, and to get there one had to ride on the Sabbath. The men didn't wear hats. The women sat with the men. The prayers were in English, and they were read out of some new book put together by some organization; they were not God's own word out of the ancient books. There was no cantor. There was nothing sacred or Jewish about these services for him, and he wanted nothing to do with them even if his own son was the Rabbi. He refused to appear there.

What he did instead was to set up a complicated series of arrangements that were a source of trouble and embarrassment to Rabbi. Sam joined the Orthodox congregation in Lanebrook, since there was none in Greenlake. He found a religious family that was willing to put him up Friday night and Saturday for just a few dollars, which he gladly paid as a tribute to his faith and to God. On Friday afternoon he had to be driven to the home of this family, and then he would walk with them to the service in their synagogue in the evening. He would walk back, stay over, sleeping on the cot they set up for him in a corner of their living room. He would spend all day Saturday at the synagogue in prayer and in talk with the few other Orthodox Jews who attended, and then on Saturday night, after the final prayers, he would have to be picked up and brought home.

It was more than a physical burden to Rabbi. It was an open, dramatic repudiation of him by his father, and many in the congregation knew about it and reacted to it. Some people had only understanding for the situation, having experienced similar differences with their own parents or relatives. But to many others it was another example of Rabbi's ineffectiveness, his inability to deal with problems tactfully. If your father feels that way, you don't have him live with you. If you're a Rabbi and supposed to be able to influence people and lead them along your path of Judaism, how come you can't do it with your own father?

And Sam, sensing somehow that by these actions, and perhaps even by his mere presence in David's house, he was in possession of a weapon against his son's betrayal of true Judaism, never missed a chance to use that weapon. To everyone he met, in every gathering that took place in Rabbi's home, he explained his views in a manner that combined indignation and sorrow.

It created so much embarrassment that Rabbi could face it no longer. But how to deal with it? Nothing that he could say to Sam would ever stop him from expressing himself, or make him give up going to the Orthodox synagogue. There was no answer, and there was no living with it.

He had a long talk with Frieda about it, and it didn't help at all. She felt he just had to put up with it. It was as if something in her upbringing, something she had absorbed in her childhood, made it necessary to consider "respect" for one's parents the greatest obligation of all.

"He's your father, David, and you can't hurt him or make him ashamed."

"But he's hurting me. And he knows he's doing it. It's deliberate."

"He's a poor little old man, David, who only knows one way to be a Jew. And when he sees what we do, how we practice Judaism, it breaks his heart. That's all he cares about. Besides . . . you have to forgive certain things in a father. You owe him that."

It was a dilemma that upset Rabbi as much as anything that had ever happened to him. Frieda being so understanding of Sam. Joshua being attracted to him and influenced by him. And he himself, the son, in a constant state of resentment and irritation, aware only of the hostility between them.

One night there was a meeting at Rabbi's house to discuss the Sunday School situation, the recruiting of teachers and how to improve the curriculum. About six people came, Bob Barrett and Dr.

Greenwald among them, and Sam Gordon took up a position in his favorite chair in the living room and sat through the discussion, shaking his head as he listened. Rabbi had suggested he stay away, but Sam had refused.

"Just to listen? What's the harm?" And he had promised not to interfere or say a word.

Everyone was aware of his presence, as sort of peripheral, disturbing factor, and a special effort had to be made to ignore him, act as if he weren't there, and his shaking of the head, his occasional "Hmmm!" were not even noticed.

Barrett had just finished some remarks about the basic goals of the Sunday School, to instill a knowledge of Judaism and a feeling of involvement with it, when Sam suddenly exclaimed:

"My God! Oy, my God!"

Everyone turned, startled. Rabbi stood up, sensing what was coming. Sam stood up too.

"I just gotta talk! I gotta say! What you people doing—"

"Dad!" Rabbi was holding his arm. "Please! I've asked you not to do this."

"So you asked. So I'm gonna do it anyhow. Since when should a Jew be afraid to fight for Jewishness—even if his own son tries to stop him?"

Rabbi gripped his arm, but Sam moved forward shaking it off. "You see? You see how afraid he is to hear the truth? But to you—" he pointed at them, "to you I'll tell it anyway."

"Please, Dad! Stop this!" Rabbi was so upset that Barrett stood up quickly.

"Rabbi, it's all right. Let your father talk. We don't mind."

"See?" Sam glaring at his son. "*They* wanna hear!"

Rabbi sat down, filled with love for his father and yet with the humiliation of it all.

"What is it you want to say, Mr. Gordon?" Barrett was handling it calmly and kindly.

"Just one thing I gotta say." Sam looked at the faces staring at him. "I hear you talking about the Sunday School, what it's gonna teach the kids. And you know what? It's gonna teach them nothing! A little history? A little bit about the holidays? This is gonna make them good Jews? Never! Let me tell you, what you'll get from that is nobodies and nothings! They'll grow up and they'll forget the Sunday School lessons one-two-three, and they'll be Jews like Hitler was a Jew! You gotta give these kids a training! They got to learn how to act, what to do, from the first prayer in the morning till the last one at night. They got to learn in *Hebrew* all the prayers. They got to be made to study and study and learn! They got to do everything like real Jews from the inside, and not like the Jewishness is something extra on the outside. You doing the Jewish people harm, all of you! Believe me what I say! You hurting the Jewish people by driving the kids away from the life that Jews gotta follow if they gonna not be wiped out and disappear! And I don't care what you think of me and how I'm talking. You think I care? What I care for is to keep the Jews alive! And for that believe me, it takes sacrifice! It takes making your whole life a Jewish life! It takes—"

He stopped. His own emotion was flowing so fully, in so many ways, he suddenly felt lost.

"That's all I gotta say."

He turned and shuffled slowly towards his room and then closed the door behind him.

In the silence, no one looked at Rabbi. No one moved for a while. Finally Barrett stood up, and the others did too. They said their farewells quietly and left. They knew it would be impossible for Rabbi to continue the meeting.

Rabbi sat there for a long time. He wasn't thinking or trying to understand. He was phrasing and rephrasing what he wanted to say. What he had to say. But it didn't seem to matter. No matter how he put it, it was the same.

He opened his father's door. Sam was sitting on the bed, a little figure of a man, his feet barely touching the floor, bent over, his hands in his lap, like a sad and lost soul. He looked up at David.

"David," he shook his head, "I don't belong here. Not in your house, not in your Temple, not with these people."

Rabbi didn't know how to answer. He sat down in the chair, and the two remained silent a long while. Maybe Sam had been hoping his son would make him feel better, say something to ease his sense of aloneness.

"You think I don't know, David? That all I do is make trouble for you? With Joshua, with Frieda, with everybody. I know. Believe me, I know. I don't belong here."

Rabbi looked at the forlorn old face of his father, at the sadness in it, the helplessness of the man.

"Dad, you're my father and you belong here! A son and a father belong together. This is your home, you understand that? Always it will be your home. But, Dad, what you—"

"—What I have to do is keep my mouth shut, my business to myself, my feelings locked up. So? That's not living for me, David. Worse than jail, that's for me. It's being dead."

"What can I do, Dad? My life and work is with these people, and you're against them and against my work. Tell me what to do about it!"

Sam looked at his son, aware of the futility of discussing this any longer. Nothing could be changed. He would rather die than give up his belief and his practices; his son could never accept them. There was no hope in it for either of them.

"I'll tell you, David. I'll tell you what. I'll go way somewhere. I'll find a place, don't worry . . . maybe with some family, I don't know— and I won't bother you no more. Finished. Your trouble-making father won't be on your hands no more."

"Dad, I want you to stay! Frieda and I both. And Josh. We love you and want you. But you must let us alone. Let us live our kind of life. You must!"

Sam shook his head, a sad little smile at his lips, knowing and understanding the truth.

"And if I can't?"

"Try! Won't you even try?"

"No, David. That's too much to ask. What I believe I believe and my way is my way. I can't give it up. Even for a home, a place to live, even to be with my son and his family. Too much. I can't."

He got off the bed and the two men looked at each other with all the pain that was in them, all the misery of the truth that couldn't be denied. They embraced suddenly and held each other, Sam patting his son's back, patting it as he held him.

"You're a good son, my David. Don't worry about that. You're a good son."

"Dad, what should I do?"

Sam stepped back and smiled. "What you should do? You should do what you have to do. Like me. I'll do what I have to do. I'll find a place, don't worry. Some family, somebody. They'll take me in. And then—I'll be able to be a Jew my way. My kind of Jew. How many years I got left anyway? So at least I'll die a good Jew."

Rabbi's arms went around the frail little figure again, wanting him to feel his love, his understanding, his concern, and in the sadness of it he started to cry.

"My David?" His father looked at him. "My David is crying for his father? So who could ask for more? A son should feel so much love for his father?"

IX

Nobody could have foreseen that precisely this Saturday night was the night of the Build-The-Temple Dinner Dance at the Sprucewood Country Club. Jack Stern had planned it months ago, made hundreds of detailed and imaginative arrangements, pushed with publicity and personal appeals, and there was now no doubt that it would be a successful fund-raising affair (at $100 a couple) as well as a big social event. The sudden developments concerning Rabbi couldn't be expected to interfere with this important function. The question was how to handle it delicately and tactfully. And Jack's decision was that the wisest step was to ignore it, to proceed as if nothing had happened, as if no danger or threat hung over them. They would go ahead with their plans and make it a great, big, beautiful, knock-out of a party.

And while it was easy enough for Jack to come to this conclusion, he realized that Rabbi still had somehow to be dealt with. The only way to do it was to have a frank talk with him. He called Rabbi on the phone. It was exactly a half hour after Barrett had left.

"Rabbi, can you spare a few minutes? I want to see you."

Rabbi sat at his desk, trying to make himself accept what had happened with Barrett, trying to feel like a whole human being again, trying to summon the strength, the understanding that should be his as a Rabbi.

He didn't answer for a moment. Then: "No, Jack. Please. I don't think I'm up to it today."

Stern had a suspicion of what was wrong. It didn't matter. He had to get to him.

"Well, Rabbi, it's pretty important. I've got to see you today."

"I'm sorry, but no. Jack, I just can't. I think—" there was no use pretending, since Stern was on the Executive Committee and knew everything, "—I think you should understand why."

Exactly what Jack was afraid would happen! "I do understand, Rabbi. But I must talk to you. It's about the dance tonight."

Rabbi held the phone in his hand and it felt like an intrusion from another world, a weapon "they" possessed that had been thrust into his own home. It felt cold against his fingers. Smooth and cold, and he wanted to drop it, push it away. The anger came now.

"Jack, I'm not going to the dance! Bob Barrett was just here! You surely can't expect me to go now!"

Dance! How strange that there could be such a thing as a dance tonight, a party at which most of the Jews in Greenlake would laugh and enjoy themselves when this was happening to him, to their Rabbi. They didn't know, of course, but that didn't make it less ironic.

Jack didn't answer. He was thinking fast, organizing. "All right," he said finally. Not over the phone. Not this way. It had to be done personally. He had to get to him. "All right, Rabbi. But can I just come and have a brief chat? Please? I ask it as a *personal* favor."

Everybody always asking a personal favor of him, that indirect and clever way of putting him on the spot, of saying: as my *Rabbi* you cannot ever let me down when I say I need you.

Jack Stern walked into Rabbi's living room a serious, subdued man. There was no sign of the cheerful Jack Stern smile and manner, there were no flip remarks. His handshake was solemn. May I sit down, Rabbi? Thank you for letting me come. I appreciate it.

Rabbi stood facing him. Let Jack feel all the guilt and shame that he deserved. Let him struggle with the problem of facing the Rabbi he had rejected. He wasn't going to make it easier for him.

"Rabbi, I want to come to the point right away. You said you weren't coming to the dance tonight."

"That's right. Do you really expect me to?"

"Rabbi," Jack stood up too now, "I have no right to expect anything of you."

"That's right."

"Rabbi, but may I say to you what's in my heart?"

"If it will make you feel better."

"Not because of that, Rabbi."

"Then you speak for my sake?"

So it would be like this. Bitterness and anger. Rabbi's sarcasm. All right, he was entitled to it. It didn't matter. It had to be done. "Rabbi, I want to say what is in my heart because what is there concerns more than just you and me."

"Ah—the greater good!" Rabbi gave a little, bitter laugh. "What a wonderful refuge that is for everyone. How it protects our own weakness."

"Rabbi—" the only way was to continue, get to it and deal with it, "the dance tonight is the biggest, most important event in the whole fund-raising drive for the Temple."

"I hope it's successful."

"In terms of money, it already is. Almost four hundred couples. A hundred dollars a couple. That's forty thousand dollars we raised to help build the Temple."

"I suppose the money has to come from somewhere. It might as well come from dances."

"It is more than a dance, Rabbi. It is an event of dedication, an expression of involvement with the great cause of building our Temple." Then summoning up the sincere look, the solemn tone, the layer of emotion in the voice, Jack said it: "Rabbi, we need you there tonight. Even with—with things like they are, the congregation needs you there."

Rabbi spoke slowly, out of the pain. It was like letting him see the wound. "I didn't think the congregation needed me for anything."

He was entitled to that. Let him have it. Pass over it. "They expect you to be there."

"To give my blessing?"

"Yes, to give your blessing. And to show to the whole congregation—"

"—that everything is fine? Smooth and lovely and that your Rabbi approves it all—and is approved by all? I have to go through with this fantasy?"

"Rabbi, I understand how you must feel. Please believe I really understand."

"Understand what?" So here was one of them. One of those who had voted for him to resign. One of those who felt he was unfit to be his Rabbi. What did this man really feel? Did he even know himself what he felt? He wanted to search, seek inside this man for some answer. "What do you understand, Jack?"

"How hard it must be for you to—"

"No!" He turned away, waving his arm. "No! What I want to know is—do you understand what you have done? You!"

Jack looked at him and didn't know what to say. "I think, Rabbi—perhaps we shouldn't—you and I—get into—"

"No! Oh, God help you, Jack! All I want to know is how much of yourself you understand after what you have done." He came up to him again. "What have you received of me since we have known each other? Have you received insight into God? Have you received help to a deeper faith? Awareness of yourself as a Jew? Have you received this? . . . Is this what you reject? Is this what you want to do without and why you ask me to leave—so that there will be no more of it? What have you done? Do you know?"

No answer. What answer could be enough? Better nothing. Better let him feel all he had to feel.

"Well, Jack?" Rabbi spoke, after a long silence, almost pitying him.

Jack stood up. "Rabbi, I can only say one thing, and you must believe me. What I did was because I thought it was for the good of the congregation. May God strike me down if there was any other reason. I swear to you!"

Rabbi stared at him, at the contorted face, the frantic eyes, the true misery of the man. He turned away for a moment before he spoke.

"I believe you."

Neither spoke then for a long time. Finally Rabbi sat down, his head back in the chair, his eyes on nothing on the ceiling, on space, on worlds out of sight. He sighed at last and then he straightened up.

"I will come, Jack." And he looked at the waiting, almost forlorn figure of the man. "As you have said: for the good of the congregation."

And the congregation for whose good all was being done, prepared itself carefully and exuberantly for the event. The men checked their tuxedos and dinner jackets to see if they still fitted or buttons were missing or if they needed pressing or cleaning, and some who had to rent them discovered that they were all gone from the tailor shops in Greenlake and they had to go to Lanebrook to obtain them. The women who bought new gowns in New York had made sure they would be delivered in plenty of time, but there were many who were still shopping in the little dress shops on Main Street as late as Saturday afternoon. The hairdresser appointments had been made long ago and the beauty salons were crowded all day and the women emerged with light scarves over their stiff and formal hairdos and drove home with the windows closed so as to protect them. Some people even had their cars washed that morning, as if in the parking lot too they would be judged.

The Sprucewood Country Club was decorated with streamers and colored paper balls and each table had a huge green candlestick from Israel (to be taken home by a lucky winner), and when people began to arrive at eight o'clock and check their coats and mink stoles and wraps, everyone reflected a sense of excitement and anticipation. There was no question it was going to be a big night, a historic occasion for the Jewish community of Greenlake.

Rabbi and Frieda didn't arrive until nine. He had put on his tuxedo almost with the feeling of a soldier preparing himself for battle at the front, a sense of going to face the enemy. Frieda had insisted years ago that he buy a tuxedo and her argument had simply been that it was a gesture, a concession to the congregation. "You ask certain things of them, that they follow your ways and accept your values. Then show them that you're big enough to go along with their ways too in certain things. They'll respect you for it." Buying that tuxedo had been a significant symbolic act on his part.

Now he looked at himself in the mirror, the stiff, uncomfortable figure awkwardly compressed into the absurd social uniform, his face like a strange, unrelated object on a body he didn't recognize, and he was tempted to tear off the whole ridiculous, repulsive outfit. But Frieda was watching him and smiling. Her blond hair combed neatly, her red evening gown hanging gracefully in a straight line to the floor, she stood beside him and took his arm. She nodded to their image in the mirror.

"We don't make such a bad-looking couple, David."

"You look nice, Frieda."

"And so do you." She squeezed his arm. "David—I know. Don't you think I know? But—" she held his hands and looked into his troubled face, "let's do it for us. Let's act as if nobody there matters except us. You and I are going to a dance. All right?"

"That's quite a fantasy."

"So we'll act out a fantasy tonight. Will you—" she kissed him gently, "do it for me?"

At the entrance to the big dining room of the Club stood Bob Barrett, Elaine, and Jack Stern to greet the guests. Frieda held Rabbi's arm tightly as they approached them, and the ordeal was over in seconds.

"Rabbi." Bob's hand. A nod to him.

"Rabbi." Elaine's tight grip. A nod.

"Rabbi, thank you." Jack's hand. Another nod.

Now they were in the midst of it, the smiles, the greetings, the handshakes, the noise, the scents, the looks, the inspection of each other's gowns and jewels, the comments, the motion, the chatter, the music, the dancing, the contact, the gaiety. And under it, in him, the reality of his own misery, the bitterness, the cruelty, the rejection, the hatred . . . and the inevitability and hopelessness of it all.

At nine-thirty, just before dinner was served, Bob Barrett made the band stop and stood in front of it to make an announcement.

"Ladies and gentlemen!" Gradually the moving bodies turned to him, the voices lowered and then silent, until finally everyone was waiting and listening. "I have three very brief announcements to make. One is that we are here to eat and dance and enjoy ourselves— so there will be no speeches, no formalities." Laughter and applause.

"The second is that the big event of the evening, the drawing of the lucky number that wins the automobile, will take place at ten-thirty." Cries of anticipation and applause.

"And the third is more serious. As we all know, our beloved Lou Mandel is in the hospital right now. Lou, as Chairman of the Building Committee, has probably done more for the cause which brings us all here—the building of our Temple—than any other member of the congregation. I don't have to say to any of you how sad we all feel that he has had this misfortune. I know—and he knows—how much our hearts are with him and how great and deep is our wish for his speedy recovery. I would now like to read a telegram Lou has sent us from the hospital: 'Dear Friends. This is a big night and a happy occasion for all of us. Let it remain as such. I send you all my sincerest wishes for a wonderful evening of joy and celebration, and my deepest thanks for helping to achieve our goal, the building of our Temple. Lou Mandel.' "

A few quick gestures at misty eyes in the brief silence that followed, then applause.

"So, my friends," Barrett continued, "with Lou's blessings, let us carry on, have fun, eat, dance, and enjoy! God bless you all!"

The band resumed, dinner was served, the party went on. Rabbi discovered that he and Frieda were expected to sit at what was designated as the Number One table, the place of honor, and that the couple sharing the table with them would be Bob and Elaine Barrett. It had all been arranged weeks before.

The four of them now faced each other in a few moments of helpless disbelief and horror. It was too late to do anything about it. Each of them realized that any overt move to change tables would be noticed. They stood in silence, confronting each other, paralyzed by their emotions.

"We might as well sit down," Frieda said. She was looking at Rabbi. He nodded to her. They all sat down, sharing the agony of tension and embarrassment.

Rabbi felt as if there was a physical pressure on him from every direction, an assault from everywhere, all at once, everything. There was no turning away, no escape. All around him the faces, bodies, eyes, the sense of being watched, observed, commented upon, judged. If he frowned or smiled, ate or didn't eat, talked or sat in silence, it was all being noted, interpreted, evaluated. Rabbi looks funny in that tuxedo. Rabbi's got a sour expression tonight. Rabbi never talks to his wife. Rabbi needs a shave. Rabbi chews his food a long time. And what did it all matter? This wasn't him they were looking at. This was a creature they had dressed up and brought here to display for their own benefit, their own needs. To make them feel they had a Rabbi who belonged and was one of them.

At his side, in a quiet turmoil of emotion, sat Frieda. He could feel the vibrations of anxiety from her, the awkward tenseness in her body. Her mouth formed a meaningless, anguished effort at a smile. Her eyes darting at him every other moment. He knew her heart felt for him, that she wanted with all her soul to help him somehow, reassure him, give him strength. And her silence was like a prayer for him. So much devotion and involvement. It was almost a burden for him. And yet, out of pity and understanding for her, he felt a need to respond to it. And at the bottom somewhere, he felt gratitude. It was all for him! All for love of him! All her being was mixed with his and suffering for him. He reached out, during a moment when her hand was in her lap, and squeezed it. She didn't look up or at him, but kept her face down. She swallowed, as if to keep the emotion in, and he could see her eyes glisten.

Elaine never looked at him. She sat with her eyes on her plate, on her hands in her lap, on her food, on some dark opening before her into which she might plunge to escape. She wasn't in her seat. She was running like a desperate creature from the horror of it. She was far away, running running running as far as it was possible to go so that no words or thoughts could reach her.

Bob Barrett's jaws never stopped moving, chewing, the muscles pulsing, the teeth clenched together tightly to hold everything in that wanted to be uttered.

Rabbi knew it was all part of the pretense that had to be preserved. The table of honor. The Rabbi and his wife, the President of the congregation and his wife. The leaders of the Jewish community. It was expected. It was as it should be.

But wasn't. Why should the deception be maintained, observed, protected? Rabbi's bitterness and anger were like a living thing inside he had to answer to. Something in him kept demanding an explanation that he couldn't provide. Not by saying "for the good of the congregation." Because he knew their good was elsewhere. What was good for them was not this pretense, but the truth.

And yet, who could dare say it was better to let them know the truth? Shock them, upset them, ruin this whole event, create a scandal, now, here? With all his heart he wanted to expose it all! His mind ached to shout it. Your Rabbi is being thrown out. Your Rabbi is being lied about, condemned for no reason! You ought to know! Let me tell you—now! Now!

And then, after a struggle, he would look around him and see everywhere the innocence of their joy, the happiness, the warmth. Look at them, he said to himself, look how they are enjoying this evening. The women as attractive as they could make themselves, proud of their gowns, their hairdos, their elegance, loving this opportunity to display their taste, admiring each other, glowing with the excitement of it. The men all more handsome somehow, formal, even standing differently, more dignified, more imposing. The festive quality of everything in the room, the very atmosphere, the happy sounds, the swirling richness of color, the sensuousness, the pleasure. And they knew it was not just another dance at the country club. It was for a cause, for the Temple, for what they believed in and wanted. How could he even dream of destroying it all?

The bitterness, the irony, the tragedy were his alone. He sensed now more than before his failure to be truly with them, one of them. For some cursed reason he couldn't be part of this in the same way they were. No matter how much he had tried and wanted to, he couldn't overcome the sense of separateness, his feeling there was something superficial about all this, that it wasn't meaningful. And he thought, sitting there, watching them eat, listening to their laughter and talk, seeing their pleasure, if only he had known how to enter into such things with their spirit, if only he had been their kind of person. . . .

When the dinner was finished and people everywhere rose to dance Barrett and Rabbi stood face to face and finally looked at each other. Barrett lost the battle for control.

"Rabbi, I want your answer."

"Now? Here?"

"What's the difference? I want it!"

"I have none yet."

Barrett moved closer. People were watching them. "I told the Executive Committee you would give me an answer at once. I want it."

"What you told—"

"Will you answer?" The words came out from between his teeth. If he could have raised his arms and choked the answer out of the other's throat he would have done it.

"No. You will have to wait."

"Then we will decide without your answer."

"If you do, I will bring it all out into the open. Everything."

"You wouldn't dare! It would destroy you!"

"And I'll—" He clenched his fists tightly. He was aware suddenly of the whirling inside him. This was too much! Unbelievable! How could this be done to him? Why control it now? Why not shatter the whole damn lie of it! Break it all apart! Now! Here! Why go on? He took a deep breath. His anger like a creature inside, at his throat, was choking him, pressing the air from his chest. He felt dizzy.

Drum beating, suddenly. The cymbals like an explosion of angry metal. Jack Stern stood in front of the band, his arms raised for silence and attention. Everyone stopped and turned.

"Ladies and gentlemen—the big moment is here! We're going to have the drawing for the grand prize—and what a prize it is! A brand new, shiny new, gorgeous Ford Mustang! Here are the keys!" He held up the dangling keys. "Who's going to be the lucky winner? We're going to find out right now! Everybody—look at your ticket—and start praying!"

Laughter, applause, tense anticipation. Jack picked up a huge glass bowl and set it on the table in front of the band stand.

"And to draw the lucky number, to award this grand prize to the winner, I now ask Rabbi Gordon to step forward! Rabbi Gordon—"

Applause. All faces turned to him. Everyone was waiting.

Rabbi stood, unable to move, his whole body suddenly cold. A total numbness in him. Everything blurred. Faces, bodies, colors. The silence had a pulse. Faces all revolving about each other like colored balls in the air. His heart pounded.

It was too much! Too much! Shout then, damn it! *Shout!* Oh you fools! You idiots! What are you doing to me?

They were waiting. Frieda touched his hand, and he was startled. Where did she come from? Where was he? Where was his body?

He heard Jack's voice from far away. "Rabbi Gordon, will you do us the honor now?"

He stumbled. A hand supported his arm to help him. Whose?

Oh God how incredible! How stupid and cruel and ugly and hateful! Oh God why? *Why?*

He was in front of them now. Round and round the faces whirled, colored balls with dots for eyes.

Silence. Waiting.

"As your Rabbi—" The words and what they meant to him—not to them—carried him through the misery enveloping him and shutting off the world, "as your Rabbi, I am glad to be able to help you perform the sacred function [he couldn't make it come out clearly,

but he kept trying] for which you have chosen me—which tonight—
is the choosing of a lucky person who will have the luck to win [was
he making sense? he had to keep going!] an automobile for his glory
and pleasure. . . ."

Jack was holding the bowl in front of him and shaking it with
both hands and whispering: Okay, Rabbi. Now. Go on. Go on!

He put his hand in the bowl and the cards felt wet and hard at the
same time. His fingers closed on something and he withdrew his hand.

Oh, all you faces staring at me! What do you see? What do you
know? Am I your Rabbi now? Is this what you want from me? I will
do it! I will do it!

A great cry from the crowd as Jack read the name on the card.
Applause and laughter and joy. He had bestowed some greater glory
on them. He had made it possible as their Rabbi. See—I am your
Rabbi! As you want me! Bestowing upon you the great, shiny, chrome-
plated gifts of the Lord!

He went home with Frieda a few minutes later, and all he could
remember was the smiling faces all around him as he walked through
the room, nodding to him, approving, accepting, shaking his hand,
thanking him, grateful to him, saying Good night, Rabbi. Good night.
Take care of yourself. Thank you, Rabbi. Thank you!

For what? He kept asking himself as he tossed in bed. For what do
they thank me? Oh God—is that what they want from me?

RABBI 9

Once, it seemed a long time ago now and unlikely, Bob Barrett had stood by the Rabbi's side and had played a strong role in a difficult situation.

The Jews in Greenlake knew that a racial revolution was going on, or at least some of them talked about it, but the excuses they had offered when Rabbi made his suggestion amazed him. How revealing they were, he thought. How much they said about the Jews' own insecurity. How superficial their dedication to justice and brotherhood could become when they felt their own position threatened.

The question was simple. Rabbi wanted to invite James Baldwin, the Negro writer, to speak to the congregation at one of the Friday night services. Was this a wise and proper thing to do?

They sat in the Barretts' living room that evening, surrounded by the conventional signs and comforts of wealth, and discussed their relationship to the Negro as if it were a matter of logistics. Barrett, Brody, Dr. Greenwald, and Rabbi. It wasn't a formal meeting, Barrett called it a "guidance session." They were merely exploring the subject together.

"To begin with," Rabbi said, "Baldwin is a writer. An important contemporary novelist and essayist. Whether he's a Negro or not."

"But Rabbi," Barrett seemed surprised, "surely you realize that no Negro writer today functions only as a writer. If he were to come to talk to us, he would talk to us as a Negro. Our inviting him would be considered giving a platform to the Negro viewpoint."

"And is that wrong?" Rabbi studied their faces. "Don't we, as Jews, support the Negro struggle, want to help them?"

"Ah—" Dr. Greenwald nodded his head wisely, "support—yes. Want to help—yes. But become involved with as a body, as a congregation, officially and formally—that we must consider carefully."

"Consider what?" Rabbi knew the area of sensitivity and he wanted to bring it out in the open.

"Come now, Rabbi. You know as well as we do. The town of Greenlake isn't exactly laying out a welcome mat for the Negro. Unfortunate no doubt, but true. Bob—" he turned to Barrett, "there are how many Negro families in Greenlake? Four? Five?"

"Something like that," Bob answered. "Living near the railroad station. Probably the smallest Negro ghetto in the state. And not likely to grow if the town can help it."

"So that—" Greenwald continued, explaining patiently to Rabbi, but also wanting to clarify the whole situation for everybody, "—we know the sentiment here, the hostility. Which we deplore, mind you. But which we must deal with. And inviting Mr. Baldwin to talk to us, however great his literary reputation, would be considered a provocative act by them."

"By them—you mean the gentiles." Rabbi was unable to hide his irritation.

"Yes, the gentiles. The community. The people among whom we must live and function as good neighbors."

Rabbi rubbed his chin hard, trying to think of how to cope with this. Here it was. The insecurity, the desire not to provoke hostility, the anxiety about being accepted as "good neighbors," and the willingness to sacrifice ethics and ideals to gain that acceptance.

"Gentlemen, is it as simple as this: we, the Jews of Greenlake, will not dare to do what is right—if it offends the prejudiced whites of this town?"

Now Bob shifted about in his chair with some annoyance. "Rabbi, that is a simplification. As Jews—as individual Jews—we are entitled and perhaps even obliged to do all we can to help the Negro cause. That's our tradition, and God knows Jews have been doing it for years and years. But this congregation cannot take an official position. In the first place, we don't all have identical views on the subject. Secondly, it would endanger our relationship with the community. And we are at a stage here where we're trying to build up that relationship, not destroy it."

Brody coughed, shifted in his chair, and spoke up finally. "I want to say something about this. Let's not kid ourselves. Like Bob said, we Jews have been helping the Negro all we can. Money, all kinds of ways. But there's a new thing around that's maybe going to change that a little bit. Or more than a little bit. I mean this anti-Semitism among the blacks. Are we afraid to talk about it? Well, I'm not! When these blacks start attacking Jews—and I mean *attacking*, like they've been doing—I don't give a damn about helping them. That's asking too much. Help them? Hell, I think we've got to stop some of them! Stop them cold—before we find out that it's we who need help!"

"Harry—" Rabbi had turned on him, "you're talking about a tiny minority, a small—"

"What do I care how small? It's small now—who says it won't grow? At a time like this, I don't want to invite *any* Negro to the Temple!"

"Baldwin is a writer. A literary man!"

"Black as any of them. Feels black, and he'll talk black!"

"I think," Barrett now wanted to sum it up, pull away from this whole area which was too sensitive to discuss this way, "I think our conclusion is this, Rabbi. We will not invite your Mr. Baldwin for the reasons given. The Jewish community will not put itself in that position. As individuals, we have the right to follow our conscience. And as Rabbi of this congregation, I trust you will not only understand what is involved, but act with good judgment and discretion. . . . I think that's about it, gentlemen. Ready for coffee?"

Rabbi gave up without a fight that evening for a reason he couldn't admit to them. The truth was that when he had heard that James Baldwin might be willing to speak at the Temple, he had seized on the idea as an opportunity, a means. Of course Baldwin was a novelist and essayist, but obviously he would talk about more than literature. And by slipping him in as a literary figure, Rabbi had hoped to accomplish what he was really after. Which was to awaken this collection of comfortable, well-established Jews to an involvement with the Negro struggle.

For how could the Jew behave otherwise? How could these people, whose entire history was of a struggle to survive as a minority, feel anything but total identity with the sufferings of this minority? How could they be more concerned with their "image" in a gentile community than with their role in the racial crisis? In fact, how could they celebrate the deeds of their own martyrs and heroes and fanatics, and hesitate to support such people who were battling in a similar tradition for the Negroes?

In his frustration and bewilderment, Rabbi felt a need to talk about it, to discuss it with an outsider, and he went to Father Lemassey's home one evening and sat with him and poured out his confusion.

"How is it, Father, that you have been able to enlist some of the members of your church in activities to help the Negro? And I have such a struggle to engage mine?"

Lemassey, who liked and admired Rabbi and felt a certain kinship with him, leaned over and patted his hand. "Rabbi, let me say first that you and I are different men. You are like a prophet, I am like a priest. You see the distant goal, I see the practical way. You demand of your people that they be better than they are, I ask only that the good in them be expressed. So your people have to undergo an inner struggle to follow you. Mine have only to make up their minds."

"But Father, our people *are* different. We have been beaten and persecuted and destroyed for generations. This is part of us. We must respond to that and be guided by it in what we do."

"Ah, Rabbi," Lemassey shook his head gently, "not everyone who has almost drowned is ready to plunge into the water to save another. It is the very terror of it that may prevent him."

Rabbi sighed and leaned back wearily and Lemassey refilled his glass of beer. Rabbi looked at him gratefully, and then asked:

"This is a strange thing to do, Father. I come to you, a priest, and I ask you for advice."

"We stand in the same place, Rabbi."

"Father Lemassey, tell me! I must do something about this. What is there to do?"

"I would say," Lemassey leaned back, his eyes upward, his fingertips together, tapping each other as he pondered, "I would say to do exactly what your Mr. Barrett suggests. Act as an individual."

"How?"

"Well now, Rabbi," and it was as if Lemassey had been preparing him for this all along, "they cannot say no to you if you as an individual do something for the Negro. Can they, Rabbi?"

"Do what?"

"Ah, there are many things. And it so happens," he stood up and fetched a letter from his desk which he glanced over quickly, "that there is something quite specific to be done." His eyes ran up and down the letter again. "Hmm. Let me see now. Well, it seems there's going to be a meeting in our adjoining community of Lanebrook this Wednesday night. A sort of protest-organizational meeting. Open to everyone, but set up by the Negro groups in town. I'm not sure of the purpose—" he glanced over the letter again, "it says: 'to prepare and organize for action to obtain our rights and satisfy our just demands.' Which is a rather general aim, but conveys the idea, don't you think?"

"It could be interesting."

"Ah—" Lemassey put the letter down in front of Rabbi, "it could also be significant. Lanebrook, our poor cousin of a town, our non-suburban suburb, is surely on the edge of something. Do you know there are nine thousand Negroes living there, in a total population of thirty thousand?"

"Isn't it sad, Father, how we naturally deduce from such a statistic that it means trouble?"

"Isn't it sad that in our society it can only mean trouble?"

"You're going to the meeting, Father?"

Lemassey pouted out his lips, stared at Rabbi, and then smiled. "I think I've just decided to go. With you, Rabbi."

They shook hands, two men in perfect understanding, both feeling a kind of defiance that was very satisfying.

Rabbi didn't feel it necessary to inform anyone officially, the Committee or the Board, that he was going. After all, wasn't he acting as an individual? As they had agreed everyone could? He sat with Father Lemassey toward the back of the school auditorium, and as the crowd began to gather he realized that only a half a dozen whites would show up, if that many.

And he felt a total stranger there, which shocked and distressed him. How indicative it was that even the mere physical presence of these people, their appearance and manner and voices and expressions were so startling and unfamiliar to him. Why is it that the Negro whom we must help, the Negro we must identify with, the Negro who is our brother—is so completely unknown and strange to us! Because there is no contact? No actual physical relationship? The servant in the house, the handyman, the delivery boy, the women in front of the drug store waiting to be picked up as maids—what else of the Negro did a white man in Greenlake ever see?

Rabbi looked at them now with the intensity of discovery, watching them come down the aisles and take their seats. Poorly dressed laborers, some in overalls, blue work shirts. Fat women in loose house dresses. Others startlingly beautiful, exotic, long necks, proud faces, smartly dressed, very assured of themselves. Children in dirty makeshifts or the brightness of sweaters and shirts, laughing and tugging at each other, sucking their thumbs, crying, squirming about. Young boys in swinging outfits, pendants, silver rings on their fingers, disdain on their faces, aloofness, not with their elders at all, but here to observe, take it in, sit in cool judgment. Girls in miniskirts and tight sweaters, their breasts moving as they moved about, giggling, talking, eyes dancing. Men in prosaic business suits, serious looking, solid.

It was as if he were seeing the race for the first time, sensing its identity, its variety, its tension, its vitality. He turned to Father Lemassey and whispered.

"We whites don't know these people. Not really. Do we?"

Lemassey smiled. "Not the way they know us, that's for sure."

When the auditorium was about three-quarters full and it was almost nine o'clock, the meeting began. And as Rabbi listened to speaker after speaker, he sensed a feeling of disappointment, a letdown, not only in himself, but in the rest of the audience. A woman complained about the housing situation in Lanebrook. The neglect, the dirt, the inadequate toilet facilities, the broken-down refrigerators. An elderly teacher spoke about the low level of schooling, the crowded rooms and oversized classes, out-of-date texts, the failure to provide the needed extra help and guidance for children of families who had recently come to Lanebrook from the South. Men spoke of the lack of good jobs, doors closed to better positions. The banks that wouldn't give credit. Merchants who overcharged. Police who were tougher on them than on whites. A town administration that didn't care, that turned its back on them, that had no plans, no program to satisfy their needs.

It was an outpouring of complaint, frustration, rejection, anger, and the audience received it all knowingly, nodding heads, grunting agreement, expressing approval. But what else? Was this all? A public self-examination? An outlet for their misery?

Rabbi was wondering and waiting. Something more had to come. Even the resolutions that were voted on and passed with mild cries of enthusiasm—a delegation to the Mayor, a committee to meet with the landlords, a watchdog group on the merchants, a petition to the school board—even these were a mere channeling of their frustration, a search for little packages to put it all in.

The meeting was about to end when a young man of about twenty-five approached the microphone slowly, almost solemnly, with an air of certainty about him, and stood there a few moments with both arms raised in the air, waiting for silence. Light-blue turtleneck sweater, a pendant against his chest like the V-sign of his attitude, the African hairdo curved tightly, bright eyes going back and forth across the auditorium, he waited.

And suddenly it was felt. The silence was a drawing in, an expectation, a readiness. Here it comes. Now.

"Ready?" He smiled. They nodded and applauded out of the tenseness of anticipation. "Well! Well, like man—we've done it, huh? We had ourselves a meeting. Good for us! So we blacks finally got together in this here pretty little high school auditorium. And we belched. And we farted. Good and loud. And man, do we feel better now! Right?" He paused, staring into their faces. Then down came his fist on the podium. "Shit! I say shit to all this self-expression we've been tickling ourselves with! Who're we kiddin'?

"I'll tell you who. Ourselves! Man—where's this gonna get us? Committees, delegations, petitions—begging? 'Cause that's all it is. Begging! We're still in the begging stage here in Lanebrook. And let me tell you something—that puts us Lanebrook blacks one hundred years back! Anybody here thinks this meeting represents progress—I mean progress that's going to bring results—he's not only deluding himself, he's doing us all harm! I say harm because he's making us fool ourselves. He's making us keep on taking the shit we've been taking!

"I say—you want to have committees, delegations, petitions, okay, have 'em. But that's not going to produce results, and we all know it in our big black bones! Don't we?"

Yells. Yes! You're so right, man! You're right!

"So I'm here to tell you what we gotta do—like man, what we absolutely gotta do! We gotta show we have reached a new stage, we have got up to a new level, we have risen to a new height of determination! We have got to scare the living daylights outta whitey in this town! We're not kidding no more. We're not crawling, we're not begging no more! We are demanding!"

The applause came now, the yells, the cheers, fists raised, out of their seats in a great release. Mouths open, eyes open, hearts open now. Tell us, man! Tell us!

"And we start that right here, right now, tonight! We start marching! We're going to march down Main Street—every black here, all of us!—and show ourselves! Let them see us! Together! We're going to march from here down Main Street and we're going to yell in the street, we're going to holler, we're going to cry out, protest, and demand! And we're going to do it now! Are you with me?"

The wild full yell came, the answer like an explosion.

"Then follow me!"

Rabbi looked at Lemassey. "It had to happen." Lemassey stood up beside him. "This may be interesting."

"Are you—" Rabbi was a little uncertain now, "going to march with them?"

"I'm not very good at yelling—but I can walk all right." He looked at Rabbi searchingly. "And you, Rabbi?"

He felt the impulse, the sense of participation, the joining with the flow of emotion all around him. "I'm with you!" He laughed uncertainly.

"With them, Rabbi."

Straggling at first, confused, the mass moved out of the building, standing, waiting, then slowly beginning to move, closer, tighter, finally as a unit. Down the middle of the street they went, stopping the cars, through the lights, marching, shouting, arms raised, fists shaking, calling out to everyone who was there, to all who were not there and must hear the cry too, bursting to cry out, say it, show it, proclaim it!

Now they moved under the highway ramp, the intersection of dark streets, with traffic stopped, cars honking, policemen's cars suddenly piercing in from all directions with roof lights whirling in red-eyed anger. There were whistles, yells against the cops, the whites, the world as they continued down the street of big iron-gated store windows, the dark closed doors like the silent enemy staring at them.

Now suddenly new sounds were heard. The clatter of glass broken, wild cries, the metal bars and fences pulled down like hated jail walls, more glass crashing to the sidewalks.

"No looting! No looting! There must be no looting!" The leaders ran up and down, shouting, pushing back, trying to control it. But the kids were grabbing, taking, running. Watches, shoes, radios, clothes, TV sets, liquor, luggage, chairs. Most of the others watched, shouting at them, but were incapable of stopping it. Little groups darted in and out of stores, quickly, laden, running.

Now the police arrived, in twos and threes side by side, swinging, holding bodies, throwing them to the street. The marchers scattered, cursing the bastard cops, even the black cops, the brutal bastard cops. They ran to the side streets with arms over their heads for protection, the women clutching their children, carrying them, the old men moaning, the march forgotten, broken, ended. It was everyone for himself now. This way, quick! Get away! Run! Beat it, man! Go!

Rabbi and Father Lemassey had stopped at the first sound of breaking glass and at the sight of small groups entering stores, breaking doors open. Lemassey had tried, with arms raised, to call to them: "Don't loot! March! This is a march!" Rabbi shouted something, but his voice was weak, he could hardly hear it himself. No one turned to listen. Father Lemassey grabbed Rabbi's arm, shaking his head, sadness and bitterness in his voice. "Rabbi, this is not for us. We can do nothing. Let's go."

They both walked quickly back to the high school parking lot, pushing through the crowd that didn't even see them, and found their cars and drove home to Greenlake.

All the local newspapers called it a "riot" and condemned it. Some pointed out that of the seven stores broken into and looted, six were Jewish-owned, and then implied or bluntly concluded that anti-Semitism had been involved as well as just plain black protest. They also printed the statements from several Negro "leaders," all of whom stressed that the rioting and looting was the work of a few wild youngsters, and that the responsible Negro citizens of Lanebrook considered it deplorable.

But then there was also an altogether different kind of statement that some of the papers had obtained in interviewing the young man who had actually conceived of the march and urged it on the people at the meeting. His name was Gayne Radcliffe, and his remarks were not only not apologetic, but there was pure defiance in them. Phrases like: "An explosion means there's something that has to explode. . . . Looting is wrong, but it's done because of wrongs that have been inflicted on the looters. . . . The Jewish stores were there—that's why they got it. . . . Waking up a community to the existence of injustice can't be done without the shock of awakening."

And many people who read his words felt that he was not only justifying and defending what had happened, he was posing a threat to them. It could happen again.

Most of the Jewish community in Greenlake responded with a nervousness that didn't even have to be expressed. Jewish stores picked out by Negroes for looting, Jewish merchants ruined, anti-Semitism in its new cloak of horror—black. They muttered about it, shook their heads, groaned and sighed and uttered some of their anger to each other. But all of them knew that something else was happening too. Inside each of them, a touching of the nerve of terror. An awakening of covered-over fears, put deep away, locked up, but never, never gone, never out of their secret awareness. It was anti-Semitism, and black or green or blue or white, it produced that clutch at the heart, that bitterness, that anxiety, that agony and anger that was always there in every Jew.

Rabbi called Barrett and told him that he and Father Lemassey had been at the meeting as "individuals." He described how it had developed and what he had seen happen. But his purpose in calling went beyond just making a report. He had an idea.

"What do you think, Bob, is the sentiment in the congregation about last night?"

"Anger, naturally. They picked out Jewish stores. And some of our people are a little scared, I'd say."

"I want to do something, Bob, that I think will be important and valuable. That will help us, as Jews, in dealing with such things. I want to invite that young Negro leader, Radcliffe, to address our congregation at Temple this Friday."

"What? My God, what for?"

"To hear what he has to say. To explain it from his side. And for him to know what we think and feel about it. A dialogue, a discussion. Let it all be aired, in the open. It will help the Negroes know what they have aroused, what such action produces as a reaction. And it can help us, as Jews, to get at certain truths we have to face—and might have to live with."

Bob realized, despite all his instincts against "inviting trouble," that Rabbi's idea might just work. It would not only provide an outlet for the expression of the Jews' reaction to this new threat, but it might have an effect on the Negroes, give *them* something to think about. And this was almost like having the Negro leader of the riot face his victims and accusers, a court of justice.

"You'll have a mob there, Rabbi."

"As long as they don't act like a mob."

"It's not going to be a gentle, polite discussion. There's a lot of anger here."

"On both sides. Let's go find out what's behind it."

"Rabbi, we'd be doing it in Lanebrook, since of course we don't have our own Temple. That's right on the scene."

"Is there a better place to settle a conflict than on the battlefield?"

"Okay! Let's do it, Rabbi. Let's do it—and pray it doesn't get out of hand."

"Right. And I would like you to be chairman of the discussion. Because I may want to speak, ask questions, and a chairman shouldn't do that."

"God help me—I'm a little scared of this—but I'm with you."

More than four hundred people showed up that Friday night and there was a restlessness among them as they crowded together into the seats, exchanging knowing looks and comments, their emotions prepared, stored up like ammunition, anger, bitterness, fear, waiting to let it all loose on this creature who had reached into them and touched that ancient, trembling nerve.

At eight-thirty exactly, Rabbi, Barrett, and Gayne Radcliffe walked out on the platform and the crowd became silent with a startling suddenness, as if a huge cold hand pressed down upon their hearts.

Radcliffe wore a close fitting suit, a white turtleneck, and looked startlingly dramatic. Vigorous, erect, calm, confident. His face expressed nothing, except perhaps a kind of serious thoughtfulness. But he revealed no reaction to the size of the crowd, to the Temple, to the atmosphere. During the services, he rose and sat down when everyone did, and seemed to listen with a remote interest, but showed no curiosity. Obviously, it already seemed to many who were studying him intently, he was intelligent and good mannered and sophisticated.

Finally the moment. "Instead of a sermon tonight," Rabbi said, "we are going to have a discussion. We have as our guest Mr. Gayne Radcliffe. Mr. Radcliffe was the organizer and the leader of the Negro protest march the other night that had such unexpected and unfortunate consequences. Since I plan to participate in the discussion, Bob Barrett has agreed to act as chairman for the evening."

Barrett was as calm as anyone could ever remember him. Poised, in perfect control.

"Ladies and gentlemen, Mr. Gayne Radcliffe has agreed to come here tonight for two reasons. One is, he feels he has something to tell us that we, as Jews, should know. The second reason is that he wants to hear what we have to say about it. And by 'it,' we don't just mean the riot that took place on Wednesday. We also mean all the larger issues and questions involved—black anti-Semitism, Negro-Jewish relations, Negro protest, Jewish involvement, the whole subject that troubles all of us.

"Mr. Radcliffe has agreed to this procedure: he will speak for about half an hour or so. Then there will be questions and discussion. One more thing: that Mr. Radcliffe has agreed to come here, that so many of you have turned out to hear him, is already the beginning of something, a step in the right direction. Let us keep that in mind throughout this evening. . . . I now present Mr. Gayne Radcliffe."

He walked up to the podium slowly, almost leisurely, and then stood there a while looking down at them with a kind of questioning expression.

"You know something? I don't know what you're expecting of me. I been sitting here and trying to think: what're these good people expecting of me? What have they come to hear?

"It can't be an apology, that's for sure! You don't think I'm coming to a Jewish Temple to apologize for my people having hurt a couple of Jews by breaking in their stores? Because you're getting no apology from me—and I figure you know that.

"What then? An explanation? Why it happened the way it happened? Why some blacks let themselves go? Broke windows? Stole? Looted? . . . All I got to say on that is—it happened because it happened. Dynamite explodes because it's got the power to explode. It's built in, you get me? And we blacks got that exploding power built into us. It's there, man—and it's been stored away in us a mighty long time now.

"No . . . I figure these good people come to hear me tell 'em—why the *Jews?* Isn't that right?" He smiled, and it was almost a kindly smile. "Why you're exploding against us Jews? Aren't we your friends? Ain't we been giving money for the good cause of civil liberties? How come you picked us now?

"And here's the answer, folks. We're picking you—because you are there! Man, you are there! We're not looking for you, not searching you out—we just turn around—and you are there!

"Where? In the stores. In the shops. In the houses. In the schools. In the whole damn power structure! You are part of it, you're holding on to it, you're protecting it—and we're moving in on it!

"Black power? You heard that, now haven't you? Black power! Let me explain that very simply. Black power means just that we blacks want in on the power structure. Every damn part of it! Businesses in town making money? We want in! Shops opening up? We want in. Jobs being handed out, contracts being awarded, graft passing around, politics being played, dirty deals going on, big dough, little dough, legitimate or illegitimate, straight or crooked—we want in on it! Because that power structure is what decides everything. It controls and runs the works—all there is to living. We want to do some of that controlling and deciding. We want our share of that power. The black share. Black power.

"And anybody stands in our way—they're gonna get it! And you folks—you are right there in our way. You Jewish folks got your hands in real deep all over this town. And you holding on tight! Houses, stores, schools—whatever—you're there! So we're hitting you, man!"

For another fifteen minutes he gave it to them as he felt it and knew it. Exploitation by Jewish landlords, job discrimination by Jewish employers, chiseling by Jewish contractors, indifference of Jewish teachers. Wherever it was, if that's what the blacks encountered in their fight for power, that's what had to be attacked.

The audience couldn't wait to answer and argue back. They shifted about, listened, muttered, stared in anger and resentment. And when he had finally finished, his last remark a defiant threat—"So just get out of the way if you don't want to get hurt!"—they let it all loose against him. Voices cried out for the floor, hands were raised and waved, people stood up. Barrett tried to calm them and control it.

The indignant, gray-haired lawyer: "Jews have been oppressed longer than you Negroes! We're a minority and we *support* all other minorities!"

Radcliffe: "Support means nothing! Move aside—and let us in!"

The mother of three children, her voice shaking: "Jews have died helping the civil rights movement!"

Radcliffe: "Old history! How about a couple of Jewish businesses dying so black ones can live!"

The high school student: "If you're against racial prejudice, how can you practice it yourself against Jews?"

Radcliffe: "We are *not* anti-Semitic! Get that straight! Look, man, we're not like some whites who grow up hating Jews without ever having seen one! We're against Jews where the Jews are hurting us. You want us blacks to say: now let's never mind being stepped on because it's a Jew stepping on us?"

The wife of a business executive: "You don't want to work with Jews who want to help you! You reject Jewish help!"

Radcliffe: "Any Jews ever asked Nazis to help save them?"

Voices: "Boo! Horrible! Are you comparing us to Nazis?"

Radcliffe, shouting: "Every oppressor's got a different name—but it hurts the same! Just the same!"

Now people were shouting, coming toward the platform. This was too much! Let him see our anger! Let him know we're not taking Jew-hate from anybody—no matter how he excuses it! Barrett called out, arms raised, asking for order. "Please! Quiet! Let's have order! Let's have a *discussion!*"

Cries of "Why help anti-Semitism? . . . He hates Jews! Let's answer him! Let's show him!" A few tried to calm the others, arguing for reason. He's making a point—listen to him! We have to understand him! Listen! But only a few, and they were brushed aside, silenced. No! We don't listen to hate against Jews!

Rabbi stood now next to Radcliffe, the three of them up there facing the anger, the hurt, the bursting out of fear. When Rabbi could finally be heard, he spoke slowly, saying what he felt was so necessary to say, so important for them to understand.

"Friends, are we unable to face our own guilt? Can we deny that some Jews are exploiting Negroes, are overcharging them, are keeping them in unlivable housing, denying them jobs? And if we are—we must face that! And deal with it!

"Don't you see—if the Negroes find Italians doing this to them, then they fight the Italians! Or Swedes, or Poles, or Catholics—whoever mistreats them and denies them what is theirs? Don't you see that is the lesson we must learn tonight? That we are guilty in so many ways toward the Negro—and that we must have the courage to admit it and remove the cause of that guilt! Don't you see that—"

Shouts of No! No! from all over the auditorium. Anti-Semitism is wrong! No anti-Semitism for any reason! Whose side are you on, Rabbi?

It was over now. It couldn't continue, and Barrett was calling out: "The meeting is over! Friends—please! We're finished. Let's have calm and reason. Let's control ourselves!"

People continued to stand about in groups arguing, talking, shouting, booing. Rabbi could stop it only by starting the final prayer, and when his words came over the loudspeaker, the solemn, heavy-hearted words pleading for peace and understanding, there was a sullen quiet in the room at last, a holding in, a struggle to control the anger.

And late that night, Rabbi alone at home, unable to sit still, unwind, go to bed, so disturbed that he kept pacing back and forth across the room, was thinking: Was Reverend Robertson right, after all? Is the Jew unable to bear the truth about himself? Does he close his heart to an understanding of his own sin? And if the Jew, with his history, his sensitivity, his ethic, if the Jew cannot be truly a brother to the black man—then who?

X

Danny was acting by instinct. From somewhere inside had come this strange guiding force that made him do it that morning. It was as if his anger, his determination to help Rabbi, had transformed him into a schemer, ready to search for help anywhere, by any means, looking for any kind of weapon that could be used.

He saw Joe Resnick on the station platform, the newspaper folded under his arm, staring across the tracks with that dazed, expressionless morning face most of the commuters had as they stood waiting for the 8:14. And suddenly he felt it might be interesting to talk to Joe. It was pure instinct. He couldn't even imagine what he would say to him. Just talk.

Joe grunted a good morning, shuffled his feet, on his face the blank, still sleepy, withdrawn look. They sat down together and both opened their papers, adhering to the respected ritual of no-conversation on the morning train. Politeness, but privacy. Danny turned the pages of his paper casually.

"Joe, you're not with Bob Barrett's agency now, are you?"

"Nope." Eyes on the paper.

"How long since you've been out?"

"Three months."

Silence. The train wheels clicking in continuous comment.

"Get to know him pretty well when you were there?"

For the first time a reaction. Joe looked at him. "Bob is an Exec. V.P. I'm a copywriter. That's a big gap."

Danny looked at Joe intently. "Got an opinion of him? I want to know?"

"Why?"

"Reasons."

Joe smiled, the head shaking a little with the train. Faint bitterness of slight smile.

"I think he's a fucked-up guy. Big success that he is, he's fucked up somewhere."

"That's interesting."

"Oh, a very complex man, Mr. Barrett."

"Tell me more."

Now Joe looked at him. "What is this? Why?"

"An inquiry. Into the character and behavior of Robert Barrett."

"Leading to what?"

"I don't know yet. Maybe it depends on what I find out."

Joe smiled. "I'm your man. Pump me."

"He had you fired, didn't he?"

"Correct. Oh, I screwed up on an account but—let's say he could have saved my job. He didn't."

"A tough man?"

"Not always. Sometimes very helpful and understanding. Then suddenly—boom! I think when he feels threatened. Would you believe Mr. Robert Barrett can feel threatened? . . . What is this? What's up?"

"Joe, I can't tell you. I'm—well, I'm engaged in a little controversy with him."

"And you want ammunition?"

He nodded.

"Do you want ammunition?"

"What kind?"

"Dirty."

"Is there any?"

"I don't know what you can do with it, but I happen to know where one body is buried."

"Whose?"

"A babe's."

"Tell me more."

"Gladly. I worked on the Lily Soap account. The group head was Bea Aldrich. Also a V.P. Also she laid Mr. Barrett. On a regular basis."

"How do you know?"

"Bea and I were good friends."

"She talked about it?"

"Once. When Barrett fired her, I bought her a couple of drinks that afternoon and—"

"He fired her?"

"Five, six months ago. Oh it's over now. Barrett makes clean breaks."

"How long did it last?"

"Two years. Maybe more."

"Where'd they meet?"

"I think her apartment. The lunchtime quickie. Maybe nights too, I don't know. Ask her."

"What?"

"Ask her."

"What do you mean?"

"Danny, what the hell are you up to? You want dirt? Here's dirt. So dig."

"Will she talk to me?"

"She might. Her attitude toward him now is slightly less than favorable."

"What's she like?"

"Nice. Quite a gal. Bright. Regular. Much too good for him."

"This could be embarrassing for her—"

"She doesn't embarrass."

"How do I—"

"—Get in touch with her? Call her. She's at BNB now."

When they reached Penn Station, Danny held out his hand.

"Thanks, Joe. Will you keep this between us?"

"If you let me know someday what it's all about."

"Someday."

"Give my regards to Bea Aldrich." And Joe walked away with the air of a man who had done his good deed for the day.

Miss Aldrich's secretary answered.

"May I ask who's calling?"

"Mr. Cole. She doesn't know me. Please tell her I'm calling at the suggestion of Joe Resnick."

"Mr. Cole?" Her voice was calm, somewhat remote.

"Miss Aldrich? This is Danny Cole. I live in Greenlake and I'm a friend of Joe Resnick's."

"Oh? How is he?"

"Fine."

"Haven't seen him for months. . . . What can I do for you, Mr. Cole?"

"I'd like to see you."

"What about? Are you a writer?"

"No, it's not business."

"Oh?"

"It's—I think I'd rather not explain on the phone. Joe thought we might have a talk together."

"I don't get it. About what?"

"It's rather personal—I mean it's just a friendly talk. Would you mind?"

"Just a minute . . . I'm looking at my calendar. . . ."

"Could it be today, Miss Aldrich?"

"Sorry, no. Got a full day. Meetings, etcetera."

"I meant tonight."

"Oh?"

"If you don't mind. It is rather personal."

"This is beginning to intrigue me. Can you give me a hint?"

"I'm afraid not."

"Hmm! . . . Well . . . Let me see . . . I should be out of here by five-thirty. Do you want to meet me for a drink somewhere?"

"You mean a bar? No, I think it'd better if—"

"Not a bar! Well, well! All right, I'll play the game. You don't sound dangerous. How about you drop over at my place? About six?"

"That would be fine. And I appreciate this very much."

"It's my sense of curiosity, that's all."

"Whatever it is, thank you."

A doorman. Nice lobby. Oriental decor. In a niche, a quizzical Buddha. A chime. Not a buzzer.

She looked very short. A cigarette in her hand like a sixth finger, bare feet, blond hair. Nice impression. Complete self-possession and something cute too. A bright awareness. Her longish green-blue dressing gown was hanging down straight, loose, comfortable.

"Mr. Cole?"

"How do you do?"

"Come in."

A big room with big things. A long glass coffee table, bearing a huge ash tray and big vase of flowers. Over the fireplace, a large, blue, Cezannish still-life and in the fireplace, a big green plant. Fluffs of rugs all over.

"Please sit down."

He picked one end of the couch. She walked straight over to the bar cart against the wall. "Bourbon, Scotch?"

"If you're having one—"

"Of course."

"Scotch. And a little water."

She curled up at the other end of the couch, legs under her, the cigarette drawn on as if for sustenance, and smiled at him.

"Mr. Cole . . . now."

He smiled. "Would you believe it that I don't know where to begin?"

"I might believe it, but I won't accept it. Let's start with Joe Resnick."

"Well, he's a friend sort of, over in Greenlake. But he's really not involved in this." He took a sip of the Scotch. At the name of the town, Greenlake, he had seen her face change. "There's somebody you know there I want to talk to you about."

"Bob?" Calm.

"Bob."

"What did Joe tell you?"

"This is the blunt, frank part, Miss Aldrich. Everything."

"Good old blabbermouth Joe."

"There was a reason. I told Joe I was involved in a controversy with Barrett. He of course is hardly a friend of Barrett's."

"So he told you about me."

"No details. Nothing. Only that—"

"—Only that we were lovers."

Danny swallowed. "You *are* a cool character."

"Let's not be childish, Mr. Cole. If you know, you know. The question is what do you want to do about it? Why are you here?"

"Well, it's not so easy to explain. It has to do with a very complicated situation in Greenlake that—"

"Mr. Cole, why are you here?"

"Miss Aldrich, I want to use this information."

"Forget it." She got up to find another pack of cigarettes, the empty pack crushed in her fist and then flung into the ash tray. She sat down, the legs curled under, the soft little girl pose unrelated to her voice, eyes, words.

"Miss Aldrich, can I ask one thing?"

"You want to use it against him. The answer is no."

"What I want to ask is: will you let me tell you what it's about?"

"It won't matter."

"But please let me tell you."

She looked at him, her head a little to the side. "Mr. Cole, whatever was between Bob and myself was our business. We no longer see each other. It's over. I still respect him. I will do nothing to hurt him."

"Miss Aldrich, could I have another drink?"

"Of course. Mind getting it yourself?"

He walked over to the bar cart crammed with bottles and selected the Scotch. Two ice cubes out of the teak bucket plopped into the glass. Water from the silver pitcher. He took a small sip and walked back.

"Miss Aldrich, can you accept this: I am not trying to hurt Bob Barrett for any personal reasons. I don't even really want to hurt him. I am trying to save a man's life."

"Very melodramatic, Mr. Cole."

"But it's true. And the man whose whole life is at stake, his career, his future, his reputation, all he is—that man is my Rabbi."

"Oh." She looked down for the first time.

"You know something about him?"

The long drag on the cigarette like an inner consultation. "Bob used to tell me about . . . about troubles he had with him."

"Then you must know. It's not just that they don't get along. The situation has reached a crisis. Bob is trying to get rid of him by making him resign."

"Is that wrong?"

"The way he's doing it is wrong. Worse. Cruel, unjust."

"Is that your interpretation of it?"

"Let me tell you . . . and you judge. He is accusing the Rabbi of immoral behavior. Of having an affair with a woman."

She remained silent a long while. "And you assume it's not true."

"I know it's not true."

She let her head fall back against the couch, the pull on the cigarette, the thinking, the long, deep pondering. Or was it a searching for something?

"I think I could use another drink too."

She reached for the glass of bourbon when he brought it and took a gulp at once, as if she needed it badly and couldn't wait. Then she set the glass down on the table, fingering it on the outside, her forefinger along the rim, contemplating something. Her sigh was like the result of a struggle not yet decided in her. Then she took another long drink. She leaned back.

"Mr. Cole, are you saying Bob knows it's not true?"

"About the Rabbi? I must assume that."

"Why!" She snapped angrily. He was startled.

"Because he knows the Rabbi."

"That's no answer!" She was sitting up. She leaned forward and took another gulp. "No answer at all."

"It is, Miss Aldrich, the complete answer. He does know the Rabbi and the kind of man he is. And what he's capable and not capable of doing. Miss Aldrich—" Danny stood up, walked about a bit but with no place to go, "Rabbi Gordon is a dedicated man—dedicated to God and religion and his fellow man. He is the most noble human being I have ever—"

The glass came down on the table with a sharp crack. "Stop it, Mr. Cole. I got the idea. What I'm trying to get at is that you think Bob Barrett would accuse him, knowing he was innocent."

"I have to think so, Miss Aldrich. He has his reasons. They must be enough for him."

"Dammit!" She was up on her feet, the glass to her lips, draining it. She walked over slowly to the bar cart and stood there, hesitating, contemplating herself, perhaps, he thought, evaluating her own motives. Then the decision and she poured it into the glass.

"Sit down, Mr. Cole. I want to talk to you." He backed into the armchair. "I want to talk. I want to talk." She moved about, stopped, took a sip and set the glass down. The next cigarette lit on the remnant of the other.

"Mr. Cole, Bob is a bastard in some ways. He can be mean. But he would not do that! I know it! As much as I know anything. He *must* think your Rabbi is guilty! He can be mistaken, have wrong ideas about it, see things that don't exist. But he believes your Rabbi is guilty! I can swear that to you!"

She plumped down on the couch. A deep pull on the cigarette. "Or—or I really lost my way." She took a slow, long sip. "I think I'm a little drunk."

"That's all right."

"I don't need your approval, Mr. Cole!" A kind of smile at him as she sat back. "I just may decide to get drunk. I just may do that little thing."

He sat watching her, his hands clenched.

"And I don't think I lost my way with Bob." She glanced at him. "You see, Mr. Cole, I am not at all concerned with my morality. I'm not ashamed of anything. If we were lovers, it was because we wanted to be. Reason enough! Because we had a need to be. He certainly had a need, God knows. How hungry he was for it! Aching for it!" She looked at Danny. "Do you know his wife?" Then she jumped up. "Don't tell me about her! I don't want to hear!"

She walked over to the bar cart, and poured into the glass again.

"No, I'll tell *you* about her, Mr. Cole. About *Mrs.* Barrett . . . You see," she was walking about with the drink in her hand, jiggling the ice as an accompaniment to her words and thoughts, "Bob is a fantastic business man. Fantastic! The way he organizes, the smooth way he operates. Everything just so. On the button. Do you know that everybody who works for him feels as if they're in a perfectly controlled universe where nothing ever goes wrong? That's security, Mr. Cole. That's what he gives his people. And he does it by hard work. You have to understand that about him. He believes in it. He works his ass off because that's his nature!

"So—one day—we're in a meeting in his office getting ready for a presentation. Very important to all of us. The agency. Him. A million details to straighten out.

"There's a call from his secretary. Mrs. Barrett is here. He can't believe it. Here? Now? She's waiting outside. Drove up from little old Greenlake to surprise him. Go out to lunch with him. He says please tell her to wait. Very calm. You know how he can be.

"Ten minutes later, Mr. Cole, that door is opened by Mrs. Barrett and she marches in! Right into the meeting, all pretty smiles and she cackles out the words: 'Oh, Bob! Can't you stop for lunch? Must you always work so hard? It's almost one o'clock. I'm sure everyone will understand if you take your own wife to lunch once in a blue moon!'

"We disappeared from that office like from a disaster area. We couldn't get out fast enough. We felt so sick for Bob's sake. We couldn't look at each other.

"That's Mrs. Barrett—devoted, loving, understanding wife, Mr. Cole! So don't tell me about her."

Danny looked down at his hands. "I wasn't planning to."

"All right. . . . So I understood him. The oldest story in history. The wife who doesn't, the mistress who does. Can I help it if I understood him? Knew what he needed? Gave him what he needed? Including in bed? Which is where the giving matters. Not just the taking—the giving!"

She took another sip. "I *am* drunk. Not . . . too drunk. Just enough. Just sweet as hell enough. . . . What are you thinking, Mr. Cole?"

"Nothing."

"You're thinking—why? Why the hell did I do it? And the answer to that is a hundred million words. And maybe that wouldn't be enough. Nobody can tell it all. There's too much. Say—" she looked at him sharply, "aren't you drinking?"

He held up his glass, "Still got plenty here."

"Good." Another long sip. "Too much. Too much. . . . Do you know, for example, that I've been living in blessed singleness for eleven years? When I was thirty-five, my husband died in an accident. Jimmy boy. He was a writer." She turned toward the bookcase, her body twisting back, and waved her arm. "Up there. Two books of his. Novels. A pretty damn good writer, Mr. Cole. . . . And he died . . . and that did it for me. Mr. Upstairs had pulled the plug on me. And I went down that drain all right. The good old eighty-six-proof drain. And then one day I woke up. I realized I wasn't even living. I would come home after work and look around me and say: why? What's the purpose of it all? For what?"

A slow sip, then staring bitterly into the glass as if it held some answer. She finally set it down.

"There is no describing a woman alone—who once was not alone. It's as plain as that. Every act of existence becomes a trap. Cook a meal tonight? Sure, it's something to do. Then to sit and eat it alone. That's hell. Keep the place clean? Dust and vacuum and change the sheets and wipe the blinds and wash the ash trays? You can't let yourself go, can you? Live in filth? Besides, it keeps you busy. . . . Ah, now it's all clean and bright and shiny. . . . And so what? For you alone, all this? And you sit there and cry. Why? Why do it?"

She looked at Danny and smiled. "I had two affairs before I had the one with Bob, Mr. Cole. One was for sex. The other guy loved me and wanted to marry me. But he was a nasty, dominating lawyer type, and he couldn't stand it that I was smarter than he was. Always had to prove he was right.

"Bob, Mr. Cole, Bob was not the answer. He was *an* answer. We sparked each other. In the office, when I worked on his account, I came up with campaigns like I never did before. We made each other tingle with ideas. We got so excited talking, exchanging, arguing, we continued it on through lunch and every minute we could anywhere. . . . And finally here. And finally in bed. And finally in what was a kind of love."

She stood up. "I think I'll have one more." She walked over slowly. "I carry it very well, don't you think? I mean, considering. Speech isn't blurred. Mind is clear. Just the . . . emotion a little stirred up." She poured, took a long sip. "Also, I was on the way to becoming a nice, ladylike lush, and I think Mr. Barrett rescued me from that."

She came back and sat down. Heavily now, wearily. "So that fixing up the place—you see?—was not for me alone anymore. Keeping it bright and shiny. Living was not for me alone. Tomorrow was not alone.

"And even more. It was good. It was warm and, in its way, very decent. We gave to each other. Whatever we had to give, we gave. And let me tell you, Bob gave to me because he wanted to. Thoughtfulness. Consideration. Attention. He would bring me flowers—but not just any flowers. Not something ordered by his secretary. He picked them up himself—big chrysanthemums, which I love. Crazy big bunches of lilacs in the spring.

"He . . . he noticed things. I didn't have a good coffeemaker. He got me the best. A beauty. My record player stank—he got me the latest model, plus new speakers, plus a stack of records this high. Are you getting the picture, Mr. Cole?

"He got me this ring—" she held up her left hand and moved it from side to side to let the light play on it—"this expensive, beautiful, magnificent hunk of gold and rubies. From him to me! . . . He brought wine for dinner every time, what do you think of that, Mr. Cole? The exactly right perfectly chosen beautifully aged French wine every time. Put a filter on that and smoke it, Mr. Cole. That's thoughtfulness. That's sensitivity. That's Bob, see?

"And nothing, Mr. Cole, nothing will make me believe that this man would destroy your Rabbi with a lie. Not with a lie. With arguments, with a clever attack, with power, anger, anything but a lie. And I will never believe it. Never! Not Bob. No! No!" She was shaking her head, crying now, wiping the tears away with her closed fist. "No! I don't believe it!"

Danny shifted in his seat. She looked at him, her smile sour.

"Which is not to say he's not a bastard. Do you know why we broke up? Mr. Barrett decided it was better for his business career! . . . You see, one or two small whispers were spreading through the agency. About us. A little guessing . . . and a little knowing. So good old Charlie Evans, he's Chairman of the Board at Bob's shop, had a little talk with his Executive V.P. If he expected to move up someday, he'd have to be clean. Upright. Untarnished. And crap like that. . . . But even more. Our biggest client, Joseph L. McCardle, the twenty-million-dollar soap and toiletries account, McCardle was a pillar of the church. The holier-than-God type. If he ever got a hint— just a breath of a hint—

"Well, you see, Mr. Cole? As Bob put it to me: I don't have a choice.—Do you think he had a choice, Mr. Cole? He thought he didn't. And that's Bob Barrett, to whom certain situations offer no choice. And that was shitty of Bob Barrett, Mr. Cole! So you know what I really think of him—just in case you got the wrong idea." She leaned back. "Oh God, I'm stoned." She closed her eyes, the cigarette between her fingers forgotten.

Danny stood up and came over to the couch. She opened her eyes, the head turning slightly, and smiled dreamily.

"What is it you want me to do, Mr. Cole?"

"Not hurt Bob. I don't want that. I want you to help me save my Rabbi."

"Bea Aldrich to the rescue! . . . What?"

"You see, all I want, Miss Aldrich, is for Bob to withdraw the accusation. And the request for Rabbi to resign."

"What, Mr. Cole? What do I do?" Impatient, drunk, tired. So tired of it all now.

"I want to—please listen, Miss Aldrich—"

"I'm listening!" Such an effort just to talk.

"I want to go to Bob Barrett and tell him I've met you."

"To give him my regards?"

"Please listen seriously." She nodded, struggling to keep her eyes open. "And then I want to say that if he doesn't withdraw the charge against Rabbi, and the request to resign, I'm going to bring this . . . this business . . . to the attention of the Executive Committee."

"Ah, blackmail! How lovely!"

"Please be serious, Miss Aldrich."

"Am! Am serious!" The head from side to side against the back of the couch.

"And—if he tries to deny it—that you will testify to the truth of it."

"Testify?"

"It's not in court. It's before the Committee. It'll never happen! But all I need is just to tell him that. That's all it'll take. You'll never have to—"

"Lovely! Lovely blackmail! You're doing his bit to him. Exactly his bit. How lovely! . . . Oh Bob Barrett baby, I think you've got this coming to you!"

"Miss Aldrich?"

"Yes?"

"Can I count on you? Can I say that to him?"

"Sure, Mr. Cole. Say it clear and sharp. Say Bea's ready to tell 'em all how he fucked me—and fucked me up. . . . Oh, one thing." She giggled.

"Yes?"

"When you tell him . . ." giggling with silly delight, "tell him I said I had no choice. No choice!" The giggles, with the head from side to side, the smiling, then the face draining, then the silence. Her head down, chin almost on her chest. She raised it with an effort and looked at him.

"Mr. Cole . . . please go. I'm . . . I'm . . . please. . . ."

Danny stood up. "Are you all right?"

"Fine! Never better. Never. . . ."

He stepped back. "I'll get to the door myself."

"Find the way?"

"Sure. You just sit there and rest."

"Sleep."

"Just take it easy."

"Sleep. . . . Sleep. . . . that's . . ."

He was in the doorway. "Goodbye, Miss Aldrich. And thank you. You've done something very—very good."

She waved her arm limply and let it fall on her lap. Her head dropped to a side against the couch.

He went down the elevator and through the lobby and out into the street and the air was like a cold caress against his face. And as he stood waiting for a taxi to take him to the station, all he could think was: Rabbi is saved! Rabbi is saved! Rabbi is saved!

RABBI 10

It was at supper one evening, about six or seven months after Rabbi had been appointed, that the idea came to Jack Stern to stage a bring-out for him.

"That's all anybody needs—just to have what's in him brought out!"

The "bring-out" was the heart of Jack's philosophy. He applied it to everything, his friends, his family, his work. He loved to joke about it. "What do you do for a living, Jack?" "I bring out." "What are you doing at the office today?" "I'm staging a bring-out." "What's happening to that new client at your shop?" "They're undergoing a bring-out."

The result was that he and Mildred and the three girls (two of them off at college) had a relationship and an attitude towards life that was open and uninhibited, to say the least. Say it! Do it! Express yourself! Be yourself! It made for an exuberant atmosphere, never dull, sometimes a little nervous-making, and when friends gathered for an evening, nobody could predict what would happen next. You really let your hair down at the Sterns'. ("And if you ask me," a neighbor once said, "I think they let their pants down too.")

That evening, he looked across at Mildred who was staring at the television set which was built into the wall in the kitchen where they were having dinner, and asked her to turn it off.

"Mildred, I got an idea."

She returned to the table and started on the salad. It's very hard to eat salad while watching TV. Fried chicken, yes. Meat, vegetables, potato, that you can handle. But spearing a salad with one eye on the set, that's tricky.

"Yes, Jack?" as if remembering he had made a remark.

"Tell me—what do you think of Rabbi? I don't mean as a Rabbi. I mean like—as a man. How does he strike you?"

Mildred held the fork with the sliced tomato, sliced cucumber, and piece of lettuce all balanced on it, and pondered a moment.

"He doesn't." Then she swallowed it all.

"Like nothing, huh?"

"Oh, a nothing he's not. When he gives a sermon you can feel the man's got a lot to say. And you can feel he feels it. But personally? Like he's wearing some kind of mask."

"And it's doing him harm, you know that Mildred?"

"With who?"

"With who not? Take for instance Bob Barrett. I mean those two really have to get along. The President and the Rabbi. Or we got ourselves a helluva impasse. Oh, it's also with most of the other people he meets. That's a whole other thing. But with the important people in the congregation, the Committee, the Board, he doesn't get through to them, you know? Can't break down and be a human being with them."

Mildred smiled craftily. "Jack, you planning a bring-out on him? Tell me!"

"Well—I got an idea. Listen. I like the guy. Basically, I mean. I want to help him. And it'll be good for all of us in the long run. After all, I'm in the public relations business, right? So I'll do a little public relations job on Rabbi."

"For instance?"

"For instance, Mrs. Stern, you're throwing a party a week from Saturday night."

"Just like that?"

"We'll pick the guests very carefully. The Barretts, that's for sure. Rabbi and his wife—"

"—Now she's something!"

"Listen, she does her best. She's trying."

"You see good in everybody, Jack. That's your trouble."

"Because there's good in everybody! No? Anyway—then I think we oughtta have the Greenwalds. With Barrett and Greenwald we got the top level represented, you know what I mean?"

"Providing he doesn't sit there like God. Looking down on us."

"Greenwald? Naah, he lets go at a party. We'll make him! . . . Then how about we ask the Silversteins?"

"Oh, oh!"

"Just because she *is* a psychologist. It'll make it interesting. Don't you see? She can open it up, make it loose and swinging. And let's say Naomi and Wilbur Pollack. And maybe—"

"Naomi?"

"So she drinks, so what? That'll be good! Get things moving. If you wanna know—I'd like to get Rabbi a little high. Make him let go. Bring him out! And let's see—"

"Enough!"

"Okay. A little gathering of a dozen friends. Let the booze flow, the conversation flow, the inhibitions flow, everybody opens up—and Rabbi has a chance for once to be himself!—You know what I might even do for him? Set up a coupla these parties. Give people a chance to really see the guy."

"Like naked?"

"Come to the Sterns and meet Rabbi naked! That's not bad."

"Bad or good—it depends on how he looks naked." The Sterns had a way of not taking each other too seriously.

The Sterns' house was oriented completely outward. A room for each child, yes. A good-sized bedroom for themselves, of course. All basic needs satisfied. But the true expression of the house to them was in terms of guests, entertaining, social and play activities, a place to relax, let go, do something. Their living room was big, informal, with lots of chairs to flop into and easily move anywhere, little tables scattered about to play games on, eat on, do something on. Open stacks of records near the hi-fi so that anyone could put on anything he liked. There was a big dining section at one side of the room, an open kitchen beyond it, and even the kitchen was a place to sit in, talk, watch TV, do something. The Stern playroom was not in the basement ("Who wants to go up and down the stairs to have some fun?") but adjoined the living room and had a ping-pong table and a pool table and a dartboard and you only had to look at it to know it was constantly used.

But Jack had organized this particular party with a definite purpose in mind. He didn't want to leave it all to chance. When Sylvia and

Ab Silverstein appeared, the first to arrive, he asked Sylvia to stroll with him toward the kitchen.

"Sylvia darling, I'm giving you a responsibility tonight."

She looked at him with a delighted smile. What a man, this Jack! Not afraid of emotions, able to make contact, ready to give, alive inside all the way.

"Anything, Jack. Just don't make me bartender, that's all!"

They both laughed. Sylvia was a dark-haired, quick-eyed, brilliant little woman, and a perfect contrast to her husband. Not that Ab wasn't a damn smart lawyer and very successful at that. But corporate law wasn't exactly a field to bring out volatility and exuberance in a man, and Ab wasn't exactly the man who had it to bring out anyway. So Sylvia made up for both of them. She was a psychologist with a masters from Columbia, and she was one of the rare women in Greenlake who commuted to New York to work. While her discipline, as they called it, was psychology, her field was social work and her job was with a city agency training social workers. She was known to have told off the Commissioner on several occasions, to have gone even to the Mayor once, to have walked out on her job in disgust and to have been begged by a high official to come back on her own terms. Sylvia could be wrong sometimes, like anyone else, but it would take a smart cookie to catch her at it, and an even smarter one to convince her of it.

"Tonight," Jack said, "not a bartender. Listen. I'm having Rabbi here."

"Oh?"

"And the Mrs. of course. And Bob Barrett and Elaine. And the Greenwalds."

"What are you up to? I smell something."

"Just this, Sylvia dear. I want people to get to know Rabbi as he is. I mean the person inside, y'know? I want him to loosen up—everybody to loosen up—and get to know each other as human beings. It's a good cause, Sylvia. It's needed, believe me. So I want your help."

"For example?"

"Anything. Do I have to tell *you*? Anything you can do to open 'em all up—do it. As a favor?"

"It might even be fun."

"That's my girl!"

The next couple to come were the Barretts. They were both somewhat informally dressed, knowing what an evening was like at the Sterns. Bob wore a sports coat, an ascot around his neck, and Elaine a tan knitted suit that was attractive and comfortable.

Naomi Pollack had a glass in her hand about two minutes after she and Wilbur arrived, and she sat down next to Bob Barrett and told him how fed up she was with her life as chauffeur, nursemaid, housekeeper, cook, and laundress, and how she wished the hell she could do something about it. Elaine sat next to Ab Silverstein and tried hard to find something to talk about.

Now Rabbi and Frieda arrived at the door. Their entrance, for some reason, stopped all conversation. The men stood up to shake Rabbi's hand. It wasn't just that Rabbi was dressed so formally in his neat dark suit and conservative tie, nor even that he held himself so stiffly, a kind of awkwardness in his manner. It was simply the fact that now there was Rabbi in the room, a *Rabbi* amongst them. It was as if one felt self-conscious about the drink in one's hand, the slouched way one had been sitting, the little dirty joke about the two fairies. . . . How the hell do you behave at a party when a Rabbi is there?

The effect was to start the evening over again. It was now a different party somehow.

The arrival of the Greenwalds broke up the restraint a bit, and luckily Dr. Greenwald seemed to be in an expansive mood, a genuinely pleasant rather than benevolent smile on his face, and for a few minutes after the greetings and handshakes there was a certain flow to the talk, a certain freedom in motion and attitude.

But as everyone sat down, each with a drink (even Rabbi, whom Jack had talked into taking a Scotch "with lots of water"), a silence suddenly came like an open expression of their uneasiness. Twelve people sitting there and not a word being said. Jack couldn't stand it.

"Rabbi—" he turned to him, expressing recognition of the presence that was in all their minds, the source of the awkwardness, "now that you've been in our town a while, I want to ask you: What's the funniest experience you've had in Greenlake?" It was a desperate attempt, but anything was better than the silence.

"Hmm. . . ." Rabbi looked up and scratched his chin. For a man thinking of his funniest experience, he had a most solemn face. "Well.

I think it was the day I applied for a card at the Greenlake Public Library."

"That's funny?" Naomi said.

A few shhs were directed at her. Was she drunk already?

"No," Rabbi smiled. "It's what happened there. I filled out the application and gave it to the young lady behind the desk. She looked at it and said: 'Please put down your affiliation.' Affiliation? I didn't know what she meant. So I said: 'What affiliation?' She answered: 'Please put down the church you're affiliated with.'"

He laughed. No one else could manage more than a smile, and some not even that.

"I think," Elaine Barrett said softly, "that it's a rather sad little story."

"Oh come now!" Bob's pooh-pooh. "She just said 'church' instead of 'temple.'"

"That's funny?" Naomi shook her pressed blond hair, her big eyes accented by the dark sickness of skin under them. "I don't get it!"

"It's funny *and* sad," Dr. Greenwald holding up his hands to indicate the obvious. "But more funny than sad."

"I just don't get it!" Naomi must have poured herself a stiff one. "What's funny? What's sad? Will somebody tell me, for God's sake!"

Rabbi looked at her, smiling that kind, understanding smile of his that sometimes seemed so unconvincing. "It's funny to ask a Rabbi what church he belongs to. And it's a bit sad, I suppose, that gentiles know so little about us that they can't—"

Endless explanation and discussion of a non-funny joke. Jack knew it had to be ended. This was deadly!

"How about another round of drinks, everyone?" He motioned to Ab and the two of them started picking up glasses.

Sylvia got into it for the first time, and by now everyone was desperately wishing it was over. "I am curious to know, Rabbi, what your reaction was? What did you say to her?"

"Ahh—" Rabbi took off his glasses and rubbed them with his handkerchief, "—interesting. I was actually wondering if I was the first rabbi she had ever met face to face."

"Here comes the booze!" Jack interrupted deliberately, hoping to turn it off. "Drink up, everyone. This is a party, not a debate! Down with the alcohol, up with the fun! Did you hear the story about the two Jewish salesmen in Africa. One says—"

"Jack!" Elaine with some irritation, surprising them, annoying Bob. "Rabbi was explaining something. . . ."

"Can I make a confession?" Jack standing, drink in hand. "I'm already tired of the whole business. Funny, sad, whatever it was. So this first salesman says: 'Tell me, Jake—' "

"Jack—?" Rabbi said it gently, but firmly enough to make Jack stop. "I just want to answer Mrs. Silverstein."

"Sure, Rabbi." Jack sat down. Deadly. Getting nowhere. Irritation already all over the place. He had to think of something.

"I decided," Rabbi oblivious to everything, and even trying to be a bit clever, "that this wasn't the occasion to inform her that rabbis are not affiliated with churches. So I wrote down Temple Israel and handed her the card."

"And?" Elaine was almost stubbornly interested.

"She filed it away. No comment."

"Of course. She didn't even realize she had—"

On and on. Jack had never seen anything like it—except that he really had. The tendency of Jews in a group to analyze the minutiae of their encounters with the gentile world. Everyone with an experience to contribute. An incident. A remark, an expression on a face, a feeling, a sensing, a reaction. The subtleties of understanding the Jew as he sits with other Jews and shares what it's like to be a Jew. There is no end to it.

Jack felt as if everyone were chewing on left-over food. The boredom of it was maddening. He moved over and sat next to Sylvia, with a heavy sigh and a plaintive look.

"Can you do something? Anything! Please, huh?"

Sylvia nodded, moved forward to the edge of her chair and clapped her hands. "Listen, everybody! I'd like to try a little experiment here. Anybody object? I think it could be fun—and very instructive."

"Your 'experiments,' " Dr. Greenwald smiled warily, "scare me."

"No, no. Nothing to be scared of. Just one thing—is everyone willing to participate?" She looked around.

"Can I just watch?" asked Wilbur Pollack, aware he had to keep an eye on Naomi.

"No watching! Everybody in it. Now come on—are we agreed?"

An uneasiness and tension pervaded the room, but a kind of anticipation too. It could be fun. Who knows? The evening might still be rescued.

"All right," Sylvia continued, "I'll explain what this is all about. I want to try something with this group that I've done many times with my people. You know I train social workers. Actually, I train people who train social workers. This is high-level stuff, I'll have you know, strictly big deal. All right. We meet for conferences, long week-end sessions and so on. Now you'd be amazed, these people get together for the first session and sit around with all the barriers up. They don't relate, don't communicate, and there's even a kind of smoldering hostility you can feel in the air.

"So to break it all down, get them to release it, express it, reach each other—with whatever they feel—I make them go through a few exercises." She smiled as she looked around at the somewhat apprehensive faces. "The results are often remarkable. I think it might be interesting for this group to try it."

"Count me out!" Bob Barrett. "I smell something—and I don't like it!"

"Me, too." Greenwald waved his hand.

"Chicken!" Jack standing up. "Oooh—you chickens! Now come on! Sylvia knows what she's doing."

"That's what I'm afraid of." Bob shaking his head.

"I will be glad to try it." Rabbi startled them all. Perhaps it was a curiosity on his part, perhaps an awareness that something significant could come of this. The effect was a silence as they absorbed what had happened. Rabbi wanting to do this! Well!

"Then that settles it!" said Sylvia, resuming control. "All right now. I'm going to suggest four different actions. Actually, all of us should participate in each one, but we'll shorten it a bit. Now we must do this with complete honesty. The truth. No hiding. No holding back. Whatever we feel, we express. From the guts! Right? Okay? . . . Now, who will volunteer for the first one?"

Naturally it was Naomi, not quite staggering as she came to the center of the room, but it was a kind of relief to everyone. It wouldn't matter what she did.

"Here I am!" She held up her arms, as if ready to be sacrificed.

"All right, dear." Sylvia was directing. "Now, I want you to give a non-verbal greeting to each person in the room."

"What the hell's that?"

"Non-verbal. Without words. Just go around the room and greet each person without using words. Do it in any way you like."

"Oooh, this is fun!" She did the expected. A deliberately polite handshake with each woman, a little bow of the head, eyebrows raised, a reluctant acknowledgment of the presence. A kiss for each man. Her husband got a little peck on the cheek, which brought the desired laughter. Bob Barrett a mushy kiss that she clung to a bit too long. Cries of Break it up! Enough! Enough! A big hug for Jack. Both hands on Greenwald's face and a rather sweet kiss for him. Then Rabbi. She stood in front of him a few moments, her hands on her hips, as if trying to decide how far to go. Then she motioned for him to stand up. He obeyed, smiling that awkward, indulgent smile. She reached out her arms as if she were about to embrace him, stepped forward, and at the last moment snapped her arms behind her back and gave him a pouting little kiss on his forehead.

Applause and laughter. Jack felt good. At least things were moving. Something was happening. Trust Sylvia.

"All right," Sylvia taking over again. "Now the next one. Who volunteers?"

"Me!" Mildred whirled into the center of the room. "I like this!"

"We should have a man," Sylvia protested, wanting it to go a certain way.

"No! Me! Me!" Mildred insisting.

"All right. Then next time. Now Mildred—you are to select a person in this group and react to him or her non-verbally, but in an unpleasant way. Do anything you want to do. Step on feet, punch, pinch, hit, anything. So—make your selection and go to it!"

"Wait!" Barrett was shaking his head. "Sylvia, I don't like this game, at all."

"It's not a game, Bob. You might call it a psychological exercise."

"You might call it that. It's a nasty little game to me."

"What do you think, Rabbi?" Sylvia turned to him, not just for his approval, but out of a curiosity to see his attitude.

"Well—" Rabbi stuck his hands in his pockets and pushed his legs straight out in front of him, "whatever it's called it obviously has its dangers. When people are asked to reveal themselves, the results are bound to be startling. The question is—are we prepared to be shocked?"

"Are you, Rabbi?" Sylvia pressed.

"I'm not sure. Honestly—I find it intriguing. There's a certain fascinating horror to this sort of thing. And sometimes such things are helpful. I know this, we'll all get to know each other better!"

"Then you agree to continue?"

Actually, Rabbi would have preferred to end it. He didn't like the premise—that acting out of hostility was desirable, that it brought people closer. And somewhere inside too, was the knowledge that at any moment, from anyone there, the hostility toward him that existed would be expressed. Would it be good for him to hear it? Learn how deep it was? Maybe it would be "helpful," which is what he had meant when he said that—but he didn't really want to go through the pain of it. But it would be worse to prevent them. He rubbed his forehead with his fingers, aware they were all watching him and waiting for his answer.

"If the others do," he said finally.

"Good!" Sylvia looked around. "Are we continuing?"

There were a few glumly reluctant faces, but no one seemed able to say no.

"All right, then. Mildred—go ahead!"

Mildred stood there, her body all tensed and ready to go, but hesitating.

"Sylvia, what if they resent it?"

"The idea is you must be willing for them to do that. Accept it. You just want to express what you feel. And remember—and this holds for all of us—complete honesty!"

Everyone was waiting now, most of them expecting her to turn to Jack.

"How far can I go?"

"As far as you want. It has to be non-verbal and unpleasant to the person. Otherwise, no limit."

"Mmmm. . . ." Mildred sighed, turned suddenly, walked over to Dr. Greenwald. Everyone was surprised. Dr. Greenwald's face registered total shock, but then slowly restored itself with an effort to smile.

Mildred motioned for him to stand up. He glanced around the room, his bottom lip out as if to indicate he shared their surprise. Then, as they stood face to face, Mildred reached up and started to muss his hair. Her fingers went through his gray, neatly pressed down hair, pulling at it this way and that as if to destroy the facade of it, rumpling, messing, disarranging, pulling, until Dr. Greenwald stood there looking suddenly like a wind-rumpled scarecrow, pained and shocked, attacked, used! Everyone reacted, but differently. A few smiled, some appeared worried, disturbed, and one or two seemed vicariously involved, somehow satisfied inside.

Mildred wasn't finished. She reached for Dr. Greenwald's tie, the dark, rich silk so neatly in place, and tugged at it until it came loose. She pulled it off and threw it on the floor. She looked at it a moment and then stepped on it with both feet, rubbing her shoes into it.

Now a tension filled the room. She was going too far! Sylvia leaning forward, her eyes gleaming with understanding, was smiling. Some others shifted uneasily, as if looking for a way out.

Mildred had more. She unbuttoned Dr. Greenwald's white shirt, exposing his undershirt. Then she pulled on the shirt, yanking it out of his trousers so that the tails hung out. Dr. Greenwald, his face white, but the expression controlled, very controlled, tightly, tightly controlled, stood there and looked at her impassively. He was a mess. She had stripped him beautifully, totally of all dignity.

She turned to the center of the room, took a few steps, and for a moment suddenly covered her face with her hands as if in shame. Then she looked up.

"Wow!" She staggered to a chair and flopped down. "Wow!" She seemed to collapse into it.

"No comments now!" Sylvia said quickly. "All discussion later. That's part of it and we call it the Fish Bowl. All discussion later."

There was silence in the room as everyone absorbed the meaning of what had taken place. Dr. Greenwald said: "Excuse me a moment." He went to the bathroom and everyone sat tensely waiting.

"We'll do the next one as soon as Dr. Greenwald returns."

"Must we?" Barrett was annoyed and uneasy.

"Oh, we've agreed to. And this gets better and better."

Dr. Greenwald returned, everything restored, in place again. He had obviously adopted an attitude toward this and he expressed it for the benefit of all. A gesture of the hand down the front of his body to indicate that everything was back as it should be, a smile on his face to demonstrate that he accepted and understood. No offense. Benevolent forgiveness. He sat down.

"I want," Sylvia broke the silence, "a man to be the next volunteer." Before anyone could answer, she pointed her finger. "Rabbi?"

"That's volunteering?" He smiled.

"I thought you were about to, but were hesitating."

"I'm still hesitating . . . ," but he was on his feet. Finally he moved to the center of the room. "All right, I volunteer." They laughed, but uneasily, apprehensively.

"The next action is as follows. And I repeat again: It must be honest, truthful. Nothing held back. All right? You are to select the person you dislike most in this group, stand directly in front of the person, and tell him or her why. Say it all. Completely. Let everything come out. Just empty yourself of all the hostility you feel for this person. Just one word to the rest of us—remember we discuss everything that's happened later in the Fish Bowl. . . . Rabbi?"

No one liked the situation. This was really too much! There was a feeling of sympathy for Rabbi, put into such a spot. There was an anticipation of something so painful and disturbing to come, they didn't want to face it.

Rabbi stood rubbing his glasses with that handkerchief again, utilizing the delaying tactic, the unconscious search for confidence, clarity, strength. His face was serious, thoughtful, troubled. He put the glasses on his nose again with both hands, then rubbed his hands together as if removing perspiration.

"All right, I'm ready."

He walked over to Bob Barrett, and Bob stood up without being asked. Somehow everyone had known this would happen. They were prepared, but wished they weren't. They wished they weren't here to see this.

"Mr. Robert Barrett," Rabbi began, his hands clasped behind his back, staring directly into Barrett's face, into the staring, cynical eyes, "this is why I dislike you most in this group.

"I consider you to be insensitive, and totally misguided. I'll say this—I think that as President of our congregation you do want to do the right thing. You work hard at it and feel deeply about it. But I think you have no idea of what is really important for the Jews in this community, and for that matter, for the Jews in the world today. You follow the wrong goals in the wrong way for the wrong reasons.

"And I think your personal character is such—your ambition, your drive, your desire to control and dominate—all this prevents you from seeing the truth and being willing to accept it. And I say this to you as a Rabbi, and as a Jew—and as a human being."

No one moved. Rabbi turned and looked at Sylvia.

"I think I did rather well."

"No discussion now." She held up a finger. "All that comes later."

Barrett sat down like a man who had willingly presented himself for an ordeal. He folded his arms and leaned back, self-control evident in his whole body, his arms clutching at himself as if to hold back, eyes on no one so as to communicate nothing, even with a glance.

Rabbi walked back to his place, nobody really looking at him in the embarrassment, only Frieda's eyes on his face, her eyes glistening. She reached out for his hand as he sat down next to her and Rabbi brushed it away, sensing how wrong that was.

"A big, stiff drink anyone?" Jack was on his feet. He looked miserable.

"Jack!" Sylvia motioned him down. "We have one more. Let's finish it."

"*Oy vay,*" Jack said, sitting down heavily. "I wish I could think of something else to say—but oy vay will do."

"No volunteers needed for the next one," Sylvia said.

"That's good!" Jack applauded and several others clapped and laughed with relief.

"This is something we all do. A group act. Very significant. The act itself is simple. The discussion of it afterward—the whys, the how we felt—that's important. Very revealing. . . . Are you all ready?"

"I'm never going to be ready!" Jack waving his arms in distress. "I can't take it!"

Chuckles, sighs, nodding of the head in agreement. But Sylvia couldn't be stopped.

"Are we ready? Here it is: Now we imagine that we have been on a ship that's gone down at sea. This group managed to get into a lifeboat and as we set out in the lifeboat, we realize that we can't make it. We have one passenger too many. We have to get rid of one person, throw him or her out of the lifeboat. The group now has to select this person."

"You mean we vote?" Jack warily.

"We vote."

"Sylvia, please—" Barrett started to protest.

"Bob, just try it. You'll see how the discussion later—"

"Sylvia!" Barrett wasn't going to be brushed aside, knowing his own emotions, sensing what all the others in the room were experiencing and thinking, "—Sylvia, I think not. No. This we don't need."

"What are you afraid of, Bob?"

And as she said the words she knew at once what it was, as they all knew now, and as Rabbi knew. This meant—of course! of course!—that it was as good as done anyhow. It was as if the vote had already been taken, the impact of it already felt. And if she agreed not to do it—wouldn't that be merely underlining that knowledge and fact? Saying to Rabbi—We're not going to do this to you? So she had to act as if that might not happen. That was kinder now. More considerate. And she thought of a change she would make. Instead of doing it verbally, as it should be done, they would do it by writing the name on a piece of paper. All this darted through her mind in a fraction of a second, as her question to Bob still hung over them all. Then quickly, "We'll do it by secret ballot. Write the names on paper. No one will know who chose whom, and—"

"Sylvia—!"

It was like a groan from Barrett, and he leaned his head back now, giving up. He couldn't press it either. It would be too obvious. And Rabbi, who understood exactly what was happening, now felt the need to show that understanding to them.

"What Bob is afraid of is the possibility that truth can be painful. To one person, to many. But since we've agreed to face truths about ourselves this evening, we might as well face this one. . . . I think we will all be facing something as we do this."

Sylvia's tone was completely changed now, and as she looked at Rabbi she said quietly: "Thank you, Rabbi."

He only nodded his head, waiting. It had to be done.

The slips of paper were handed out in a troubled silence. People seemed to be afraid to look at each other. The writing was done quickly, the papers folded, held, the waiting for Sylvia to collect them in a tension of anticipation.

Sylvia sat down with all the papers in her lap and they watched her. She unfolded them, glanced at the name, put one under the other. There was no expression on her face, no reaction. She was acting as if she were reading an ordinary list of names, not a sentence of death.

Everyone was wondering how she would manage to say it to them.

She was finished. She didn't hesitate, she began to tear them up. All the papers into little pieces in her lap, in shreds, so no names could be read.

There was a silence. Then Rabbi stood up and came over to her. He looked down at her and there was the pain of a smile on his face.

"Thank you, Sylvia. I know of course, why you did that."

"You're assuming—"

"No, no," he waved his arm, "not assuming. It's all right. I know. We all do."

He turned to them, and as they watched him they felt not only a sympathy for the man, but a sharing of the pain of this moment, the humiliation of it.

"Will you forgive me, friends," Rabbi held his hands clasped, his eyes half closed, as he was formulating the words, seeking the expressions that would convey it to them, "—if I say something to you now?"

How could they not let him do this? It was like allowing a condemned man to make his final statement to the world, that act of self-justification that makes dying possible to accept, both for the death-dealers and the victim.

Rabbi wanted it to be more than that. It had to be for him so much more! For was he not a man of God, a teacher of His word, and thereby committed to using every moment of life, every deed, as a means of helping his fellow men to understand life and to understand themselves? He knew it would sound like a sermon, but he couldn't avoid that.

Smiling, his expression almost asking their forgiveness, he said: "Permit me to make a symbolic interpretation of this little game, this exercise we have just been through. A group of people must choose someone to sacrifice, get rid of, so that they may survive.

"Let us—indulge me in this, please—let us think of that group not as a dozen people in a room, but as the Jews in Greenlake. Or America. Anywhere. And let us think of the person they have chosen to be removed—not as a person at all. Not their Rabbi—but their faith. For that is what he symbolizes, what he really represents.

"Now . . . now I can say to you: I understand what you have done, and why. In your lives, in the meaning of your lives, there is really no important place for religion. Not if you must choose what to sacrifice. Your homes, your comforts, your pleasures—these you will hold on to and save. And it is Judaism you will allow to die.

"If the choice must be made." He looked at them intently. "I say— *if* that choice must be made. And that is why this game is false, why its symbolism is false. For that choice need not be made. Judaism can and must be part of your lives—yes, even the way you live right now, right here. It can enrich all that you have and all that you do— if you will only let it. Accept it, allow it to dwell within you and to guide you."

His eyes moved across the room. "Do you all feel a guilt now because you have voted to sacrifice your Rabbi? No need to feel that. I do not feel rejected. I am alive and will continue to work and teach and inspire that coming closer to your faith, that involvement with Judaism. . . . Yes, I will go on.

"If there is any guilt to feel—let it be for what is not yet in your hearts, not yet in your lives, not yet part of you. The beautiful and holy and joyful and meaningful closeness to God and to Judaism. . . . With God's help, I will continue to try to lead you to that."

He didn't move for a few moments when he had finished. In the silence, the emotion in the room was as tangible as his presence. No one knew what to do next, how to continue. Rabbi understood this, and turned to Frieda.

"Let us go now."

She came up to him quickly and then the two moved towards the door. No one had spoken yet, responded. The moment was aching with the emptiness. Then suddenly Barrett walked over to Rabbi and held out his hand.

"Rabbi, I want to say thank you."

Nothing more had to be said, and they all knew it. But it released something for them and they were now able to come up to Rabbi as he stood at the door, each one to shake his hand. Nothing more than that, no words.

And the miracle of it was, that as Rabbi clasped their hands, as he looked into their eyes, into the gentleness there now they were trying to express, into the openess of their emotion for him, he felt a kind of joy and a hope. They can be reached, he was thinking. They can be reached!

XI

At four o'clock in the morning the phone rang. Rabbi picked it up groggily. Frieda was already upright in the bed.

"Rabbi Gordon? Sam Beskov."

Rabbi couldn't clear his throat for a while, swallowed, tried to sit up.

"Rabbi Gordon?"

"Yes. . . . Yes, this is Rabbi Gordon."

"Sam Beskov. . . . Rabbi, I want you to come here. To my house."

"What?"

"Right now."

"What? I don't understand. . . ."

"Rabbi, my mother just died. She just died, Rabbi. She just died. . . . Rabbi, I . . . I don't know what to do. Will you come here?"

Rabbi coughed, confused. Beskov? Calling him?

"I . . . if you—"

"Right away, Rabbi. You know where I live?"

"Yes."

"Thank you. I'm waiting."

The town was asleep, the street through the center of it gently, softly glowing from the overhead lamp posts. Here and there a store window was half lit up for protection. A police car was moving down a side street, cruising on its patrol. The long drive down Beach Road led toward the bay, the dark trees like huge silent guardians of the night, standing with arms linked.

Beskov calling him? He wasn't even a member of the congregation. The man they all considered a renegade. The Jew they wished not a Jew. The multi-millionaire who used his money, his power, so ruthlessly that even the gentiles were afraid of him. Beskov? But how could Rabbi have said no? Beskov's mother had died. He was reaching out for help.

Rabbi could see now, above him at the top of the hill, a dim light in one of the upper rooms, another room brightly lit upstairs, and the whole lower floor glowing with light. He drove up the driveway through the archway of trees and stopped the car in front of the huge house.

Beskov came down to the car. Dressed in white slacks, a sport shirt, he was smoking a cigar.

"Rabbi Gordon? We've never met. Sam Beskov. Thank you for coming."

A tremendous, powerful grip of the immense hand. Encompassing. Rabbi followed him into the house.

"This way."

The living room was enormous. All the lights on. Like an assertion. A declaration.

"This is my wife, Gloria."

She was holding a drink in her hand. A weary, blond face. A blank look.

"I'm having a drink. I need it. Sam needs it, but he won't take one."

"All right, Gloria. All right."

She went to a chair and fell back into it, legs stretched out on the foot rest, her head back. She couldn't do any more for him. He wouldn't let her.

"Rabbi, my mother's dead. An hour ago. Upstairs. She's upstairs. I called because—"

"I understand."

"No. Because I don't know what to do."

"Have you called a doctor?"

"Why? She's dead!"

"You need . . . there are certain formalities—"

"To hell with it! She's dead! I don't need a doctor to tell me."

Gloria jiggled the ice in her glass. "You need a death certificate from a doctor, Sam."

"I know what I need! I'll get it later. She's dead!"

He sat down for the first time, on the edge of a chair. His legs were spread apart, his arms resting on them, drooping. From the cigar's white ash rose a reluctant curl of smoke. His big round face, red, was turned downward, the flat strands of black hair pasted down across the skull from side to side like strips of rug on a bare floor. The man just sat there, heavy in silence.

"I'm sorry," Rabbi finally said.

"Me too." He turned suddenly to his wife. "Gloria, wake up Charlotte. Let her make some coffee. Maybe the Rabbi wants something."

"Oh no, nothing—"

"Sam, let her sleep. She'll have a full day, believe me. I can make coffee."

He was back to his dead mother, the maid an irrelevant interruption. "It's mama. It's mama." He turned to Gloria. "So make the coffee? Like you said? Please?"

"All right all right all right." She managed to stand up, breaking the embrace of the chair, and shuffled into the kitchen, the drink still in her hand.

"You'll have some coffee, Rabbi. Eh? Me, I think I'll take a brandy."

He walked over to the bar, an immaculate white structure at one end of the room, more elaborate than the altarpiece in a great church, ten black leather bucket seats in front of it, a gleaming brass rail along the bottom, the sparkle of glasses and decanters and bottles in its depths like the glittering treasures of a cathedral. He returned with a large brandy snifter, the golden liquor swaying back and forth.

"Some doctor—I read somewhere some doctor said cognac is good for the heart. Also like when you're tense. So—" He held up the glass to Rabbi as if in toast and then took a sip. "Excuse me—maybe you want some?"

"No, thank you very much."

"It's funny, I thought a Rabbi, you know—? But you're allowed to have a drink, aren't you?"

"Of course. But not now, thank you."

"Yes. Yes, yes, yes. Yes." He was still standing, thinking of his mother. "So she's dead. . . . Cancer. . . . Eh, I knew it a long time ago. You know, nobody kids themselves about cancer. They opened her up eight months ago, the doctor says—can't do a thing. He didn't operate. Closed her up. Only . . . only he told her—we said it was a good operation. Everything would be better now. Hmmm. . . .

I wonder. I wonder if we really fooled her. She knew. People know, y'know? Sure they know."

He sat down, stretched his legs out. The look of wisdom and acceptance we all get in the face of death, Rabbi thought.

"Gloria—you got that coffee for the Rabbi?" His voice became suddenly confidential. "She's so tired she don't know what she's doing. Been up with me all night. She's asleep on her feet."

"I'm in no hurry."

"So I got you up at four o'clock, Rabbi—and here you are, and we don't even know each other."

"I've heard a bit about you, Mr. Beskov."

"I'll bet!" He gave a throaty chuckle. "Ha! I'll bet!" He sipped the cognac slowly through thick lips. "Good of you to come." He stood up, restless. "Your mother dies . . . your mother dies right in front of you . . . you don't know what to do, you know? You need someone. . . . Even me, who don't need anybody. Because death, y'know—" He shook his head. "Hmm. Look at me. I feel lost. Me!"

He sat down again. "She knew. Of course she knew. When I moved her here from New York. Two weeks ago. You know, the pains were getting . . . I had nurses twenty-four hours a day. They were holding her hand all the time. She wanted somebody to hold her hand all the time. Like a little baby, y'know? We get like little babies when we die. Afraid of the dark. The big dark in front of us. . . . Uhh . . . uhhhh. . . ." A huge sigh was accompanied by a shaking of the head. "Hmm, Rabbi? Nothing helps. Nobody helps. At that moment, you're alone."

He stood up, restless, restless. "I gave her everything she wanted. For the last ten, fifteen years? She lived like a queen! Five room apartment for herself on Central Park West. A maid who did everything but wipe her nose for her. A car and a chauffeur.—That was the thing!" He was smiling now in recollection. "When I gave her that— a car in the garage downstairs with the chauffeur always waiting—she said: 'Sammy, tell me the truth. You making this money honestly?'"

Rabbi smiled. Beskov looked at him.

"She couldn't believe it. The first job I had, I was eleven years old, a delivery boy in some market, I brought home the three dollars I earned for a week's work, she said: 'Sammy, you made this money honestly?' Same question! Funny? . . . Oh—so you managed to make the coffee? You all right?"

Gloria was pushing in a cart with a coffee pot, cups and saucers, napkins, sugar, cream, silverware. "I've got my eyes open, haven't I?"

"I tell her to go to sleep—she stays up!"

Gloria waved her hand, dismissing the idea. "Would you mind helping yourself? I—" She flopped into a chair.

"Of course." Rabbi went over to the cart. "Thank you very much."

"We knew it was coming." Sam sat down again. "The nurse told us, seven, eight o'clock. So we knew."

Rabbi brought his cup of coffee back to the end table near the couch and set it down. He stirred it calmly, raising the spoon and lowering it into the cup again, as if inspecting the coffee.

"Rabbi, I want to give her a Jewish funeral. You know—whatever that—I don't even know what—"

"Of course. I understand."

"Will you—uh—?"

"Yes." He took his first sip. "Do you have a family plot?"

"No. Funny, I own all that real estate, streets in New York, all this land here, acres and acres of land—I don't own a couple of feet in a cemetery to bury my mother."

"Our congregation hasn't yet purchased its land for a cemetery. We plan to do that, but as yet—"

"So what do people do?"

"Well, individuals make their own choice. Their own arrangements. . . . There is a Jewish cemetery in Lanebrook. It's Orthodox."

"That means—?"

"Well . . . the services, the ritual, you know. It has to be done a certain way. I know the Rabbi and can arrange—"

"Wait." Sam came over and sat down near him. "Can *you* do it?"

"Do you want that?"

Sam stared at him, and it was like a man reaching out for a hand, for support.

"I want you to do it."

"All right."

"Thanks, Rabbi."

"I am glad to help."

Sam looked at him, studying him, sizing him up. "You're an interesting man, Rabbi."

"Yes?"

"I mean—look at this. I call you at four in the morning and say come over. You come. To Sam Beskov, the one Jew in town all the other Jews hate. Your whole congregation maybe hates me. . . . But you come. Without a word. And you sit here . . . and you don't lecture me, you don't give me no religious talk. You don't try to give me sympathy, nothing. You're like—just here. You let me talk. You listen. . . . Which is, I guess, what I want. Or need. And you must know that. So you do it for me."

"A Rabbi is there to help all Jews."

"Even one like me?"

"Are you not a Jew?"

"Am I?" He stood up, the hand around and around in a little circle, the brandy in the bottom of the glass whirling. "Of course I am! And you know—I got a right to be the kind of Jew I am! Yes?"

"Every Jew has the right to be himself."

"And still be a Jew. Right?"

"It's not something that can be taken away from you."

"Right! And I can be a Jew even if—"

"Sam," Gloria had drained her glass, "—so you're a Jew. I don't get it. What is all this? Your mother's dead upstairs, and you're sitting here proving you're a Jew."

"Gloria—do me a favor? You're so tired you don't know what you're talking. Go to sleep—huh?"

Gloria stood up a bit unsteadily, weariness, alcohol, emotion, all pulling at her. "Goodnight, Rabbi. Thanks for coming. . . . 'Night, Sam."

He kept looking at her until she was out of the room, as if walking out with her, beside her.

"So there's a wife for you! Would you believe it? Looks like a dumb blond broad and got a heart one hundred per cent pure gold! You know, most people think she married me for my money. Don't you believe it! She loves me, that crazy broad! I met her—" He smiled at the remembrance, his mind obviously needing to wander off, talk about anything, everything. "—you know where, Rabbi? Next door! Right over there—that house. She was visiting my neighbors what's their name, Allenby or something, and one day I'm taking a walk and happen to look over to their house—and there in a lounge on the lawn, practically stripped down to her naked body, there's this beauty of a blond, with the sunglasses, with the stretched out body to get a sunburn, *laying* there! So I start a conversation, very gentlemanly, we get acquainted, I invite her over with her friends for cocktails—and bingo! What am I going to tell ya? A brain trust she's not. But not so dumb either. The basics—you know what I mean?—the basics she's got down cold. To respect a husband, be with him day and night wherever he goes, pay attention to his *mishegas*, to put it plain—to love him!"

He looked at Rabbi with a pleased smile. "You know what tickles her? What she gets a big kick out of? I put her in my advertising! You seen the ads? Big, full pages. She's right up there top of the page, winking at you and pointing to the stuff—the supermarket, the real estate, whatever. I call her 'Goldie' in the ads. Goldie invites you to enjoy life, buy, see—whatever it is. . . . Ehhh! Why not? Let everybody see I'm proud of her, all them wise guys who think I'm stuck with a dumb broad who married me for my money. And I'll tell you something, Rabbi, she's made me a million times happier than my first wife—that real *Yiddishe mama!*—who's now sucking blood outta me with alimony you could support a hundred families on! . . . Anyway, where were we? Why am I telling you all this? See—you make me want to talk. Like I feel I can *talk* to you." He patted Rabbi's knee. "So tell me, do I have to follow anybody's idea about how to be a Jew? Does anybody have the right to criticize the kinda Jew I am? I want to hear this!"

"It is written: And what the Lord doth require of thee: Only to do justly, and to love mercy, and to walk humbly with thy God. . . . Notice the word 'only.' That's all."

"But I don't walk humbly with God! I don't need God!—I'm an atheist, Rabbi!"

"But still a Jew."

"Ahhh. . . ." He sat down and leaned back. "But still a Jew. . . . You know when you realize it? Oh—all the time in a kind of way, I suppose. Everytime a goy opens his mouth some kinda nerve in you gets a signal. But that's only—"

"—Negative response."

"Yeah. Like instinct or something. No, I mean you realize it in a strange way when death comes. To me—like take my mother here, lying dead upstairs. To me it would be some kinda crime not to give her a Jewish funeral. Go through the services. Bless her soul in the old Jewish way our fathers and their fathers have done. Put her in the ground with the same kind of prayer. And listen to me—I'm an *atheist!*" He stood up. There were tears in his eyes and he was ashamed of them. He moved over to the bar. "Rabbi, do me a favor? Have one with me?" He held up the brandy bottle.

"All right."

"Good!" He brought the two glasses over and set one down in front of Rabbi. "Because God created even this. Right? If He did anything—He did everything."

Rabbi took a sip. It was soothing, rich, warm.

"Rabbi, you really, really believe in God, don't you?"

"Yes."

"That's all you're going to say?"

"Now. I don't want to define what that means to me—now. Come to Temple. Listen to me there. You'll understand."

"You know—I might just do that!"

"You'll be welcome."

"Think so? Sam Beskov—that bastard—welcome in the Temple?"

"By me."

"Yes. That I believe." He took a sip. "Good stuff, huh?"

"One of His better creations."

"Tell me, you think it's a shitty world?—Excuse me. I forgot—"

"That's all right. Talk any way you want to talk."

"Because it is a shitty world, isn't it? Life is just a bowl of chocolate-covered shit, that's all it is. You know? I mean the wars, the fighting, the murders. People hungry. People hating each other. A lousy struggle all their lives.—I haven't forgotten that. Never forget it. The number of days—weeks!—I didn't have enough to eat. My poor mother. There was a time once—she was a proud lady—there was a time when everybody in the neighborhood was practically starving. No jobs for the husbands. Nothing. Friday night, the women supposed to be in the kitchen, cooking Saturday dinner. *Shabbes* dinner. The kitchens were dark, lights out. Nothing to cook. But my mother, she kept the shade up, the lights on. She stood in front of the window, a big pot full of water, and she stirred the water and threw salt in the water and tasted the water, and all the neighbors thought—look at the Beskovs. They're eating. They got what to eat. My mother did it because she was proud. For my father's sake. Crazy. What a world. And the sickness. And struggle. All leading to death. It's a shitty world, Rabbi."

Rabbi smiled. "I remember reading a reference to something Van Gogh had written. He put it as an artist. He said more and more he was beginning to think that God shouldn't be judged by this world. It's one of His sketches that turned out badly."

"So what do we do, Rabbi? What do we do?"

"The best we can. As each of us sees that best."

"And you're trying, Rabbi. Huh?"

"I am."

"Getting anywhere?"

"In what way?"

"With these people here? These shnooks? These creeps? You're not getting anywhere with them, I know that."

"What do you mean?"

"Rabbi, tonight—I should say this morning—what the hell, you and I sitting here, let's be honest with each other. What've we got to lose? I know you're having problems. It's no secret. Barrett, that slick bastard, Greenwald, pompous ass, all those others—they don't dig you. You know something, Rabbi? I—me, Sam Beskov—I dig you better than any of them! What do you think of that?"

"It could be."

"They hate your guts. You think you're going to last with a bunch like that after your neck? Take it from Sam, start looking around, Rabbi. That's practical advice from a guy who lives by facts."

"As a matter of fact—" And Rabbi couldn't quite understand why he was saying it, whether from the bitterness stirred up by Beskov's remarks, or something about the man, his directness, his honesty, his reaching out and establishing more contact with him than almost any man he had met in this town, but he had started now and wherever it would lead he would finish—"as a matter of fact, they have asked me to resign."

"Aha!" Sam stood up, a triumphant smile. "Aha! So there you are! Those bastards got to you already! You gonna do it?"

"I don't know yet. It's a situation with many—"

"Look, Rabbi," Sam interrupted, sitting down next to him. "Let me cut you off. Don't get sore."

"It's all right."

"Look. I'm Sam Beskov. I got how many millions I don't know. I got power, I got influence, I also got *chutzpah*. I also got an itch for a good fight. Rabbi—I say screw those bastards and don't quit. I say fight 'em like you're fighting for your life. Which you are. Fight 'em and fight 'em—and Rabbi, I want to help you! Me. I'll fight with you. Whaddya say?"

"You're not—"

"A member? So tomorrow I'm a member! They'll turn me down? Ha! Five of them were up here two years ago. Begging me. They were going to put me on the Board. The Executive Committee. Sam Beskov's money was going to be given big honors! In ten minutes I'm a member, Rabbi. But you gotta let me really fight those shitheads. Because I don't fight to lose. And I don't fight according to no rules."

"Why . . . why do you want to do this?"

"You care why?"

"Yes. It's important to me."

"Will you believe me, whatever I tell you?"

Rabbi looked at him. Sam was gripping his arm, leaning forward, holding him. "Yes."

"Rabbi, it's—" Suddenly he stopped. He got up and moved away, then turned around. "Rabbi, will you believe that it's because I'm a Jew? In my crazy way. In my own dopey way. Maybe—my mother dying. Maybe, talking to you. I'm feeling, Sam Beskov is feeling like a sonofabitch of a Jew—and there's something wrong going on! A man like you, this kind of Rabbi you are—they need you, these dumb shmucks! They need you!"

He walked over to the huge sheet of glass that was a window, and stood there looking out at the bay, the softness of dawn teasing its way upward into the sky, the water changing from dark blue to gray, the last stars still clinging weakly to life.

"Rabbi—I'm also saying thank you."

"That's not necessary."

"For me it is." He came back and stood looking down at Rabbi. "For what you did for me. Okay? I gotta say thank you."

"But it—"

"Stop! I'm not going to let you talk! . . . Hey, I got an idea. I'm going to make a little contribution. They're building a Temple, right? I'll give them a quarter million."

Rabbi stared at him. "A quarter of a million dollars?"

"What is it? To Sam Beskov? Are you kidding? Maybe I'll make it a half.—And you know what? It'll be in memory of my mother. Let 'em put up something with it. A building, a wing, whatever it is. Rachel Beskov's Building.—I wanna do it, Rabbi! I'm going to! Don't argue with me."

He reached down and grabbed Rabbi's hand. The two of them looked at each other. Sam pulled the Rabbi to his feet.

"Come on. I want you to see the dawn coming up over the bay. Y'know it's dawn already? A new day, Rabbi. A new day!"

They stood at the window, the light crawling upward, reaching up, leaping up over the sky, the water sparkling as if all the lost stars of the night had fallen into it and were there now.

The way Rabbi had discovered a brand new kind of Jew, and a brand new kind of anti-Semitism, was through Billy Grossman.

The boy was bursting out of his skin, his pants, his shirt, his shoes. The energy was packed in so tight that the need to release it was like holding in an explosion.

Rabbi looked at this creature roaming his living room, slamming his fists together, flicking his head like a tensed-up bull, restlessly pacing, driven by the current in his nerves, the pulsing in his muscles. It was a new specimen to him. The Jewish athlete.

His father, Paul, was a clothing manufacturer, plumpish, the stomach not hanging so much as sitting up there in solid demonstration of the good life. Bald, of average height, he was more or less relaxed. And although he was obviously agitated now, he was nevertheless able to show self-control.

But his son—ah, what a fascinating phenomenon! Rabbi smiled wonderingly, somewhat appreciatively at him. The bulky body, thick arms, thighs bulging. The round stump of a neck. Shoulders like a slab of cement the body was carrying around.

Remarkable! See what America has done to us Jews. Milk, vitamins, orange juice, fresh air, exercise, steaks, freedom, opportunity, competition—all these things produce athletes, not scholars. After generations and generations of dwarfed, pale, long-fingered, frail students—this new species.

"Rabbi," Paul Grossman slid his thumb in the air toward the boy, "I ask you—is that a football player?"

Rabbi smiled, "Something special he is—I'm not sure what!"

"Look at that build, huh? How much you weigh, Billy?"

"Two-oh-five."

"Two hundred and five! Enough, huh? But he can move! Fast, tricky. He can get around like a damn monkey on that field. Stamina, drive. You name it, he's got it."

"Aw, Pop—all right!"

"Let me tell Rabbi how it is! And the most important thing, Rabbi, he loves the game. He's a natural, crazy about it! Spends every minute throwing the ball around. Practicing. He loves it! He wants to play like he wants to breathe."

"So?"

"So—" Grossman stood up as if to deliver a bomb, "he's not good enough to make the team! Would you believe it? The dinky football team, Greenlake High, he's not good enough for it. Is that something?"

"It does seem a little strange. What exactly do you—?" Rabbi couldn't understand why Grossman had brought the boy to him, why he was telling him all this.

"The thing's plain and simple, Rabbi. They got a coach there, the football coach—what's his name, Billy?"

"Angstrom."

"That's it! Angstrom. Sounds German to me, you know?"

"He's not German, Dad."

"All right, all right. So this Angstrom guy, after Billy tries out for the team, says he can't make it. He drops him from the squad!"

"And why," Rabbi asked patiently, "did you come to tell me this?"

"Because it's plain and simple, Rabbi. The guy's an anti-Semite! Hates Jews. There isn't a Jewish kid on the squad. Greenlake High football team—no Jews allowed. What do you think of that?"

Rabbi looked at Billy, who sat now red-faced, embarrassed by all this. "You think that's true, Billy?"

"About there being no Jews on the squad?"

"And his attitude?"

"Well, no Jewish kid's on the squad."

"And you believe that's deliberate?"

"He—he once said something."

"What?"

"I was trying out. I want to play quarterback. He had me throwing the ball. I was—well, I wasn't doing too good. So he said: 'That's what I expected.'"

"Meaning—?"

"He said: 'It's not in you. Not your game. Jews can't play football.' "

"He said that?"

"What'd I tell you?" Paul was standing. "A dirty anti-Semite!"

"That is rather open." Rabbi sat scratching his chin. Could it be true?

"Oh, he'll deny it! Face him with it. I'll bet he denies it!" Grossman sensed Rabbi's doubt.

Rabbi sat pondering the situation a few moments. The angry, disappointed father. The frustrated, rejected son. The high school football coach who had possibly indicated some prejudice. And of course he was expected to deal with it. Rabbi, go show up that coach. Rabbi, get my son on the football team. Rabbi, stop this new kind of anti-Semitism that keeps Jewish boys out of sports. They came to him with everything. It was natural, and maybe even a good thing. The trouble was, he couldn't really feel it was very important. So many bigger problems! So many more vital needs.

"What do you want me to do about it, Mr. Grossman?"

"You tell me! You're the Rabbi."

"Mr. Grossman, maybe I'm going to shock you. I'm not sure we should do anything about it."

"What? Anti-Semitism in the school and you say—"

"There are different kinds of anti-Semitism, Mr. Grossman. *If* this is anti-Semitism. Not all kinds can be controlled."

"I don't get it, Rabbi! My kid's not allowed to play on the team because he's Jewish and you think maybe we shouldn't do anything?"

"Wait. Fighting anti-Semitism when it does harm, that's one thing. We take action. We do something. But reacting to a feeling some people may have about us, that's another."

"This ain't doing harm? Right in the high school of our town a man—"

"Mr. Grossman," Rabbi didn't want to become involved in the argument now, "I will go and have a talk with this Mr. Angstrom. Let's see what happens. Allow me to consider what to do after I talk with him."

"All right. If you say so. You're the Rabbi. But I think he ought to be exposed. This ought to be a scandal!"

"I assume, Mr. Grossman, you want your son to play on that team?"

"Right!"

"Then let me see how we can achieve that objective."

Dwight Angstrom had a way of looking at you and of moving his body about at the same time that was very disconcerting. He would be arranging things, shifting objects here and there, and yet always staring at you as he did it. It was as if he wanted to distract you with his movements while he himself watched you carefully.

"What can I do for you, Rabbi Gordon?" He did not sit down, although Rabbi sat across the desk, looking at him as he moved around putting papers in drawers, files into a cabinet, adjusting the blinds in his tiny office.

"Well, Mr. Angstrom, it's not so much a question of doing something. I . . . I wanted to have a chat with you. Thought we might get to know each other. I certainly want to know the man who's so important in the lives of the young people of this town." Rabbi piled it on a bit, trying hard to make it casual.

"Me—important?"

"The football coach of Greenlake High? You're a decider of destinies. You're at the heart of a very emotional area of activity."

Angstrom now decided to sharpen a few pencils, glancing over his shoulder as he did so.

"It's a sport to me, Rabbi Gordon. A beautiful sport. That's all. I don't encourage any other emphasis on it."

"So you see the young people who participate in your football as sportsmen? Athletes?"

"Nothing else. A beautiful sport." The pencils sharpened. He had apparently run out of distracting little enterprises and he finally sat down opposite Rabbi. The left leg was placed high up over the thigh of the right. He made an adjustment of a sock, re-tied a shoelace. Then a tapping with the pencil against the the sole of the shoe.

"And you judge them—evaluate them, shall I say—purely as athletes?"

"That's it. They've got it or they don't." Now Angstrom gave him a direct, sharp, and unafraid look into the eyes, the confrontation taking place beneath all the subterfuge.

Rabbi decided, too, that the point had been reached. "Mr. Angstrom, you really know why I'm here, don't you?"

"Haven't the faintest."

"No idea?"

"Tell me." The calmness of the challenge was like saying: "You expose yourself first."

"All right. Please understand this is by way of a discussion. Not an accusation. I have no intention of arguing with you. It's a—let's say an exchange of views. All right?"

"I'm here."

It wasn't going to be easy. Angstrom wouldn't let it be. That was obvious. "Well, it's about a young man. Billy Grossman."

"Grossman?" Eyes upward as if searching his memory. "Oh yes."

"He applied—or whatever the phrase is—"

"Tried out."

"Thank you. Tried out for the football team."

"Yeah. Quarterback. That's what he wanted. Quarterback."

"And, as I understand it, he didn't qualify."

"Nope."

"I'm—well, you know I'm a Rabbi. My knowledge of football is zero. But it does seem to me—judging from his build, his interest, enthusiasm—"

"Not enough. Ability, that's what counts."

"And he doesn't have it?"

"Nope."

"Mr. Angstrom, we're in a—well a slightly delicate area. But I'm going to be frank. This is your objective opinion?"

"What are you getting at?"

"You indicated to him that his lack of ability was a racial characteristic."

"Such as?" He continued tapping the pencil on the edge of his shoe.

"Well, he's Jewish and that Jews can't really play good football."

The direct, intense blue eyes stared right at him. "That's my opinion."

"I see."

"Sorry. My opinion. And experience."

"Well, I can't discuss your experience."

"Or my opinion. I have it." Now standing up, he adjusted some papers on a little table in a corner. "Negroes make good runners. Great in track. Italians have it in soccer. Got a knack for it. Australians in tennis. Jewish people? I don't know—maybe handball. Things like that. Football's not their game."

Rabbi tapped the ends of his fingers together. His smile was indulgent.

"Do you realize, Mr. Angstrom, that's a prejudiced statement?"

"No—it isn't." The reply was uttered with calm assurance, almost indifference. "It's an opinion based on experience." The round face remained bland, the eyes now staring at him with remote equanimity. Suddenly. "Let me ask you something Mr. Gor—Rabbi Gordon. You think Swedes are as good at playing the fiddle as Jews? You think the Irish are as smart with the book stuff as the Jews? Or let me put it this way—you think the English are as good at cooking and that kind of thing as the French? Get it? Then you've got prejudices too. Or do you consider them opinions based on your experience?"

He was standing over Rabbi now. "Let's get one thing straight. I pick the kids for the squad on ability. Period. That Grossman kid hasn't got it. The build, yeah. Sure. But he can't throw a pass to save his life. No control. I tried him out, didn't I? He hit the receiver twice out of ten passes. The other times he didn't come a mile near 'em. That's not going to win games for Greenlake. He don't play quarterback for me."

Angstrom did not pause. He just stopped talking. Then:

"Anything more you want to discuss?"

Rabbi stood up. "No, thank you. I think the situation is clear." But he was unable to resist the final pinning-down. "If he could—pass, is that it—"

"Yeah. A quarterback passes the ball. Throws it to a receiver down the field."

"If he could pass, he'd have a chance for the team?"

"Yup. Ability, that's all I'm interested in."

"Thank you." To show something, he was not quite sure what, Rabbi held out his hand. Angstrom shook it. The smile on his face was confident, a sense of having won.

Paul Grossman brought Bob Barrett into the situation, something in him so strongly aroused that he didn't know how to deal with it. Now the three of them sat in Rabbi's living room and Barrett had to be told the whole story from the beginning and when Paul was finished, Rabbi waited a few moments. He leaned back, trying to think it out quickly. Paul Grossman with a declaration of injury: An anti-Semite crushing his son. Bob Barrett sitting there expectantly, waiting for a Rabbi's wisdom. And he knew that they would find it hard to understand his position, perhaps battle with him over it. But he felt confident of his judgment. This had to be dealt with in a special way.

"Let me put it briefly," Rabbi said. "I went to see this Angstrom. He *is* prejudiced, full of racial nonsense."

"Anti-Semitic?" Paul pressing it.

"He doesn't think so."

"Anti-Semitic or not?" Paul demanding now.

"Rabbi," Barrett's almost condescending chairmanship of the meeting, "Paul has a right to know. Don't you think?"

Rabbi shaking his head. The eternal other side of the problem. No matter how non-Jewish the pattern of their lives, despite all the efforts to escape from a label and classification and even an identity, just whisper something that could be interpreted as anti-Semitism and you get the crackling response, the bristling, the impulse to attack and fight. The reaction was good and natural, but it had to be directed, used where it mattered.

"No," Rabbi said. "He's not anti-Semitic."

"All right," Paul moved about, pulling up his trousers, almost like a fighter in the ring about to stalk his opponent. "I don't care what we call him—what do we do about it?"

Rabbi, putting aside his resentment at Paul's pushing, aware of Barrett's quiet waiting, said calmly, "We do nothing."

"What?" Paul, indignant, glanced from Rabbi to Barrett to Rabbi.

Barrett sensed something. "Why, Rabbi? Why do we do nothing?"

"Gentlemen," Rabbi paced about a bit, arranging his thoughts. "I don't want us to make fools of ourselves. We cannot, as Jews, hope to wipe out in the minds of idiots, like this man Angstrom, the prejudice that's there by making demands. By creating a public scandal. By fighting it in the newspapers. By applying pressure. It's not going to change what he thinks and feels about Jews."

"But Rabbi, he's part of the school system."

"Agreed, Bob. But he's not teaching anti-Semitism. He's a gym instructor. If he were teaching or publicly expressing lies about Jews, I would urge the strongest possible action to get rid of him. He's the football coach. It's a voluntary activity at school. He runs the team. He can decide who plays on any basis he chooses."

"Even an anti-Semistic basis?" Barrett was trying to understand.

"It's not on that basis." Rabbi faced the two men. "According to him, Jews can't play football. And all he wants is to win football games. So he won't put Jews on the team."

Barrett was now curious and interested. "Rabbi, you're leading up to something."

"I am. It's as simple as this. He thinks Jews can't play football— we'll show him he's wrong!"

"How?"

"I suggest we make Billy good enough. So good that Angstrom can't afford to keep him off the team. Let's just make him a great football player!"

"How're you going to do that?" The boy's father looked at him skeptically.

Rabbi pointed to Paul. "You're going to do it. This is the idea. There are professional football players in New York, and I assume they are interested in making extra money. You approach one of them— I don't care who or how—and pay him to give Billy lessons in throwing that ball. Intensive lessons. Hours at a time. Seven days a week if necessary. Make that boy of yours so good that this Angstrom idiot won't be able to turn him down."

The silence of the two men was full of surprise and wonder. They looked at each other. Paul stood up and held out his hand to Rabbi.

"You know that's brilliant! A great idea! Oh, baby! To show up that bastard! Say—and will Billy love it!"

"If I may twist the old phrase," Rabbi said, smiling, "if you can't join 'em—beat 'em!"

The arrangement Paul made was simple. It was training season and the New York Giant team was in Fairfield, Connecticut. Paul approached one of the passing coaches and offered him five hundred dollars to work with Billy. The setup was for Billy to drive from Greenlake to Connecticut after classes every day, arriving about five in the afternoon. The coach then gave him from two to three hours of personal, intensive, professional instruction in the art of throwing a football accurately, fast, and far.

It was a seventy-five-mile trip each way. Paul gave Billy the Chrysler convertible to use for these drives. The maid was told to have a dinner ready to serve him each night when he returned home about nine o'clock, a pound of prime shell steak every night. He would start his homework at ten and have to work at it until one in the morning sometimes.

The coach was either a slave-driver, a sadist, or a hypnotist, Billy couldn't decide which. He had him practice gripping the ball to get it ready for the throw a hundred times before he let him toss it once. His right hand felt as if it had been stretched on the torture rack. He had to drive home using his left hand only and could barely manage to hold a pen in class for days.

Billy had sixteen days to learn how to be a good enough quarterback for Greenlake High (after that the Giant team was leaving for its first exhibition game). At the end of the first week, he felt so good about his improvement that he wanted to rush to Angstrom to try out again.

The coach said: "You're just starting to learn maybe a little bit. You got a long way to go, kid. A long way!"

It was discouraging, and his reports to his father, who wanted to know every detail, reflected this.

"But you are learning! That's what counts." Paul would try to cheer him up.

"A little, Coach says. Not much, Dad."

"Wait! Wait! It's only a week. You'll make it, Billy. Don't worry!"

But Billy did worry. He would try with all his concentration to master everything the coach was pounding into him. "Hold the ball this way—you're holding it too far back. Open the hand, grab it, like this!" Billy tried with a desperate determination. "The arm! The arm! Where's your goddam arm, kid? Raise it like you meant it. Fast. Get it up there!"

His shoulder ached so much he could hardly lift the arm, but he would try to snap it into position. And the coach wasn't even letting him throw the ball down the field. Just urging him to get rid of it, out of his hand.

Ten days. The coach was letting him throw a little more now. But he couldn't get any distance, couldn't even approach accuracy.

"You know, kid," the coach said to him that day, "you got outstanding ability for lousing this up. You're throwing like a girl, so help me! Get some zilch into this for chrissake!"

"I'm doing my best, Coach."

"I don't want to hear that. If that's your best—Mama mia!"

The discouragement was enough to upset the whole Grossman family. Paul stood in the kitchen as Billy ate his dinner and pumped him to get at what was the matter.

"Not enough power? Is that it?"

"I don't know, Dad. I give it everything."

"Wrong grip?"

"Maybe. I don't know."

"Tell me! What? What? We gotta find out what's wrong! It's ten days and you sound like you're throwing worse than before. To hear you tell it, the coach thinks you stink."

"Maybe he does."

"Why should he?"

"Maybe I do. Just stink. Maybe I'm no good."

"Don't say that! You're going to be a great passer and you're learning from an expert. You're going to knock Angstrom on his ass when you show him!"

"Maybe I just haven't got it, Dad."

"You? With that build? That natural ability? You're out of your mind! You have got it—and how! Listen—" Paul sat down at the table beside Billy, pulling his chair close, "—you know what? Tomorrow I'll go up with you. So I'll take a day off, so what? And I'll talk to this Mr. Coach character—and I'll find out what's what! . . . Now eat that steak. Don't be so goddam discouraged for God's sake!"

Paul approached the coach on the field with a great show of respect. He held out his hand, smiled generously, and said: "Coach, I want to thank you for all you've done for my boy. It's terrific!"

The coach, a heavy-faced man with deep lines that made him look as if he were perpetually growling, pushed back his cap and scratched his forehead.

"Don't know if I've done anything."

"Well, I know he's improved, he's learned. He's getting there— isn't he?"

"Getting there? You want it straight, mister? I feel like giving you back the money. He's not throwing any better. Not so it matters. He's not doing it like I show him and teach him and explain it. Honest, I feel like giving you the money back."

Paul turned to Billy and motioned him to move away, out of ear-shot. He wanted to talk to the coach privately.

"Listen, coach. I want to ask you a simple question: Why? Why isn't he doing any better?"

"It's like this, Mister. Some got it, some don't. Your boy—" he shook his head, his lips out, "if you ask me—never. It's not in him. But chrissake not everybody's born to be a quarterback. Maybe some other position. Let him try that."

"And give up?"

"It's up to you. We got five more lessons—I'll finish 'em. If you want it."

"I want it. He wants it! We're not going to give up!"

"Your dough." The coach shrugged his shoulders and walked away towards Billy. "Okay kid, we'll go through it again. . . ."

On the drive back to Greenlake that evening, Paul sat there in a turmoil of bewilderment and anger. How could this be? A kid like Billy, built for it, eager for it, working his balls off to learn, and getting nowhere. Why? Could that idiot Angstrom be right? Jews can't play football? Crazy! What a stupid notion! Like saying Jews can't be soldiers—and look at that Israeli army knocking the shit out of the Arabs! Some dumb Negro out of nowhere could be a super-super quarterback—and a Jewish boy with intelligence couldn't? Crazy! Or those dumb guys out of some dinky college in the South you never heard of, and the Polacks and the Italians, just think of the kooky names in football! Shmalowski, Pastorelli, Bourgadnik, who the hell were they that a Jewish kid like Billy wasn't a hundred times better? Maybe that Giant coach was anti-Semitic too! Why not? How many Jews on the Giant team anyway? So they got a Jewish head coach—big deal! No, no, no—there was something fishy about all this. He just had to believe that.

When the lessons were finally over and the day came when Billy was to approach Angstrom again, Paul wanted to go with him, wanted to be there and see if that anti-Semitic bastard was going to try it again. Let him just say that Billy Grossman wasn't good enough for the crappy Greenlake High football team!

But Billy persuaded him not to go. It would be too embarrassing.

No father had ever shown up to try to get his son on the team. And Paul agreed reluctantly.

Billy walked onto the field where the squads were practicing, and came up to Angstrom. It was the most difficult thing he had ever had to do in his life and he was sweating and he wasn't even sure he could see straight.

"Mr. Angstrom?"

The coach looked at him calmly, as if he had somehow suspected after the Rabbi's visit that something like this might happen.

"Yeah?"

"I'm Billy Grossman. I tried out for quarterback before . . . and . . . and didn't . . ."

"I remember. Yeah?" Angstrom was really curious now.

"Well . . . I'd like to try again. Please. Can I . . . will you give me a chance?"

"Sure." Now Angstrom had an idea of what had happened and he was curious to see the results. "Grab some balls and toss a few. Go on. Here—" he called to another sudent, "Sandy, get a few balls over here. Grossman's going to try out for quarterback again."

Billy's hands were wet and he wiped them on his pants. A few people on the field were watching.

Billy wished he were dead. He hated his father at that moment, along with Rabbi, Coach Angstrom, the Giant character, and whoever had invented football. It was hard for him to breathe and he opened his mouth and took a few grasps to get the air into his lungs.

Finally he was ready and he gripped the ball and flung it as far as he could. Lousy. Well, that was only the first.

By the time he had thrown ten passes, in various directions and of the type Angstrom was suggesting, he knew it as surely as he had ever known anything. But now a strange thing happened and Billy was unprepared for it.

"Listen, kid—" Angstrom put an arm on his shoulder, "let's take a walk."

The two moved across the field to the benches of the stands and then sat down side by side.

"Tell me, Grossman—you been taking lessons?"

Billy had thought about being asked this question and decided he would tell the truth. Why not?

"Yes."

"From a pro? Something like that?"

"Yes. One of the Giant coaches."

"Well—I admire that, you know? At least you didn't give up. That's not bad for spirit. . . . Well, what do you think of your passing now?"

Billy, a little overwhelmed by Angstrom's being so direct, almost friendly with him, let it burst out.

"I think it still stinks!"

He looked at Angstrom. The man was laughing, his head back, laughing and shaking his head.

"You know what, Grossman? You're right! . . . so why don't we forget it, huh? This quarterback business?"

"I guess so." Billy was looking down at his hands.

"But—" and now Angstrom came out with his idea, "—we just lost a lineman. Reynolds. Broken ankle." He was watching Billy for his reaction. "And I think you might just make a pretty damn good lineman. . . . Want to try it?"

Billy looked at him in wonder. "On the team?"

"Where the hell do you think? Of course on the team!"

Billy covered his face not to show anything, the red eyes he knew were there.

"Thanks, Mr. Angstrom."

"How much you weigh, Grossman?"

"Two-oh-five."

"Hey—we could use a hunk o' beef like that!" He slapped Billy's back. "Go find a uniform in the locker room—and get out here in five minutes. Five minutes! you hear me!"

Billy was running already, as fast as he could.

The Friday night services after Billy had played in his first game, Rabbi came up to Grossman.

"Tell me something," Rabbi said, "so Billy's on the team?"

"Well, he let him play anyway."

"And he played well?"

Grossman scratched his forehead. "He didn't take him out."

"He played the whole game?"

"Kept in the whole game!"

"Why do you think he did it?"

"Angstrom? That lousy goy—all he wants to do is win. Billy can help him win, he lets him play."

Rabbi looked up, smiling. "I wonder what an anti-Semite would have done?"

"What do you mean?"

"An anti-Semite would rather lose—than win with a Jew's help."

"And you know what?" Grossman smiled too now. "It would serve him right, the shmuck!"

XII

Danny discovered he had a greater sense of decency than he had imagined. When he went to bed that night after seeing Bea Aldrich, everything seemed clear and simple. He had been adding it up all the way home. The long, straggling train ride, the drive from the station with that sense of isolation that comes from being alone in a car on the dark, sleeping streets of a small town, the getting undressed quietly so as not to awaken Alice, the lying down finally, the light out, the darkness, the end at last, the conclusion to all the thinking, feeling, reacting. *I'll do it.*

But in the morning everything looked and felt dirty. The drunken, self-destroying figure of the woman, fighting against the pain of being abandoned. The sordid behavior of Barrett. The messiness of the whole business. He didn't want to touch it, be involved. He had a strange awareness inside of poor, unhappy humans, struggling for something to live for, and the knowledge that he could only hurt them by exposing it all. He was afraid to go ahead, unable to decide not to.

Danny finally determined not to commit himself. He would approach it delicately, see what developed. He called Rabbi in the morning, before leaving for the station, and said he wanted to see him that night. Rabbi agreed.

"Alone please, Rabbi."

"Of course, if you wish."

But Frieda was there. The woman had an instinct. She had that damn incredible instinct for detecting trouble, or vital decisions to be made. She opened the door, and Danny felt as if he were living through an experience again, the time he had come to Rabbi's home right after the meeting. She had the same expectant, terrified look on her face, the same suggestion of stubbornness in her manner.

"I have to tell you, Danny," Rabbi said, "it was no use. I say to Frieda—I want to be alone with Danny, and that's all that's necessary. She decides to be present too."

Frieda didn't even mind these references to her as if she were some remote object.

"If it's about David—it's about me. What happens to him—happens to me."

Rabbi shrugged his shoulders. "You see?"

They finally sat down in the living room, Frieda this time without apron or dish towel or sign of other preoccupation. She had the coffee made in advance, and the electric percolator was plugged in right there in the living room on a side table.

Danny found it impossible to begin. It all flooded through him again. How do you suddenly reveal the dirty secret of another man? How do you indicate that you went searching into his private life and want to use what you found no matter how filthy it is? Danny looked at Rabbi as if attempting to find in him again the justification for all he had done and planned to do. Rabbi, with that rather abstracted expression. Rabbi, with the smile that seemed so remote. Rabbi, with the abrupt intensity, the outburst that came from stored-up frustrations. Rabbi, the dedicated man who was always above other men, out of reach. Full of weakness, perhaps, ineffectual in so many ways, yet in him the essence of all Danny believed in, the concern for one's fellow man, the values, the search for meaning in life. It had to be done for him. Such a man had to be saved.

"Rabbi, this isn't going to be easy."

"I can see that," Rabbi smiled. "You look like you have some terrible message to deliver."

"More trouble?" Frieda tensely.

"No. Oh no," he reassured her. She was sitting there like a woman about to be told her fate. "It's not like that at all. Rabbi—we have an important decision to make." It was so hard to get to it, so awkward to explain it all!

"About what?"

"Rabbi—" Danny looked at him, "just so we understand each other, I believe with all my heart that you must remain here as our Rabbi."

"Thank you, Danny. Thank you very much. I know that."

"All right. Now what you said to me last time was that you wanted to do what was best for the congregation. An open fight, you said, bringing this whole business out in the open, might cause a split, break up the congregation into factions, endanger the building of the Temple."

"I still believe that."

"I know you do, Rabbi. But what would you say if I told you there's a way to win your fight without bringing it out in the open?"

"I don't know. That would depend."

"Rabbi—to stay on here you have to *do* something. You have to agree to fight in some way."

"Ah . . . in some way. That's why I say it depends. . . . Look, Danny. If you told me you could have Bob Barrett assassinated, shot by a gangster, that might save my job here as Rabbi. Without Barrett— who knows? But would you expect me to approve?"

Danny shook his head. He looked down at his hands, a bit frightened suddenly. Why had he started this? Had he gone too far? It had all seemed so easy and right, and now he was frightened. He found himself worrying about the way it would be seen by others, interpreted, what Rabbi would say. But it was too late. It had to be faced.

"Funny that you should say that."

Rabbi laughed. "You weren't actually thinking of assassinating Barrett, I hope!"

"In a way, I was."

"What?"

Frieda and Rabbi were staring at him incredulously. "In a way, I guess that's what it amounted to."

Rabbi leaned forward. "Are you serious, Danny?"

"Rabbi, here's the story. Please let me tell you the whole thing first, before you react. All right?"

"I don't like the way this sounds, Danny."

"Please—Rabbi? Now listen. You are accused by Bob Barrett of . . . of . . . well, immoral behavior."

"An excuse! Yes?"

"Now that's . . . that's an outrageous thing. Isn't it? Against any man. Especially a Rabbi. Especially when he knows it isn't true! And what does it make him? Mr. Bob Barrett? It makes him appear to be a man of high ethical standards. The protector of virtue. The upholder of moral behavior. The man to whom sin—"

"Get to it, Danny!"

"I am, Rabbi! . . . Now such a man should himself be leading a clean life. Shouldn't he? If he tears you down before our Committee—then he should be virtuous, moral, upright, decent! Shouldn't he, Rabbi?"

"Danny—what—?"

"Well . . . well it so happens that Mr. Bob Barrett, the President of our congregation, is himself a sinner!"

"How?"

"How? In the vilest way! As dirty as you can get! He has—or had—a mistress."

Rabbi for some reason looked at Frieda. She sat like a tight spring, glaring at him. No one moved or spoke for a long time. Then Rabbi felt the sickness in him. A nausea enveloped him as if Danny had coated him with it, spread it over him—a sick kind of filth.

He turned quickly. "Danny, I want you to go home! Now!"

"Da-vid!" A cry came from Frieda. "Listen to him! Listen!"

"Rabbi. . . . Rabbi. . . . Rabbi, listen to me." Danny said, almost pleading. "Listen. I met this woman yesterday. I was at her home. I know her name, where she lives, where they met, everything that went on. She was his mistress for more than two years! Mr. Bob Barrett's mistress!"

Frieda was strangely shaking in her chair, back and forth, rocking. "I knew it. I knew it. I knew it. The kind of man he is. I knew it!"

"Frieda!" Rabbi's tone was incredulous. "What kind of thing is that to say!"

Frieda continued the rocking, hands clasped in her lap. "I knew. I knew. Thank God thank God thank God thank God. . . ."

Rabbi wanted to turn away from Frieda's face all twisted, Danny staring at him like a man holding out a knife and waiting for him to grasp it. But there was no place for him in all this.

"What does this have to do with me?"

Danny moved forward now with the eagerness of a conspirator. "Everything, Rabbi! This can save you!"

"Barrett's private life—"

"Just listen! All I have to do is go to him. You don't have to do a thing—I'll do it! Confront him with this. Tell him I know everything. The name, the person, the place. She has even agreed to swear it's true! Don't you see? He'd have to drop the charge against you. He'd have no choice!"

Rabbi stared at Danny as if at some creature he had never seen before. "You would . . . threaten to expose him?"

"Of course! Before the Committee! The noble, virtuous man who accuses—"

"You want me to do exactly what I condemn him for?"

"Fire with fire!"

"Evil with evil! . . . No! No, Danny! Never! I don't want anything to do with this! No!"

At that moment they noticed, but didn't really notice, that Frieda had stood up. An awareness of her off at the side, standing. Maybe leaving. Going to the kitchen. Somewhere.

But her face was twisted, like that of a woman in pain. The mouth open, the lips shaped as if in a cry of pain. She came up to Rabbi slowly, reached out and took his hands, gripping them.

"David, you're going to let Danny do it."

Rabbi had only to take one look at her and it was clear to him. The eyes, the expression, the grip on his hands.

"David, you're going to let him do it. You are. You are."

He didn't know how to deal with it. Her hands were so tight, the nails digging into his flesh. The head was now moving, the tears coming, the body swaying a little.

"You are!" A cry into his face.

He pulled his hands away. He stepped back. Frieda slipped to the floor. To her knees. Her hands clasped as if in prayer.

Danny watched, frightened. Rabbi's face was taut with agony.

"Frieda—" he was staring down at her, aware of the need for strength, firmness. He had to shake her out of it. Stop it. End this! End this! "I am not going to let him do it. It's not the way I live! And if I have to pay a price for that, I'll pay it!"

"Price?" What was almost laughter came from her. "Who's paying a price for how you live? Me! You hear that? Me! Me! Me!"

"Frieda—" He reached down, tugging at her hands, trying to make her get up from the floor. Where did this come from? What had she kept in her all this time that it could suddenly burst out like this? What had she hidden from him? He didn't want to hear it, believe it. She was hysterical, that's all, frightened by what might happen to him—to them—and she was reacting like a scared child. He pulled at her hands as if to draw her back into reality.

She broke loose from his grip, fell back. She was swaying, moaning. "Me! I'm paying! For everything you do. Over and over. One congregation after another. Fights, troubles. Always, always troubles. I don't pay for it? You think it's easy to be your wife? What they do to you they do to me. What they say. Behind our back. To our face. The looks. The pity. Poor Frieda. Poor Frieda—I don't want to be poor Frieda any more!" She was moaning, her body swaying. "No more! No more!" Now she was deep in her own dark recess of torture, in her own private hell, with all her memories, with the frightening uncertainty of all these years. The tears were coming, the sobs. Her body back and forth, still on her knees on the floor. "For me! For me—do it! . . . I'm tired. I'm tired of moving. Tired of not knowing what I am, where I am. I'm tired of your being too good for the whole world. Too good to be a human being! Be a man who fights for your family! Help me! Oh God, help me! Help me!"

Rabbi bent down on his knees beside her, stroked her head, her back.

"Frieda, Frieda darling. It'll be all right. Don't worry."

"How? How?"

"You're just scared. I didn't know, Frieda. I had no idea. Why didn't you ever tell me?"

"Protecting you. Always protecting you. . . . Protect *me* now, David!"

"I will, darling. You'll be all right, we'll all be all right. Whatever happens—there's nothing to be afraid of."

He looked up at Danny standing motionless, in shock. Rabbi gestured for him to help get Frieda up on her feet. Danny came over to the other side and together they started to lift her, support her. She was shaking.

"I'll get her into bed, Danny. She has to lie down."

Frieda turned her head slowly to Danny, looking for him, as if she had to find him somewhere.

"Danny—do it. Do it! Do it, please!"

Rabbi motioned Danny away now and started to lead her toward the stairs, his arm around her, holding her to keep her from swaying. "Come to bed, Frieda darling. Lie down, you'll feel better. It's going to be all right, don't worry. . . ." And he took her up the stairs slowly, guiding her, supporting her.

Danny stood at the bottom of the stairs. The noises above became muffled. He sat in the car a few moments before starting it. How could Rabbi not do it now? How could he refuse to fight for his life and Frieda's after this?

But in his heart he knew, Rabbi would not do it.

D anny Cole had once made an effort to share the discovery of this man with some of his friends. He wanted others to see and experience what contact with Rabbi could mean.

Whom to ask? Should they be Jewish? This was debated at length between Danny and Alice. Rabbi might actually find it more stimulating to talk with some of the bright gentile couples they knew. But Danny realized that what he really wanted to happen was for some of his nonbelieving, noninvolved, non-Jewish Jewish friends to discover what they were missing. The kind of Judaism they were cutting themselves off from. He wanted them to see and understand what it was that had engaged him and Alice so profoundly.

After a great deal of evaluating, the selection was made. Joe and Eleanor Laskow, Marty and May Baron. Joe was a free-lance writer, which meant in practical terms that he wrote anything for money. Articles for magazines on automobiles or prize-fighting, scripts for TV documentaries on the Negro problem, or the conservation of natural resources, a ghosted book for a Senator on his trip to South America, a sexy novel about a Hollywood couple that was published under a pseudonym. Joe's description of himself was: If it's done with words, Laskow can do it.

Marty Baron had graduated from Harvard, *magna cum laude,* at the age of twenty, had done secret work of an organizational nature on nuclear matters, worked for a big electronics firm for a few years, and now had his own company in what he described as the "computer parts" field which was prospering.

Neither the Laskows nor the Barons were members of the congregation. Both Joe and Marty considered themselves Jews, never denied or hid their Jewishness, but felt absolutely no need to act upon it.

They were part of that younger element in every Jewish community that finds itself in a state somewhere between rejection and dissociation. Rejection of their Jewish upbringing, the preservation of ritual, the affiliation with a congregation, the acceptance of "organized religion," the making of any aspect of their life specifically Jewish in character or tone. And a sense of dissociation with the Jews who did, a feeling that they were different, not on the same intellectual level, that there was an alien quality to the pattern of life these others followed, from the holiday observances to the involvement with Jewish causes, events, drives, even the identification with Israel.

Rabbi knew the type well. He thought of them as "the wandering-away Jew," the Jew who had looked for and found other causes to be involved with, politics or social protest, and who derived a greater reward and fulfillment from them than from anything Judaism could offer. In the life and affairs of the congregation, these were the missing: the intense and the concerned, the bright, articulate voices of the young. They had wandered away—they would have to be brought back. But he did not know how.

But Rabbi had so much more on his mind at the time, the problems of dealing with the actual affairs of the congregation—from ritual changes he wanted to introduce to Sunday School programs he felt a need to enrich—that he regarded this as a peripheral matter. And besides, there was something about Danny's attitude that he resented. Come and meet my Rabbi, the man who has changed my life. See why I've been influenced by this man. Engage him in conversation and discover the joy of a profound intellectual encounter. He had the feeling that Danny was "showing him off" and at the same time justifying the validity of his own experience. Rabbi agreed to come that evening very reluctantly.

He showed it at once in the manner with which he introduced himself to the two couples.

"I'm that strange phenomenon you may have heard about—a rabbi."

The Barons and the Laskows smiled, as if they expected a rabbi to be defensive. When it was Marty's turn to shake Rabbi's hand, he said:

"And I'm that strange phenomenon you don't want to hear about, a Jew who is anti-rabbi."

"Wait a minute!" Danny almost physically separated them. "This was going to be a pleasant evening of talk!"

Rabbi smiled, but the bitterness was already there. "Am I allowed, Danny, to feel pity for them?"

"Oh, God!" Danny turned away, aware now that it was not to be at all what he had hoped for.

Marty seemed unperturbed. "Rabbi, we'll accept your pity—if you'll accept our indifference to it."

So, everybody now knew, it was going to be that kind of an evening. But first they all made an attempt to observe the amenities and they settled down with a sense of suspended hostility. It went along for a while, calmly enough.

A stack of Mozart quartets on the hi-fi playing at a background level. Comments about a local event or two (there had been a police raid on a party of teen-age kids smoking pot in Greenlake), the selection of drinks (Rabbi: "Just color the water with a drop of Scotch"), the careful sizing up of each other.

Marty said: "When I make enough money, I'm going to quit business and teach high school here in Greenlake." Joe said: "You have more than enough money now." Marty said: "I hate bastards who spoil people's illusions about themselves." Rabbi said: "Nobody can destroy all your illusions about yourself. It's impossible to live without them."

Danny demonstrated the color television set they had just bought, then defended it against the sneering attacks, then championed it as part of identifying with life today. Joe said television had replaced religion as the opium of the people. Rabbi pointed out that opium was actually a stimulant, and said it was the advertising on television that was the danger. They talked back and forth, making observations, comments, getting a feeling about each other.

Then, in a quiet moment, staring at Rabbi with a kind of quizzical look—Joe began it. Suddenly it was as if all the underlying differences had to be revealed, the recognition that a Rabbi was present, a man dedicated to a life of religion in today's world, a man outside their own concept of life. Perhaps out of curiosity, or the need to explore his own feelings and attitudes, Joe began to question Rabbi. He probed, directly, cynically, as if Rabbi were a strange phenomenon that needed to justify itself. It became a cross-examination. On faith. Judaism. The essence of what Rabbi was and believed in.

"Do you mean, Rabbi," Joe was smiling, the way one does when one knows in advance that the other's response will not be acceptable, "that you really, actually believe there is a *God?*"

Rabbi was not surprised. How many Jews had already asked him this! The self-destructive honesty of their questioning. The inherent Jewish skepticism. The refusal to surrender something in the self. Why was it so hard for Jews to believe in God? Rabbi sighed, clasped his hands, looked at him calmly.

"Yes. I believe there is a God who created our universe."

"A being? Rabbi—?" The response was incredulous.

"Yes. A transcendent being. Certainly God isn't nature. Nor is He some abstract concept, an impersonal force. I believe God is a living Will."

"And Rabbi—can you speak to this God?" Joe's expression was amused, and he spoke now as if testing Rabbi's simplicity.

Rabbi looked at them. Here it was, the cynicism, the sophistication, the denial. The generation without faith. He knew then that he would play this game of intellectual exploration with them all the way, as far as they wanted to go.

"Speak to Him?" He smiled, his eyes half-closed, thinking of how to explain it. "Since God exists and has created us—are we to assume He is indifferent to us? How can we? God feels and is affected by man—so that means He listens. And so we can speak to Him."

He leaned forward now. "There are many ways of approaching this. Buber has said: God cannot be expressed, He can only be *addressed.* God is a Thou. . . . My only answer to your question can be a spiritual one. You see, in Judaism there is actually very little concern with defining God, explaining His nature. He exists for us only in relation to man. And so our relationship to Him is that He is our creator. We don't study Him for Himself. We accept Him as our ruler."

"I think," Marty said, getting into it, trying to be honest and truthful about himself, expressing his own problem, "that one of the reasons people like Joe and myself and many like us have so little to do with Judaism today—is that God is still part of the picture. It's very hard for me—and a helluva lot of people like me—to really believe in God."

"Why is it hard?"

"I think it's because of all the evil in the world. The injustice. The wars, the horrors, the killings. For me, it's as simple as that."

"An ancient cry." Rabbi leaned back, rubbing his forehead. What answer could satisfy this? "The message of Job is that man is not the measure of the universe. What man suffers is beyond man's understanding, but not beyond God's. Besides, we don't know the end. How do we know what He has in store for us? How it will all be balanced in some way. Of course evil exists, but does it exist in God? No—in man! And how do we know God isn't punishing that evil? Wars, revolutions, all the horrors that happen—how do we know they are not God's fulfillment of His judgment?"

"But Rabbi," Marty persisted, "suppose I don't accept this? Suppose I still cannot believe? According to you, I must believe in God or I cannot be a Jew."

"Don't expect Judaism to change to accommodate you to the extent that we can quietly drop God. Man must have a relationship with God. That's the essence of Judaism. . . . You know, a man like Martin Buber didn't accept all of traditional Judaism either. But one thing he did feel: That Biblical Judaism expressed what was most essential to him—the dialogue between man and God. And it is through this— accepting and believing in the kingship of God—that man finds his path in life. For us, that path is to live by God's ways and His rule."

"Ah—" Joe was not attacking really, but seeking an answer, "that's exactly it. I believe a man can lead a good life, serve his fellow man, without God."

"And why," Rabbi asked, smiling gently, "why do you want to help your fellow man?"

"Because it's the right thing. Because I believe in justice. Isn't that enough?"

"Well, now." Rabbi sat back. "Let's see. According to Judaism, the answer is no. Justice is not enough. Judaism goes beyond doing right, beyond justice. It includes love. To do good because we believe in good is not enough. We must do it because we want to be good, as God wants us to be. It is part of our relationship with Him. We have been called upon to imitate His ways—and that means to love one's fellow man. And our fellow man deserves our love—not because of some abstract principle of justice, but because he is a creature of God. Each man has God's love—so he must have ours."

Rabbi looked at them, and what he felt was a sense of sadness, the need to make Jews feel that Judaism was the way. Here were two good and intelligent men, born and reared as Jews, so totally lost from the faith of their fathers. Why? Why could nothing he said reach them?

"Are you saying, Rabbi," Joe squeezed his hands as if pressing out the thought, "that if I live a good life without faith in God, I cannot be considered a good Jew?"

The good Jew not wanting to be a Jew! No commitment. No involvement.

"I can only answer that without devotion it isn't Judaism. Without the relationship with God, you are not really a Jew."

"That's ridiculous! I am a Jew because I feel like one. I have a link to all the tradition and heritage and culture of the Jews. That's part of me. That makes me a Jew, doesn't it?"

Jewishness without Judaism. Was it something they feared? "What you feel, Joe, is good and valuable. But Joe, I am talking of *Judaism*. A Jew is a Jew not because of what he feels, but because God has chosen the Jews for His people—and therefore a Jew has to have a relationship with God.

"What is the heritage and tradition you identify with, if it is not the history of the Jews. Jewish religion is Jewish history. Their experience is your experience. At the Passover seder, do we celebrate the freeing of our forefathers? No. We celebrate our being freed from Egyptian bondage. The words we say are: God brought me out of Egypt. What every Jew of all time has endured is in every Jew living today. And what the Jews have endured has meaning only in terms of their relationship with God. And so to be a Jew is an act of commitment—to God, to a relationship with Him."

Rabbi felt that they understood, but they could not accept. The separation was like a physical barrier between them. This was only a kind of intellectual discussion to them, a little more than a game, but not much.

"This relationship with God you keep talking about, Rabbi—" Marty was shaking his head, "that involves ritual. But I find the ritual in the Temple unsatisfying, meaningless. Why do we need ritual to be Jews?"

Nothing about Judaism was right for them. How defend this now? And why the need to defend it to his own people? He felt sorry for them.

"Yes, Marty. You have a point. Much of the ritual we have is unsatisfactory for the Jew of today. That's why Reform Judaism has changed and is changing it. To make it more meaningful in terms of modern life. But don't reject it totally! Ritual is vital to our existence as Jews. Without it, Judaism cannot be brought into the daily life of man and into all aspects of his life. Ritual is a means, a way of making man think of God and feel Him. It is a link with our ancient tradition, with all other Jews of today and of all time. And it is a way of teaching. Judaism needs ritual to survive."

"I know," Joe replied smiling, "that you, as a Rabbi, feel deeply that Judaism must survive. But why should I feel it? Or millions like me who live in this country as Americans, as part of a country that believes there should be no differences? Why does Judaism have to survive?"

And Rabbi stared at him, the words and the question so painful. How many were there like him? What a tragedy for his people. Rabbi felt like someone who wanted to shake an unconscious man into life again. Live! Don't die! Come back to life! But there was no reaching them that way. Arguments. Reasoning. They were thinking their way to death.

"Let me say first," he wanted to do it calmly, "that we have no choice. Neither you nor I. Is the survival of Judaism something that *we* can decide? It concerns all Jews of all times. Why have they tried to survive through the ages, through all the horror and despair? How can we face what they have done to survive, what they have endured and suffered for being Jews—and not struggle to survive?

"And secondly, I believe Judaism has something to give the world of great meaning and value."

"Unique?"

My God, to ask that! Don't you know? "Yes. Unique. It consists of living and thinking in a special way. In a special relationship with God that the world needs. What is your alternative, Joe? Assimilation?"

Joe was very calm about it. "Don't you think that's where we're heading? Eventually? All over the world? Equalization. The wiping out of differences. Including the sense of uniqueness. And isn't it better that way?"

"So then," Rabbi holding back as much as he could, "you feel you are an American more than you are a Jew? Tell me, what is an American? Who is an American? Can you define one? We live in a country where we still don't accept the Negro as an American—and now he is not sure he wants to be one. Are you ready to give up your unique identity as a Jew for a concept so confused and full of conflict?

"But even more. Assimilation means acceptance of another world—the gentile world. Disappearing into it. Are you willing to accept that world? That idea of society and way of life? Has it shown itself to be so worthy that you want to be a part of it?"

There was no answer. And in the silence there was an awareness that there was really no more to say—on either side. No touching. No understanding.

Rabbi decided to end it. He smiled: "At the end of every show on TV there's a commercial. Let me give mine. Come to Temple. See what it is to belong, to participate, to be involved. Judaism is engagement. Become engaged. I don't know what kind of experience you've had before, how going to a Synagogue or Temple has affected you. But every Temple is an independent body. It acts alone, within Judaism. As a Rabbi, it is up to me to decide how I shall lead my congregation. So in my Temple you will experience *my* approach to Judaism. I think it will have meaning for you."

If there were only a nodding of the head now, a sign, a gesture of acceptance. But there was none. Joe sat back, the drink in his hand, taking a sip finally. Marty looked down at the floor. Danny stared at Rabbi in an agony of identification and disappointment.

And Rabbi felt himself in the presence of death. Their God, their history, their ritual, their Temple, their Judaism—all dead. A generation of Jews proclaiming the death of Judaism.

And it was they who were dying.

Rabbi had come resenting the evening, the purpose of it, Danny's desire for this encounter. But at the end he was grateful for the understanding it brought him. Oy, Rabbi, Rabbi, he said to himself, what a job you've got ahead of you. This is where you're really needed. This is where the most work is to be done . . . converting Jews to Judaism!

XIII

Sam Beskov acted fast. He called Bob Barrett the day after his mother's funeral.

"Sam Beskov."

"Hello, Mr. Beskov."

"Sam."

"Hello, Sam."

"Bob—you know my mother died?"

"Yes. I'm so sorry, Sam. I want to extend my deepest sympathies."

"All right. Thanks."

Barrett waited, his mind jumping in all directions. Why the call? Beskov was up to something. Watch out. But still—maybe this was an opportunity. A man's mother dies, you never can tell. Call me Sam. That's a clue. A desire for intimacy conceals other desires. But Beskov was a clever bastard. A one-purpose man, and that purpose was the advancement of the interests of Sam Beskov.

"Is there—anything—?" Bob didn't want to push it, yet he had to make Beskov feel the way was open.

"Bob, my mother's dead. That's a big blow to me. Ya know how it is? You got a mother—suddenly, gone. I want . . . I want to do something."

Barrett's excitement began jumping, anticipating in spectacular visions. But using the exactly correct tone, going with Sam's, like a singer doing a duet, he said "I understand, Sam. I understand."

"Bob, you're President of the Congregation—"

"Right."

"You got this Executive Committee it's called—"

"Right."

"That's the top? They run things?"

"That's our top Committee. In charge."

"Okay. As President you can call a meeting?"

"Any time."

"Tonight?"

"What?" He was being pushed, already feeling being pushed. The Sam Beskov push. Right away. Direct.

"Yes or no? Bob—?" The Beskov impatience was already there, the voice saying now come off it. Quit crapping around.

"What is all this about, Sam?"

"Important. Very important to the congregation. Would I ask otherwise?"

"All right, I'll try."

"Tonight—a meeting of your Executive Committee. Yes or no?"

"Yes." How Barrett hated this pushing! But he had to find out. With a man like Beskov, it could mean anything.

"You're inviting me?"

"Yes, Sam. I'm inviting you."

"My house."

"What?" Goddam sonofabitch! Already feeling the power. Grabbing control. The goddam Beskov power play.

"My house. You heard me."

Screw him and his money and everything connected with it! He wanted them to come crawling to him. But Barrett knew he would have to do it. Too much was at stake. You don't miss an opportunity to help build the Temple, help the entire congregation and its future— on account of pride, or even dignity and self-respect. Your self-respect and integrity live in your dedication to the cause, to the great goal of the Temple. . . . Screw the bastard—and use him!

"The meetings are usually held in my house—" a final feeble effort.

"Not this one. It's an unusual meeting. Nine o'clock. My house."

"All right, Sam. I'll do my best to get everybody who—"

"Just get enough members to decide something."

And he hung up. Barrett was in his office in New York. He looked at his watch. Eleven in the morning. He wanted to sit back a while and think about what had happened. Digest it, analyze it, plan a reaction to it. But there was no time. He had to reach the others before lunch and before they made commitments for the evening. And to give them a chance to break any commitments they had made.

Whatever he felt about Sam Beskov, the combination of pure, sheer hatred and disgust, the resentment, the instinctive resistance to his push and power, he knew that what might come out of this could be very important for the Temple. He let himself feel the glow of dedication to the cause of the Temple, the warm satisfaction of a sense of higher responsibility, and it was enough of an antidote. Within a half hour he had reached all the members of the Executive Committee except Lou Mandel, who was in the hospital, and of course, Rabbi.

Danny Cole simply asked: "What's it about?" And Barrett said: "I don't know. I'm not sure. But his mother just died and I think he wants to do something about it." Danny said: "I'll be there."

Jack Stern and Harry Brody grasped the idea at once. First, it was better to have Sam Beskov involved with the Temple, on any basis, than have him outside it. The image of the richest man in Greenlake as a Jew who had no relationship with the other Jews in town was somehow discomforting. It was like an admission of a failure on their part, of what they represented and wanted to accomplish.

Secondly, the way he acted in town, buying up property and putting up shopping centers, speaking out on every issue that came up, taxes, school budgets, police efficiency, whatever, all of this they felt was creating hostility toward Jews in Greenlake (because such things, in the undiscriminating eyes of the gentiles, rubbed off on all of them). Now at least, they might be able to suggest points of view to Beskov, work on him in some way, guide him a bit. It would be a surrender of his independence of action, and that could remove the constant threat he represented to their image.

Finally, there were the Beskov millions. And millions. And millions. What this could mean to the building of the Temple! All the problems solved. All their hopes realized.

Have an Executive Committee meeting in his house? They'd meet him in a bar if he wanted to! It was for the Temple. How many times have good Jews had to humble themselves to achieve worthy ends? Let him have his show of power and arrogance. Every Jew in Greenlake would benefit from their indulgence of him.

It was Dr. Greenwald who surprised and shocked Barrett.

"I'm not coming, Bob."

"Why?"

"I was planning to call you and get together with you tonight."

"About what?"

"I don't want to do this on the phone."

"Is it important? Because this meeting could mean—"

"Important, Bob. Very important. To me—and to the congregation."

"Can we discuss it at the meeting?"

"No. I want to talk to you first, alone."

"Can't you tell me what—"

"Bob, be at my house at eight. I want to see you."

When Barrett arrived at Sam Beskov's that evening, the others were already there and it was obvious that Sam had established the mood and atmosphere he wanted. They were all relaxed, sipping some of Sam's twelve-year-old Scotch, or aged bourbon, and there was a sense of their being encompassed by the sensual comfort of the room, its aura of wealth and power.

They noticed the tense look on Bob's face, the tightness around the mouth that indicated the striving for self-control, even a certain distraction in his manner. But they assumed this would all change as he too became part of the Beskov scene.

When it didn't, when Bob maintained that anxious manner, even a certain gruffness of tone, they felt it was because of his attitude towards Sam. Everyone knew how Bob Barrett resented Beskov. Originally, Sam was to have been one of Bob's "accomplishments." He had announced that he, personally, was going to win him over to the congregation, to membership in the Jewish community, to support and work for the Temple. It was going to be a demonstration of his ability to persuade, of his efficiency as President. And Beskov's rejection had been so blunt and harsh that most people assumed Bob could never forgive him. According to one report, Beskov had said: "I'd quicker join the Ku Klux Klan than your shitty Temple. That's what I think of all you jerky Jews."

But now, tonight, here, it was Sam's home, Sam's environment, Sam's hospitality, Sam's overwhelming presence. He wasn't going to let any silly past incidents or remarks spoil it. He greeted Bob as he had all the others, with the huge, acquisitive grasp of the hand, the clasping of the other arm, the grin of a man at ease, the voice of a man taking over, the Beskov control.

"So how many we got here now?" he asked Bob after shoving a drink into his hands. "This is your Committee?"

"The Executive Committee has seven members," Bob answered, no effort to conceal his tension. "We have four here. Lou Mandel, Rabbi, and . . . Dr. Greenwald are not coming."

"That's enough for a vote? A decision?"

"Yes, by our rules."

"Good!" Beskov had a bounce about him as he moved across the room, an exuberance that surprised them a bit. With his mother's funeral the day before, they had expected a solemnity, perhaps even signs of sadness. But not Sam. His voice came out with a joyous ring, his manner had a bantering quality about it.

"All right," he said, sitting down at last so that he faced them all, "let's start the meeting. Bob—how d'you start these meetings? You want to start it?" The assumption of power, the natural way of running things, directing, organizing, taking charge.

Barrett swallowed, looked down a moment, then managed to answer. "I called this meeting of the Executive Committee . . . at . . ." a sigh he couldn't control, "at the request of Sam Beskov. I assume he has . . . something. . . ." It was really hard for him to speak. "Something of importance he would like to tell us. . . . So in view of that . . . the special circumstances . . . we'll suspend preliminaries, procedures and all that, and get right on with it. . . . Sam, why did you want to speak to this Committee?"

"Oh!" Sam had thought of something and was grinning. "I forgot— I'm not even a member of the congregation. How do—"

Jack Stern, in his excitement and anticipation (after all, he was Chairman of the Fund Raising Committee and all this was almost too good to be true) burst out: "You're a member!" There was laughter. "I mean—to join the congregation you just say: I want to join. Right, Bob?"

Barrett nodded. "We have no rules for membership. Any Jew who wants to join our congregation can become a member."

"Great! So I'm a member. I'm telling you, it's easy to be a Jew! . . . Look, lemme get down to it now. What this is all about. . . . As you know, my poor mother died and was buried yesterday. Rachel. Now me, I'm not going to kid ya, I've never been religious. Nothing. Never had a thing to do with it. Nothing against it, mind you. I never hid the fact I was a Jew—and you all know that. Open about it. Sam Beskov—Jewish. But religious? Forget it.

"Now the thing is, with my mother, with Rachel—that's different. To her it meant a lot. She was here two weeks with me—these last two weeks—you know she *bentshed licht* every Friday night? I swear! The candles, the works.

"All right. She's dead. So I want to do something in her memory. In her name. I want to give something that'll be a memorial for her. Rachel Beskov."

Jack's eagerness became uncontrollable. "Mr. Beskov, are you thinking of—"

"Jack—" Barrett raised an arm to cut him off, to indicate he was handling this. Then quietly he said to Beskov, "What do you have in mind, Sam?"

"Not just money. Let's make that clear. I want something solid. Something you can *see*."

"A memorial?" Barrett was uncertain too.

"Look—what am I? I'm a builder. I got skyscrapers, apartment houses, shopping centers. I build. I like to see a structure, you know what I mean? Something standing there!"

Jack Stern and Harry Brody exchanged glances, trying to think fast. Danny Cole sat back. A building! How they all translated their love, their devotion, even their faith into solid brick and concrete.

Barrett cleared his throat, balancing things in his mind. "Do you . . . have any suggestion?"

"How the hell do I know? You're putting up a Temple, so what do you need? I mean, I don't want no garage or anything like that. No parking lot, tennis courts, swimming pool, what the hell."

"A Temple," Barrett spoke with cold intensity, "doesn't have tennis courts or a swimming pool. It's a place of worship, not a recreation center."

"All right, so you tell me!"

"Perhaps," Bob now had a certain remote look in his face, as if there were a special plan in his mind and what was happening might just fit into it, "if you could give us an idea of—"

"How much? The money?" Sam wasn't going to let them get away with this phony delicacy. They were here for his money—why pretend otherwise? He decided to prolong it a bit, let their tongues hang out.

He stood up and walked over to the bar, poured some more Scotch
into his glass, lifted it, examining the light gold as if it were a chemical
specimen. Everyone was watching him and he knew it and enjoyed
it. He put the glass down, reached for a brandy glass and poured in
some cognac. He sniffed it slowly, and then whirled it around in the
bottom of the glass, as if this were all he was concerned with. Then
he deliberately turned to face them, lifted the glass as if in a toast to
them, and took a long sip.

"Ahhh. That's good. Very good cognac. . . . The money. Let me
tell you, fellas—" But he wasn't going to tell them that quickly. He
enjoyed the sense of their sitting there and waiting to find out how
much they were going to get from Sam Beskov. The abject hopeful-
ness, the anticipation. "—did you know that I once went to college?
Yeah, me. Sam Beskov. For two whole years! City College. And they
didn't kick me out either, I quit. I had to. Couldn't even afford to go
to a free college. Had to get a job. Help out at home. Bring in some
money so the family could eat. But—I figured those two years did
something for me. They opened up the world for me. So . . ."

He took another sip of brandy, and then smiled at them all, relishing the attentiveness, the eagerness with which they were listening to
him.

"—so I was going to give a little donation to the college. Set up a
fund, scholarship fund or something, you know? But now—" The
pleasure showed in his face as they hung on every word, "—now I
figure I'll give that same amount to the Temple. For my mother's
sake. The same amount."

No one dared speak, utter the words, ask the question. Sam took
another sip.

"Half a million."

The silence was like a sudden pain. Each of them was aware of the
need to breathe out, recover. They all looked at Barrett.

"That's a very generous offer, Sam." Bob spoke in a quiet, un-
emotional voice.

My God! Is that all he could say? Jack burst out: "It's magnificent!
A magnificent gift!"

"Mr. Beskov—" Brody was groping, shaking his head in wonder,
"you don't know what this means! Wonderful! Great!"

"But—" Sam held up his hand, "I don't want it peed away. I want that money used to build something. I want a Rachel Beskov Memorial Building that'll mean something!"

Again they turned to Barrett for guidance. And Bob, for some strange reason, was looking down at his hands, clasping them tightly, struggling with something.

"What do you say, Bob?" Beskov sat down and leaned back. "Got any ideas?"

Barrett sighed, and then finally decided to do it. It had to be faced and done, and the moment for it had come. He looked up, arranging the thoughts, the words.

"We are building a Temple, Sam. And a Temple has certain basic things—the sanctuary, offices, and so on. It is also going to be used for our Sunday School of course, so there are classrooms, a library, and all the rest. Now a Temple can also have other facilities that could be quite important. For example, a meeting place, an auditorium . . ."

Suddenly everyone staring at Barrett in shock. What was he saying? An auditorium?

". . . a place to hold lectures, put on performances, use for receptions. Such an adjunct to the Temple would have a stage, dressing rooms and so on. It would have a kitchen, storage space, many other features."

Barrett wasn't looking at any of the others, just at Sam. Avoiding their eyes, the puzzled expressions, the confusion.

"Now a member of our congregation, Dr. Greenwald, had pledged a certain amount of money—I might as well tell you, it was three hundred and fifty thousand dollars—to build such a structure. It is actually incorporated in our architect's plan, the space provided for, all worked out. The Greenwald Auditorium."

Now one quick look at all the others, as if in response to their tension, their waiting. He unclasped his hands. They were wet with perspiration and he rubbed his palms back and forth on his trousers.

"Today . . . just tonight in fact . . . I was informed by Dr. Greenwald that he was considering withdrawing that pledge."

Sam began to laugh. His head back, the voice guttering from the throat in pleasure, the laughter in full, rich uproar. "I'da guessed it! The no-good shitty bastard! He's full of hot air! Greenwald? That's just like him!"

The others were so stunned they sat motionless. Greenwald withdrawing? This was unbelievable! The auditorium was the great dream of his life! Something must have happened. Something terrible. No wonder Bob had looked so upset, so tense, when he arrived. Suddenly Danny stood up.

"Why? Did he say why?"

Barrett glared at him. "I don't want to discuss that now."

"Why!" Danny moved toward Barrett. "I think I know why. . . ."

"Danny—" Barrett controlled his voice, "we will not discuss that now." The jaw muscles actually quivering with his tension.

Danny stepped back. "Well, what do you know? He actually did it!" He sat down, smiling, nodding his head. The others stared at him, wondering what it was all about.

"Look—" Sam felt himself now too long out of it, "so Greenwald backed out. All right? Whatever the reasons, the hell with it. . . . You're saying to me, Bob, that this auditorium can now be mine? I mean, I can have it built for my mother. Her memorial . . . the Rachel Beskov Auditorium. Is that right?"

Barrett was not just uncomfortable now, but suffering the humiliation of the situation, the need to hold back all he felt, to play the right role.

"If you would like to—we—the congregation—would welcome it."

"And for half a million you could have some auditorium, huh? A beauty!"

Brody, already dreaming: "We could give it everything, Mr. Beskov. We could add things that we couldn't afford before. We could—"

"Harry—" Barrett spoke almost wearily, restraining Brody with his voice, expression, "—let's wait till we hear that Sam agrees to this. Take it easy."

Sam just looked at him and said it. "I agree." He stood up. "It's a deal."

Like a collapse. The tightness released, the nerves loosened, the emotion out of the throat muscles. The relief in all of them.

"Only—"

What? Sam was holding up his hand as if to stop the process. They stared, unable to respond to the sudden fear.

"Only—I got one condition." He could have said it then, uttered the words, but he wanted the question asked. He wanted to hear the appeal in some voice.

Barrett gave it to him. "What is that, Sam?"

Now there was no smile, no relaxed manner, but a closing up of the face, a harshness over it, almost anger.

"My condition is that Rabbi Gordon stays. And—" He moved in quickly to push it all the way, cut out the doubts, hesitations, questions, "—and there are no buts, no ifs, nothing. He stays. Period. Otherwise—forget the whole thing. Right now."

Only Danny was able to sit back normally. He stared at Beskov, not even smiling, but overwhelmed by the wonder and strangeness of it all, by the emotions he couldn't sort out in himself. The others were looking at Barrett, and away.

"Sam—" Leave it to Bob. Quick mind. Executive. Ready for anything. "—what makes you think there is a question of—"

"Cut the crap! I know! See? So drop it. . . . Now I want this Rabbi here because I think he's a goddam good Rabbi, that's all. And I think this dopey, jerky, half-assed congregation needs this Rabbi. So he stays—or I don't give you a cent. Now what is it? Yes or no?"

Barrett had the look of a man living through an ordeal too great to express. His body had become stiff, his face writhing, his lips unable to form the words. He finally put his hands in his pockets, a desperate gesture at self-control.

"Sam, our Executive Committee must make that decision."

"So make it!"

"Sam—" the voice so tight it was painful, "—this requires discussion. And—" before Sam was able to blurt out again "—this is not the time or place for it." Barrett was pretty damn good at controlling things too. Power in him too, when it got close. "We will have that discussion. We will make a decision. And we will let you know."

"When?"

Goddam sonofabitch of a goddam pushing bastard! Bob turned away. The words were in his mouth, all said, but he didn't utter them.

"As soon as possible. Gentlemen, this meeting is over."

He began to move toward the door, acting out its end. It was finished. No more. The others were standing, uncertain at first, and then slowly moving too.

Jack Stern stopped. "Thank you, Mr. Beskov."

Sam didn't answer. He was watching Barrett. Brody at the door chimed in: "Me too. Thanks, Mr. Beskov."

Danny walked up to Sam and held out his hand. Sam looked at him, felt the tight grip in Danny's fingers, answered with his own.

He smiled. He didn't escort them out, but let them all find their way through the foyer and out to the front terrace and down to the driveway and their cars.

Then he finished the brandy with one gulp.

While Frieda never had had a sense of security, having learned that a rabbi's job could be as unstable as a salesman's or office manager's, she had begun to relax after six months or so in Greenlake, able to make an effort to enjoy life more and to turn to things, personal matters, that disturbed her and try to do something about them. And the most important of these was what she always thought of as "the problem." It was like a secret reference in her anxiety and unhappiness file.

The problem, it seemed to Frieda, was that David didn't consider there was a problem. He wasn't running from it or avoiding it, he wasn't even dismissing it as unimportant. He was just totally unaware of it.

In trying to understand why this was so, she had to probe into her own involvement with him. Was it the difference in their feelings for each other that created the problem? Do I really love him?

By now, I do. At first no. At first there had been such a mixture of resentment and gratitude that she could hardly deal with it. The overwhelming shame of the arrangement. She had been sold by her father, accepted by David as a means of attaining his education. How could she respect a man who would agree to marry a woman under such terms?

And the crazy, conflicting, contradictory thought: Hadn't she done something equally horrible? Agreed to marry a man on the basis of a financial arrangement. But in an odd way, it was more acceptable for her. After all, there were such things as dowries for brides, and weren't they a means of buying husbands?

David was a strange man, the most unusual and difficult to understand that she had ever met. There was a dissociated quality about him. He was not like other men in his involvement with this world, its patterns, attitudes, values. He lived somewhere on another level of sensitivity, responding to other needs. He seemed able to go through life untouched by everyday things. They didn't exist for him. He had gone into this marriage on a certain basis, and that was that. All considerations of its implications for their relationship were over. He probably never thought of it again. Now he had a wife, and it was Frieda, and they were together, and there was nothing to question, nothing to ponder about.

And Frieda knew that this was good in a way, even lucky for her. Another man would have been unable to resist bringing it up, somehow torturing her with it. With David, she escaped that humiliation. And she was grateful for it. Not so much grateful directly to him— he was behaving this way unconciously—but grateful for the situation itself. It was like buying a car and finding that it provided no mechanical trouble. You couldn't be grateful to the car, but you could be glad you had this particular one.

And David's strangeness, his intensity in certain things, his tremendous involvement with his work which was so different from all other men's work, his essential goodness, his concern with what he believed to be the most important things in life—faith, God, justice, one's fellow man—all this dedication frightened her a little bit at times. But it also made her respect him.

She did love him. She knew it and believed it when she found herself transferring that love from merely what he was, to the man himself. To the David, the physical reality of him. To his presence, his closeness. To the contact with him.

And she began to take pleasure in the intense, dark eyes that stared into unknown worlds and then suddenly returned to you, directly, totally. The face that looked so solemn and even sad when he confronted his problems, hopeless or betrayed when he struggled with himself trying to find answers. And yet could be so young and innocent looking when he was pleased, that could grin like a boy's when he was happy. There was nothing ever shallow in that face. It was always alive and vital. And she learned to see in it the signs of what he was experiencing, all the range of his reactions and moods. And she came to love it. It was her David. He was good to live with.

But somewhere too, and this was a secret sadness for her, there was in David only an acceptance of their marriage. It was not a negative attitude on his part, and perhaps there was even no holding back, but there was not much giving either. What he gave of himself was like the performance of a ritual, the observance of the ritual of marriage. Not the nurturing of it. Not the desire to deepen it. Not the need to explore it for greater joys and significance. What it added up to for her was a disappointment, a sense of loss, of a need unfulfilled because he didn't know it existed.

She would look at herself sometimes in the mirror, wondering if the fault lay in her physical appearance. That big, longish face. The mouth she wished were more delicately formed. The awkwardness of her body, so that she couldn't walk as gracefully as some other women did, but seemed to stride in a kind of unfeminine way. And she would think: If only I were beautiful, or more delicate looking, he would respond to me in a deeper way. I would exist for him as a woman he wanted to be with, as well as his wife. He would want to make me respond to him.

Sometimes, standing in front of the mirror when she was dressing, she would examine herself, trying to see her body as David saw it. She would look at her breasts and think—here there is no difference between me and any other woman. They are breasts, full enough. And the rest of my body is good. Not fat, the stomach still firm after two kids, and my thighs aren't flabby. My body is for him and he can want it and enjoy it and be satisfied with it as much as with any woman's.

And yet. The question. The problem. It seemed as if all he were able to do was *accept* this body of hers. It was there, his wife's, part of her, part of the relationship, part of the ritual of marriage. But there was no yearning in him for this body, no desire for it, no passion in seeking and taking it. No hunger. And no real joy. She never felt, in all the times they had been together, that he had ever derived an ecstasy of gratification that her body had given him, that the possessing of it, the being with it, had ever filled him with some overwhelming satisfaction. And that meant somehow to her that she wasn't really wanted by him. And not being wanted deprived her of a sense of being taken. And whatever the writhing and the moving and the cries, it wasn't fulfillment really. It wasn't physical love. It wasn't feeling completely woman. And it was denied to her because David was innocent of the need.

What led her to try what she did that particular evening, what gave her the courage for it, was this belief in his innocence. She remembered the way—and she laughed making this comparison—she actually had to teach him to enjoy eating. That food on the table was not like air in the room that you took in unconsciously. You paid attention to it. You noticed differences. Chicken paprikash was a different experience than veal cutlet. You responded to a sauce, or a spice, you reacted to an interesting flavor. You let your senses not only feel it, but long for it. He had never told her what to cook, what he preferred. And after literally making him taste the food, describe to her what he felt while he was eating it, he had begun to relate to it, enjoy it, and finally want certain things and look forward to them.

She had taught him to enjoy the sun, the feel of cool grass underfoot, the pleasure in sitting outdoors on their little back terrace and listening to the cries of birds, the sight of leaves gently shuddering in cool twilight. He had been closed to that kind of experience, unaware of the existence of this kind of joy, like a city-bred boy to whom the outdoors was only a place to pass through on the way to somewhere.

Now she felt she had to teach him about this other, too. Open his eyes, his awareness to it. Show him it existed, and that there was a capacity for it in him, and that he should let it come out and experience it.

It was a summer night, comfortable, not too warm. The kids were asleep. She had told David she was going to bed and would wait for him. He was reading and looked up.

"Wait for me?"

"I mean I won't be asleep. Will you come soon?"

"Oh, sure. A few minutes. Just finish this chapter." He assumed nothing. A remark about going to bed. He read on.

Forty-five minutes later, when he entered the bedroom, he was surprised to discover that Frieda was not in bed. She was sitting in the little armchair near the window, reading. She closed the book quickly, put it away on the floor between the chair and the wall.

"Not asleep yet?"

"Don't you remember? I said I'd wait for you."

"Oh yes." Then, only a partial awareness, a perfunctory curiosity. "Anything wrong?" He was taking off his shirt.

"No." She sat watching.

Suddenly another glance, noticing for the first time. "What are you wearing?"

"This? A nightgown." It was light blue, delicate, transparent, a long gown with no collar, open at the top, a low curve across the top of her breasts.

"Never saw that before."

"No. It's new."

"Oh."

She was waiting, watching him get undressed. He did it slowly, almost wearily, not hiding himself from her but merely turning his back when he slipped off his trousers, standing facing the wall as he put on his pajamas. When he turned to get into bed, she came over quickly.

"David, wait."

She stood in front of him, looking at his face, a softness in her eyes, a smile, a seeking and hoping.

"David—do you love me?"

"Of course." He was beginning to wonder. What was happening?

She put her hands on his arms, holding him. "Don't you know that's the wrong answer? No woman wants to hear 'Of course.' "

For the first time, he really looked at her. "Frieda, what's the matter?"

"Just answer my question first."

"All right. I love you."

"Really?"

"Really."

He started for the bed. Her insecurity again. Her self-doubting. Oh, this constant need to reassure her. But she took his arm again quickly and stopped him.

"What's the matter, Frieda? What is it?"

"Don't get into bed yet. I want us to talk."

"About what?" He spoke not with impatience, but a growing sense of something emerging, demands and probing and questions. Demands of some kind, always demands on him.

"About us. I think it's important. Please?"

He looked at her face and seeing the need gave her a kiss.

"No."

"What do you mean no?"

"Don't kiss me like that. It's . . . it's like kissing a baby goodnight. I . . . please, David. Sit down with me."

Why did a woman constantly have to probe into her relationship with a man? Want to seek out nuances, determine depths, explore meanings of remarks and behavior? Why couldn't a woman just accept what was—if it was good? And their relationship *was* good. He decided not to let her make this too analytical, to treat it lightly and casually.

"All right. So we're going to have a meeting." He managed a smile. "I'll sit here." He walked to the other chair near the window and sat down, his hands clasped in his lap. "All right, Frieda. Now, what's on the agenda?"

"David, it's—" she went to her place and sat on the edge of the chair, leaning toward him, "it's about us and it's important. To both of us. So—" She shook her head helplessly. "I don't know where to begin. But I'll try."

He leaned back, receptive, but a tenseness inside too, preparing himself.

"The only way I can do this, David, is to talk right out. Frankly. And please listen to me with an open mind. Don't be against me. Wait and listen."

"You have the floor, Madam Chairman. Speak!"

"Don't joke about it." She sighed, and then began. "David, I think we love each other. I know we love each other. We show it in many ways. You to me, and I hope I for you."

"Agreed. We love each other."

"Between two people who love each other, many things happen. Or are supposed to happen. They're supposed to feel something for each other that—that expresses itself in certain ways. In their—" She didn't want to say sex, or intercourse, and she couldn't think of how to put it for a moment, "—in their physical relationship."

Aha! So that was it. What was wrong now? What bothered her?

"There's supposed to be, David, a physical love between them. For each other. A physical wanting of each other. Enjoyment of each other."

"We have—" he had to clear his throat, "—we have a physical relationship, Frieda. I assume it's a normal one."

"A relationship—but not a physical *love*. Not real enjoyment."

"Are you—" Extraordinary! Who would have believed it? "—saying to me that I leave you . . . well, I believe the expression is . . . unsatisfied?"

"No, David. Not that. I know you try, and want to make me happy. But I just feel we're both missing something. And that it's right and good for us to have it."

"And what is that 'it'?" My God, who would have imagined Frieda capable of this? This kind of nerve in her he had never encountered. "What 'it' are we missing?"

"I told you. The enjoyment—for both of us—of each other."

"I don't—" he suspected, but wasn't sure, wasn't sure of the extent of her meaning, "—I don't really know what you're saying."

"I know you don't, David. That's why I feel I can talk to you. This is not something deliberate on your part. You're—maybe the kind of man who just never realizes how—how it can be."

The defensive instinct rose up in him, the rejection of an implied criticism. He sat up straight, not angry yet, but something inside beginning to shape itself. "Kind of man." That easy form of attack on him. "You're a special kind of man." The denial of his normal, human quality. Yet when he looked at her, his sharp retort about to be uttered, he saw such an intensity, such a reaching out for him, he stopped himself, and it came out clumsily.

"Can you be more—specific?"

"All right." She was soft, gentle with him. "All right. David, I want us to do more things when we make love. Different things. Take more time. To try—to enjoy each other more."

He felt sudden awareness of the foolishness of his own reticence. She was being totally herself, giving to him the fullest honesty about herself she had ever exposed. No other level made sense now for him either. But good Lord, it wasn't easy to put any of this into words.

"Do you mean . . . do you mean . . . positions?"

He couldn't believe he had said it. Positions! Did other couples talk like this? Discuss the act of love like a mechanical exercise? What would she do next? Demonstrate coital positions she wanted him to practice? He almost held his breath as she answered.

"Yes, but there's more to it than that. David, I want you to love my body. It is for you."

Was this Frieda? Where did she get the courage to talk like this?

"You try to make me happy. You do, David. But I want *you* to feel the excitement. Because . . . I want you to love me as a woman."

"Frieda . . . I don't know how to answer you. I really don't. What I feel—about our relationship—is good. How do we—I don't understand."

"There are ways, David. If this were a problem just for us, that would be one thing. But millions of couples have it. It's not unusual. It just takes—a little guidance."

"What? From whom?"

"Well, David—there are books on the subject. Books and books."

"Pornography? Frieda, are you—"

"No! Books by doctors. Books by psychologists. Good, serious books. . . . David—" she looked directly at him, "I have one of those books."

"What?"

No, this was incredible! Frieda, his Frieda, his subdued, accepting Frieda had gotten a book on *sex*? How can you hope to understand a woman? What crazy, private world of—who knows? Maybe strange, perverted desire?—what had she been experiencing? And now he was supposed to read God knows what silly sex manual she had found somewhere and to perform according to the text? Follow instructions? It was almost funny. For a moment he saw himself in the scene: Rabbi gets directions for having better sexual intercourse. Put the penis here. Have orgasm from left to right while partner hangs from the chandelier. Who knows? Anything was possible now!

She reached down beside the chair and picked it up. "It's. . . ." She read from the cover. "*How to Achieve Greater Sexual Satisfaction in Marriage*. By a doctor. Dr. Alfred M. Hersch."

"Give me that!" He reached out and grabbed it. "Where did you get this?"

"In a bookstore in New York. Bookstores have a lot of these books. Millions of people read them, David."

He held the book tightly, pressed down in his lap, refusing even to glance at it.

"Frieda, I want to—" What? Suddenly he wasn't sure. The emotion without purpose. Reaction, but no direction. He felt, and knew what he felt, but now he didn't know if it was right to say it. That he was hurt? How could he justify being hurt, even though he felt the pain, as if he had been attacked? She was talking of love, offering love, offering herself, and he was hurt. How could he defend himself? What had he done, how had he functioned in their relationship? That would gain nothing. She had been too open, revealed too much. But if not defense—then what? He didn't know. "I . . ." he was groping, "I can't believe that the relationship between two people . . . that what they feel for each other . . . can come out of a book."

That was it. Mechanization. Organization. Prescription. Method. That was wrong! That, at least, he could say.

"Not what they feel, David. That doesn't come out of a book. But how to express it. How to enjoy what they feel."

"What is it . . . a textbook or something?" Still not looking at it, he was clasping it tightly, squeezing it out of existence. "I don't know what to call it. It's . . . advice . . . and . . . suggestions . . . as to how . . . how two people can. . . ."

He glanced at it finally to finish her sentence for her, "Achieve Greater Sexual Satisfaction." The words read from a remote uninvolvement. A disdain. "Is that . . . is that what you feel is missing?"

"Don't you? For both of us?"

Trying to make him say he had this need too. When all of it, the marriage, the being together, all contact between them on every level had all been settled, established, accepted. What it was, it was. To be lived with. Accepted. Enjoyed to the extent that it was enjoyable.

"I don't have a sense of something missing, Frieda. What we have is . . . is the way we have our relationship. I think we have good feelings for each other."

"David—" She had never been so articulate, so clear. It was as if all the awkwardness and confusion of her life was part of another world, but here, in this, there was an essence that was herself, and it came out simple, and certain, and unafraid. "—It says somewhere in that book that emotional love and physical love must be thought of together as part of married life. And that . . ." Trying to remember, trying to put it objectively, "and that to have a harmonious married life, the couple cannot be ignorant or unconcerned about sex. They have to actually learn about . . . about techniques in sex. There is nothing shameful, David, when two people in love want to make each other happy . . . and find out how. And find out how to enjoy each other."

There was no answering. There was just no answering. He stood up without knowing why or what to do next. "I. . . ." He didn't know what to say. He opened the book at random. "Frieda!" He blurted it out as he read from the page. " 'Oral-genital positions! Mutual kissing'—Is that what you're interested in?" What he had expected! Perversions! Sickness! Degradation!

"You happened to open to that page. There are all kinds of—"

He was turning the pages, reading. The shock in his voice. " 'Male sex movements. Female sex movements' " . . . More pages. " 'Rear entry position'—My God, Frieda!" He flung the book down on the chair. "I can't believe it! I just can't! It's not what—"

"—not what you think of as love?' She came over to him. She stood close to him and then slowly raised her arms to touch his. Then his shoulders, his throat. Her hands touched his face gently, slowly. She kissed him. He didn't respond, but she held her lips on his a few moments, her hands along the back of his head, at the neck, stroking his hair lovingly.

"David—we do make love, don't we? We do lie with each other, our bodies close. We do that. And if it is right one way—then why not another?"

"Is that what you want?"

"Yes. And that you should want it."

He didn't answer, but let her hold him close. He was not looking at her, out of shame perhaps, out of embarrassment, but out of some kind of realization too.

"Whatever, David. Whatever would make you and me feel good. Whatever."

Suddenly—God, from where?—Julia. He was eighteen. Julia undressing him. Julia making him hold her breasts. Julia looking at his body and laughing. And the disgust at her body. At the sight of it. The naked ugliness. All the parts just parts. Not goals of secret desire, not the fulfillment of dreams. Just organs, parts. Ugly, sweating, hairy, stinking skin and masses and clumps of flesh. Damn Julia! Why was he thinking of her?

With a determination like summoning his self from some other existence, he looked at Frieda. At her face, the eyes watching him and waiting for him to return to her. *This was Frieda.* You are with her. And she is holding you, in love, in the giving of herself and the wanting, in the yielding, in the offering. This is Frieda. Open to him. Allowing him. Wanting him to feel all that had ever been in him, in his senses and desires. Saying yes to it. Yes! Feel it all! Let it come out!

He hugged her. Suddenly he felt freed from the tight holding back. He hugged her and held her close to him. They stood there a while, their bodies against each other, everything flowing, the release, the giving, the taking.

Finally he looked at her and kissed her on the lips. And now it was all gentleness. All a tenderness for her. A thankfulness.

"I think I understand, Frieda. I think I do. I want us . . . to be happy."

"That's all we need, David. If we both want it, we will be."

He stepped away, his hand through his hair at the awkwardness of the moment, at the prospect of the next step.

"What . . . what do we . . . I mean how—"

She smiled and kissed him happily. "Well, here's the book. Let's get into bed, without any clothes, lie side by side . . . and read it together. And if something we read . . . something that we . . . want to do . . .

My God, it was happening! The excitement of it now, the freedom of all he was feeling. It was easy if you only allowed it. And she had made it possible, to feel it, want it, do it. She had opened the gate where it had all been locked in, put away and buried. She looked beautiful to him now, smiling, warm, accepting. She made him feel alive, able to reach out, take!

"All right?" She was looking into his eyes, to see the joy in him, to feel his joy.

"We're . . . we're supposed to—to do this?"

"It's in the book."

They both laughed and fell back, lying there. After a while he turned to her.

"Well . . . in that case . . . if you're sure it's in the book . . ." he said, and picked up her hand and put it on him.

XIV

B arrett told the others he would be in touch with them the next day and a meeting of the Committee would be called, then he drove away from Beskov's home with a mixture inside of him of fury and defeat.

He sat at the wheel, his arms, his hands like conductors of his anger, from him to the car, to the lunging weight of it grinding against the road, pushing into the darkness, pounding the violence forward, fast, tight, hard.

How he despised that Beskov! He had always felt him to be a crude and insensitive creature who used his money the way other people used their hands, who expected the world to see him as money, and who seemed to feel that the acquisition of all that money was a sign that Sam Beskov had been chosen and designated to exercise absolute power. But Bob had hoped that he would eventually win Beskov over. Work on him as a human being and a Jew, soften his aggressiveness, influence his attitudes towards the community, involve him with the congregation. Every man needed to belong to something, didn't he? He had hoped to make Beskov realize the rewards of acceptance and respect. Now he felt it was hopeless. Now Beskov was determined to get some idiotic, personal satisfaction in keeping Rabbi. Now Beskov had become more than a lost cause—he was an enemy.

And Greenwald! Manny Greenwald. For him to threaten to withdraw his pledge "unless the Executive Committee reconsiders its action regarding Rabbi"—since when the hell had he begun to use his money as a weapon? It had always had a positive function for Greenwald. Bestowing. Granting. Endowing. Helping. Providing. It had been Greenwald's aura, the glittering cloak of his personality that caused the eyes of all those around him to sparkle with gratitude and appreciation, and that sparkle itself then reflected in his own eyes, happily absorbing the praise and admiration. All that benevolence! All that dedication to the causes and drives and needs of others. All that impression of concern with what was good and right for the community, for his fellow-man, for his fellow-Jews! Now using his money as a weapon?

Gripping the wheel, his eyes on the turning dark road, little stones at the edge snapping and flying under the tires, he felt the hard anger, the desire to strike back, strike down, to hurt as he had been hurt. But Barrett was aware of something inside that was neither anger nor hate. A thing he was running from, avoiding like the secret knowledge of some sickness that was too awful to face.

Defeat. He had failed. Been repudiated. He, the President of the Congregation, had been defied. His purpose, the advancement of the congregation, the correction of a disastrous fault in its structure, which was Rabbi, all this had been brushed aside and rejected. What did they know about the rightness or wrongness of keeping this man in office? Only he knew the complete story, all the harm his continued presence would cause, all the trouble that could follow if he weren't removed. And they were not accepting his guidance, his leadership.

He wanted Rabbi out to save the congregation, to assure its survival and growth. Didn't they understand his purpose? Didn't they realize his involvement with their good, his dedication, his work, his giving of himself? How could they question his judgment now, and in that questioning defeat him, destroy him, as well as themselves?

By the time he reached home, he was in such a state of tension, confusion, bitterness, he didn't know what to do with himself. Sleep was impossible. He didn't want to drink. He couldn't be still, sit in a chair, lie down, stand. He walked into his study, aware that the lights were still on all over the house, Elaine awake somewhere and probably waiting, and slammed the door shut. He started walking back and forth in front of his desk, stopping at the window to look out without knowing he was stopping, not looking, not seeing, and then once more walking, the pacing out his anger and frustration.

Elaine waited a few moments after she opened the door, even though he had glanced at her and seen her from a distance.

"What happened?"

Not sympathy in her voice, not curiosity even, but a kind of asking for a report. Bob didn't answer, then stopped after a while and faced her. Too much. This was too much! Not Elaine now to deal with.

"Now look, Elaine." His voice was tight, flat between his teeth. "I don't want to talk. I don't want to do anything. So just go. All right? Just go!"

"You had a meeting at Sam Beskov's house. What happened?"

There was a sense in her that she had to know, that some kind of turning point was involved. And out of it a determination, and a strange fear too. But there could be no backing away. Not tonight. Not now.

Barrett, almost as if needing this to get release, to let something flow out of him, stopped again and stared at her.

"Damn you, Elaine! What do you want? Is it going to be one of those nights again? I've had all I can take tonight! Goddammit, it's enough! Let me alone! Go!" Already he knew she wouldn't. He could see the cold resistance in her face, the stubbornness, the unyielding demand. Already he was preparing himself for the confrontation, anticipating her reaction. Seeing her absorbing the news and using it against him. He was facing it all inside himself already.

Elaine closed the door behind her and went to a chair. She lit a cigarette slowly, dropping the match into the ash tray on his desk like a flare to indicate her position. She sat down, the smoke pouring out of her nostrils like a declaration, the sitting back like a pitching of the tent on the battlefield.

"You'll have to throw me out, Bob. And if you leave, I'll follow you. I want to know."

"Goddammit—why?"

"Because if it's about Rabbi, I'm involved. Remember? I'm very much involved, thanks to you."

"What makes you think it was about—" Not really sounding as if he expected her to believe his question. Elaine dismissed it with a shaking of the head. No use. Don't even try that.

"Tell me. It might as well be now."

This, too, was part of it, of the whole situation, the battle, the betrayal. It had to be faced like the rest.

"I will put it—" Barrett gave up this struggle at least, now almost relishing the complexities and effect of it, "—to you the way you would never see it. But the way it is. Your Rabbi, your no-good louse of a Rabbi, has lined up some very fancy people to fight for him. Somehow he got to them, and for some idiotic reason they're on his side."

"Who?"

"Who? Well, just guess! You'd never believe—God, what's the use? Greenwald. Yes, Greenwald! And that bastard Beskov. Satisfied?"

"What did they—"

"What? Greenwald, our great benefactor, our noble patron, has threatened to withdraw his pledge to the Temple unless the Committee reconsiders about Rabbi. —I'm almost tempted to sue him. And we could! . . . And Beskov told us we could have half a million of his filthy dollars if we—only if we—kept Rabbi on. . . . A situation, huh? It makes you feel good? You like it?"

She felt no satisfaction, no sense of triumph, only an awareness of something significant, an incredible development. There had to be more to it.

"Why are they taking this position?"

"Don't make me laugh! Does it matter?"

"Of course it matters! Is it because they believe he's—"

"They don't know a thing! Why? Their motives? How the hell do I know?"

"They must believe that the accusation—"

"Crap! Beskov said he thinks Rabbi's good for us! We need him. Beskov! The non-Jew Jew! Now he's a judge of Rabbis! Now he's telling the congregation—which he spit on all these years—telling them what's good for them. That's a laugh! That's unbelievable! This congregation—" the bitter sarcasm in the parody of Beskov's voice, "—needs a man like Rabbi."

"And Dr. Greenwald?"

And Dr. Greenwald? Barrett rubbed his face, his brow, as if to straighten out the confusion, the bewilderment, the insane clash of thoughts and questions.

"Greenwald? I don't know! How the hell do I know? Does it matter?"

Elaine took a long pull on the cigarette, looking at his face with the sense now of all that was involved. "I think it does."

"Why? Is he so wise? So all-knowing? That if he changes his mind

—we all have to wonder about ourselves? He's like anybody else! He can be stupid, and wrong!"

"But a man like Dr. Greenwald must have a reason."

"A good reason? Who says so? Maybe . . . maybe that sonofabitch Danny Cole got to him? How do I know? Somebody influenced him— but it doesn't matter!"

"Dr. Greenwald's motives are not—"

"—not what? Impure? If you're so sure about his—why do you question mine? Why do you doubt me, but not him?"

"Because I know why you did what you did."

"Oh do you?" All his bitterness now found a place to go, a target. All the anger, all the reaction to defeat. "You think you understand me—know me. Of all the people in this goddam world, *you* know me least! Have you ever—ever, ever, ever—ever accepted me for what I am? Did you ever believe that I really love this Temple, this congregation? What it means to me? Did you ever understand what I feel? I am a Jew in every bone of me. And I have worked as a Jew day and night, all my energy, all the time I could give and more, to *help*. To do something good and right for the Jews here. To give them a unity, to lead them to some goal, a strong congregation, going somewhere, building, growing. That's my motive—and nothing else! Nothing. Do you think I want Rabbi out for personal reasons? That's stupid! That's how much you know me! I want him out because he's no good for us! He's weak—yes, morally weak. I believe that! And he has let us down. I can't respect a man like that and have him as our spiritual leader. That would be a farce!"

"But that's just what he is. A spiritual man who—"

"Bunk! Crap!" He turned away, clenching his fists, holding in the rest, controlling it. Then he turned to her. "Look, I don't want to discuss that. He is not a man to lead this congregation. He must be removed. However it's done—I don't really care how it's done! He must be removed!"

"And to do it, you would sink to any level. Lies, accusations—"

"Stop it! I know what I know about a man! I know it! He's a weak, morally weak man!"

"Not weaker than you."

The words hovered in the air, penetrating and returning, hanging over them, alive in the sudden stillness.

Barrett stood motionless. He swallowed, the jaws clenching back the words, his eyes expressing it all. Then finally: "What did you say?"

"Are you so pure?"

"What the hell are you saying?"

"I don't have to go into it. You understand. I think you understand very well."

"Goddammit!" Almost tearing at her, his hands were open, ready to grab her. "Say it! What? What is this?"

"A morally weak man—if that's your description of Rabbi—doesn't it describe you?"

"Elaine—say it! What?"

"What? . . . Well. . . ." She moved away, as if holding the explosive in her hand, ready to go off at a word. Her heart so tight, the pain ready to burst out. "I guess . . . it's now. It's time." But she couldn't face him. She was looking down, and the words came out quietly, out of anguish, not anger. "I know about Bea Aldrich."

Forty-eight hundred thousand decisions whirling in his mind. Yes. No. Admit. Deny. Fight. Strike. Run. What? He did nothing, staring at her.

Elaine looked at him now, and the tears were for all of it. For all that had been and no longer was, and was never to be again. The loss, the hurt, the sadness to come. "Bob—I don't want to go into it. I know. I found out a year ago. By accident. It doesn't matter how. But I've known. Don't try to explain it. Just don't try to explain it. Don't try!"

The tears came now. She was unable to stop them, unable to feel anything but the sadness of it. The loss of it all, like something draining out of her. Going out. Gone out of her now for always.

"All right, so you know." He was marking time, thinking. Thinking, thinking. What? Was this—? Or maybe—? What?

"I know everything. There's nothing to hide any more, Bob."

"I don't want to hide it. But there's something that does matter. It's over. That whole thing is over. It's been over for a long time!"

"So what?" She was looking at him, the foolishness of his face, the words. He understood so little. "What difference? It was there. You—and that woman."

"Not love! Nothing! She was a friend!"

"In bed? In her bed—for friendship?"

"Because you and I—" What was he trying to do? He wasn't sure yet. Not justify. Not explain. He was pleading. As he had done with her all these years. Always begging for something she didn't give, "—we were like enemies. You know that. Enemies!"

"We hurt each other. Yes."

"More than that! It's one thing to hurt—but to destroy a person by not understanding, not accepting anything about him! You made me feel alone. Always, in every way. I couldn't stand to be alone any more."

"And wasn't I alone?"

"All right—it was bad for both of us. I had to—I needed—you were destroying me. I needed that—whatever—whatever it was I got from her. Can you understand that?"

"And can you believe that I did understand, in some way? That's why, for a whole year, I've never said, never told you that I know. Don't you see?"

"Then why now? Why?"

But in her search for the answer, in her reaching into her thoughts and emotions, the attempt to understand their truth, there was only a deadness. Only a nothing. The sickness in her, the cells of death. The body eaten away. That's what there is in me, and I am dying. There was no other answer.

"Why? . . . Because now it doesn't matter any more. I've given up."

"Why didn't you—" Disregarding this, not wanting to accept the words, not able to hear them, "—tell me before? Why now?"

All right. She would do it his way, leave it at the incident, not the significance, the moment, not the lifetime. "I bring it up now because you want to destroy Rabbi in a way you have no right to. Not you. Not you, Bob."

"I brought it up a week ago! The meeting was a week ago! Why now?"

"I felt—" She sought for the words, the logical explanation, the putting it in order for him, the organizing of the chaos for his need, "—that if I brought it out then, it would be like putting it all on the same level. Do you understand? You say Rabbi is immoral, well—so are you. That would have been like balancing it off. Like accepting what you said of him. Like saying he was no worse than you."

"And now?"

"Now there are others fighting for him. Who believe in him. A man like Greenwald. . . . Now what *you* are makes a difference. Now you have no right to attack him. Not any more."

"I don't understand you!"

"I don't care."

"I don't understand you! God, I don't understand!"

"Have you ever?" She shook her head, the simple cold fact of it, the truth at the end of it all. "We have never understood each other. Not really ever. So why go on, Bob? Why?"

"What do you mean?"

"I want a divorce."

He sat down in the chair as if the weight of the words pressed him down, the meaning too much to hold. She hadn't known she would say it. The words came out as if of their own force, from a source inside that was hardly a part of her. They came out and she recognized them, the words, the meaning, and only then realized they had been in her for ages, for so long she couldn't even know when they were born.

"For that?" Like at a meeting. She felt him getting the arguments and points and reasons all straight and clear before proceeding.

"For everything. For the nothing that we have. That's what we have—nothing. . . . I want a divorce."

Now it was a strength in her. Now the words were something to grasp and push at him, to fill the void between them.

"Don't keep saying that! We're talking!"

Oh, that sudden strength. That knowledge. How good it felt. To say it all. "No we're not. We're deciding. And I've decided. It's over and it's finished. Whatever it was. I don't want it any more."

"Do you realize what—"

Oh God, not arguments! Not now. Not back and forth.

"I realize everything! The kids, our lives, everything. I want a divorce, Bob. There is nothing more to talk about. Don't you realize that?"

He walked slowly to the chair behind his desk and sat down. The hand on his face, the rubbing of his brow, was like a mechanical gesture, the body's reaction. His mind was on a hundred things. The children. The Temple. The house. The living. Incredible, how stupid little details were already in his mind! A minute ago they didn't exist.

Moving out. The settlement. The bank account. Alimony. Lawyers. Where he would live. Telling people. All of it crowding into him. They weren't important! Why was he thinking of these things? This was crazy. Papers, court, legal procedure, announcement, settlement, custody, possessions, separation, details, details, details! He couldn't stop it! Why?

And he knew why. Because it had come. The time. The truth. The reality of it. It had happened. It was. It was no use. It was.

"You think—" not as an argument now, but as someone trying to be apart from it, "—you really think it's wise?"

She actually smiled. "Wise? What a word to use! God, I don't know! But I don't care. It's what has to be. And I think you know that."

"Elaine—" What was he clinging to? He didn't even know. Amazing, the solidity, the hard, impregnable solidity of what was there between them, coming out of her. More than will and determination. A kind of truth that she wouldn't let go. It was between them and there was no reaching her anymore. "—Elaine, do you—?"

"Yes. No question in my mind. I know. We both know."

Suddenly she couldn't bear it any more. All the emptiness in her. Everything was suddenly gone. She wanted to cry, bawl, shriek. It was dead. Everything dead. Dead!

She ran out of the room and up the stairs, unable to see the steps through her tears, the blurred hallway, the light vibrating, her feet running without her, her hands out groping for the door, the room, the bed, like a sea to plunge into, deep encompassing empty sea of nothing and herself in the midst of it, sobbing, her whole body sobbing, and the pain writhing inside of her, the awful pain out of the emptiness. . . .

Whatever the degree of involvement with religion and the Temple, it becomes necessary for every group in the congregation to establish some kind of relationship with their Rabbi. It is one of the miracles of Judaism. We are what we are, but let Rabbi know us. He is our Rabbi, let us know him. The relationship may become close and deep, or it may remain so distant that it has no meaning for either side, but the effort must be made. It's as if two parts of an organism that function independently still sense an underlying unity.

The country club element among the Jews of Greenlake perhaps felt the least need for this, and so they waited longest. But when Rabbi, after more than a year in office, had delivered that particular sermon, they felt the time had come. They invited him to come out to the golf course.

He accepted the invitation more or less as a joke. They pressed it on him with such enthusiasm and conviction that he decided he would indulge them. But to him it was actually like being invited to a house of sin and being told: When you see how enjoyable it is, you'll forgive our wanting it so much.

A golf course. A group of members of the congregation were building a country club and golf course that would be theirs, that would be Jewish, and everyone would know it was theirs and Jewish.

The facts were simple. Jews were not welcome at any of the country clubs in and around Greenlake, except for Sprucewood, which was practically a community club, inexpensive to join, easy to be accepted in for membership, overcrowded in all its facilities, with one lousy eighteen-hole course that had mobs of players on it at all times and was poorly maintained. What was a Jew who loved golf and had a bit of money to do?

The three men sat in Rabbi's study and put the question to him. Alex Bardnoy, Sherm Walters, Len Strobin. Rabbi realized that he hardly knew them. Members of his congregation, three of the wealthiest Jews in the community, and yet they were strangers to him. They belonged to another species of Jewish life that Rabbi couldn't understand or relate to.

Very decent men, successful in business, respected by their friends, they lived in elegant homes with quietly happy families, somewhat inconspicuous in the community, and uninvolved in Jewish affairs. They sent their kids to the Sunday School, came to services on the High Holy Days, contributed generously to the various drives for funds and aligned themselves with the Jewish community, but played not part in it. It was not just conscience money they gave, nor a sense of guilt that made them join the congregation. It was a natural and uncomplicated acknowledgment of their Jewishness. It was done sincerely. It said: Of course we're Jews, so we belong. And then it said: That's enough.

The fact that the private clubs around Greenlake excluded them from membership was hardly even resented. They expected it. People wanted to stick with their own. Oh, you could mix in business, get real close in making deals. But socially? Who needs it? Let them have their circles, their life, we have ours. It's natural.

And so they wanted a country club and golf course of their own simply because it was an easy solution to the situation, and because it would provide them with a comfortable environment in which to enjoy themselves. There was no crusading aspect to it, no bitterness. It was the acceptance of a social truth.

Maple Hill, as it was called, had been founded by fifty Jewish families, each of whom had contributed ten thousand dollars. They figured another seven or eight thousand from each family would eventually be needed to finish up all the work, complete the clubhouse, get the course in perfect shape, apply the final polish here and there.

These fifty families owned the club. They weren't seeking any more members, they had no plans for expansion. They were concentrating on developing it into a lovely place to spend a day playing golf.

It wasn't even intended to be a social gathering place, though it did have a small and elegant bar in the clubhouse, a wide terrace with chairs and tables under the trees and umbrellas. But it wasn't a place for parties or dances. Maple Hill existed for golf. Now what was wrong with that?

Rabbi looked at the three men in his study, and didn't quite know how to answer. They had come at their own request. Alex Bardnoy had called for an appointment to have a talk after Rabbi's last sermon.

The subject of the sermon had been "The Unity of the Jewish People." Rabbi had pointed out that it was this unity, this deep and meaningful bond between them that had enabled the Jews to survive through persecution and crisis and separation. And he felt that now, perhaps for the first time, it was in danger of being lost. It was disappearing because to some Jews it no longer served a purpose. That unity had been for survival, resistance, help to each other. These were no longer problems in the United States. There was no longer any need for them to "stick together," even in terms of an emotional tie. And in Greenlake, Rabbi had said, there was in fact no Jewish community as such. There were thus and so many Jews, but they lived lives unrelated to each other.

And then he had said (it was only one of the examples he gave): "Take those Jewish families who have built their own, private, exclusive, rich man's country club. They have created their own world, for their own enjoyment, isolated themselves from the rest of the Jewish community. But they have also done more than that.

"We are building a Temple. We are *struggling* to build a Temple. Hundreds of our members are working hard to raise every penny we can get to achieve that goal—a place of worship for our whole congregation.

"Yet these Jewish families have spent hundreds of thousands of dollars to create a place where they can play golf. Can one say that *these* Jews have a sense of unity with us? Can we believe they care, are concerned with the basic needs of their fellow-Jews when at this very moment they are putting all that money into a golf course? Is golf more important to them than the building of the Temple?"

Word of this sermon got around immediately of course, and while many members tended to agree with Rabbi ("Those rich bastards don't give a damn and never did!"), there were others who felt Rabbi had not only overstepped and been indiscreet, but had revealed again that ignorance of the facts of life that made him the strange man he was.

"Each of us," Bardnoy told Rabbi, "every one of the fifty members of the club has contributed most generously to the building fund of the Temple. Surely you know that, Rabbi?"

"As much as you contributed to the golf club?"

Bardnoy sat back and shook his head. How to make Rabbi understand? "No. Not as much. But the congregation has—what? Four hundred families? Five hundred? The money is supposed to come from everybody, be spread around."

"Each family," Rabbi said, "should give what it can. As much as it can. And you people haven't done that. You've put golf first—now that's a fact!"

Sherm Walters, stoutish, genial, with a quiet, restrained smile, a tolerant manner about him, leaned forward.

"Rabbi, the Temple building fund is not a tax. It is a voluntary contribution. We have given to the Temple because we believe in it and want it built. But all of us also have a private life. That's our own concern. If I decide to install a swimming pool on my property, should I feel it's wrong to spend ten thousand dollars on it? When I can afford it? Shouldn't I take a trip around the world with my family if I'd like to? I have two Cadillacs. Is it wrong to spend money like that—for my private satisfaction? Golf is something we enjoy very much. It means a lot to us. Why shouldn't we do whatever we want to make it possible to play golf? We're not hurting anyone."

"To the extent that this money could have helped build the Temple sooner and build it better—you are hurting the congregation."

"But Rabbi," Walters was still smiling gently, "it wasn't a choice. Either the club or the Temple. We want both, and we all gave to both. And we gave what we felt we should—our just share to the Temple, and we put in what we had to put in to make the club possible."

"Let me ask you something," Bardnoy said. "Rabbi—have you ever been out on a golf course?"

"I've seen them of course."

"No, I mean out on the course with a set of clubs and played the game?"

"No."

"Then, tell you what. Come out to Maple Hill this Sunday. I'll pick you up. We'll have a set of clubs for you, and just . . . just play a round of golf with us."

"What will that do?"

"Rabbi," Bardnoy was looking at him intently now, "forgive me for saying this, but it may be that there are some things in life you don't know about. That you haven't seen or experienced. I think this may open your eyes, will help you understand that a man can be a good Jew—and love to play golf too! It's as ridiculous and simple as that."

Rabbi's casual clothes consisted of an old pair of pants saved from a worn-out suit and a striped shirt he didn't like so he wore it "around the house." Alex Bardnoy, driving him out that Sunday morning, glanced at him from time to time and smiled. Rabbi almost had the air of slum-area kid being taken out to the country for the first time.

Alex was a happy man. Everyone who knew him felt that his outstanding characteristic was his humor, his kindness, and calmness. He gave out a sense of well-being and contentment. Alex had worked out his version of the good life, and enjoyed it serenely. The printing business he owned was now being run chiefly by his son and his partner, though Alex was still active. His investments had been solid and profitable, his holdings were, in the language of the trade, "substantial."

He was not an intellectual, knew he wasn't, and didn't care that he wasn't. "Remember," he'd say, "being intelligent is not the same as being an intellectual. I'm intelligent." His wife enjoyed classical music, he didn't care for it. His children read books and did beautifully at college, he was proud of them without understanding the nature of their achievement. He didn't even want to live a life of the senses, and indulged himself very little. Food was relatively unimportant. A good steak was about it. He never had wine with his meals, though Bessie always served it for company. His clothes were hand-tailored and expensive, but restrained in style. His cigars were excellent. His passion was golf.

It was not the "exercise," which so many others of his age talked about. It wasn't the need for an activity to kill time. It was love of the game itself. He got a thrill every time he sent that ball two hundred yards down the fairway. He relished the concentration on each stroke. He played it competitively, and he could spend hours afterward over a couple of drinks describing what had happened at each hole. He was a damn good golfer.

How could he convey any of this to Rabbi? To this man who was so involved with another world, so absorbed in matters of spirit and religion and Judaism that he was like a relic of the ancient ghetto existence that had long ago disappeared?

Many of the members of Maple Hill were there that day, since Rabbi's sermon had disturbed them considerably and the idea of having him come out to the club had aroused their curiosity. There was, in fact, almost an unofficial committee on hand to greet him.

The foursome consisted of Rabbi, Bardnoy, Walters, and Strobin. A set of clubs had been set aside for Rabbi, a pair of gloves to prevent blisters, a cap to shield him from the sun, which he put on and surprisingly enough looked good in, a pair of golf shoes which he refused to wear, and they set off in the electric carts for the first hole.

It was impossible for the three others to believe that a man could be so uncoordinated as Rabbi. After six swings he managed to get the ball off the tee and it rolled down the hill about five yards almost as if to escape from Rabbi rather than because it had been hit. He wanted to give up then and there, but they persisted.

Within a half hour, they realized that it would be torture for all concerned to pretend at playing the game. Rabbi would glare at the ball as if it were an enemy that was meant to be destroyed. His swing was that of an executioner. And his inability to hit it despite all his efforts made him first feel frustration, then irritation, and finally to decide that this whole business was sheer, utter stupidity.

Golf was a form of organized idiocy. The concentration by grown men on propelling that ball, the determination involved, the complexity of the skills required, the training, practice, and expense that went into it, the technically precise equipment, the satisfaction attained, the prestige and honor accorded, the time spent in discussing it, the space given to the facilities, all for the purpose of propelling that little white ball—this was a sickness. If you had never heard of golf, went to an insane asylum and saw the inmates occupied this way, performing exactly what these people were doing, you would conclude they were poor, sick creatures. Their minds hopelessly gone!

It took Rabbi twenty-two strokes to get to the first green, and of course no one was counting any more. It took him eleven putts to drop the ball in, and despite their cheers and good-natured pretense of recognition of this triumph, he decided to stop.

After considerable persuasion, Rabbi agreed to at least accompany them on the first nine holes. Just to watch them, they urged, see how it's done, how much fun it could be once you learned. They regretted this almost at once. For there was something in Rabbi that made him turn against what he didn't understand. And the hostility emerged, without his being aware of it, in what he considered to be "joking."

When Sherm Walters got a good drive off and looked elated, Rabbi smiled and said: "What an accomplishment! You feel proud?"

"Of course! That's a two hundred and twenty yard drive."

"So you'll want to be remembered for that? He hit a little ball two hundred and twenty yards?"

When Len Strobin, a dignified man of sixty, sank a ten-foot putt and grinned with delight, Rabbi turned to him: "This is something to pass on to your children, ha?"

Len couldn't resist answering. "They respect me for being an active man at my age. For doing things. Playing."

"And who will respect them for having such values?"

When Alex was teeing off, standing over the ball, taking two or three preliminary swings, Rabbi broke into the silence. "If you knew how to pray—maybe you'd say a prayer."

Alex stepped back, his concentration broken. He controlled his irritation and stood there a moment staring at Rabbi.

"Rabbi, I happen to know very well how to pray."

"I just hope that the most sincere prayers from your heart aren't offered here on the golf course."

It was no use. They gave up after the fourth hole and headed back toward the clubhouse in the two carts.

There were about thirty or forty people sitting around on the terrace, and there was an air of expectancy among them. Rabbi out on the course! This ought to be interesting. Maybe he would begin to understand something about people at last, see them as human beings instead of as worshipers and Jews.

Rabbi agreed to sit down and have a drink with them. Orange juice. The others ordered Bloody Marys and martinis and his expression almost made them feel guilty about it. You just couldn't relax with Rabbi. He had no way of letting go. Even his sense of humor, they now felt, was basically destructive. Always at the expense of something or somebody. Now they sat there in a tenseness they didn't know how to deal with. People at other tables were staring at them from time to time, expecting.

Finally Alex, uneasily and with a feeling of the inevitability of it, said to Rabbi: "So—what do you think? Have you any impression of . . . of what this is all about? Why we enjoy it?"

"I have an impression all right, but you're not going to like it."

"Tell us! We want to hear it. Let's try to understand each other."

People at various tables near them were turning to listen. There was a silence on the terrace.

"Rabbi," Alex suggested, "why don't you speak to all of us? I know everybody would like to hear this." He stood up. "Friends, you all know Rabbi was invited here today so he could see what happens here. Why we built this club, why we like to come here, what it means to us. I've asked him to give us his impressions. I'm sure you'll all be interested." He sat down. Chairs were moved, people coming closer or turning so they could sit facing Rabbi.

He rose slowly, almost reluctantly, the smile on his face had that forced quality about it, the smile that never deceived anyone.

"Well—a Sunday sermon! On the golf course yet!"

They all watched him, waiting, a certain apprehension in the air.

"No. I'm not going to give you a sermon. From what I understand, most of you feel I've already given one sermon too many. . . . That's why I was invited out here, I guess. As Alex put it to me—how did you say it?—to help me understand that a man can be a good Jew— and love to play golf too."

A few smiles now. Not too bad. He was starting off okay. Maybe he was all right after all, if you gave him a chance.

"So now Alex asks me to give you my impressions. . . . Well, those of you who know me—and by the way, it's rather interesting that I know fewer people in this group than in any other group I've been with—"

Aha. He was beginning something, a bad note. Here it comes. They all felt it, like witnessing the loading of a weapon.

"—know that I'm frank and say what I think. . . . So . . . take another sip of those Bloody Marys, because here it comes. . . ."

The humor didn't help. It even seemed unnatural with him. They were ready for it now and already resentful and angry. Who needed this? What was the good of it?

"Can a man be a good Jew and love to play golf too? Of course he can. A man can be a good Jew and love to dance, to see plays, to read books, to go sailing, camping, climb mountains, do anything. And that's simply because his Jewishness is not being tested by any of these experiences and activities. They are unrelated to his existence as a Jew. A Jew who is living in a particular place, at a particular time, facing particular problems.

"So—how is golf different? It isn't different. It is you who feel differently about it. You have made it different. You have made the playing of golf—and everything that's involved with it, the time, concentration, money, your dedication to it—you have given this an importance in your lives that I consider unworthy.

"Because no matter what you may think—and Alex has expressed this to me—it does constitute a choice. A choice of where to put your energy, your time, your interest, your devotion . . . and . . . since we are building a Temple . . . your money.

"Why is it that there are so many of you here now, out on the golf course—and so few at services? I don't think I've seen more than three or four of you at Friday services ever. Why have you poured so much of yourselves into building this place, and none of you are on the Building Committee of the Temple, or on the Fund Raising Committee—or on any committee that is devoted to the work of building our congregation?

"It's very simple, isn't it? This is where your interests are. This is where you are involved. This is your concern—and not the congregation, not the Temple.

"Is it only because I am a Rabbi that I feel this way, and object?

I don't think so. It is because as a Jew I see your loss and ours. What you are denying to yourself, and what you are keeping from the rest of us. You have alienated yourselves. You have no involvement in those areas that matter to the preservation of Judaism. And without it Judaism will die.

"Of course this golf course isn't the whole picture. It is only an example, a symbol . . . of Jews without Judaism. . . . You . . . all of you . . . are to that extent lost to us."

He sensed their silence, their heavy, uncomfortable silence. He decided to stop.

"That's all I have to say. You asked for my impressions. I've given them to you."

He sat down. No one quite knew what would happen now, but something did have to happen. It couldn't end like this.

Alex Bardnoy stood up. His quiet manner, his calmness, the gentleness in his face, all of this contradicted their own feelings. But they waited.

"Thank you, Rabbi." A nodding of the head. A quiet dignity. "We appreciate your speaking to us so frankly."

Rabbi nodded back, uncertain too. What now? He waited with the others.

"I wonder if you would mind, Rabbi, if I said a few words?"

Rabbi smiled and waved his hand generously. Of course. Speak.

"I can't make a speech, because I'm not a speech-maker. But I would also like to talk frankly. . . . You know, as I look around, I can't help thinking: When did this ever happen before? A religious discussion on a golf course? A Rabbi and some Jews—talking over the problems of Judaism on the terrace of a golf club?

"Something new, isn't it? Does it make sense?—Why not? Because we are living in a new world, in new times. So we don't have to sit in a dark little room in an old synagogue and talk about Judaism there. We can do it here. Because just as the place of discussion has changed, so what we are talking about has changed.

"Judaism has changed. Rabbi, I am not a scholar and you are—but I tell you that I feel more about how Judaism has changed than you do. All of us do. Because we are living the new Judaism.

"We are Jews in the U.S.A. in the twentieth century. Yes, Jews in the suburbs. Jews in the country clubs. Jews in the night clubs. Jews anywhere, doing anything. We are part of today's life. And the question isn't: Why shouldn't we be? The question is: How can we help living like this? This is the world around us. This is what our children are being born into, growing up in. This is what we see, breathe, feel, and experience everywhere we turn. This is us, Rabbi. The Jew of today. Crazy about golf, or skiing, or whatever.

"The Temple can't mean to us what it used to mean to our grandfathers in the old shtetls in Europe. Going to services is not as important to us as it was to them. It just isn't.

"Judaism itself is not to us what it was to them. Any more than Catholicism is what it used to be in the Middle Ages. We take out of Judaism what we need. And if we only need this much, then it can't be helped.

"And it's you, Rabbi, who has lost touch. By not understanding your own people. You say we're making a choice. And I say—we have no choice. We can only live in a way that has meaning for us. We can only take out of Judaism what we need. It is the needs that have changed, Rabbi. The needs. . . . Someday, we hope, you will understand that."

Applause. The crisp clapping like a release. Smiles. They were looking at each other, pleased. Good for Alex! He told him. The truth! He'd better face it. The discussion was over. The impasse exactly where it had been before. So be it. . . . Now, how about some golf?

It was so awkward in the car, Alex driving Rabbi home, that neither one could say anything for a while. Then Rabbi, like a professional handler of awkward situations, the man whose function it was to relate to people, touched Alex' shoulder and smiled.

"Let's not be upset about this, Alex. It was a dialogue, a discussion. It served a purpose."

"Thank you, Rabbi. I'm sorry if I said anything that—"

"It doesn't matter. As long as there is discussion. As long as we think about the problems and face them."

But the smile was bitter, and a little sad. In the driveway of his home, Rabbi stood a moment beside the open car, and then reached out and shook Alex' hand. Alex responded eagerly, so glad Rabbi was showing no resentment.

"I invite you," Rabbi said, the little smile at his lips, "and all of those people there, to hear my next sermon. It's going to be called: 'God Is Dead and He is Buried on the Golf Course at the Country Club.'"

XV

Fay called and said it very simply.

"Lou's dead."

It was six in the morning. He had died at three-thirty in the hospital. Nobody had been with him. The doctors hadn't expected it, another quick and final stroke.

At the time Fay called Rabbi, there were already half a dozen people in the waiting room on that floor of the hospital. Barrett was the first one to arrive. Jack Stern. Dr. Greenwald, driven by his wife Rebecca, so stirred and shaken by Lou Mandel's death that he could only sit in a chair, his head down, staring at the floor in bewilderment. Harry Brody with that look of obvious solemnity that certain faces assume to indicate sorrow, like the wearing of the tragic mask. But there was no question Harry was upset. Lou Mandel gone! My God! My God! Shaking his head unbelievingly. A brother of Lou's from New York, who had been staying with Fay during the last week or so. And Fay herself, the gaunt misery almost unbearable to look at. She wasn't crying. Her face was so tight, so haggard and drawn, it was like a silent wail of anguish.

No one tried to console her with words. The touching of her hand, the look into her eyes, the arm quickly around her shoulders just to express what couldn't be said.

She walked back and forth in the little square waiting room, in front of the brown leather chairs, the shiny aluminum posts with ash trays, past all of them sitting and standing about, past their sympathetic glances, aware of the emotion in the room, feeling the flow of their sorrow.

The whispers among them were of details, facts, filling in answers.

"Three-thirty."

"Suddenly?"

"Just like that."

"They didn't expect it?"

"No. They thought he was doing fine."

"No doctor there?"

"The intern on duty. Already too late when he got there."

"So—in his sleep."

"God bless him. God bless him. My God. Poor Lou. Poor Lou."

And then suddenly Fay stopped and looked around. Suddenly she was in the room with them all, seeking something.

"Where's Rabbi?"

They looked at each other. Barrett stood up and came over to her. "Fay, I don't think that—"

"What do you mean? Where's Rabbi? Didn't anyone call him?"

Barrett tried to take her hands. "Listen to me, Fay. To bring him here . . . this isn't . . . well, most of us feel—"

"I want Rabbi here!" Not anger. A need. A desperate reaching out. She stood there in the center of the room, looking into her purse, her fingers fumbling, unable to see through the tears.

"What are you looking for, dear?" Rebecca wanting to help.

"A dime. I want to call Rabbi."

"I'll call him for you, dear."

"No!" She held her hand out in a gesture of pain. "Will somebody give me a dime, please!"

Jack Stern gave her the dime, trying to look at her. But she didn't even glance at him. Rebecca walked with her into the hallway to the phone booth.

Fay sat down on the stool inside and turned away. She put her head against the wall, collapsing into grief, crying, sobbing, and Rebecca stood beside her, rubbing her back, her arm over Fay's shoulder and touching her head gently.

"I know, dear. I know. It's all right. You call him. You do what you want. It's all right."

The others in the waiting room were talking, already beyond Lou's death, involved now with the implications, the practical matters, the way to handle it, the question of Rabbi being part of this too.

"It's wrong to have Rabbi here," Barrett said tensely, bitterness in his voice, "—doesn't she realize it?"

He shook his head in the anger of his disapproval. "If not for him —if Lou didn't have to go through what he did—" He looked toward the door quickly. Fay was coming back. "Rabbi must be no part of this. Nothing!" A restraining hand went out, an expression to indicate: Not now. We'll talk later.

When Rabbi arrived at the hospital it no longer really made any sense to be there. Lou's body had been moved out of his room and the funeral home had taken over to begin its work. Stern and Brody had left, after the touching of hands with Fay, the eyes locked in sadness.

"Anything I can do. Anything."

"I know, Jack."

"And me too."

"Thank you, Harry. Thank you both for coming and being with me."

They walked out with slow steps, as if it were sacrilegious to make noise.

Barrett, Greenwald and his wife, all remained for different reasons. Greenwald found himself affected almost more than he could explain. He hadn't been that close to Lou. They seldom saw each other socially. But somehow Lou had become a kind of symbol for him, and a means too. The symbol, or perhaps it was more like a living example, was that of a man totally involved. The building of the Temple had become Lou's life, his whole being. Such dedication of self was beyond his own range, and he recognized it as something he could never experience. He admired it and respected it and felt in awe of it. He knew its rarity. He knew it was a phenomenon he might never see again.

But Lou had also been of tremendous and sympathetic help to him in his own need. As Chairman of the Building Committee, it was Lou more than anyone else who had been responsible for the idea of the Auditorium, for the concept and the practical plans, the making of it into a meaningful expression of Greenwald's feeling about himself and his Jewishness. Lou had helped him channel the vague urgings, the desire to identify with the the congregation, into something specific and useful. And Lou had understood. How gently and tactfully he had shown that understanding of Greenwald's desire for a "monument," a need to bestow glory on himself, a hunger for recognition, almost a compulsion to impress. And he had made him feel good about it, rather than guilty, had spent hours with him going over details, pointing out all the ways this Auditorium would benefit the congregation, making Greenwald feel that it was their need that was being met more than his own.

It wasn't only a sadness that Greenwald now experienced, it was an intense sense of loss. Lou wouldn't be there anymore to reassure him and guide him, to support him, to cast this aura of virtue over the project. He wouldn't be there anymore.

And the strange thing was that Greenwald, in the involvement with Lou's death, in the reaction to the tragedy of it, seemed to forget completely what he had told Barrett, his demand that the Executive Committee reconsider or he would withold the money for building the Auditorium.

That was all changed now. Lou's death placed a new responsibility on him and all of them—to continue his work, to fulfill his dream, to make all the dedication that Lou had poured into this task have meaning. Now there could be no question of witholding support or money for any reason—the Temple had to be built, and the Auditorium, and it would be like saying: Not only for us, Lou, but in your name we do this, in memory of your devotion, in gratitude, in tribute.

All this whirling through his head, all this emotion like waves surging and clashing within him as he sat there. He seemed unable to move. He leaned back in his chair, the hand covering his eyes from the light, the darkness a shelter from his sadness, his confusion.

"Are you all right?" Rebecca leaning over him.

"Yes. Just . . . just. . . ."

"I know. I'll be over there with Fay."

Barrett waited for Rabbi's arrival. He didn't want Rabbi taking over the situation. It had to be made clear to him at once that Lou Mandel's death was a tragedy for the congregation that Rabbi couldn't share, and that even his presence at anything that was to follow, the services, the funeral, would be resented by most of the members.

Rabbi had to understand that! All of them had been working with Lou, joined together, part of his all-consuming involvement with the Temple—and Rabbi was like an intruder in this. And even worse, a divisive force, a source of trouble to them, a threat that had brought agony to Lou, maybe even produced in Lou the shock and pain that was responsible for his tragedy. How could Rabbi now try to be part of this? Lou's death and all that would follow from it, belonged to *them*.

The problem was Fay. Her desire to have Rabbi here was probably due to the emotional confusion she was experiencing. She was in no position to realize the effect of her action. She was groping, responding to her grief. She needed guidance, and Barrett stayed on to provide it. He would be with her as much as he could.

When Rabbi walked into the waiting room, Fay looked up from her seat, from the numb isolation she had sunk into, and stood up at once. Rabbi came up to her and embraced her. He held her, the way one holds a frightened child, and she clung to him and started to cry.

He was saying something to her in a low voice and she was nodding her head, sobbing without control, her head nodding and letting him hold her in the support and shelter of his arms.

The others watched, and understood something of it, projecting into her grief. Yet—how naturally she had gone to him! How simply and easily he had embraced her. How close the two of them were, as if all this had happened before.

And of course it had. And what Fay knew and reached out for now was that same complete understanding Rabbi had given her when her son died, the total acceptance of all she felt, the letting her feel it the way she had to. And the reassurance that flowed out of him on so many levels, not just the friend sharing sadness, not just the human being experiencing with her the agony of the loss, but a kind of bestowal of spirit, of deeper significance, a man of God making it all seem a part of life and God's way.

No one said anything for a long time, even when Rabbi led Fay gently out of the room. He walked with her down the hall, his arm around her shoulder, down to the far end of the hospital hall, and they stood for a while near the window as he talked quietly to her.

Barrett watched it all and knew that at this very moment he wasn't seeing what was there, he was looking beyond and planning what he had to do. And he felt it was right of him, despite the moment, even despite Fay's need, to plan how to handle it as it should be done. As it must be done.

When Rabbi and Fay came back to the waiting room, Fay's face a little different already, less tight, less gaunt somehow, a softness in it now, she looked at them and said: "Rabbi is taking me home."

Barrett spoke calmly, under complete control. "Fay, can I talk to you a minute?"

She came over and Barrett took her arm, moving off to the back of the room.

"Fay, forgive me for bringing up such things now, but we must face them. There are decisions to be made."

She only looked at him, waiting.

"Well, there will be a service of course. And you have to decide where."

"Where?"

"At the Temple in Lanebrook—"

"No!"

"You don't want it there?"

"No. That wasn't Lou's Temple. It didn't mean anything to him."

"All right. Then . . . I suppose . . . at the funeral home?"

She held her head up, swallowing. The image of it all suddenly clear and before her. She couldn't answer.

"I'm sorry, Fay, but. . . ."

"Yes. At the funeral home."

"Now Fay, please understand. I only want to do what is right. I want to talk to you when you get home about—"

"Rabbi?"

He was startled. It was as if she had revealed an unexpected strength, in the midst of all this a clarity and determination.

"Yes . . . but not now."

"Now!" She was staring at him. "Rabbi will conduct the services. No one else."

"Fay, let me talk to you later—"

"No!"

"There is more involved than—"

"I don't care! I want Rabbi."

"Fay, if Lou could—"

She looked at him, and there was the strangest suggestion of triumph on her face, of the revealing of some battle that had been fought and won.

"Lou? . . . Lou would have wanted it too."

"Fay, you know about all that has—"

"I know! But what you don't know, Bob, is that. . . ." Suddenly hard to say, hard to express Lou's words, utter them. "Lou told me . . . in the hospital . . . lying there . . . as I held his hand . . . he said: 'I have been wrong. I have done wrong.'"

Barrett, losing everything, not wanting it to be decided now, but controlling himself. "Fay, don't decide yet. I want to talk with you later when—"

She stepped back. "It's decided, Bob. All decided. And it's Lou's decision."

She turned away. Rabbi had been standing apart, near the door, not watching Fay and Barrett, not wanting to look, not wanting to know what he knew. Fay came up to him.

"I want to go now."

She put her arm in Rabbi's, as if to lean on him, as if to feel again the contact that was like a release, a channel. And Rabbi led her out of the room.

Barrett decided to talk to Rabbi first, before he approached Fay. He drove to Rabbi's home that afternoon, feeling all the anger that a sense of rightness could bestow. After all, was it to deprive Rabbi of anything that he was doing this? To deny him anything? Even to question his role? It was the desire to honor Lou Mandel's memory as it should be honored, with the full and open love that the whole congregation felt for him. It was to cherish the spirit of Lou's dedicated life. And Rabbi's presence would violate that. It would destroy the unity of the emotion. It would bring regret and bitterness into the hearts of so many if Rabbi were to be there at this moment.

"Rabbi, I want to put it very simply. At a time like this, only Lou Mandel counts. No one else. No procedure, no ritual is important. Only Lou, only his spirit and what he stood for . . . and you were not part of that, Rabbi. You didn't understand Lou. You not only felt differently, you hurt him in many ways. That's why, to many of us, just your presence at the services would be wrong. Do you understand?"

"I respected him as much as anyone."

"Did you?" Barrett confronting him directly. "And I tell you that Lou felt you were his enemy!"

"I did nothing to make him feel that."

"You think so? Lou controlled himself—he was too decent a man to express what he felt openly. But everyone knew. He was a sick man, Rabbi. Every fight, every argument, every obstacle, every problem you created—helped kill that man!"

Rabbi did not know what to do with his anger. "How can you be so cruel, Bob?"

"How can you be so insensitive?"

"Fay has asked me to conduct the services."

"The services are not for her. They're for Lou Mandel!"

"I will let her decide what is for Lou Mandel. Not you!"

"She's confused because of her grief. She can't think. She doesn't know what she's doing."

"She knows what she feels. Lou is dead. She has to live. I have to help her now."

"For the last time, Rabbi—since I can't stop you, and she does have the right to decide, I ask you to rise above yourself. Understand something bigger than two individuals, you and Fay. Lou was the spirit of the whole congregation. He was our solid rock. His death is the congregation's tragedy. Respect that! Let the congregation have this moment for its own sorrow. Do that much for the congregation!"

"I can only do what I feel must be done. I am needed there by a woman who lost her husband. And I will be there."

Barrett, driving home, felt such a sense of bitterness, such an intense frustration and violence in himself, that he knew it would be unwise even to see Fay. He couldn't face another confrontation with her. He decided to let Rabbi conduct the services, and to make up for it, to do what had to be done for Lou.

There were people standing in the back of the chapel, in the doorways and outside in the corridor, so many had come. The coffin was in front, closed, a rectangular object. It wasn't Lou Mandel, had no relationship to him. The gentleness and softness of the man could not be locked into a box. It was impossible to think of Lou Mandel being there.

The flowers, on either side of the coffin, along the steps to the raised platform, along the sides of the chapel, on the platform, cascades, mounds of flowers, heaps and bunches of flowers, vases full, wreaths. All meaning lost in them. Like a formula for mourning. The expression of sympathy now became a huge design, an arrangement, a thing to stare at and be in awe of. So many flowers!

The atmosphere was wrong, something nervous about it, subdued, but a sense of strain in it. It was as if the sadness they all knew they should feel and were feeling, was being pushed aside by something else. The grief acknowledged and then the awareness of other emotions contending. The friends, neighbors, relatives, fellow members of the congregation, fellow Jews, fellow humans, other creatures due to die, sat there in the cells of their own uncertainty, their private relationship with death, their piece of sadness, and yet, in almost all of them, a sense of anticipation, an anxiety. Coming from where? No one seemed to know, but everyone seemed to sense it. Fay's quick glances, the nervous seeking of the eyes out of that bone-projecting face, Rabbi looking at no one. So withdrawn that it was like a preparation, a storing-up for the encounter. Barrett talking in a corner to a group, the three or four men watching his face intently, absorbing, agreeing, sharing something.

Finally the hush, self-imposed, passed through the crowd, through eyes, fingers to the lips, sighs, turning away of faces, the bodies sitting back. Now silence.

Rabbi was on the platform, at the podium, directly above the coffin. He did not look into their faces at all, but opening the Bible began to read.

> "I will lift up mine eyes unto the
> mountains.
> From whence shall my help come?
> My help cometh from the Lord,
> Who made heaven and earth.
>
> He will not suffer thy foot to be
> moved;
> He that keepeth thee will not slumber.
> Behold, He that keepeth Israel
> Doth neither slumber nor sleep.
>
> The Lord is thy keeper;
> The Lord is thy shade upon thy
> right hand.
> The sun shall not smite thee by day,
> Nor the moon by night.

> The Lord shall keep thee from all
> evil;
> He shall keep thy soul.
> The Lord shall guard thy going out
> and thy coming in,
> From this time forth and for ever."

With the closing of the Book, Rabbi gripped the dark wood, holding it as if to keep from swaying, as if to gather strength.

"Let us now offer a prayer for Louis Jacob Mandel, dearly beloved husband of Fay Mandel, brother of Herman Mandel, father of Susan Mandel, friend to all of us here. O Lord, in your kindness and mercy, receive the noble spirit of this rare and wonderful human being, who seemed to dwell among us only to do good, only to help his fellow man, only to serve Thy will. Bless him with Thy love, O Lord, as he blessed all of us by his devotion and his sacrifice. Give him the peace and the reward of Your everlasting kindness unto the end of time, as he gave to all who knew him the joy and the beauty of his love, his gentleness, his understanding, and his magnificence of spirit. Amen."

Fay was crying, and the sounds of the suppressed tears and the soft moans of sadness were all through the room, many heads nodding in agreement and awareness as the words touched their own grief for Lou Mandel.

Rabbi opened the Bible again.

> "The Lord is my shepherd; I shall not
> want.
> He maketh me to lie down in green
> pastures.
> He leadeth me beside. . . ."

The beloved, familiar words. The simple comfort of God's assurance.

> ". . . my cup runneth over.
> Surely goodness and mercy shall follow
> me all the days of my life;
> And I shall dwell in the house of
> the Lord for ever."

Rabbi closed the Book. He looked up into the faces, and then at Fay in the first row, directly behind the coffin. He reached into the pocket of his jacket under the white robe, and was taking out the folded sheets of paper, when he became aware that Barrett was on the platform moving towards him. He was the last one in the chapel to realize it, to see him. Everyone was staring, waiting.

Barrett stood beside the podium now, directly beside Rabbi, and it was as if he were pushing him aside, his presence, his standing there, his manner, the expression, a declaration to Rabbi to move away and yield to him.

Barrett looked at Rabbi and said: "I will deliver the eulogy."

The two men regarded each other for a moment of total confrontation, naked before each other and before them all. Barrett then faced the mourners, his eyes upon them as if for support and approval, his claim made.

Rabbi took an everlasting, agonizing second to look at Fay. Her head was down, her hands clenched, her face plunged down into her misery. Then Rabbi stepped back and turned around, looking for a place to go. There was a row of chairs at the back of the platform and he walked quickly to them and sat down. The folded sheets of his speech were still in his hand, and he suddenly realized this and put them back in his pocket.

Barrett was still waiting, standing alone now before them, but unable to begin yet; his face was a tight cage inside of which all was controlled. He couldn't start.

Everyone knew. They knew exactly why he couldn't begin to talk yet. It flowed out of him like a vibration. And they knew also that this was an act of courage and defiance. The formula, the practice was that a Rabbi conducts the services and delivers the eulogy. No one else. And they sat there tense, uncertain, wondering and yet understanding, accepting. Somehow this had to be done. Barrett was the one. Not Rabbi. Barrett. It was right. For Lou, it had to be Barrett. No one else.

Barrett was now able to clear his throat, the last effort of holding back, the words now able to be uttered.

"Lou Mandel is dead. I have decided to speak here now . . . not so much about him . . . as for him. For Lou."

He paused, like the putting down of a huge weight. The first words were out. Now he was ready to begin.

"Lou Mandel didn't die of a heart attack. He died of a broken heart. He died of a broken dream. He died of a broken hope.

"Is there anyone here who cannot say—who doesn't know and

feel—exactly what that dream was? Lou's dream? How well we all know it! How much a part of us he made that dream!

"For it was not a building that was his dream. Not the putting up of a structure, bricks, walls, glass. The Temple. . . . No, that was not what Lou was working for, living for, and what he died for.

"The Temple that Lou was building was in our hearts. In our souls. In our spirit. To want to have a place of God in our midst, a place of worship and dedication. To want to meet together there . . . our congregation . . . and together to seek God's guidance. To want to be involved with each other in this work of building a house of God. This was what Lou wanted for all of us. Not the building . . . but the unity and love and faith that this building would bring to us.

"Why do I say he died of a broken heart? Are we not building that Temple? Are we not moving forward according to plan? On schedule? The work being done? . . . Yes, the building is going up. The foundation is already there. . . . But what Lou realized . . . to his sorrow . . . to his despair . . . was that the unity and spirit that were to give that Temple its meaning—these were threatened. These were in danger.

"I cannot—as a man, as a member of the congregation, as a friend and mourner for Lou Mandel—I cannot let this moment pass without letting that be known. Lou felt that the whole meaning and purpose of our Temple and our congregation could be destroyed!"

He paused and looked at the faces staring in shock and wonder at him, many shaking their heads in disbelief, some nodding, knowing, suspecting, and all of them hurt somehow by what was happening, Lou's funeral, the man lying dead there in the coffin, and such words and thoughts, such emotions being expressed. Even if they had to be. Too bad. Too bad.

"He saw," the voice now trying to express the sorrow in Lou, "he saw it as a tragedy for us. For all of us. Because he felt for all of us. Because his heart took in all of us. He saw the tragedy that could befall us . . . and his gentle spirit, his beautiful soul, grieved for us.

"I said I would speak for Lou Mandel. But don't you think I know—as you all know—that no one can speak for him? No one can even have a fraction of that magnificent dedication, that holy—that noble and holy—sense of dedication that was only his.

"That is what speaks for Lou here, now. And will speak to us all as long as we live. It is now part of us. It is a blessing we carry within us.

"And it is more. It is an obligation. He has bound us all, by his work and his spirit and his love—to do what must be done. To build a Temple. And to make that Temple a sacred symbol of our unity, our dedication, our faith in God.

"No one . . . no one can be allowed to stop that from happening now!"

He swallowed, gripping the podium, looking with all the intensity of his being at them, driving his meaning and his emotion into them.

"God bless him."

He turned and walked slowly off the platform and down to his seat in the front row.

The long silence in the chapel was like a stopping of breathing, a holding back, an inability to let the moment end and have the next one begin. And then slowly, the tensed backs softening, slumping, the hearts pumping again, the consciousness returned. It was like a great sigh signifying the restoration of life that filled the room.

Rabbi stood. He just stood there at the back of the platform without moving, as if unable to come forward. His face was like that of a man lost somewhere, removed, in a distant, private world.

He came forward slowly and it was as if someone else was walking for him, moving his body. Then, in a voice that could hardly be heard, coming from some mechanism in him that wasn't really part of him, he said,

"I accept . . . with all my heart . . . as we all do and must do . . . the message and its meaning that Bob Barrett has spoken to us. No one must destroy the work that Lou Mandel gave his life for. No one must destroy the unity and wholeness of our congregation. . . . It will not happen. So be it."

Then slowly, as people glanced at each other, wondered, understood, felt shaken and frightened in the significance of the moment, felt for Rabbi in his own agony, felt the sadness and the truth of what had happened, the inevitability of it, Rabbi said the closing prayer, the *El molay rachamim*.

The services were over. The coffin was wheeled away by four attendants of the funeral chapel. The people stood and looked at each other as if they had all returned to reality. But there was no peace in that reality.

XVI

The meeting was set up at Lou Mandel's funeral. During the standing around in the driveway of the cemetery, the gathering in small solemn-faced groups, the awkward waiting when all felt ashamed of their impatience, ashamed of their irritation at the delay, as if that conveyed a desire to bury Lou quickly, put him in the ground and get it over with, during this time Bob Barrett moved about quietly, a motion of the head, a finger barely raised, a stopping alongside a silent figure. Greenwald, Stern, Brody, the word passed, even to Danny Cole, a meeting of the Committee tonight, nine o'clock, my house, like the fulfilling of a plan, the last act.

Barrett realized that after the funeral a great many people would return to the Mandel home to be with the mourning family. A dozen women had already brought food to the house, casseroles and stews and roast beef, salads and rolls, so that Fay would have to prepare nothing, do nothing. And close friends would stay late into the evening, sitting with her and the others as an act of devotion. Barrett felt that it was precisely this situation, this moment, this sense of tragedy, that made it proper to hold the meeting. It was, to him, a part of the tribute to Lou Mandel, an expression of dedication to his spirit.

There were other reasons too. His eulogy of Lou at the services had opened up the whole business about Rabbi. It was no longer a Committee secret, no longer a matter for them to deal with alone or in secrecy. In effect, he had proclaimed to the congregation that a threat to its future existed, and that action had to be taken. Rabbi had spoken in a strange way, said something he had never expected to hear . . . I accept. . . . No one must destroy the unity of the congregation. It will not happen. . . . Did that mean he was ready now, at last, at last, to resign? This had to be determined at once. The whole question—now that it was out in the open—that had to be settled immediately.

And somehow, for himself, too, the time was now. Not just because of the conflict with Rabbi, not just a question of his leadership and position with the congregation, but in a personal sense too.

Elaine's idiotic demand for a divorce produced a reaction in him that expressed itself in the need for action. It was the way Bob always responded to a threat or an attack. With decisiveness, with positive motion. Just taking action, showing strength, moving forward, indicating determination in some area, this helped. It would be an acknowledgment of defeat if he were to allow her demand to cause him to withdraw, or halt his momentum. Yes, he would have to deal with Elaine, face it out with her, reach an "understanding," whatever that would be. But meanwhile, positive action, strength, the Barrett push and drive had to be shown. It was an instinctive answer for him, as well as an escape.

Rabbi wasn't told of the meeting until five o'clock. Barrett waited until he saw him leave the Mandel home because he didn't want Rabbi to react to the call in the presence of these other people. Then he reached him in his study.

"Rabbi, the Executive Committee is meeting tonight at my place at nine o'clock. We ask you to be present."

"Is this meeting about—"

"You know what it's about, Rabbi! Just be there, please."

Rabbi's long delay in answering irritated Barrett and he couldn't control himself.

"Is that understood?"

"Yes, it's understood." And both men hung up without another word.

Rabbi didn't want the confrontation. There was no need for it now. Hadn't he indicated with his words at the funeral services that he understood and accepted? He had been brought to it only by the sheer horror of the situation, the degrading brutality of it. Barrett condemning him openly and at a time and place like that had suddenly made it clear to him. If Barrett could do that, then it was because he had no uncertainty about how it would be received, how the congregation would react. In effect, Barrett had made it impossible for him to fight to stay on. And in fact, he no longer wanted to. Enough. He had gone through enough. Even the self-examination, pondering, searching for an answer, had become a torture.

It was just that he wasn't quite ready yet. Not tonight, not at a meeting. He didn't want it that way. It was a humiliation of the spirit, and Barrett should have realized that and spared him this. After what he had said at the services? Didn't he deserve this consideration now? He felt a bitterness at the way people couldn't wait until the emotions could develop a protective cover, but had to deal with them when they were still quivering with raw pain.

When Bob mentioned to Elaine that there would be a meeting that evening, he expected her to make an effort to be present. After all, as she had so often reminded him, she was involved in the matter. But instead, she had delivered a brief and uncomplicated lecture to him at the dinner table. She spoke with the new freedom of a person who has learned the language of honesty.

"You did a terrible thing at the services, for which neither God nor Fay will ever forgive you. And you're following it up with this meeting. You're acting like an executioner!"

"Thank you, my loving wife."

"I'm not your loving wife! Don't forget that! Or don't you take me seriously?"

He didn't answer.

"Well, it doesn't matter. See? No more! It doesn't matter. I'm just trying—not for your sake—but for Rabbi's, for the congregation's, to make you realize that you're acting like a monster. No human feelings, no mercy, nothing! Having this meeting tonight is like something out of a horror story!"

"Has it ever occurred to you—that if I were one-thousandth as bad, as vicious, as you think I am—I couldn't live with myself? How is it that I feel good about what I'm doing? Justified! And that the others are with me?"

"Because evil can't see itself!" She threw down her napkin and stood up. "I'm getting out of here. I can't stand this—or you anymore. I'll be at Fay's."

And she left. Bob, still holding the knife and fork in his hands, looked at the roast beef on his plate, the pink meat soft and juicy, and he sliced off another piece and started to chew on it.

Danny was the first to arrive. He walked up to Bob directly and said: "I want to talk to you. Right now."

Bob took him into the study, and Danny closed the door.

"Yes, Danny? What's on your mind?"

"This meeting tonight is to ask Rabbi to resign, isn't it?"

"Exactly."

"You're determined to do this to him?"

"I am determined to do this for us—for the congregation. But you know all that, Danny. Now what is it?"

"I just want you to know something about Rabbi. About this man you detest. If he does resign, it's not because he has to. If he wants to stay—he very easily can."

"Yes? How?"

Now Danny put his hands in his pockets, as if to help himself remain in control, not show his emotion. "Rabbi—" he said it as calmly as he could "has certain information that he could use. That might make you change your mind."

"Such as?" Barrett was uncertain of what was coming. This kid Danny was capable of anything.

"Such as information about you, Mr. Barrett."

"Stop playing games! What?"

Danny stepped back, needing the security of space between them. "Bea Aldrich."

Barrett stroked his hair back with the palm of his right hand merely because some release of energy was necessary. He could only hold so much in. He was phrasing and re-phrasing his response in a hundred different ways, and he knew that each one could reveal something horrible. Finally he accepted the truth of the moment and the situation. There was no time for denial, nor for anger, nor for a battle with Danny. Nor was there any escape.

"How did he find out?"

"From me." Danny was still, in the remote shelter of his being where a hope can live on nothing, waiting for something to happen, to be said, that might change everything.

"You found out?"

"I met her. She told me."

"And you told Rabbi?"

"Everything."

With all the intensity of his being, Danny was waiting for Barrett to say something, to utter one word that would indicate a new direction, a retreat.

Barrett turned and walked to the door, and stopped there with his hand on the knob.

"Just two things, Danny. One is: You're a stinking little no-good punk, no matter how noble you think your intentions are. And the other is: I'll take my chances." He opened the door and walked quickly to the living room.

Everyone except Greenwald had already arrived. Barrett took a chair and set it up between the two couches, the position of the chairman of the meeting. Jack Stern and Harry Brody sat side by side on one couch. Rabbi, following some instinctive need to set himself apart, picked up a chair from the other part of the room and brought it half way over. Danny sat down at the end of the couch at Rabbi's right, quite close.

Then Greenwald arrived, the most solemn of the solemn, the face intended to make clear an awareness of tremendous responsibility.

They were ready now. Barrett leaned forward, his hands clasped in front of his knees.

"We'll start the meeting now. No formalities or anything. I have called the Executive Committee together to arrive at a decision, and we'll proceed." He didn't look at Rabbi, but addressed him.

"Rabbi, the question is whether you are to continue in office or not. That's all that's involved." Then he looked down at his hands, the words so hard to say now that he was unable to face Rabbi. "I want to make it clear to you that we're not going into that matter I talked to you about when the Committee requested your resignation before. We're not going to discuss it." He paused, and it was as if he and Rabbi had just had a long conversation, an exchange of understanding and awareness of each other's thoughts. "We just want your answer. Nothing more."

Rabbi didn't answer at once.

"Oh, one other thing." There was now a certain calm in Barrett's voice, "—I don't know what you've heard, but let me enlighten you.

You probably know that Sam Beskov offered the congregation a considerable amount of money—with a certain condition attached. That you be kept on as Rabbi.

"We have rejected Beskov's offer. Completely. So that's understood. . . . You may also have heard that Dr. Greenwald, at one point, raised the possibility of withdrawing his contribution. And that—" he hesitated about the phrasing of it, "—that his reason for this was that he wanted the Committee to reconsider its decision about you.

"As of now, that possibility is ended. Dr. Greenwald has told me that Lou Mandel's tragic death has caused him to change his mind. He is more determined than ever now—and as a tribute to the memory of Lou—that the Temple be built as Lou had planned and worked for. The contribution stands. . . . Is that right, Dr. Greenwald?"

Greenwald, looking down at the floor, solemn, the weight of the occasion on him, nodded his head. There was a pause, as if everyone was waiting for more.

Greenwald responded to it. "The Auditorium, the Temple, must be built. It is going to be."

"All right," Barrett now sat back. "This is just so that you have no misconceptions, Rabbi. . . . We are now ready to hear from you."

He looked at Rabbi and something in him suddenly went soft. He knew, surely and completely, that Rabbi was not going to bring up that matter in any way. And the certainty of it, as he studied Rabbi's face, the absolute knowledge, produced such a surge of relief, and gratitude in him, that he almost wanted to say: "Thank you! Thank you, Rabbi! For being so decent. For not trying to save yourself that way. For sparing me.

But Rabbi had no notion of this. He had not given the Bea Aldrich thing another thought. He had never even considered it. His emotion now was only of hurt, of their cruelty to him.

So, it was going to be just like that. We are ready to hear from you. A formality that was going to be observed, nothing more. Weren't they even going to express some human decency and warmth—say just a word that would soften the horror of this? Acknowledge his pain somehow?

And then it was as if Greenwald had heard him, sensed what he was feeling, and had the need to let something else flow into the tense atmosphere.

"I think," he said it slowly, "that Rabbi should know this isn't easy for us either. This is an unhappy and painful moment for all of us. I wish—we all wish—we could have avoided this meeting and what it represents. . . . But we no longer can, Rabbi. We must face the reality, bitter though it is for all of us. We must come to a decision. And there just doesn't seem to be any other way to do it now. . . . We ask you to understand that, Rabbi."

Rabbi heard the words and all they meant to him was that it had been decided. By them. By him, too. The truth of it had been faced by everybody and there was only the need to utter it and acknowledge it. And the need for this decision could not be denied. . . . Yet, something in him was still struggling to deny it. He couldn't help it. Something was still saying: Why? Must it be? Must it be? He could do nothing to still this questioning in himself. No matter how much he understood it with his mind, the questioning remained. And he had to let it come out.

"I feel . . ." he said, "I feel that . . . will you allow me? . . . I would like the opportunity to do something now. I would like to . . . to ask each of you a question."

He was looking at Barrett for approval, but he didn't wait for his answer.

"Each one of you . . . Dr. Greenwald, do you want me to resign as Rabbi?"

Silence. The tension tore at them like an agony that had suddenly been thrust into them and had to be dealt with.

Everyone was looking at Greenwald. He knew he had to face Rabbi at this moment, no looking down at the floor, no façade of overwhelming sorrow.

"I'm sorry, Rabbi. But I do."

"And Jack?" Rabbi didn't let the moment last, like a quick swallowing of the pain. "What do you think?"

Jack turned to Rabbi as if forced by Greenwald's example, even though it was against his nature, even though he wanted to do it in kindness, without looking at the man.

"I'm also sorry, Rabbi. But I . . . I think that would be best for the congregation."

"Harry? Tell me, please?"

No hesitation here. It was not cruelty with Harry, but a simple factualness of manner. "I agree. That's the way I feel."

Rabbi looked at Danny's mournful face and expressed somehow a tenderness for him, an affection and awareness of his despair.

"I know how you feel, Danny. And I thank you."

"I don't have to say anything, Rabbi."

"No, you don't . . . and . . ." Now a direct look at Barrett. Cold. The calm comprehension. Almost a disdain. ". . . and neither do you, Bob. I know your position."

He stood up, and everyone wished he hadn't, but everyone understood his need to, like the need of a man who has been struck to recoil under the blow.

"So . . . well. . . . Then there is really nothing more that any of you . . . that this Committee has to say to me. . . . And perhaps there is nothing really that I can say to you.

"I just . . . I suppose it can't be helped that I want to express something at this moment. . . . What? Well, please believe this, if you believe anything that I say. I think that all of you who feel I should resign as Rabbi—really do feel this way out of a concern for the good of the congregation. I cannot ever doubt that. I couldn't make myself believe that men such as you—who think of yourselves as good Jews, and are—in your way—good Jews, that you could have any other motive. I must believe that. And I do."

He gripped the back of the chair, his head up, his eyes up, as if seeking a path for his emotions, thoughts.

"So. . . . So. . . ." There was no other way except to say it. "I hereby resign as your Rabbi. It's done. You have it. . . . But I must say this: The reason I resign is not because you here, or any other members of this congregation, think I should.

"I do it only because I think I should. I am resigning because I have failed. Not failed in your terms—but in mine. I came here with a vision, a goal, a purpose—and I couldn't accomplish it. Was this because of some inadequacy on my part? Lack of skill? Am I a Rabbi unable to do his job?

"I don't think so. I am just . . . not the Rabbi for you. And the truth is . . . I don't want to be. I cannot be. My concept of Judaism is not yours. My idea of how a Jew should live and act in today's world is not yours. My way of reaching a deep involvement with our religion, making it a meaningful part of our life—that is something you don't share with me.

"Yes, you have your Judaism. And there are millions like you today. A kind of Judaism does exist for you. It is part of you.

"And that's enough for you. To you—being a Jew is being Jewish. To me, being a Jew is living as a Jew, acting as a Jew, taking on the responsibility of being a Jew.

"You feel—I suppose, I don't really know—that this is old-fashioned, dated, not for our times, not for this life we lead in this world of today. I don't condemn you for that, because I don't really understand it.

"Maybe that's my problem. Why I failed. I cannot understand the Jew of today and his Judaism. To me, Judaism is a way of life, or it is nothing. And it may be that today, here, among people like you, it is destined to be nothing. In which case, God help us. God forgive us. We have departed from His way, and denied His gift to us.

"Perhaps you know the story Rabbi Simlai tells. It is well known. Of how all the commandments that were handed down for Jews to follow were reduced to fewer and fewer in order to get at the essence of Judaism. First by David . . . then by Isaiah . . . then by Micah . . . and finally Amos reduced all the commandments to one: *Seek ye Me, and live.* . . . There must be love of God as well as love of man. There must be both. One without the other is not Judaism. And I cannot be a Rabbi for people who want to live with one and without the other.

"So . . . I am leaving you. I won't be annoying you anymore. You won't have to say anymore, 'What should we do about that crazy Rabbi of ours?' "

He looked at them, and now the bitterness, the pain, came out. "I hope the new Rabbi you get will do for you what you want and need. I hope he'll play golf with you and go bowling and sailing, and be a big hit at the dances and raise money for you and bring in new members and all the other things where I have failed you.

"But also I hope—for your sake—that he will find time and have the desire to teach you. And I hope he will be able to teach you how to be *Jews* . . . even in today's world, even in the suburbs, even in Greenlake, even in your homes . . . even in your empty hearts."

He turned and walked out quickly.

Danny stood up at once. "I don't suppose it means much to you, but I am resigning from this Committee and from membership in this congregation. God help you! That's all I have to say. God help you!"

Nobody tried to stop him with a word or gesture as he walked out after Rabbi. The four men sat there, a shaken, silent group, somehow drawn close under the impact of the emotions, the turmoil in them, the wondering mixed with resentment, the questioning, the confusion despite all the certainty.

Barrett stood up and so did all the others, in a kind of awkward, unconscious gesture of unity.

"Well . . . I guess this has been a day. Lou Mandel put to rest in his grave . . . the Rabbi leaving. I know how we all feel. And I know this too, and I want to say it for all of us. We *are* Jews. We do live as Jews. In our way. The only way we want to and can today. And it is a good way. Because it is for us. It's our Judaism.

"And we're going to live with that Judaism and work for it with all our hearts and devotion. We are going to build a Temple that will serve the cause of that Judaism . . . and it will be a beautiful Temple . . . and we will worship in it . . . and meet in it and enjoy it and use it in a hundred different ways.

"It will be a Temple for us . . . and for our time. . . ."

* * *

Now all the things were packed, as they had so often been before. And Frieda thought: as they probably will be again. The cartons and cartons of books, the clothing carefully folded, the dishes (which she had packed in barrels herself to save money), the children's toys in a jumble in several boxes, all their possessions. Nothing would be left behind.

Or would it? Something of David would surely remain in Greenlake. In Danny, in Elaine, in a few others. Greenlake, she felt, would not soon forget Rabbi David Gordon.

And the next congregation? She looked at David, puttering about, making sure every book was secure in its box, and knew that his mind and heart were already there. Hoping this congregation would respond to him, understand his purpose, measure up to his demands. For they were demands, and demands hard to live up to. But the quest would always go on with him.

As if sensing her eyes on him, and her thoughts, he looked up from a book he was holding and shook his head.

"It's here. Heschel says it so well in this book. Listen: 'We are the only channel of Jewish tradition, those who must save Judaism from oblivion, those who must hand over the entire past to the generations to come. We are either the last, the dying, Jews or else we are those who will give new life to our tradition.'"

She came over to him and held his hand lovingly. "You will give it that new life, David."

"I will try. God help me, I will try."

And they stood close together in the silence, amidst the clutter of their past, and both felt a deep and wonderful kind of hope.